HIS SPLENDID TOUCH

"I love you, Jennifer," whispered Damon, but his words soared into the silence of the ship's cabin, expanding the sound into trumpets of joy that played a love song in Jennifer's heart.

"Damon—oh Damon," she whispered. "I love you in a way I've never loved anyone."

With a low moan, he pulled her into his arms, burying his lips in the thickness of her long, blonde hair. Then his mouth was on her throat, her eyes that had fluttered shut, her lips, stopping her words of love before she could utter them. His eyes, black with passion, searched her face, reading the surrender reflected there. . . .

When their first passion was spent Damon propped himself on an elbow, looking down at her with eyes still bright from lovemaking. "I want to marry you. That's why I brought you out on the bay—to ask you to be my wife." He hesitated. "I hadn't planned to seduce you," he said.

Jennifer's face went hot at his words, embarrassed even though he had explored every curve and swell of her body. "Oh, Damon, I want that too, and soon. But for now, we'll have to wait." Then Jennifer forgot everything as Damon's fingers once again began to search her body. . . .

North to Destiny

Donna Carolyn Anders

BANTAM BOOKS
TORONTO · NEW YORK · LONDON · SYDNEY · AUCKLAND

NORTH TO DESTINY

A Bantam Book / January 1986

ISBN 0-553-25266-6

Published simultaneously in the United States and Canada

Bantam Books are published by Bantam Books, Inc. Its trademark,
consisting of the words "Bantam Books" and the portrayal of a
rooster, is Registered in U.S. Patent and Trademark Office and in
other countries. Marca Registrada. Bantam Books, Inc., 666 Fifth
Avenue, New York, New York 10103.

PRINTED IN THE UNITED STATES OF AMERICA

O   0 9 8 7 6 5 4 3 2 1

For Ruth, Lisa, Tina,
my beloved daughters

I

Distant Hills

Chapter One

Jennifer Carlyle's gaze fastened on the horizon, where the distant cotton fields and pine-covered hills provided a sharp contrast to the July sky faded by the hot afternoon sun. A slight breeze rippled the surface of the Savannah River, which lazed along beneath the bluff where she stood, a solitary figure. She had never felt lonelier in all of her nineteen years. The breeze stirred the Spanish Moss that draped the live oak tree above her, and for a fleeting second, the moss caressed her sunburned face.

Suddenly, her large blue eyes burned with unshed tears as she thought of her father, who had died three months ago from yellow fever. Fighting to control herself, she turned her gaze back to the Carlyle plantation house, which dominated an even higher bluff above a sweeping curve of the river. The magnificent mansion, with its gleaming white marble columns and tall shuttered windows, had once been a showplace in the Old South.

Not caring that her dirty fingers might leave muddy smudges on her face, Jennifer brushed away a tear that had escaped. "Damn the Yankees!" she cried out angrily. Even though it was twenty years after the Civil War, a war that had been over before she'd been born, she hated the North for destroying Georgia. It was small consolation that the Carlyles were among the lucky few who still owned their plantations. Each year saw them taking a bank loan to buy their cotton seeds and pay the wages of disgruntled field hands.

A vicious circle, Jennifer told herself, her anger choked off by the knot of fear that had been growing within her since assuming responsibility for the plantation. She knew that to break even the crops must yield enough to repay the spring planting loan as well as pay the property tax. She wiped her hands on her skirt, adding more soil to the cotton print. But the crops never did yield enough . . . there was never enough money.

Her long lashes blinked furiously as she glanced at the twin headstones that reminded her that she was alone in the world . . . *truly alone.* "George Joseph Carlyle 1823–1885," and "Katharine Ann Davis Carlyle 1836–1869." Her parents had left her a legacy of debts, labor problems, and High Bluffs, the deteriorating mansion that had presided over this stretch of the Savannah River since before Washington was President of the United States.

The white walls of the mansion shone with dazzling brilliance under the Georgia sun. Jennifer sighed, the shabbiness of the house and grounds was not apparent from where she stood.

"Somehow I'll manage," Jennifer whispered. "Papa, I'll keep it going until—" she broke off. Until what? she asked herself. Until she married an eligible man who would restore the Carlyle fortunes? Or until her older half brother, Joseph, returned from the West, where he'd migrated fourteen years ago? She kicked the dirt with a savagery that jolted her whole body. There are no eligible men here, she reminded herself. And her brother, a man she hardly remembered, hadn't written in years; he was obviously not interested in the family plantation. "Undependable and selfish," her father used to say about his only son, the offspring of his first marriage. "Just like his mother."

Jennifer shifted her gaze back to the headstones. "I swear I'll not lose High Bluffs," she said, giving words to her fears. "I'll work the land until my last breath."

Suddenly, someone cleared his throat. She whirled around and faced Zeb, the old black man who'd been with the family since his birth, the only former slave still at High Bluffs.

"Miss Jennifer," he said, his calm tone belying the rigid set of his thin shoulders. "You best git back to High Bluffs. We's got trouble."

"Trouble?" Jennifer repeated. But she was already head-ing back along the path that edged the riverbank and led to the house.

"It dat Big Sam," Zeb said, hurrying to keep up. "He tellin' dem niggers dat dey ain' gonna git no pay now dat yo' papa up and died."

"Damn!" Jennifer exclaimed, her grief and worry forgotten as she braced herself to confront Big Sam, a laborer who was constantly causing trouble—a man her father shouldn't have hired.

"What you gonna do?" Zeb asked. "Big Sam's a bad nigger if you rile him."

Jennifer shook her head. How could she handle the matter and retain her authority? she wondered. Some of the blacks had already left; she knew that backing down now would guarantee losing the workers she needed until after harvesting time.

When they reached the driveway, the crushed oyster shells slowed her pace. She could hear Big Sam's bass voice telling the crowd of blacks to demand full wages now or risk losing them if they waited until after picking time. A murmur rose from the workers as they were swayed by his words.

"Ask the mistress if she has the money for your wages now," Big Sam said as Jennifer strode boldly into the crowd. Her gaze was caught by his, and his black eyes challenged her. Her slim girlish figure was only two inches over five feet, while he stood six-and-a-half-feet tall. As she hesitated the field hands closed in around her, waiting.

Nervously, she licked her lips, and her gaze darted over the men. She began her attack. "*Why* aren't you all working?" she demanded, hoping her fear wasn't apparent in her tone. "How *dare* you ask about wages when you haven't even earned them yet."

There was an abrupt silence, and Jennifer seized the moment. "Have you ever been cheated out of wages at High Bluffs? Have the Carlyles ever lied to you?"

A low murmur of agreement rippled through the crowd, and Jennifer felt sympathies shift away from Big Sam.

"My father always paid up after the harvest . . . and so will I." Her gaze circled the group, and her voice was more confident as she continued. "You agreed to lower wages in return for food and a cabin at High Bluffs." She paused, breathing deeply. "That, and your final pay, is more than any other plantation is offering."

Again there was a murmur of agreement.

"Then get back to work," Jennifer told them.

"Wait!" Big Sam shouted as the crowd began to disperse. "This here girl is alone, and she ain't gonna keep this place goin' nohow. Y'all best leave now . . . with me."

As the workers hesitated once more, Jennifer whirled to face Big Sam. "Get off this plantation!" she cried, knowing she had to stand firm now or all was lost. "You're discharged!"

Their stares locked, blazing blue fire and glowing black coals. He grabbed her, his giant hands imprisoning her small arms. "Big talk for a little gal," he said, his tone tight with fury.

"Let me go!" Jennifer demanded. "How *dare* you touch me."

"I dare," he said hoarsely, and as Jennifer twisted and squirmed his powerful fingers tightened painfully.

"Let Miss Jennifer go." Zeb rushed forward. "You's in trouble now, Big Sam."

With one quick motion the old man was elbowed aside. As a hush fell over the crowd Jennifer saw that the other men had no intention of helping her. They stood as though carved from ebony, their skin glistening with sweat, waiting to see what would happen next. My God, she thought in terror, I'm at their mercy.

Suddenly, pistol shots shattered the charged silence; one bullet ripped into the pink blossoms of the oleander bush behind Big Sam. He stumbed backward, releasing Jennifer, as blood blended with sweat on his cotton shirt.

"Stand back," a man's voice commanded. "Or I'll shoot more of you black devils!"

Jennifer's gaze flew to the short, thickset white man who'd arrived unnoticed and who now stood in his buggy waving a smoking pistol: Judson Carr, her neighbor and a hated carpetbagger, but she was so relieved to see him, she could have thrown herself into his arms.

Immediately the workers began to move toward the fields beyond the old slave quarters. Zeb stepped forward to take the reins while Judson Carr descended from his buggy, his pistol still pointed at Big Sam.

"I could have you strung up," he told Big Sam, "molesting a white woman."

Big Sam stared back, his eyes defiant and unyielding. "I done nothin' wrong."

Her confidence restored, Jennifer stepped forward. "I told you, get off my property," she said, her gaze steady on Big Sam, "or I'll have you arrested."

Big Sam's glance flicked between Jennifer and Judson Carr's pistol, then he spun around, picked up the bundle of his belongings at his feet, and strode down the drive toward the road.

"Goddamned nigger," Judson Carr said, putting his gun away and pulling a handkerchief from his pocket to mop away the sweat blistering on his upper lip and forehead.

"Uh—thank you." She gestured with her hand, indicating her relief at Big Sam's departure and the workers' return to the fields. He nodded, his dark eyes watchful. She had no choice but to invite him into the house.

Feeling Judson Carr's eyes on her, she suppressed a shudder, trying not to dwell on her distaste for the man. Hadn't he save her from—from what? A revolt of her workers? Or worse . . . an assault by Big Sam?

That doesn't change my feelings for the man, she told herself in the welcome coolness of the hall. She had not relished all the visits he'd made since her father's death, visits that he claimed were to check on her welfare. Maybe he's genuinely concerned, she thought for a moment. Maybe she was being unfair because he was a northerner, a carpetbagger, and much older than she.

Zeb followed them. "Bring coffee and brandy to the drawing room," she told him.

"Just coffee for me," Judson said, his eyes on the paintings that hung along the wall. "Who was the artist?"

"My mother did the ones in the small gold frames," Jennifer replied coolly. The paintings of prewar Georgia were her only legacy from her mother, her only connection to the vaguely remembered woman who'd died after a miscarriage when Jennifer was three years old.

"Nice." He nodded, his gaze shifting abruptly to her. "You paint too?"

She shrugged, having decided that it was none of his affair that she'd inherited her mother's passion for painting or that her father had allowed her to have special art instruction each winter when she'd attended school in Savannah. She wanted to keep him out of her personal life. "Please come into the drawing room, Mr. Carr," she said instead. "Zeb will bring the coffee directly."

She walked to the doorway of the room, then stood aside for Judson to enter first. Sunlight streamed in through the tall windows that stood open to the veranda, allowing the heavy fragrance of the flowering shrubs into the house. He paused, impressed as always by the setting, elegant despite the faded oriental carpet and frayed brocade draperies and worn furniture. She watched his admiring glance move from the floral print of the French wallpaper to the marble mantel of the fireplace, to the carved black walnut woodwork.

"Magnificent house," he said quietly.

She nodded, acknowledging his compliment, the same one he gave each time he entered the house. "Please sit down," Jennifer said politely, suddenly aware that his eyes were assessing her now, noting her soiled work dress and how it clung to the curves of her body. She tilted her chin up, annoyed. Damn the man, she silently cursed.

He seated himself on a gold velvet, high-backed chair, his stare unwavering, while Jennifer chose a hassock. Because I spent the morning in the fields doesn't mean I'm inferior to Judson Carr, she reminded herself, and sat up straighter, exuding all the dignity she could muster.

Jennifer was relieved when Zeb brought the coffee. Although grateful to Judson for saving her from Big Sam, she was eager for him to leave.

Judson sipped his coffee, his appraising eyes making her more nervous. "I came with a proposal for you," he began, and then cleared his throat.

"A proposal?" She stared, noticing that his face was flushed from the base of his thinning hair to his fleshy jowls.

Judson shifted position, crossing his booted feet. "I may

as well come to the point," he said, his smile revealing stained teeth.

"I wish you would," Jennifer replied, her hand trembling as she pushed a strand of blond hair back under the scarf she wore turbanlike in the manner of the Negro women.

"High Bluffs is having labor problems . . . like today," he began, his tone hardening. "A lone girl can't handle that kind of thing."

"But—"

He waved her to silence, rudely continuing his flow of words. "Your father's death made you an orphan, and I understand you have no living relatives."

"I have a half brother."

He nodded curtly. "So I heard. A man eighteen years older than you who went West and never came back. . . . Isn't that true?"

Jennifer stiffened on the hassock. "No, I don't expect my brother's return is imminent," she said coldly. But that's none of your damn business, she thought to herself.

"You're alone in the world, and so am I." He paused, running his tongue over his thin lips. "As we own adjoining property, I've been giving thought to the advantages of an alliance." He waved his hand as Jennifer was about to speak. "Let me finish," he said, his words running together, so that she had no chance to interrupt. "I've come to propose marriage to you."

Jennifer jumped up, her empty cup and saucer falling from her lap to the carpet. "What? You can't be serious."

"But I am, my dear." He stood now, looming over her, and Jennifer cringed involuntarily.

Something flickered in his eyes. Anger? Or embarrassment? she wondered, knowing he must see that she wasn't interested in him.

His eyes narrowed, but he stepped back. "Just think about it. I don't need your answer today." He picked up her cup and saucer, and placed them on a table. "But in the meantime, I do want you to consider another offer—a sincere, neighborly offer to help you keep your field workers in line."

He'd progressed from marriage to labor problems with

such speed that she had hardly had time to formulate her objections.

"You must see that you'd benefit from my help—a man's authority, if you will," he said, his tone stiff. "The alternative is to have no workers to harvest your cotton."

"I've got everything under control now," she said, not wanting to admit that he'd just voiced her own fears.

"Like hell you have," he retorted. "Only until the next incident, when they'll all leave for sure." He turned and strode to the window, the back of his shirt damp with perspiration. "A young woman of genteel upbringing has no business in the fields beside blacks." He spun around, his critical gaze moving from her sunburned, dirt-smudged face to her stained work dress and dusty shoes.

A great wave of anger hit her as she stood facing him, trying to decide whether to tell him to leave or to leave herself. A southern gentleman would have had the good manners not to remind a lady, by word or by look, that she didn't appear her best.

But before she could decide, he picked up his whip and hat, thanked her for the refreshment, and walked out to the hall. "I'll be back in the morning," he said over his shoulder.

"Mr. Carr . . . wait!" She hurried after him. "I can't possibly accept your help," she said primly, displaying all of her Carlyle pride. "It—it wouldn't be proper."

"You can, Miss Jennifer," he replied, his expression hard, "because you have no other choice if you're to manage your hands. Blacks are rebellious even with a man as an overseer. But a girl?" He shook his head, then continued out through the wide front doorway. "I'll see you tomorrow," he said. "And in the meantime, you'd do well to consider my other offer." After a final glance, he got into his buggy, cracked the whip, and was gone in a crunching of wheels against shells.

Jennifer closed the door against the brilliant sunshine and leaned back against its polished surface. God help me, she thought as her whole body began to tremble. What next? Tears of frustration welled up in her eyes. How would she ever manage, a lone woman in a world designed by men . . . to be run by men.

She yanked off her turban and tossed it across the hall. Skirts whirling, she spun around and then started up the wide sweeping staircase to the second floor. She would take a bath, wash the dirt and sweat from her body and hair. But how could she wipe Judson Carr's words from her mind? she fumed, words she knew she had no choice but to consider.

"I'd rather be dead than married to him!" she cried out to the empty second floor of her house. Yet, as her glance slid over the familiar walls she remembered her earlier words at the graves of her parents, words vowing to keep High Bluffs at any cost, and that meant harvesting the cotton.

Chapter Two

Jennifer still couldn't believe it. The final days of July and the first two weeks of August had gone so well . . . and now this. She sat on the window seat and stared at the moon-haunted landscape of High Bluffs, where the first glimmer of dawn was a blush of light on the horizon. She shivered, pulling her sheer robe closer around her body. Her feet, tucked under her on the velvet seat, were numb.

Shifting position, she stretched her limbs, gritting her teeth as her legs prickled back to life. Then she pulled up her knees to rest her chin on them, unable to stop thinking about the tax server's visit the morning before, or the banker who'd arrived in the afternoon.

As Jennifer listened to birds awakening in the magnolia trees and oleanders, she finally admitted to herself that there was only one answer to her problem: Judson Carr.

Her mind made up, she yanked open the doors of the cupboard. Feeling around in the darkness, she took out her favorite blue dimity gown and placed it on the chintz-covered bed.

"Papa, today I cannot wear a black mourning gown," she whispered as she lit the candles on her dressing table, "forgive me."

Jennifer poured tepid pitcher water into the bowl, then bathed herself and donned fresh undergarments before stepping into the dress. When she adjusted the bustle, she realized she'd forgotten her corset. No need for it, she decided. She'd become so thin from the long hours of work that the damnable thing was too big anyway.

Sitting before her dressing table mirror, Jennifer arranged her long blond hair into a chignon, then stared at her image in the glass. Her blue eyes glowed with reflected candlelight, and her cheeks were fevered from worry. God help me, she thought, and with a quick motion, blew out the candles.

Judson will understand, she thought. Since the morning after the confrontation with Big Sam, he had been overseeing the workers. And he'd always been polite, not pressuring her for an answer to his proposal of marriage. Although she didn't love the man, she was coming to respect him—even like him. Judson will lend me the money, she decided. But her hand shook as she grabbed up her straw hat, and her knees quivered as she strode to the door and out into the hall.

She couldn't help but wish it were September instead of August, so that she already had the money from the crops. Then she wouldn't have to ask anyone for anything. If only there were someone to talk to. She started down the steps and her thoughts shifted to the people she'd always considered friends. She couldn't go to any of them for help now: the Picketts, with whom she'd boarded while she attended school; the minister of Christ Episcopal Church, who'd married her parents; or the girls from the female academy. Her hand tightened on the banister. They'd all been avoiding her for some time. They never came to call anymore and had stopped inviting her to their social gatherings. At first she'd believed it was because she was in mourning, and it had come as a shock when whe discovered the truth: the old families of Savannah disapproved of her working in the fields with blacks. They would certainly never forgive her for accepting a carpetbagger's help in running the plantation, either.

"Damn hypocrites," she told the quiet house. They were treating her like she was a—a what? Someone with a contagious disease? Or someone as unacceptable in society as the infamous Savannah madam, Nellie Thornton? They didn't understand that she'd had no choice, not if High Bluffs was to survive.

As Jennifer rode beside Zeb in the buggy the sun climbed above the pine hills, burning away the dew that webbed the flowering shrubs and live oaks lining the avenue. She kept her gaze on the house that sat like a dull

blister on a patch of scorched grass, a square red brick
building not nearly as elegant as High Bluffs.

Her heartbeats suddenly fluttered with alarming speed.
Within minutes she'd be facing Judson to ask for money.
Fear knotted her stomach. What if she couldn't save the
plantation? What if she lost it because of back taxes?—taxes
she hadn't realized her father owed until the tax server had
arrived with the eviction papers that gave her until the end
of the week to pay the full amount. Twenty-five hundred
dollars; for her it might as well have been a million. She
clenched her gloved hands and sighed. She was down to
her last hundred.

The mist was rising off the Savannah River as Zeb reined
in the horse next to the veranda steps. A black servant
immediately came forward and took the bridle.

Jennifer stepped to the ground unaided and then was
suddenly assailed by doubt. She adjusted the bustle of her
dress, hoping the dimity looked as fresh as when she'd left
home, that the neckline wasn't too low, that wisps of hair
hadn't come free of the pins.

"You is lookin' pretty as yo' mama 'fore she die," Zeb told
her, sensing that she needed reassurance. "And yo' papa
sho buy you fine dresses 'fore he go to da Lord."

Jennifer smiled at Zeb; his words had restored her
confidence. Her father had always bought her new gowns
each year after the harvest, insisting that she look like the
mistress of High Bluffs. God, she sighed inwardly, how she
missed him—his loving concern, his sense of fairness, the
companionship they'd always shared.

Suddenly Jennifer was hit with another disturbing
thought. Her father couldn't have afforded new gowns or
his many trips into Savannah. That money should have
gone for back taxes and bank loans.

Too late for recriminations, she told herself, knowing
now that her schooling at the academy, her winter board at
the Picketts, and her painting lessons had also cost more
than the plantation could provide. Lifting her skirts,
Jennifer started forward. As she reached the porch the
paneled door opened and Judson strode out to greet her.

"Jennifer," he said, his eyebrows arching in surprise. "An
unexpected pleasure." His black eyes flickered over her,

noting the low cut of her gown and that she'd discarded her mourning black. He took her arm and led her into the house.

It smelled of stale tobacco, dust, and mildew, and looked in need of a proper cleaning. No wonder Judson coveted High Bluffs, she thought as he led her into the dining room.

"Won't you join me for breakfast?" he asked, pulling out a chair.

"I've already eaten, thank you," she lied, knowing food would choke her.

Judson hesitated before rounding the table to sit opposite, and Jennifer felt his scrutiny. Her thoughts whirled as she searched for the words that would give her what she needed . . . money.

He resumed his meal, alternating mouthfuls of congealed eggs with gulps of coffee and bits of conversation about the cotton crop, unmindful of his crude table manners.

She shuddered. His breeding wasn't much above that of the blacks. Jennifer forced her mind away from the thought of intimacy with him, remembering why she was here . . . to save High Bluffs.

Abruptly he pushed back his plate, the full force of his dark eyes on her. "Well," he drawled. "It's obvious you're here for a reason. What is it?"

Jennifer's stomach lurched, sending tremors into her limbs. Nervously, she licked her lips, hating his insensitive manner. God, she pleaded silently, let my voice sound normal.

"Well?" Judson prompted.

"I need money," she began, knowing she must take a direct approach with Judson. "I've—I've come to ask you for a loan."

"A loan?" His tone reflected surprise, but his eyes narrowed. "Your cotton is almost ready for harvest—can't you wait for that money?"

Her lashes fluttered, but she kept her gaze steady. "I need twenty-five hundred dollars by Friday."

His lids lowered, hooding his eyes. While she waited, her nerves tingling, he pulled a cigar from his shirt pocket, lit it, and blew some smoke. Beyond the windows the plantation was alive with activity, but in the room the silence stretched into minutes. Was he thinking about marriage? she wondered. During the night she'd decided to accept Judson's proposal even though she didn't love him. But she'd felt it would be a bad beginning to do so before paying the back taxes. Once they were paid, she could stave off foreclosure until she sold her crops. The money from the cotton would repay Judson and take care of the wages for the workers. After they were man and wife, Judson could pay the planting loan, as High Bluffs would then belong to him.

"I'm sorry, Jennifer," he began, interrupting her thoughts. "But I can't lend money blindly."

"You won't—"

He shook his head, his eyes opaque behind the smoke.

She twisted her hands together, knowing she had no choice; he wasn't making it easy. "There's a planting loan against High Oaks," she began and hesitated, hating to reveal her financial problems. "The bank is foreclosing on Friday."

He crushed his cigar in his plate. "All planters have loans and the bank will wait for the harvest." A brief smile twisted his lips. "You're upset over nothing, my dear."

Tears of frustration burned behind her eyes. "But—uh—there are back taxes—delinquent taxes I didn't know about." She broke off, willing her throat muscles to relax so she could go on. "The tax server says the plantation will be seized if I don't pay." She glanced away. "And the bank is calling their note before the property is confiscated."

"Jesus Christ!"

"I'll pay you back right after the harvest," she said, unmindful that her voice had taken on a pleading tone.

He stared, his expression closed, suddenly reminding her that he was a northern carpetbagger.

"Of course I wouldn't ask had you not proposed marriage, and had I not decided to accept your proposal," she said, trying to ignore his stony silence.

"I'm shocked," he said finally. "I'd always believed that the Carlyles still had money to go with the land." He gave a laugh, a sharp bark that sent shivers of foreboding down her spine. "I believed the neglect at High Bluffs was due to it being run by an old man and then a girl."

Jennifer's face burned with humiliation. Damn him to hell, she thought. She'd caught the implication in his tone. He was the master of the situation and enjoying the fact that she was begging for money.

Pushing back his chair, he stood up, giving her no choice but to do the same.

"I can't give you a decision until I review my own finances." Judson rounded the table, took her arm, and directed her back to the front entrance before she could think of a reply. "But I'll let you know soon," he added coolly.

Suddenly Jennifer knew that her one hope was fading faster than the echo of Judson's words. She freed her arm and faced him. "It's imperative that I get the money," she said, mustering all her dignity. "And important for both of us if we're to marry." She drew a ragged breath. "Can't you decide right now?"

"No," he replied curtly, as though he were a stranger, not the man who'd proposed marriage to her.

As she walked to the veranda, her emotions swinging between anger and hopelessness, Jennifer knew she would just have to wait for Judson's decision. Without another word, she swept down to the buggy, climbed in, and signaled Zeb to drive them back to High Bluffs.

As the vehicle lurched forward she again met Judson's unreadable gaze. "I'll see you soon?"

He inclined his head, then turned away and disappeared into his house.

Jennifer's body shook. Dear God, she thought, she hadn't expected cold indifference from Judson, not for one moment had she imagined he wouldn't give her the loan.

Twisting on the seat, she glanced back at the empty veranda. Even the hot sun couldn't take away the chill that raised gooseflesh over her body.

Turning back to the road, she forced her mind away from disturbing thoughts. Don't panic, she told herself. Judson, the man who wanted to marry her, would save High Bluffs. He loved the plantation almost as much as she did.

For the first time in weeks Judson didn't appear in the morning to check on the field hands. By Thursday after-

noon, the day before bank foreclosure, Jennifer was
exhausted from the days of hard work and the long nights of
sleeplessness.

Unable to work, she determined to pay Judson another
visit. As she crossed the hall the sound of wheels crunching
up the driveway sent her running to the nearest window.

She hurried to the door, then slowed to a sedate walk
before stepping onto the veranda. Her gaze fell on Judson,
who was tying the reins of his buggy to the hitching post.
When he turned to face her, his expression was set in hard
lines, and his inscrutable black eyes sent a cold chunk of
fear to the pit of her stomach.

"Come in, Judson," she managed to say, striving for calm.

"I can't stay, Jennifer," he replied, his words clipped.
"I've been in Savannah, and I want to be home before
dark."

She stared, her body tensing, anticipating his next
words.

"But I want you to know that—um—uh—I can't lend you
money." He toed shells as the silence swelled into a
monstrous presence that threatened to choke the breath
from Jennifer. "It's just not possible for me to do so at this
time."

"I'll—I'll lose High Bluffs." Seemingly of their own
volition, her legs propelled her forward, and she grabbed
his arm. "You can't mean it—you must give me the money."
She didn't care that tears spilled from her eyes—that she
was begging. "You asked me to marry you . . . doesn't
that mean keeping High Bluffs?"

"Pull yourself together, Jennifer," he said, shaking off her
hand. "I *am* sorry, but there's nothing I can do." He turned
away from her, untied the reins, and leaped back into the
buggy.

"Judson!" she cried as the vehicle jerked into motion.
"You can't do this . . . what about our marriage?"

He glanced back, his expression closed. "We'll discuss
that later." He cracked the whip, and the horse went from
trot to gallop, quickly taking Judson beyond her voice.

Jennifer stared until the buggy was only a dust cloud in
the distance. Then she went back into the house and up to
her bedroom, where she closed the door on the world.

* * *

From her window seat Jennifer watched the moon rise to cast a silver spell over the hills and fields. The house had been silent for a long time, as if it sensed that everything was about to change—that she would be leaving forever. Even Zeb had finally stopped coaxing her to eat. Poor Zeb, she thought. He had no family but for his grandson Noah, who'd gone west with Joseph. And Zeb, like Jennifer, had nowhere to go; High Bluffs was the only home they'd ever known.

Impulsively Jennifer went down to the front door and a moment later was outside, moving like a specter across the eerie landscape, following the river toward the oaks, where the moss-draped branches beckoned, black witch-fingers against the luminous night.

At the graveyard Jennifer paused. Then she crumpled, sobbing, onto the damp earth that covered her parents, She was conscious of nothing but the fact that she'd failed. It was unthinkable . . . impossible . . . but true. She, the last Carlyle, was losing High Bluffs.

Struggling to her feet, she stood on trembling legs for her final goodbyes.

"Mama and Papa," she said, her words whispering like a gentle wind through the Spanish Moss. "Whatever happens I'll always remember you—try to make you proud of me." Jennifer paused, forcing back more tears. "I'll never forget the tradition of the Carlyle family—to endure no matter what the future holds."

Slowly she turned away. Then, hesitating, she glanced back for the last time. "Somehow, someday, I'll make you proud of me."

Chapter Three

The next morning Jennifer was determined to go on as though disaster didn't hang like a thundercloud above the plantation. As noon approached she began to hope that the threat of foreclosure had been a bluff.

"Someone comes," Zeb informed her shortly after lunch.

Jennifer hurried to the door, her heart stopping momentarily when she recognized Mr. Penn, the portly man from the bank.

"I'm sorry, Miss Carlyle," Mr. Penn said as she went out to meet his buggy. He reached into the pocket of his frock coat and pulled out a paper. "This grieves me but—uh—I'm afraid High Bluffs no longer belongs to you."

"What?" Jennifer's gaze darted to Zeb, who looked as stricken as she felt.

"Perfectly legal," Mr. Penn said, and paused to clear his throat. "Unless you have the money for the back taxes . . . do you?"

Jennifer shook her head, dazed. "Please, can't the bank wait until my cotton is harvested?"

He blinked nervously. "The tax people won't wait, and bank policy is to call in the loan in such circumstances."

"But the bank could pay the taxes—add the amount to my loan. I'd pay it all back within the month." She hated to beg, but she'd give up her soul to save the plantation.

He waved a hand, silencing her. "Your yield couldn't possibly repay both the loan and taxes. These are hard times, and the bank must protect itself. Someone else has put up money to pay the taxes and mortgage." He glanced away, avoiding her eyes. "The bank must accept this sale if you're unable to meet your debts."

For a moment the afternoon went dark; Jennifer clung to

the hitching post, fighting an urge to faint. It was as though she'd stepped into a nightmare, yet the sun was still shining over the land that was no longer hers.

"Who?" she whispered.

"I can't say—until tomorrow when your grace period is up."

A light breeze rippled through the flowers and shrubs, while beyond the old slave quarters, the field hands sang a work song. *Nothing will ever be the same again,* Jennifer thought numbly as she watched Mr. Penn take up the reins.

"The new owner will harvest the cotton—recoup some of his money," he told her. "And—he requests you be gone as soon as possible." Mr. Penn glanced away. "You know, of course, that your father included the furnishings as collateral for the loan?"

She caught her trembling lower lip between her teeth. "No," she said, her tone so faint, she doubted he heard her.

After inclining his head for a moment, Mr. Penn was gone, leaving Jennifer to wonder who'd paid her debts. No one had extra money these days; no one but carpetbaggers.

She stood rooted to the ground, oblivious to the burning sun. What could she do now?—Where would she go? *Judson,* she thought in reply. She'd send him a note, again ask for his help.

"I want my mother's paintings crated up," Jennifer told Zeb the next morning as she removed the four small pictures from the wall.

By early afternoon the crated paintings were propped against Jennifer's trunk and boxes in the hall. She'd decided to seek help from the Picketts in Savannah; they'd been like family to her when she'd lived with them while attending school. She'd stay with them until she heard from Judson— and decided whether or not to marry him.

Suddenly a knock startled her. She whirled around and then stepped to the open doorway, where a slender young man was standing. He handed her an envelope.

"A message from Mr. Penn," he told her.

Jennifer stared at the envelope, her hopes soaring. *Maybe I'm not being evicted after all,* she thought, waiting until the man was galloping down the drive before tearing open the seal.

Yanking out the letter, her gaze flew over the page. "God! It's not possible." She slumped into the nearest veranda chair, the paper fluttering to the floor.

Zeb rushed to her side. "Miss Jennifer," he began, but was silenced by her expression.

"Zeb." Her voice shook. "Judson's the one buying High Bluffs."

Zeb's eyes widened. "Mist' Judson?"

"Mr. Penn has written that Judson is giving me several more days before I have to leave."

"But Mist' Judson wants you to marry up with him," Zeb said, his expression puzzled.

Hatred seared through Jennifer. "I'd die before I'd marry him now." She leapt up. "All I did by asking that devil for a loan was to give him the chance to take High Bluffs. That northern carpetbagger . . . scum!"

She whirled and faced Zeb. "If he stood here now I'd— I'd kill him!"

Zeb wrung his hands, shaking his grizzled head. "Miss Jennifer, doan talk like dat. Yo' mama and papa would be right upset with yo' language. It ain' right nohow."

"Is what Judson did right?" Her tone was shrill. "And what about you, Zeb—where will you go?"

He shook his head again, torment in his eyes.

"You'll come with me."

A large tear glistened in each eye. "I can't leave High Bluffs," he whispered. "If'n I go, Noah won't know where to find me."

"But—but he and Joseph aren't coming back. Not ever." Jennifer took his hands. "You can't stay for that."

Tears slid down the lined face. "An' den I'll look after yo' mama and papa's graves. If you's not here no more, I'll do dat, 'cause someone has to. 'Sides I's a heap too old to go."

"But Judson won't want you here."

"Den I'll stay with some sharecroppers down da road a piece."

Suddenly she was hugging him, the old man who was like a grandfather to her. Her eyes burned and her throat ached, but her sorrow was beyond tears. She needed strength now—to face the future alone.

"I love you Zeb . . . and I understand." With a final kiss, she fled upstairs for one last, sleepless night.

Jennifer awoke to birds chirping outside her windows. She dressed quickly, went out to the veranda, and stood gazing at her beloved cotton fields. As she turned back to the house to find Zeb she swallowed hard. It was time to leave.

Suddenly Jennifer heard the familiar crunch of oyster shells and stopped short, her eyes on the man reining in his horse below the veranda steps.

Hatred boiled through her veins. "Yankee carpetbagger!" she cried, flinging back her long hair haughtily. "You—you northern scum!"

Judson's dark eyes narrowed dangerously, but his reply was cold and controlled. "So they told you, eh?" He paused. "There's no need for hysterics, my dear Jennifer."

"Hysterics?—You—you—" she sputtered, groping for words to express her hatred. "I wouldn't marry you if you were the last man on earth."

He shrugged, but she could see anger tighten his features. "I no longer have a need to wed you," he said, and got ready to dismount. "But I'd have done so to get your land—uh—my land now," he corrected himself.

Speechless, Jennifer stepped next to his horse. "You were using me to get what you wanted . . . High Bluffs."

His mouth twisted into a mocking smile. "I was quite willing to marry you until I realized it wasn't necessary."

Jennifer lunged forward and slapped the horse's flank. The animal reared, almost unseating Judson before bolting down the drive. "I hope you break your neck!" she screamed. Rage consumed her; she had but one thought . . . revenge. And there seemed only one obvious way.

She ran across the lawn to where a black woman was washing clothes in an iron tub over an open fire. Grabbing the woman's broomstick, which lay near some kindling, Jennifer dipped the dry straw into the coals, impatiently waiting as the sprigs reddened and finally ignited.

Scared and astonished, the woman whined, "Miss Jennifer? What's you doin' with dat broom?"

Ignoring her, Jennifer ran with the flaming torch to the

edge of the cotton field and, with one quick sweep, set it on fire. Smoke billowed upward almost immediately, a churning, dark cloud that spit hot cinders onto more cotton. Surprised cries from the field hands sounded above the crescendo of the flames, and from the corner of her eye she saw Judson wheel his horse around and start back up the drive.

Momentarily hypnotized, Jennifer watched as the fiery monster gobbled up the cotton. A fickle breeze was spreading the flames in all directions.

A flash of satisfaction shot through her. She stared at the wall of flames that was roaring over the rows of plants and at the blacks running to escape the fire. The crop was doomed; months of work would be destroyed in minutes. Judson Carr would never profit from her work. Before she had been born, the Yankees had burned their fields. Now she was doing the same thing. She had her revenge.

Exultant, Jennifer ran back to the house, slamming the door behind her. Judson had taken her plantation, but he wasn't getting her crop, she told herself. As she calmed down, however, she realized she must leave quickly.

"Zeb," she called. "Hitch up the buggy." Her words echoed into the silent house, but there was no answer from Zeb.

Suddenly the door banged open, shaking the windows and jolting the paintings that still hung against the wall. Jennifer's gaze flew to the man who stood in the doorway, his face a mask of fury. Behind him the field was a red sea of fire.

"I should kill you," he said hoarsely, slapping his whip against his leg.

Jennifer stepped backward as an almost paralyzing fear shot down her spine. "Get out of here."

In a second he was across the room, grabbing her arm roughly. "You're going to pay for this."

"That cotton was rightfully mine . . . not yours."

"Wrong!" His free hand encircled her waist, yanking her against him, until his face was inches above hers. "You'll compensate me—in the only way you can." His breath smelled of garlic and stale tobacco.

Repulsed, Jennifer twisted, trying to free herself. "Let

me go you—you smelly snake. This is still my house until I leave . . . which I intend doing right now."

"Wrong again." His lids lowered. "You'll leave when I'm done with you." He pulled her into the drawing room while she kicked and struggled against his superior strength. "Yes, you'll pay . . . with your body."

Panic-stricken, Jennifer managed to squirm out of his grasp and stumbled backward. When she regained her footing, she ran for the door.

She'd only gone a few steps when his arms came down hard on her shoulders, knocking her to her knees. "You little vixen," he said, growling the words. His face was an ugly red and dotted with sweat.

His arms held her like a vise as he pulled her to him again. God help me, she pleaded silently. She knew her prayer was futile when she saw Judson's dirty hand reach for the neck of her gown. With one sudden motion he ripped her bodice open to the waist. His eyes gazed at her white breasts for a moment. Ashamed, Jennifer again tried to twist out of his grasp.

"No escape this time," he hissed at her, dragging her to her feet. When she braced her heels against the carpet, Judson grabbed her hair with a vicious yank.

Jennifer's scream echoed into every corner of the house, drowning Judson's cruel laughter. He threw her onto the sofa, pinioning her arms and legs to the velvet with the weight of his body.

"Please!" she pleaded. "You mustn't—" Her voice broke.

"But I must, my dear." He fondled her breasts, pinching her nipples. She cringed, and his fingers tightened painfully.

Jennifer tried to roll out from under him, desperate to escape, terrified by what was about to happen. Freeing a hand, she clawed at him, raking her nails down his face.

Judson winced. "You spitfire—never learn do you." He slapped her hard, stunning her.

She started to cry out, but he silenced her with his mouth, his kiss wet and brutal. A sob caught in Jennifer's throat as tears flooded her eyes. Oh, God, where was Zeb, she cried silently.

"You devil—you Yankee pig. I'll kill you for this!" she shouted against his lips.

His laugh was harsh, but his breathing came in short gasps as his legs forced hers apart. She could feel him fumbling with his trousers. Jennifer knew there was no way she could stop him now.

"Let go of that girl, Judson," a female voice demanded from the doorway, "or I'll blow your cheating, conniving head off your body."

Judson jerked his head up in surprise. A moment later he was on his feet, his eyes on the strange women. "What in hell are you doing here?"

Trembling, unable to believe she'd been saved, Jennifer scrambled off the sofa. She, like Judson, stared at the buxom woman dressed in an emerald velvet traveling suit, an attractive woman apparently in her late thirties . . . a woman with a gun in her hand.

"Who are you?" Jennifer asked shakily. It was obvious from the daring cut of her suit, and from her rouged and powdered face, that her rescuer was not a "lady."

"Nellie Thornton, a friend," she replied, keeping her gaze and her gun leveled on Judson while she swept into the room.

Jennifer's eyes widened. Nellie Thornton was the madam of the most notorious brothel in Savannah.

"Get out," Nellie Thornton told Judson. "While you still can."

Judson hesitated. Nellie fired, her hand jerking upward as a bullet thudded into the French wallpaper behind him.

"Jesus!" Judson's face drained of color. Then, as Nellie tensed to fire again, he strode quickly to the door, where he paused only to glance back at Jennifer. "You were lucky, but not for long. I'll have you arrested for what you did."

"Git!" Nellie repeated sharply. "Right now . . . clean off the property."

Within seconds they heard his horse's hooves scattering oyster shells.

Nellie Thornton placed the gun in her handbag. Behind her, Zeb suddenly appeared in the doorway.

"Miss Jennifer, how dis happen?" he asked anxiously.

"God forgive me, I set the field on fire so he couldn't take my cotton."

Nellie handed Jennifer her shawl. "You'd better cover yourself."

Embarrassment warmed Jennifer's face. How could she have forgotten about her state, she scolded herself.

"Now then," Nellie went on. "I heard about your being evicted, and I'm here to help, because I was your father's friend."

"But what—" Jennifer began, a dozen questions whirling in her mind.

"There's no time to discuss this now," Nellie said, ignoring Jennifer's incredulous expression. "Judson'll be back with the law. If you're still here, God only knows what'll happen to you. That man has no mercy." She hesitated. "You'd better come with me."

"Zeb'll take me to Savannah," Jennifer said, abruptly cool. Nellie Thornton might have saved her from Judson, but Jennifer would not allow such a woman to interfere in her life. What was happening, she wondered, first carpetbaggers and now madams?

"And if you meet Judson on the road?" Nellie asked.

Jennifer tilted her chin. "I can take care of myself."

Nellie closed the space between them, grabbing Jennifer to shake her. "Christ! This is no time for proprieties. Your reputation is already ruined from working with blacks and from allowing yourself to be courted by a carpetbagger with a reputation for using women." She took a deep breath. "Do you want to end up in jail next?"

Jennifer stared, trying to read Nellie's intentions. The woman looked genuinely concerned for her.

"Think of your father—what he'd want you to do." Nellie paused. "Besides, who in Savannah will help you now?"

"My friends will help." Jennifer hesitated. "And I *had* to work with the blacks—to save High Bluffs. And I believed Judson wanted to marry me, because—because he cared for me."

"That's the past," Nellie said sharply. "It's the present we have to worry about now."

"We?"

She nodded. "I told you I was your father's friend."

Jennifer finally agreed with Nellie. Zeb would be in danger driving her to Savannah. Sadly Jennifer watched as her trunk and the paintings were quickly loaded into Nellie's carriage.

Jennifer's gaze swept over the smoking fields. The acrid smell of burned cotton hung in the air, but it was Zeb's stricken face that made her cry. She threw her arms around him.

"Oh, Zeb, I love you, and I'll—I'll miss you . . . terribly." She clung to him, knowing she might never see him again. Then she climbed into Nellie's carriage.

"I love you too, Miss Jennifer," Zeb said softly, tears streaming from his eyes as the vehicle started toward the corridor of live oaks, leaving him standing alone.

Jennifer turned away and fixed her gaze on her lap, willing herself not to break down again in front of Nellie Thornton. Papa, she thought, swallowing hard, I'm glad you're not here to see a carpetbagger take the plantation.

Suddenly Nellie leaned out the window to signal the driver and the carriage rocked to a stop. "This is the last place where you can see High Bluffs," she said kindly. "I thought you'd like a final look."

For a moment Jennifer was tempted. In her mind's eye she saw the Corinthian columns of her home, the brilliance of the flowering shrubs, the live oaks, and the cotton fields. She would carry those memories forever. Slowly she shook her head, knowing she couldn't bear it.

"Thank you," she whispered, again close to tears. "But . . . I can't."

Nellie covered Jennifer's clenched hands with her own. "I understand," she said, signaling the driver to continue on.

Jennifer stared with burning eyes at the passing scenery, wondering if she would ever return. She would miss the magnolias and white dogwoods in spring, the smell of river mist, the fragrance of warm earth, and the bonfires that lit the slave quarters at night. Suddenly she realized that she no longer belonged anywhere, or to anyone.

They were sitting in silence when the carriage approached Savannah. The vehicle slowed as it moved along cobblestoned streets lined with stucco-and-brick houses adorned with lacy wrought iron balconies and stair rails. The city was a mass of parks and squares, flowering shrubs and shade trees. As they approached the Picketts' house Nellie finally spoke.

"Jennifer, please come with me—Judson will find you here."

"My friends will help me," Jennifer replied, hoping she was right.

Jennifer glanced beyond the filigreed iron fence to the narrow, brick house; the shuttered front windows did not convey a sense of welcome. What if the Picketts wouldn't take her in?

"Jennifer? We must talk soon—I have something important to tell you."

Jennifer breathed deeply of air fragrant from the nearby sea. She wouldn't be seeing Nellie again. She'd worked with field hands and been deceived by a carpetbagger, but she wouldn't stoop to associating with a madam. She couldn't do that to her father's memory.

But she was grateful to Nellie. "Thank you," Jennifer began, realizing that Nellie's concern was sincere. "I appreciate your bringing me to Savannah." Then she turned away and stepped out of the carriage.

Moments later Jennifer stood staring after the departing vehicle, feeling a strange security in knowing there was one person in the world who seemed concerned for her welfare. That thought gave her the courage to go up the shaded walk and knock on the front door.

Maybe she should hear what Nellie had to say. What do I have to lose, she mused, my reputation? She smiled wryly as the door opened.

Chapter Four

Jennifer stood in the vestibule by the front door, waiting for Nellie's carriage; her belongings were piled beside her. She could feel the Picketts' disapproval even as they stood silently. When Jennifer had boarded with them, they had treated her almost like a granddaughter. Never having been blessed with children of their own, they were lonely and had taken her to their hearts. However, when the gossip about Jennifer's behavior had horrified Savannah society, their weekly letters to her had abruptly stopped. Yesterday they'd only begrudgingly allowed her to stay the night. When Nellie's note had arrived the first thing in the morning, requesting a talk, offering a "respectable solution" to Jennifer's dilemma, Jennifer had been relieved and sent back her acceptance with the driver.

"You're really meeting with this—this woman?" Mr. Pickett finally asked, coldly.

"I have no choice," Jennifer replied equally coolly, trying to hide her hurt. "And, as I told you, she saved me—"

"Mercy." Mrs. Pickett fluttered her fan, interrupting Jennifer. "Spare us the details."

Jennifer stared at them. They'd chosen to ignore her plight, yet were shocked that she'd meet Nellie Thorton, the only person who had offered help. Jennifer clenched her hands nervously. She didn't like associating with Nellie either, but as she had nowhere to go and almost no money, she had few options.

"If you go with her, you won't be welcome here," Mr. Pickett said, his face pursed into a mass of loose wrinkles.

"Are you saying I can stay if I don't go with Nellie Thornton?"

"I'm saying that you've almost ruined your reputation already—to be seen with that woman will guarantee your downfall," he replied. "As it is, no decent man would marry you."

His wife nodded. "You're too headstrong, Jennifer, too determined to do as you please, regardless of proprieties."

"You're both hypocrites," Jennifer retorted. "You condemn me, but you won't help me."

"See—see." Mrs. Pickett's spectacles slid down her nose so that her small eyes peered over the lenses. "Your father was too permissive—allowing you to be friendly with the Negroes, buying you Paris gowns when you were a schoolgirl, and—and painting lessons . . . indeed." Her huge bosom heaved from the effort of her rising anger. "What good will painting pictures do you? Will it give you a home? Find you a husband?"

"My father was a good man." She tilted her chin haughtily. "How dare you condemn him."

Mrs. Pickett gasped. "You're an unmannerly chit—and as willful as your mother; if she hadn't kept painting while with child, she might not have died."

Although her mother had died when she was only three, Jennifer did have vague memories of a loving woman who smelled of lavender water and turpentine, and who sang and told Jennifer stories while sitting before her easel. Jennifer faced Mrs. Pickett. "You cruel old lady—I wouldn't spend another night in this house if you begged me." She broke off, close to tears.

With relief, she heard carriage wheels on the cobblestones outside. She quickly turned away from the Picketts and grabbed up her toilet case. "I'll send for my things," she said angrily, and ran out the door, slamming it behind her. She knew she had doomed her future in Savannah forever. Everything she had believed to be the foundation of her life was gone: family, home, and friends.

She hurried through the gate to the waiting carriage. I'll make my own future, she vowed.

Jennifer stepped into the carriage, seating herself across from Nellie, who greeted her with a sympathetic smile. As the vehicle jolted forward she glimpsed the angry faces of the Picketts peering from a front window.

"They disapprove?" Nellie asked, looking every inch the madam in her tight satin gown.

Jennifer nodded, suddenly apprehensive. God, let this be the right thing to do, she thought. Her decision was an irreversible one, she knew. Leaning back against the cushion, Jennifer waited for Nellie to speak.

"I told you that your father and I were friends," she began, and then hesitated.

Jennifer stiffened at the thought of her father and a madam. But then probably most of the male citizens of Savannah knew Nellie Thornton, she reasoned.

"We were more than friends," Nellie went on, her blue gaze unwavering, although her words had quavered. "We had a child . . . a boy."

"What?" Jennifer stiffened again. "You . . . I don't believe you. Stop the carriage! I won't listen to lies." She twisted on the seat, turning her back on Nellie. "I'll walk back." For the moment she had forgotten that she had nowhere to go.

Nellie grabbed her arm, restraining her. "Wait, Jennifer. I loved your father, and he loved me." He voice broke from emotion. "Please, let me explain so that you'll understand—that I want to help you—that I can help."

Slowly Jennifer turned back to Nellie, surprised by the compassion in the older woman's eyes. "I'll listen . . . but I won't promise to understand."

When Nellie spoke, the words ran together in her haste to explain. "I met your father back in 'seventy, the year after your mother died. He was devastated by her death, and even though he never loved me as much as her, he did care for me." Her eyes sparkled with tears. "I loved him more than I've ever loved anyone aside from Jamie, our son."

"Then why didn't you marry?" Jennifer asked. "After you were expecting a child?"

"It wouldn't have worked," Nellie replied, her tone sad. "Your father and I both knew that. Neither of us could cross into each other's world."

"When—"

"Jamie is thirteen now," Nellie said, anticipating Jennifer's question.

"How? . . . I can't believe this."

"I'm telling the truth, and I can prove it." Nellie reached into her purse and pulled out a letter, which she handed to

Jennifer. "Your father wrote this; it confirms my claim that George Carlyle is Jamie's father."

Jennifer scanned the page, recognizing her father's handwriting. "Why would my father write this?" she cried, once again feeling betrayed, this time by her own father.

"Because he was an honorable man who trusted me not to disrupt his life . . . not to hurt you. But he also loved Jamie, and he knew that his son would need confirmation of his birth one day."

Jennifer stared. "Why tell me now? . . . Why betray my father's trust?"

Nellie busied herself returning the letter to her purse, and Jennifer noticed that the jeweled fingers trembled. "I hadn't planned to," she began, and then looked up. "But when I found out that you'd lost High Bluffs—that you were completely alone—I wanted to help."

As Jennifer started to speak Nellie gestured her to silence. "I've sold my establishment and am leaving Savannah shortly, taking Jamie out to California to start a new life, a respectable life. I want you to go with us." She paused, shaking her head. "I wouldn't have broken my promise to your father, but I believe he would want me to now—to offer you a chance for a new life."

"But you don't know me. Why would you care what happens to me?"

"Because of your father and because you are the half sister of my son." She hesitated. "And because I was once in your situation—cast onto the street with nowhere to go."

"What did you do?" Jennifer asked, her curiosity aroused.

"The only thing I could," Nellie replied. "What you might have to do if you stay in Savannah."

Her words chilled Jennifer. She hadn't allowed herself to think about the future.

"Come with Jamie and me to California." Nellie covered Jennifer's clasped hands with her own. "I have a brother who is a respected businessman in San Francisco. I haven't seen him in years, but I know he'll help us get established properly."

"I—I don't know." Jennifer knew she should say no at once, but the idea of going to California and starting anew

appealed to her. She no longer had roots in Georgia, and
then, there was Judson. Would he actually have the law
after her? she wondered. Could she really go to jail? She bit
her lip. She hadn't believed she'd lose High Bluffs
either . . . and she had.

Something flickered in Nellie's eyes, and Jennifer knew
the woman sensed her indecision. "I understand. Before
you refuse, I'd like you to meet Jamie."

Jennifer nodded, relieved that the decision had been
postponed.

A feeling of unreality hit Jennifer as she walked into the
elegant drawing room in Nellie's waterfront establishment.
As Nellie ordered a servant to bring tea Jennifer's fears
returned, stronger than ever. She was about to have tea in a
brothel with a madam, a woman who wanted to share a
future with her. A woman about whom she knew almost
nothing.

The black serving woman returned and placed a silver
tray on a dainty French table. As the woman was leaving
the room she paused at the doorway to let a young boy
enter, a boy whose dark eyes darted from Nellie to Jennifer.

"Come in, Jamie," Nellie told him.

Jamie flicked another glance at his mother, nodded with a
hesitant smile, then stepped forward, his eyes now on
Jennifer.

Jennifer's heart lurched in her chest. The boy's complexion was dark, as was his hair; he looked like her father.

"Jennifer, I'd like you to meet Jamie," Nellie said,
moving forward so that the three of them formed a triangle.
"And Jamie, this is Jennifer."

At once Jamie offered his hand. Although he was small
for his age, and his whole bearing far too solemn for
thirteen, Jennifer was impressed. Something stirred within
her, feelings she'd not felt for a long time.

"I'm happy to meet you," Jamie said in a voice not yet
matured into manhood.

Jennifer nodded slowly. "And I, you." He knows who he
is and who I am, she thought. Nellie's told him about me,
and he's as curious as I am.

As she watched, a shy smile lit Jamie's face, and she

realized he wasn't ashamed of his background—that he loved his mother. But her most intense realization, one that filled her with unexpected joy, was that the polite, soft-spoken boy who was unmistakably her brother had inherited the Carlyle family pride.

She stepped closer, her gaze held by eyes identical to her father's. "You know?" she asked him.

He nodded.

Instinctively she hugged him. The gesture took even Jennifer by surprise. She didn't care who Jamie's mother was—*he was her brother*. Loneliness and grief welled up in her, sending tears streaming from her eyes. "Oh, Jamie. I'm so glad I found you!"

"I'm glad too," he said, looking startled even though his arms had crept around her to return her embrace.

A smiling Nellie stepped forward and hugged them both, her tone low with emotion as she spoke to Jennifer. "Then you'll join us, come with us to California?"

Jennifer swallowed hard, then nodded, unable to speak.

"C'mom, Mom." Jamie pulled away, now embarrassed. "Hugging is for girls. Besides, the tea's getting cold."

After Nellie had sent the carriage to collect her trunk and paintings, Jennifer realized that it was too late to change her mind. She was going to California with her half brother and his mother, the only people on earth who cared about her. Funny, she thought, the fact that the woman was a madam and her brother a bastard no longer shocked her.

Within the hour the driver returned with Jennifer's belongings, reporting that the Picketts had been obviously happy to see the last of her.

"They said Judson Carr and the sheriff had been there earlier, looking for Miss Carlyle," the driver told them.

"Did the old gossips tell them where she'd gone?" Nellie asked sharply.

The driver shook his head. "They said they wouldn't help a carpetbagger even though Miss Carlyle had behaved inappropriately."

"How considerate," Jennifer snapped. The reaction was typical of southerners clinging to the Old South. But, she thought sadly, I no longer belong to either the Old or New South.

"Confound it," Jamie said as Jennifer captured his king.

Jennifer grinned, recognizing their father's favorite exclamation. "Surely you don't mind me winning *one* game; you've won all the rest."

He glanced up. "Ummm . . . guess not. I'm glad to have someone to play chess with now that Papa is gone."

"Our father taught you?" When he nodded, she went on to tell him that she and her father had often played chess on winter nights. "He was hard to beat."

"So are you." He stared, his expression abruptly serious. "Isn't it too bad that we couldn't have been a family?— shared our father together instead of separately?"

Jennifer nodded. During the past three days since she'd been staying at the brothel, she'd decided that her father and Nellie should have married . . . and society be damned. But she also realized that Jamie hadn't suffered adversely: he'd lived in elegant quarters, isolated from Nellie's business, he'd attended a good school, and he'd seen his father often. But he had admitted that living in a brothel had caused him embarrassment.

"Come and eat," Nellie called from the doorway.

Later, while they ate, Nellie told them about a change in plans.

"Judson isn't convinced that I'm not hiding you," she told Jennifer. "We can't wait for the ship at the end of the week; we're leaving tonight."

Jamie was excited, but Jennifer's stomach lurched. Judson had come to the brothel with the sheriff that afternoon, and while she hid in a trunk under Nellie's gowns, they'd searched the rooms. He'd been angry when he hadn't found her, threatening Nellie and her servants, and Jennifer feared he planned to waylay them when they boarded the ship.

"He knows our departure date is the last Friday in August, so if we go tonight, Wednesday instead of Friday, on another ship, we might fool him," Nellie said slowly. "But to be on the safe side, you'll have to be transported to the ship in my trunk."

"Me too? . . . They'll be looking for two women and a boy."

"No, Son," Nellie said, affectionately ruffling his hair. "This is serious business, not a game."

"He's still out there," Nellie said.

"Careful, or he'll see you." Jamie's tone was edged with excitement.

"Damnable Judson," Nellie retorted. "He's making sure we can't sneak out."

Jennifer nodded but kept on dressing. They'd changed their plan again after realizing the house was being watched, knowing Judson would have all the trunks searched when they left. It was Jennifer's idea, to disguise herself as a man and walk boldly out of Nellie's and down the street. Once safely past the brothel, she was to be picked up by a servant and taken to the ship. She shuddered. God, it had to work. If she was caught, she would go to jail.

"I don't know, Jennifer," Nellie said. "It's risky."

"I have no other choice." Jennifer plopped a hat over her pinned-up hair, trying to hide her fear. "Besides, it's the one thing Judson wouldn't expect me to do. He thinks women are helpless cowards."

A flash of anger shot through her, and she said no more. That bastard! Because of him, not only had she lost her home, but she might go to jail. Yet she still did not regret burning the cotton. She was convinced that her father would have understood.

She took a final glance in the mirror, pleased that she didn't recognize herself, then walked to the door. Her heart raced and her legs felt shaky, but her voice was steady. "I'll see you on board."

Nellie stepped forward and hugged her. "Be careful, Jennifer. And—and if the worst happens—that is, Jamie and I won't go without you."

Jennifer nodded, suddenly unable to speak, not allowing herself to think about being caught. Before she could reconsider, she opened the door and stepped into the street. She concentrated on a longer stride and in keeping her posture erect. But as she approached the man who slouched in the shadowy doorway of the next building, the urge to run almost overpowered her.

She felt the man stiffen as she passed and knew his eyes were studying her. From the corner of her eye she saw him take a step and hesitate. Fear exploded within her. It *was* Judson!

Somehow she kept walking, as though she belonged on the waterfront, as though she were a man who often paid a midnight visit to a brothel. She expected a hand on her shoulder at any moment. By the time she turned down a side street, she was trembling so hard that she wondered how she could still walk straight.

The buggy was waiting in the next block, and she immediately scrambled up onto the seat. As she rode through the quiet city Jennifer calmed down. She'd fooled him. . . . she'd really outsmarted Judson Carr. The thought lifted her spirits; she'd needed revenge, needed to get the better of the man who had tricked her. He would eventually learn how she'd eluded him—that she'd walked right past him . . . and he'd let her go.

Once on board Jennifer's fears returned. She knew she wouldn't feel safe until the ship cleared the harbor. By the time Nellie and Jamie arrived, she was already in her cabin, afraid to watch the coastline of Georgia disappear into the night, knowing she'd probably never return.

"Oh, God," she said into the darkness as she lay in her bunk. "Please let this be the right course for my life—and take care of Zeb—and watch over High Bluffs—and—" Her thoughts slowed, her eyelids fluttered over her tears . . . and then she slept.

Jennifer stood at the rail with Jamie and Nellie and watched as the ship passed through the Golden Gate, the final approach into San Francisco's harbor. The long trip around the Horn had passed quickly once they had gotten over their seasickness. Jennifer had gradually realized that she'd been right in joining Nellie and Jamie. Her feelings for both had grown over the past weeks; she'd come to understand why her father had fallen in love with Nellie.

Turning away from the looming city, Jennifer glanced at Nellie and wondered what the future held for them in San

Francisco. Because Nellie hadn't discussed her past beyond
mentioning that her older brother had made a fortune from
logging the giant California redwoods and that he'd married
years earlier, Jennifer had often wondered about it. How
had she ended up in a brothel? Nellie's comment about
being cast into the street had surfaced in Jennifer's mind
many times. Why hadn't Nellie's brother helped her then?
Had he already gone to California? There are so many
things I don't know, Jennifer told herself. She had no choice
but to trust in Nellie's belief that her brother would help
them get established in a respectable life.

The ship plowed through the turbulent bay, and Jennifer
could feel Jamie's excitement: his eyes were shining, his
cheeks were glowing, and he couldn't stand in one spot
longer than half a minute.

"Jen, look at all the ships. . . . Where'd they all come
from?"

"All over the world I expect: China, England, India
. . . maybe Africa."

His head kept moving, his gaze taking in the capping
water, the city of steep hills, and the seabirds swooping
above them. "One day I'm going to all those places; one day
I might be a ship's captain."

Jennifer reached an arm around his shoulders and gave
him a hug. Sometimes she couldn't believe how much she
loved having him for a brother; it was as though she'd
known him all her life.

He shot her a grin, then returned his attention to the
harbor that teemed with life. Jennifer felt a surge of pride;
Jamie was intelligent and even-tempered. The latter trait
was undoubtedly inherited from Nellie. The Carlyle men
had always tested their courage with daring, impulsive
actions that had sometimes gotten them into trouble.

"I've made arrangements with the captain for you both to
remain on board until I've seen my brother and know
where we'll be staying," Nellie told them as the ship
slipped into its berth.

"Can't we go with you?" Jamie's expression went from
anticipation to anxiousness.

Nellie smiled but shook her head. "It's easier this way.

We don't want to drag trunks through the streets when we don't know where we are going."

Suddenly uneasy, Jennifer watched as Nellie disappeared into a street crowded with men. To pass the time, she told Jamie about High Bluffs, one of his favorite topics, and they talked about what they thought their new life in San Francisco would be like. Jamie couldn't wait to go ashore and start exploring their new home. He was excited about meeting his uncle. "Will he be very rich?" Jamie asked her. "Will he like me?"

It was two hours before Nellie returned with the news. "My brother doesn't live here anymore," Nellie said, and Jennifer could detect disappointment—or was it fear—in her voice. "He's left his California holdings with a partner and moved north to Seattle, in the Washington Territory. I heard his first wife died and he married a second woman several years ago." She waved a gloved hand. "So we'll continue on to Seattle with the ship.

"It'll be just fine," Nellie said, seeing that they needed reassurance. "Seattle'll be as good a place as San Francisco for beginning a new life."

As Jennifer stood between Nellie and Jamie at the rail, watching the ship leave the Juan de Fuca Strait to turn south into Puget Sound, her spirits lifted. The ocean journey had taken over five months including stops in South America and San Francisco. Now in early February of a new year, 1886, they were finally reaching Seattle, a city they knew almost nothing about.

"Jamie," she said, turning to her brother. "Remember, I told you about Joseph, our older brother?"

He nodded.

"Did I mention that his last letter came from Seattle?"

"No," Jamie replied, excitement edging his word. "Do you suppose he's still there?"

Not wanting to get his hopes up, or her own, Jennifer tried to reply casually. "It's possible." She was vaguely aware that for some reason her words had made Nellie stiffen. But that impression faded as the ship headed southward through the heavily wooded islands that were like giant stepping-stones between the larger masses of land. In every direction they looked they could see high, ragged mountain peaks draped with snowy capes.

Jamie's face was glowing from the pure sea air, and from his growing excitement. The splendor of the place was beyond description. The three watched in silence.

It would be heaven to place her feet on solid ground, Jennifer thought. The soil of a new land . . . their new home.

II

The Hills Are Mountains

Chapter Five

Against a backdrop of high, snowy mountains the dense evergreen forests were like exquisite carpets woven in an infinite number of green hues, covering the islands all the way down to the tidemark of the bay. Above the ship the gulls rode the wind currents, their cries a plaintive welcome to the wild and majestic frontier where Seattle, the city named after an Indian chief, had been established three decades earlier by the Arthur Denny party, the first settlers in the area.

"It's . . . so different." Jamie looked away from the town looming before them to the steamer that had followed their wake past Whidbey and Bainbridge islands and into Elliott Bay.

Jennifer nodded, watching the growing shoreline of wharfs and wooden buildings as the ship slowed and deckhands scrambled to get ready for docking. A gust of wind touched her face with prickles of moisture, sending a shiver of apprehension down her spine. She pulled her shawl tighter, suddenly oppressed by the dark clouds billowing across the faded blue February sky, cloaking the awesome Mount Rainier under folds of silky gray mist.

Nellie, who stood between them, grabbed Jamie's hand. "I think you'll love Seattle."

Jamie gave a quick laugh. "I'd better. There's nowhere else for us to go."

Nellie smiled, but Jennifer saw that her expression was strained and nervous. "You'll see," Nellie said. "We'll all love it here."

Did Nellie really believe that? Jennifer wondered. Or was she trying to maintain a brave front? As Jennifer continued to stare she realized that Nellie's smile was forced.

Jennifer shivered again, this time at the thought that most of her clothing would not be appropriate for the dampness of the Northwest. She swallowed, fighting the tightening of her throat. Don't think about High Bluffs, she told herself, or the Georgia sunshine, or Zeb, who'd been left behind to tend the graves. That was all in the past.

Jamie put his arm around Nellie. "You're right, Mother. We'll make it our home, be a real part of this city, respected by everyone."

Nellie nodded, seriously. "That's a worthy ambition, Jamie. But for now we'll take each day as it comes. And the future . . . who knows? We might even move some of these mountains around here."

He shot his mother a grin, then returned his gaze to the approaching wharf where men in knit caps and dark jerseys were loading lumber. "We'll build our own mountain, by establishing a good life."

Jennifer stared. Jamie was doing it again, surprising her with his mature insights. He'll succeed someday, she thought, but he'll need a good education and acceptance in proper society.

They stood in silence now. The wharf stacked with lumber had caught Jennifer's attention; she remembered the captain's description of the logging camps on Lake Union and Lake Washington beyond the hills of Seattle. "Fortunes to be made in Washington Territory for those with the courage to do it," he'd said.

We'll do it, she thought suddenly. We'll help make Seattle into a great city, and in the process make our fortunes. She was worse than Jamie, she realized, creating an empire before she'd even stepped onto dry land. But somehow she felt better now about the buildings and strange little clapboard houses that clung precariously to hills so steep that she had to tilt her head to see the tops of them.

The ship slipped into a berth, and within minutes the deckhands had everything secured and Jennifer, Nellie, and Jamie were ready to disembark. Nellie had already arranged for their trunks to be held until they'd found lodging.

"Follow Main to Commercial Street and turn north," the captain explained as they stepped onto the gangplank. "Several good hotels up in that area."

Nellie thanked him, and they continued down to the wharf. The clouds had lowered, completely obscuring Mount Rainier, a gray ceiling on the city that blotted out the Cascade Range east of Seattle and the Olympic Mountains to the north. Jennifer smelled the rain before the first drops hit.

"Let's get going," Nellie said. "Or we'll be soaked."

Jennifer nodded and pulled her shawl over the perky straw bonnet that sat atop her upswept curls, aware that her black traveling suit was too lightweight for the weather. Shivering, she hurried along to the rutted dirt street called Main that led up a hill away from the water.

"If it keeps raining, the street'll be nothing but mud," Jamie said, his dark eyes glowing with anticipation of a new adventure. Suddenly he was all little boy. "The captain said a person could sink plumb out of sight in the stuff."

Jennifer grinned at him, glad that Jamie's fears had receded, even though she was now greatly dismayed by Seattle. Jamie didn't appear to notice the bearded men with bold appraising eyes, or the flimsy wooden buildings that looked as though the first gust of wind would blow them into the bay, or the rat-infested piles of garbage . . . or the fact that there were no women on the streets.

Glancing at Nellie, she was not surprised to see her fears reflected on the older woman's face. God, help us, Jennifer thought, trying not worry about how they'd survive in such a place. But each tap of her heels against the wooden boardwalk was in tune with the doubts whirling in her mind. I shouldn't have come—I shouldn't have left Georgia after all, she kept repeating to herself.

Abruptly the sound of angry voices brought Jennifer's attention back to the street. "What's happening?" she asked. Her glance moved to a mob of men ahead of them.

"Looks like a lynching," Nellie said in a low tone, grabbing both Jamie and Jennifer, bringing them to a stop.

Jennifer watched in horror as the mob suddenly ran out

of control, pushing and shoving and screaming profanities. Then she saw the focus of the crowd's rage: a group of cringing Chinese who were trapped within the circle of angry men.

"Get these Chinese bastards onto the *Queen Of The Pacific*!" someone shouted. "We don't need these yellow dogs taking our jobs—working for almost nothing."

"Captain Alexander says he can't take them all—and he wants fare of seven dollars a head!" another man cried.

"Then kill 'em—throw 'em into the bay!"

"Yeah . . . drown 'em," others shouted, joining the outcry against the small Chinese men and women, who, in their cotton pants and high-collared jackets, straw hats and pigtails, were a striking contrast to the larger-statured white men.

"Men!—I order you to disperse!" a newcomer cried above the voices.

"Who the hell are you?" someone demanded.

"William White," the man shouted. "United States Attorney for the territory. I'm ordering all of you to leave these people alone. This matter can be settled in the court . . . or Governor Squire will declare martial law."

"We ain't letting this heathen horde stay," one of the mob leaders said. "You and who else is gonna stop us?"

"Sheriff McGraw's deputies, that's who," the attorney retorted.

Jennifer watched, incredulous. The mob was about to take on the law.

"They're going to kill those people!" Jamie cried, and would have started forward but for Jennifer's having restrained him.

"I think we'd better get out of here," Jennifer said.

"But those people need help," Jamie began, only to be interrupted by Nellie.

"Jennifer's right," she said. "This is no place for women."

"Let's go," Jennifer said.

They turned around and almost crashed into two men who were hurrying to join the crowd. The men quickly blocked their way.

"Goddamn!" the taller man cried. "More whores arrived in town."

"They sure ain't Mercer Girls," the other man chimed in.

"Stand aside," Nellie demanded coldly.

"Don't git uppish with me," the taller man said, his expression hardening.

"When ya opening for business?" the other one asked, a grin twisting his scarred face. "Ya look right tempting, sister," he said hoarsely, stepping up to Jennifer.

Jennifer's fear instantly vanished in a flash of anger. "My friend told you to let us pass."

"Jesus . . . a spitfire!" the short man cried. "But I'll soon have ya purring."

"The hell—maybe I want the blond," the first man said. "The old one looks like she's sampled every cock between here and the Atlantic."

"You—you take that back!" Jamie cried, and leapt forward, flinging himself at the man who'd insulted his mother. Flailing his arms, Jamie beat his fists against the man's broad chest. "I said take it back."

"Jamie—" Nellie rushed to help him and was blocked by the other man.

"You're being called, Boy." The man grinned, his jagged-toothed grimace angering Jamie still further. His fists had little effect on the man. "Hey, kid, stop it now. Ya ain't big enough to hurt Al Cox."

"Not until you apologize to my mother."

"I said stop it. It ain't funny no more." With a savage motion, Al Cox grabbed Jamie's arm and twisted it until the boy cried in pain.

Nellie and Jennifer sprang forward only to be stopped by more men who stepped between them and Jamie.

Jennifer found herself trapped by the laughing, mocking men, but Nellie elbowed through the crowd until she stood before Al Cox. "Release my boy at once," she demanded.

"Fuck you," Al Cox retorted, and twisted harder. Jamie screamed, his face drained of color.

"Let go . . . you bastard!" Nellie lunged at him, her cape flying open, unmindful that her language and her low-necked gown confirmed their belief that she was a prostitute.

Several men grabbed Nellie and held her away from Jamie. As Jennifer watched helplessly Nellie's gown was ripped from bodice to waist, her hat flung into the street, and her hair yanked loose from its pins. Her face was bright red with anger, but the gaze that met Jennifer's was filled with terror.

"I knew it," the man with Al Cox cried. "These here women ain't nothing but common whores."

The crowd roared approval. "Let's give 'em what they want right now!" a voice shouted.

Hatred shot like fire through Jennifer. She had a sudden memory of Judson Carr. But this time she was not without protection. She slid her hand into her reticule, found the small revolver, and pulled it out.

"Get back, you . . . you, scum!" she shouted. As they hesitated she fired a shot above their heads, the sound echoing over the clamor.

There was immediate silence as the men stepped back, their eyes on the gun in Jennifer's hand. "My next shot won't miss one of your filthy bodies," she said with a chilling calmness.

The men backed off, releasing Nellie, who stumbled forward to join Jennifer. But Al Cox still held Jamie.

"Lookee here, missy," he said. "Put down the gun—or the boy'll get hurt." He glared, his eyes challenging her.

"I said let him go." Jennifer waved the gun. "Right now!"

He stared, measuring her. Then his lips twisted maliciously. "Grab her, men. She ain't gonna shoot."

"Women are scared of guns," a voice cried from the crowd.

The men surged forward. Without hesitation, Jennifer fired; the bullet struck Al Cox in the lower leg. He stumbled backward, releasing Jamie as he collapsed onto the boardwalk.

"Sweet Jesus," Al Cox's companion cried, backing into the crowd.

A murmur of shock swept through the crowd. Every nerve and muscle in Jennifer's body was poised for action. Heartbeats drummed in her ears as she waited; Al Cox lay moaning on the sidewalk. Shouts filled the air from the mob at the corner, and Jennifer realized she'd forgotten about the poor Chinese. The sky had darkened, weeping a steady drizzle of rain.

"Thank God for your gun, Jennifer," Nellie whispered

as she fumbled with her dress. "Mine's in my trunk—didn't think I'd need it when I became a proper lady."

The men began to shuffle their feet, impatient for action. "Come on," someone said. "Let's get outta here. Whores ain't worth getting shot."

As the men hesitated, a tall black-haired man shouldered through them. "What's going on?" His dark gaze flickered over the crowd, coming to rest on Jennifer.

For several seconds Jennifer was caught by a strange emotion, suddenly unsettled by—by what? His attractiveness? Or his strength? "Stay back," she told him.

"I asked a question," he replied, his thick brows lowering over the blackest eyes Jennifer had ever seen in a white man.

"These men accosted us," Jennifer said, making sure that the range of her gun now included the newcomer.

"That's right," Nellie added. "That one"—she pointed to Al Cox—"hurt my boy."

Jamie stepped forward, his face streaked from dried tears, and briefly explained what had happened. "These men tried to hurt my mother and sister—Jennifer was only protecting us."

The stranger's gaze shifted from Jamie to Nellie's torn gown and unpinned hair, then beyond them to the men. The outline of his face seemed etched from stone as his aristocratic features tightened. "We don't detain women against their wishes."

Al Cox struggled to his feet, his trousers stained crimson with blood. "They're whores. No decent woman would be walking on the waterfront. Ya know that's a fact, Mr. Polemis."

"Get the hell out of here," Polemis said. "That means you, Cox."

Jennifer wasn't surprised when the men obeyed; Polemis had an air of authority that commanded respect. Within seconds the crowd was swallowed by the larger one herding frightened Chinese toward the ship moored at the foot of the hill.

Al Cox glared at Jennifer as he limped past. "Ya heard my name . . . remember it. Cause ya ain't seen the last of me." His tone lowered so only she heard his next words.

"Damon Polemis ain't always around to save fuckin' whores."

"Move Cox, or you'll get worse than a limp," Damon told him coldly.

Seconds later Cox disappeared around the corner. For a moment Jennifer felt relief, then her body began to tremble. She stepped back and leaned against a clapboard storefront, trying to regain her composure.

"You can put your gun away now . . . Jennifer, isn't it?" Damon said beside her.

Her thick lashes, which had fluttered onto the top curve of her cheeks, snapped open, and she looked into eyes as midnight black as hers were midday blue. "I—yes," she stammered. "I'm Jennifer Carlyle."

He reached out and took the gun from her hand. "You don't need this anymore."

She straightened, aware she'd forgotten the gun, conscious that her wet clothing clung to her body. "Thank you," she said stiffly, taking back the gun and dropping it into her reticule. He watched silently, assessing her, and Jennifer was suddenly stricken by more nerves. What was the matter with her? she wondered. He made her feel self-conscious. Was she merely embarrassed to be found in her predicament by such a handsome man? But whatever the reason, she knew proprieties dictated that she thank him for his help. Before she could open her mouth, Jamie stepped forward and thanked him instead.

Damon nodded. "I'm glad I happened by." He smiled at Jamie, the transformation of his features almost stopping Jennifer's breath in her throat. "You know my name—what's yours?"

Jamie told him, then introduced his mother, explaining that Jennifer was his half sister.

Jennifer averted her eyes, watching the last of the crowd disappear toward the bay. But she felt Damon watching her as Jamie told him they'd just arrived from San Francisco and were looking for a hotel—that they intended to settle in Seattle.

"Seattle has a great future. . . . You'll like it here," Damon said, turning as a big blond man and a small girl approached. "Andy, I forgot you were waiting." As the blond man shrugged, a grin softening his square features, Damon made introductions.

"This big Swede is Andy, who works for me and—" he dropped an arm around the small girl whose brilliant blue eyes stared from an Indian face, "this is Martha, Andy's daughter."

Jennifer soon learned that Damon was Greek and owned a steamship company. She also noticed that Jamie wasn't paying attention to their conversation; his gaze was on Martha.

"Are you—" Jamie began, then blushed scarlet.

"*Ja,*" Andy said, anticipating the question. "Martha is half Nootka Indian."

"I . . . didn't mean to be nosy," Jamie told the girl, his tone tight with embarrassment.

A shy smile touched Martha's lips as her long lashes lowered. Nellie spoke, breaking the awkward silence. She thanked Damon Polemis, explaining that they had to be on their way to find lodgings.

Damon looked thoughtful as he considered Nellie's words. "I can help you," he began, but Jennifer cut him off. She didn't want him to think they were helpless.

"We've already decided to stay in one of the hotels on Commercial Street," she said, anxious to be off the streets and away from everyone . . . especially him.

His lids lowered, hooding his eyes, but not before Jennifer saw the glint of anger. He wasn't used to a woman dismissing him, she surmised.

"As you've learned, the waterfront can be dangerous," he said coolly. "You'd be wise to accept my offer."

Jennifer's gaze was held by eyes as hard and dark as coal, and it occurred to her that under the right circumstances he might be even more dangerous than a frontier waterfront. His attitude toward them was probably the same as the mob's.

"As I said, this boarding house is clean and reasonable," Damon Polemis said, his words jarring her as she realized she'd missed part of the conversation.

"You're very considerate, Mr. Polemis," Nellie said. "We'll only be needing rooms until we establish our contact here."

Damon's brows arched his forehead in a question. When Nellie didn't elaborate, he flicked a glance at Jennifer. She tilted her chin. Let him think our contact is questionable, she told herself. Let him think the worst.

Jennifer stood with Nellie and Jamie on the boarding house porch, waiting for Damon. Several minutes later he returned, explaining that he'd arranged everything. They followed him into a narrow, dark hall that smelled of fish and tobacco and baking bread.

"This is Mrs. Coray," he said. "She has three rooms."

A plump woman in her early sixties stepped from the shadows, wiping her hands on a soiled apron as she peered into their faces. "But only for a week . . . no longer," she said, her words heavily accented.

Jennifer bit her lip as a wave of humiliation swept over her. It was obvious that Damon had persuaded the woman to accept them. "I think we'd better go to a hotel. It's Sunday—we're imposing here and—" she broke off as Nellie interrupted.

"We'll take it," she said, and shot Jennifer a warning look.

"Good," Damon said. "With the governor in town and all the people involved in the Chinese riots, hotel space might not be available." Unreadable dark eyes held Jennifer's for long seconds. "Until next time," he said, his tone echoing strangely in the hall. With a final salute, he disappeared into the gray day, where the rain still fell, an ominous beginning for their first day in Seattle.

Jennifer hardly heard Mrs. Coray reciting the rules of the house. But she did hear the final order. "Remember, only a week, then you're out."

Jennifer went into her room and closed the door, hardly seeing the high bare walls, the brass bed with its sagging springs or the small window that looked out at another unpainted wall. "It's only for a week," she said aloud. "Until Nellie finds her brother." She removed her damp skirt and jacket, throwing them onto the only chair in the room. Then she stretched out on the bed, pulled the patchwork quilt over her, and stared at a ceiling of rough boards.

God, she prayed, it has to be different . . . it must be.

Chapter Six

That night Jennifer was too tired to join Nellie and Jamie for supper. Instead she snuggled deeper under the quilt, enjoying the feel of a real bed again, a bed that didn't move with the waves. In the morning she felt rested and optimistic as she washed in cold water from a cracked pitcher and then dressed for the day. Breakfast was served early to accommodate the other boarders, all of them men who worked on the wharfs.

"The city regraded twenty-eight streets last year," one man was saying as Jennifer, Nellie, and Jamie entered the dining room.

"They'd better cut more streets through the hills. Men need jobs this year," another said. "Those yellow bastards took work from white men. I hope they rid Seattle of 'em for good."

"I don't know—Governor Squire declared martial law yesterday and requested federal troops from the Fort Vancouver barracks. The law—" The first man broke off as he saw the women.

Silence settled over the room, and Jennifer felt all eyes on them as they sat down at the long table. Someone passed a bowl of cereal and then thick cream, which she poured over the lumpy oatmeal. Her first spoonful gagged her, but she swallowed it anyway. After the initial quiet the men ignored them, continuing their conversations, unmindful of profanity or subjects not suitable for discussions when ladies were present.

Fallen women, that's what they think we are, she told herself angrily. After a few more mouthfuls Jennifer pushed the bowl away; she had to get out of there. What would her

father think if he could see her now? she asked herself and
shuddered.

But she lifted her chin haughtily as she swept into the
hall. Jennifer knew it wasn't simply Nellie's fault that they'd
been marked as "fallen." Society just didn't trust women
who traveled alone and stayed in a man's boarding house.
The hell with them all, she decided, ignoring the fact that
her own thoughts were far from ladylike.

Later in the morning their trunks arrived from the wharf,
and as Jennifer was sorting through her wrinkled clothing
Nellie came into her room announcing, "I've located my
brother, and he's coming to see me. While he's here, I
thought you and Jamie might want to look around Seattle."
She busied herself nervously patting her elaborate hairdo.
"Just stay away from the waterfront."

Jennifer realized that Nellie wanted to be alone when she
met with her brother. Grabbing her jacket, she went to find
Jamie, trying not to worry about what Nellie had once said
about being cast out as Jennifer had been. Why hadn't
Nellie's brother helped her then? What sort of person was
he?

When Jennifer and Jamie stepped outside into the gray
day that threatened more rain, the air was surprisingly
warm and Jennifer felt her spirits lift. Maybe now, with the
help of Nellie's influential brother, their fortunes would
change. Jamie shared her optimism; they enjoyed their
walk over the steep hills even though they had to stop often
to catch their breath. They passed Indians carrying baskets
of salmon and stevedores who gave Jennifer bold glances.
But Jennifer hardly noticed them; she was listening to
Jamie who had found out who the Mercer Girls were. He
explained that they were marriageable women from New
England, who'd been brought to Seattle by Asa Mercer
back in the mid-sixties to marry eligible men—that the
women were now respectable matrons. The thought gave
her hope. That the Mercer Girls had been accepted boded
well for her and Nellie.

A light rain began falling, and they decided to start back.
At Main Street they waited for a buggy to pass, the driver
holding his bay horse under tight rein for the descent.

Jennifer recognized Damon Polemis and was startled when his gaze suddenly found hers. He nodded and Jamie waved. Before Jennifer had time to acknowledge him, he had already passed, leaving her feeling awkward, as though she'd snubbed him. As they reached the boarding house they heard shouts from a mob in the next block.

"The Home Guard's been called out. Gonna protect the Chinese dogs who didn't get on the *Queen*."

But Jennifer's fear of the mob was soon forgotten when she reached the upstairs hall. The loud, angry voices from Nellie's room brought back all of her other fears.

"Jesus Christ, Nellie. You track me down, after all these years, and expect me to welcome you into my family?" a man asked, his voice tight with anger.

"I mistakenly thought you would," Nellie answered, and Jennifer could hear a pleading note in her voice. "I *am* your only sister."

Jennifer felt Jamie stiffen beside her. Both of them stared at Nellie's door, which was ajar.

"That's too goddamned bad. I feel no obligation to a whore."

"I'm not a whore!" Nellie retorted. "How dare you call me that just because I've had to work for a living."

"You can't fool me. I can tell by looking at you that you're a whore. And once a whore, always a whore."

It was several seconds before Nellie spoke. She sounded tired suddenly, defeated. "I only want a chance, so my son can have a decent life."

"Let me put it this way, Nellie," he said, obviously cold to her hopes. "As far as I'm concerned, I have no sister."

"You can't mean that," Nellie said. "I have nowhere else to go—what about my son—and—"

"As I told you, that's your problem, not mine," he said, interrupting her. "I have my position to think of—my own family."

"But your wife would understand. I—"

He broke in rudely. "No she wouldn't. Her parents were early settlers here, with the Denny and Terry and Boren families, and were highly respected people. Women like my wife don't speak to prostitutes, let alone accept them as family members." His voice lowered menacingly. "I *won't* have her finding out that you were the madam of Savannah's most infamous brothel."

Nellie drew in her breath sharply. "You knew?—and you never tried to help me?"

He laughed harshly. "Help you?—and ruin my own life? Surely you jest."

"You bastard! You rotten, filthy bastard!" There was a sharp crack that sounded like a slap. "And I believed you would have helped me had you known my circumstances."

"You bitch!" he retorted furiously. "You're leaving Seattle on the next ship! The whole town is talking about yesterday's shooting. And no one in this town is going to know that one of the whores who shot Cox is my sister . . . I'll see to that."

Jennifer grabbed Jamie's arm, instinctively knowing that he was about to run to his mother's side. Nellie shouldn't know that they'd witnessed her humiliation.

"That—that rotten skunk. He can't do that to my mother," Jamie whispered angrily, but his voice shook and his eyes threatened tears.

Jennifer tried to push back her own growing hopelessness. They were stranded in Seattle—the end of the earth—with no means of support. What kind of man could do that to his own sister? A man like Judson Carr? No, even Judson wouldn't have been that despicable.

"I'm staying," Nellie said, and though her tone was low, she was no longer pleading.

"I'll have you run out of town."

"Try it . . . and I'll tell everyone who I am." Her voice was stronger, more the old Nellie.

"I'll pay your passage—I'll—"

"Get out, you bastard!" she cried. "Get your fat ass out of my room."

Nellie's doorknob turned, and Jennifer pulled Jamie toward her room. "But mind my words," Nellie was saying. "I won't reveal our relationship so long as you leave me and mine alone. If you don't, so help me God, I'll—"

Jennifer didn't catch the rest of what was said, as she'd closed her door, not wanting to be caught eavesdropping. A moment later Nellie's door banged and heavy footsteps hurried toward the stairs. Long seconds of silence swelled in the room as Jennifer and Jamie waited, unsure of what to do next. Then Nellie burst into the room.

"You heard?"

Jennifer and Jamie exchanged looks, neither wanting to admit all they'd heard.

"Enough to know that your brother wants nothing to do with us," Jennifer said finally.

Nellie nodded, blinking quickly, as though trying not to cry. "Imagine, my own brother." She hesitated. "I can't talk about it."

"Don't then," Jennifer said. "It's enough that we know where we stand."

"We don't need that old coot," Jamie said, hugging Nellie.

"No, we don't, do we." Nellie stood up straighter. "And I don't want either of you to worry. I have some money left, enough to buy a boarding house better than this dump. It isn't what we'd planned, but it's a way to make money. What do you think?"

Jennifer stared at her. What other choice did they have? Slowly she nodded. "Let's get started right away because . . . because I hate this place."

Chapter Seven

Nellie found a suitable building down on Front Street, but three thousand dollars was more than she could afford. Nellie finally bluffed the owners into believing she would buy another place, and they agreed to her terms, fifteen hundred down and another two thousand in six months. The owners had hesitated at first, but the extra five hundred they'd gain by holding the note, and the encouragement from Dr. Seth Andrews, the tenant who was moving out, had swung the deal in Nellie's favor. "Buyers at that price aren't easy to come by," Seth Andrews had told the owners.

Afterward Nellie worried to Jennifer that the boarding house might not make two thousand dollars in six months. "I gambled that it would," she said to Jennifer. "And I can always open a saloon if necessary." She turned away, but Jennifer heard Nellie's last words. "At least I won't have to do what I did at seventeen."

Nellie's words hadn't reassured Jennifer; she knew that she had to find suitable work on her own. She hated the thought of running a saloon. Now, as she stood waiting for a response from the proprietress of the millinery shop where she'd gone seeking work, she realized how badly she wanted this respectable job.

"You say you want work—are good at keeping ledgers?" The woman peered at Jennifer over spectacles that had slid down her nose.

Jennifer nodded, but before she could explain further, the woman interrupted her.

"Now I know who you are," she announced triumphantly. "It's women like you who give us honest, hardworking ones a bad name." She stepped closer, her huge bulk looming over Jennifer. "Get out, you trollop. I've heard all about you—you shot a man."

Jennifer backed away. "But . . . you can't hold malicious gossip against me. It's not fair."

"Fair?—fair?" The woman wagged a thick finger at her. "Don't try to fool me with your southern belle drawl and your Paris gown. Are you telling me you didn't shoot the man?"

"I . . . no. But—"

"Get out," the woman repeated, her tone rising. "And don't show your face in here again."

Anger swelled in Jennifer, begging for release. She stared at the woman, who stood like a lump of lard in her gray muslin dress. Straightening to her full height, Jennifer stepped closer, her chin raised haughtily. "I wouldn't work in this —" She hesitated, glancing over the shabby room, where thread and remnants of material lay among clumps of dust on the board floor, "Hovel!"

"You . . . harlot!" The woman's expression was incredulous. "I'm calling for help if you don't go at once."

Jennifer's anger slipped away then, leaving humiliation. Damn that woman, she thought. Damn them all.

Without another word, she spun around, petticoats and velvet skirt flaring, and strode to the door. Pausing, she faced the woman again. "Lordy Lord," she began in her best southern drawl. "I must confess, I couldn't possibly work with a seamstress who didn't even know the difference between a Paris gown and a Savannah traveling suit." She pulled on her gloves and then adjusted the tie of her hat. "That would simply be too, too much for this . . . southern belle."

As the woman sputtered in anger, Jennifer stepped into another dreary afternoon of dripping sky. The rain is good for one thing, she told herself. It kept people from knowing that the drops that slid down her cheeks and onto her jacket were tears.

The rain intensified, and she quickened her pace along Front Street, passing the huge Frye's Opera House. At the corner of Marion she lifted her hem so that it wouldn't drag over the wet planks of the street, then darted between two buckboards, while trying to avoid the mud splattering from under loose boards. As she approached the opposite sidewalk her foot slipped off the planking and was sucked into the mud.

"Damn!" she cried. Bracing herself against a hitching post, she pulled against mud that felt like quicksand. Then, with a quick twist, her foot suddenly popped free. She would have fallen into the same mud but for the post that supported her.

"Damn—damn!" she muttered when she saw the condition of her shoe. "It's ruined."

Someone clucked his tongue behind her. "Temper, temper," a familiar male voice said.

Her gaze flew to the sidewalk, where a man dressed like a stevedore in black jersey and knee boots stood watching her with obvious amusement.

Damon stepped forward, extending a hand. "You'd better get out of the street before the mud ruins more than your shoes." His glance flickered from her hat, which drooped wetly over her ruined coiffure, all the down her navy suit to the mudddy shoes. As she hesitated he grinned, relaxing the stern set of his features and belying the arrogance of his posture.

He took her hand and helped her up onto the boardwalk. "Thank you, Mr. Polemis," she said coolly. Damn, why must this man always see me in such embarrassing predicaments, she thought to herself.

"You're welcome, Miss Carlyle . . . Jennifer?" Dark slanting eyebrows arched upward in a question.

She glanced and looked away. "Yes, Jennifer will be fine."

"Well then, Jennifer, where are you going in such a hurry?"

"Back to the boarding house. But as you see, I got caught in another rain shower. I can't step out the door without getting soaked. Doesn't the rain ever stop for more than a day in Seattle?"

"Better get used to it if you're planning to stay," he said, bluntly. "Rain goes with the territory—it's what keeps the forests green. Course you can always move on if you don't like it here."

She glanced up, meeting the challenge of his words. "We plan to stay."

A sudden silence swelled between them. The sound of the town receded beyond the curtain of rain. Above them, a flock of gulls flapped away from a nearby building to wing their way back to the water. Almost in slow motion, Damon's hand came around her shoulders. "You're soaked," he said softly, his cultured voice incongruous with his rough workman's attire. The infinite blackness of his eyes imprisoned her.

She nodded, shivering. Her heart thumped in her chest, its beats pounding faster than the raindrops hitting the wooden walk. The air was fragrant with the salty smell of the bay, which lay at the bottom of the street, and as her teeth began chattering, Damon swung her around to propel her along the street toward the boarding house.

They hurried along in silence, and Jennifer wondered why he was accompanying her. Didn't he have work to do, appointments and responsibilities? she reflected. As they neared the boarding house Damon grabbed her hand and they ran the final steps to the porch.

Jennifer started to thank him but was caught by another awkward silence. Then he grinned, and the moment passed.

"Has Jamie's mother made her contact yet?" he asked suddenly, and she wondered if he felt the strange tension that throbbed between them.

Jennifer hesitated, then looked directly at him and lied. "No, the person no longer lives in Seattle."

His lids lowered, hooding his eyes. "I see."

Glancing away, she continued before he asked more questions; she had the impression that he knew she'd lied. "Nellie bought a building and plans to open a boarding house."

"I'm pleased you're staying even though you have no family here," he said, his abruptly cool tone contradicting his words.

"That's not completely true," Jennifer said quickly. "I have a brother who migrated to the Northwest years ago. I intend to locate him if he's still here."

Something flickered in his eyes, and although he hadn't

moved, she felt his body stiffen. "Your brother's name's Carlyle too?"

She nodded, now expecting him to say he knew Joseph. When he didn't, she smiled wryly. "I didn't expect you'd know Joseph. It's been so long since he wrote home that he could be anywhere by now."

Again, Damon looked uncertain. But when he took her arm and directed her to the door, she decided she was mistaken. "Get out of your wet clothes," he said, all trace of his earlier humor gone. "Being wet won't hurt you but getting chilled might." He pushed her into the hall, and when she turned, he was already closing the door. "I'll be in touch" were his parting words.

Jennifer didn't mind the hard work she shared with Nellie and Jamie during the following weeks. When they'd opened the boarding house for business in March, the three extra bedrooms had rented immediately. She and Nellie split the work, Jennifer doing the bookkeeping and shopping, while Nellie tended the bar in the small saloon they'd just opened in the front room. They'd hired an old Chinese cook, one of the few Orientals left in Seattle after the deportation. Jennifer stayed away from the saloon; it was a decision Nellie understood.

Jennifer was longinng for a real home and a respectable place in the community. She thought often about Joseph and wondered if she'd ever see him again—if he were still even in the Northwest. She'd asked everyone if they'd heard of him, had even inquired at the post office and newspaper. When a stevedore said he thought he'd met Joseph down at Yesler Wharf, Jennifer went immediately to inquire. But no one remembered her brother. She followed up on every lead and finally came to the conclusion that Joseph was not in Seattle. But she didn't give up; she continued to ask about him everywhere. If he was still in the territory, she meant to find him. He would see to it that she was treated as a respectable woman, of that she was convinced.

Damon Polemis stopped by frequently, and Jennifer found herself looking forward to his visits. She knew that although he didn't approve of the saloon, or of the women it attracted, he didn't voice his disapproval; he always treated her with respect. She'd long since relaxed around him, even though their awareness of each other continued to grow, sometimes creating odd silences between them that filled her with a longing to touch him and be held in his arms.

"Did you ever locate your brother?" he asked one evening in May as he watched her wash the supper dishes.

Her hands stilled in the soapy water as she shook her head. Then she glanced at him, a Greek God dressed in black jersey, and wished she wasn't gowned in gingham and that her long hair wasn't tied back with a ribbon, making her look like a child.

Abruptly, the chair leg scraped the floor as he stood up from the table and moved to stand behind her. "This is no life for you, Jennifer. You don't belong in this place . . . doing servant's work."

She twisted her head around to face him. "Perhaps not," she replied, her words almost a whisper, her eyes caught by tiny points of light in his. "But I have no other choice."

She averted her gaze, not wanting him to read her thoughts. She knew that the "good ladies" of Seattle believed she was a whore, even though she, not they, had been born the aristocrat. It was frustrating to be condemned by former Mercer Girls and scrubwomen. She wiped her hands on her apron. It was totally . . . unfair.

"Jennifer?" Damon said softly, startling her. "Did you know that Nellie has . . . expanded her business?"

She'd known that Nellie had acquired the adjoining building, and she had suspected what that meant. Jennifer had told herself not to interfere, although she was concerned about its effect on Jamie.

"I guessed she had," she answered finally, feeling slightly annoyed with him for bringing up a subject that didn't concern him.

Damon's eyes narrowed, and although he hadn't moved, Jennifer sensed that every muscle and nerve and bone of his body stood rigid with disapproval. "You must move out of here, Jennifer," he said, the note of command unmistakable in his tone.

Her annoyance flared into anger. "Is that right, Damon."

She stepped back, tilting her chin defiantly. "Since it's so easy for you to give advice, where do you suggest I go?—a First Hill mansion?—a respectable job?"

"I wasn't attacking either you or Nellie," he retorted.

"And I don't know those—those women, and I don't associate with the men in the saloon. I'm not a prostitute as everyone in Seattle believes." She gulped a ragged breath. "I know I'm the subject of gossip. But I'll show you all . . . because I'm going to make something of myself one of these days." She whirled away from the shocked look on his face, afraid she might have ruined their friendship, afraid she might burst into tears.

At that moment Jamie and the cook came in through the back door, their arms loaded with firewood.

"We'll talk again," Damon said casually, but as she watched him a little muscle twitched above one eye, telling her that he was angry. Then he was gone, leaving her with the pile of dirty dishes.

Damon didn't return for over a week, and Jennifer heard that he'd gone with one of his steamers to Olympia in southern Puget Sound. When he returned he brought Andy, and over the days that followed, it became a routine for both men to stop by when they were in port, sometimes accompanied by Martha, Andy's daughter. Jennifer's outburst was never mentioned, but Jennifer knew Damon's opinion hadn't changed. Yet she realized that Damon's feelings for her were deepening, despite their differences.

During the late spring and into the summer, Jennifer enjoyed her friendships with both men. She became a confidante to Andy, who told her about his Nootka wife, who had gone back to her tribe, leaving him to raise Martha.

Jennifer still knew very little about Damon. She saw that Andy respected him enormously and often mentioned how well liked Damon was by his business associates. Damon had never talked about his own background, aside from once mentioning that he'd been born in New York and still had relatives there.

One evening, as Jennifer was rushing around the kitchen to get ready for the supper crowd, Damon suddenly appeared at the back door with another tall, dark man beside him.

Jennifer stared at them, a strange feeling rooting her feet to the floor. Behind the two men, black clouds were closing over the summer sky. A rumble of thunder shook the dishes in the sideboard, muffling the sounds of food simmering on the stove and voices from the saloon.

Then a sudden flash of lightning zigzagged beyond the door, reflecting for a moment in Damon's dark eyes. He appeared pale and tense as he waited for—for what? she wondered.

When his words came, they had gathered momentum, like the storm that was building in awesome force over Seattle.

"This is Joseph," Damon said. "Your brother."

Chapter Eight

"Joseph?" Jennifer stepped closer, her gaze fastened on the stranger. Then, as the resemblance to their father became apparent, the dishcloth fluttered from her hand to the floor. "Joseph," she repeated, unable to tear her eyes from the tall, bearded man, whose expression suddenly altered from a frowning question to outright astonishment.

"My God! It *is* Jennifer." As she nodded mutely, he sprang forward, closing the distance between them. "What are you doing in Seattle?—in this place?"

"I . . . had no choice," she whispered, trying not to think of the accusation in his tone.

A moment later she was wrapped in his arms, her head resting against his wool plaid jacket that smelled of saltwater and machinery. Her legs began to tremble, and she clung to him, willing strength back into her limbs.

Abruptly, he stepped back, holding her at arm's length, staring down into her face. "Little Jennifer . . . as beautiful as your mother."

She smiled shyly, her eyes measuring the man she hadn't seen in fifteen years. Her first impression had been right; he did resemble their father, although his bone structure was larger and he wasn't as handsome. His raven hair was streaked witht gray, and the lines in his face were deep.

"I've asked and asked after you, but no one in Seattle knew you. How—"

"Damon Polemis," Joseph interrupted, anticipating her question. His features tightened suddenly with—with what? Jennifer wondered. Disapproval of Damon?—or of her?

"You know Damon?" she asked, glancing at the man who

still stood by the door. Why hadn't Damon told her that? He knew she'd been looking for Joseph.

Joseph nodded. "I just met him when he came to tell me about you—this afternoon, after I'd brought my steamer up from Tacoma."

"A steamboat?"

He nodded again. "I recently moved my business from southern Puget Sound to Seattle. Polemis and I are competitors."

Her gaze again shifted to Damon. "You knew about Joseph . . . and didn't tell me?"

He shook his head. "Only since someone told me that the Carlyle Steamship Company was moving here. I didn't want to mention it before I'd made sure it was the right Joseph Carlyle."

Jennifer's eyes were held for a moment by his as he read the gratitude on her face. Then she returned her attention to Joseph, hardly believing he really stood in the same room with her. "You've been gone a long time. Why didn't you write and let us know about you?" She hesitated, remembering her father's disappointment and subsequent harsh words about Joseph. "If only Father had known you were safe before he—" She broke off; Joseph couldn't know their father was dead.

"Before what?" Joseph asked sharply.

"The plantation—" she began and stopped, trying to gather her thoughts. "Father died over a year ago . . . from yellow fever."

Joseph recoiled, turning away so that she couldn't see his face. A deadly silence swelled in the room. Damon averted his gaze to the yard beyond the doorway. As thunder rumbled and a sudden gust of wind capped the bay into frothy foam, Joseph turned back, startling her by his expressionless face.

"It must have been hard for you, Jennifer," he said in a low tone. "More so than for me, who hadn't seen him in years."

He straightened suddenly, as though he were trying to master his emotions. "Why are you here . . . in Seattle? Why did you leave High Bluffs?"

"I—I—" she began. "A carpetbagger has the plantation

now," she said finally, not wanting to explain further in front
of Damon.

"A carpetbagger?" His eyes widened. "For God's sake
. . . you didn't sell High Bluffs to a carpetbagger did you?"
His accusing words dropped between them.

"No, I didn't sell the plantation," she answered, abruptly
cool, suddenly aware that he disapproved of her plain dress
and soiled apron and tied-back hair. He had no right. He
was the one who'd abandoned Georgia and his responsibilities to the family, not her. "It's a long story; I'll explain
later."

Joseph pursed his lips. "You didn't sell?—Then why did
you leave Georgia?"

Couldn't he see that she didn't care to discuss it now—in
front of Damon? "I said I'd—" she broke off, her eye caught
by movement as someone stepped from the stoop through
the doorway . . . a huge black man of about forty who
resembled old Zeb.

Without hesitation she moved forward. "Are you Noah?"

He inclined his head, his lips curving into a grin as he
looked down at her from a height of at least six and a half
feet. "I sure is, Miss Jennifer."

She smiled. "You look like your grandfather."

"How is ole grandpappy?"

"Fine, the last time I saw him," she replied, sobering as
she pictured the wizened Zeb in her mind. "But he's very
old, and he waits, every day, for word of you."

Noah glanced down at his scuffed boots. "I'm not good at
letters." He hesitated, embarrassed. "I only learned to read
and write a couple of years ago. By then I figured
everyone'd forgotten me at High Bluffs."

Jennifer touched his arm, immediately lifting Noah's
gaze. "Zeb never forgot . . . you're all he has. I can tell
you where to write if you want to."

He nodded. "I'd appreciate that a heap, Miss Jennifer."

"Jen?" Joseph said behind her. "You still haven't answered my questions." He cleared his throat. "We have a
lot to catch up on."

Why was he so concerned when he'd never bothered to
write? she wondered. He seemed more concerned about
the plantation than about his father's death. Had she

somehow put him in an awkward position by being in Seattle? Maybe he wasn't glad to see her—wouldn't welcome her into his life. "When I've finished my work, I'll have time to explain everything," she said, forcing back her disappointment.

"Why not now?"

"Because there's no one else to do my work," she said tartly, irritated by his selfishness. She glanced at Damon and wondered why he'd stayed. To make sure she was all right?—or because he was curious? Either way, he should have excused himself and not eavesdropped.

His lips twitched, threatening a grin, and Jennifer had the uncomfortable feeling that Damon read her thoughts and was amused by them, that he shared her impression of Joseph and wanted to be sure she was all right before he left.

Disregarding both of them, she directed a question to Noah. "Do you work for Joseph?"

As Noah nodded Joseph interrupted. "Noah was once a slave on a ship that traveled between Savannah and New England; he's been invaluable to me in my shipping business. But all that can wait. When can you talk?

"Can you come back around eight?" Jennifer asked.

"I suppose I have to if I want to find out what's happened," he said, obviously exasperated.

It was apparent that Joseph disliked any opposition to his wishes. She remembered her father's words.

"Annie'll sure be surprised when she hears my sister now lives in Seattle," he said, moving to the door.

"Annie?" Jennifer asked.

"My wife," he replied, glancing back at her. "Her parents came right after the Denny Party settled at Alki Point in the early 'fifties. We have a thirteen-year-old daughter . . . Rachael."

Jennifer stared back, seeing a dark stranger whose life was a mystery to her. But his expression had relaxed at the mention of his family, and Jennifer felt her spirits lift. Joseph does have tender feelings, she told herself.

A flash of lightning flickered in the shadowy room, followed by a clap of thunder. Then the door to the saloon opened, and footsteps sounded on the kitchen floor. All eyes went to Nellie in her crimson gown.

"Nellie!" Joseph cried, his deep voice shrill with surprise. "Christ Almighty . . . Nellie Thornton!"

Nellie stopped short, her rouge suddenly too red on her whitening face. "Joseph Carlyle," she whispered, her words ringing like a death knell in the silent room.

Startled, Jennifer's gaze darted between them. Why hadn't Nellie mentioned that she knew him?

Within seconds Nellie had regained her composure and, stepping forward, extended her hand to Joseph. "This is a surprise. It's been a long time."

Joseph hesitated, unsure. Then, following her lead, he shook Nellie's hand. "A long time . . . years," he replied, his words stilted, his mouth pursed from—shock or anger? Jennifer wondered.

Shock, she decided. At discovering his sister living in Seattle with Savannah's infamous madam. Of course he'd have known Nellie, she reminded herself. Everyone had known Nellie.

An awkward silence was broken by Damon, who strode to the door. "I apologize for overstaying my welcome," he said, his eyes on Jennifer. "But I wanted to know everything was settled before I left." He lingered seconds longer, as if he wanted to reassure her that she could count on his friendship, then stepped around Joseph into what had become a downpour that was turning the yard to mud.

"I'll return at eight, and between now and then I want you to consider moving in with my family," Joseph told Jennifer. After a curt nod in Nellie's direction, he followed Damon out with Noah a step behind him.

Nellie turned to Jennifer. "I think you should consider Joseph's offer—not because I'm overly fond of him, but because it's a way for you to live a respectable life." Nellie hesitated, and Jennifer could see she was very upset. "What I'm trying to say is that Jamie and I love you and you'll always have a place with us. But I also want you to have more than I can offer . . . a respectable future."

* * *

Alone, Jennifer waited for Joseph's return. He reappeared on time, and Jennifer explained why she'd left Georgia.

"Goddamned carpetbagger!" Joseph exclaimed when she'd finished. He banged the tabletop with his fist. "I can't believe High Bluffs is gone. I'd always intended to go back . . . after I'd made enough to restore the place and show—" He broke off, his features tight with old resentments.

"Show Father?"

He inclined his head, but his expression was noncommittal. "I expect that you've thought over my request—that you've decided to live with Annie and me," he said, abruptly.

She was suddenly unsure; he *expected* her to obey his wishes. Did she really want to leave Jamie and Nellie? "I've thought it over."

"And?"

She glanced beyond him to the lines of rain slashing against the window. "I don't know," she said finally. "Nellie has been good to me, and then there's Jamie."

"Who's Jamie?"

Disconcerted, Jennifer searched for words; Joseph didn't know about Jamie.

"Our half brother," she said quietly, again knowing she must be direct. "The son of our father and Nellie."

Instantly he was on his feet, the chair crashing over behind him. "*Father?* That's a lie," he said hoarsely. "A filthy lie."

Somehow she stayed calm and explained that she knew it was the truth. He listened, but his face was closed. As she finished he picked up his chair but didn't sit back down.

"I'll never believe it. Nellie Thornton is nothing but a—a madam," he said, altering his intended word. "And a goddamned liar."

"You're wrong. Jamie's—"

"Silence. I won't listen to another word."

"But he looks exactly like father . . . and looks very much like you."

He stared, his mouth working, trying to formulate words. "Jennifer, I want you to promise that you'll leave here. My God—what next? If this got out, I could be ruined. Here I am, trying to get established in business, and in Arthur Denny's Loyal League Party to help the election campaign, and now this. I've met Mayor Yesler and other leading citizens. . . . I can't jeopardize my future in Seattle."

She stood up and moved to the fireplace, her thoughts in a turmoil, no longer hearing what he said. It was true that she wanted to make a decent life for herself . . . and for Jamie. But could she do that and stay in a boarding house saloon? she asked herself. Wouldn't she be trapped forever?

"I could use your help in setting up my office on the waterfront," she heard him say. "Doing the bookkeeping as you did at High Bluffs.

She spun around and faced him. "You mean you'd let me help in your business?"

He nodded, then glanced away. "I couldn't pay much, but you'd have your room and board as well."

Hope flickered, then flamed to life within her. She was sure that if she could work, she'd be able to make a place for herself, a respectable place. And as time went by, she reflected, Joseph would surely get used to the idea that he had a younger brother and eventually accept Jamie.

"I agree," she replied, outwardly calm.

He nodded, and the satisfied smile that lifted his lips took years from his face. "When can you go?"

"Not right away," she said. "I'll want to explain to Nellie and Jamie." She went on quickly as his expression hardened. "I owe her that consideration."

"Would two days be enough?" he asked, stepping to the door.

She nodded, sensing his unhappiness with the compromise.

"I'll return then."

Chapter Nine

"You do understand that what Jennifer is doing is for the best?" Nellie asked.

Jamie nodded. "I just wish things were . . . were different. Why can't people like us? We don't hurt anyone."

"I love you, and I'll still see you often," Jennifer said, hugging him.

"I know." He toed the leg of the table. "But Joseph won't want you to have anything to do with us. . . . I know he won't."

Jennifer tried to reassure him, but she had her own doubts. She just hoped that Joseph wasn't a narrow-minded bigot. Her father hadn't been, and neither was Damon or Seth Andrews, the friendly doctor who frequented Nellie's saloon.

Jamie smiled sadly, and Jennifer felt awful. But she knew that she had to go with Joseph; she had to win the respectability they both needed.

She watched Jamie as he went outside to join Martha. Then she went upstairs to finish her packing.

Jamie sat with Martha on a dock timber and watched Damon's *Sisyphus* load and then steam out of port. He was glad of Martha's silence; his own thoughts were on Jennifer. He suspected that Damon, who was probably only five years older than Jennifer's twenty, was interested in his sister. Maybe they'll get married one day, he told himself, wishing they already had, so that she wouldn't have to live with Joseph. Then another stern-wheeler arrived from Bainbridge Island, and as a small group of passengers disembarked Jamie stood up.

"Time to get home for lunch," he said. "You hungry?"

For a moment the brilliance of Martha's eyes was on his face, and he caught his breath. She was a beautiful child, he thought, despite her dusky complexion and black Indian hair. As though she read his thoughts, her long lashes fluttered and she looked down at her small hands clasped against her gingham skirt. Slowly she nodded.

He stared, wondering when she'd ever get over her shyness. This was the first time he'd been alone with her; Andy had brought her for the day after his housekeeper had suddenly quit. Now Jamie saw his chance to ask the questions he'd been curious about. "Do you go to school yet?"

She shook her head, her eyes still downcast. "But I have a teacher, and I can read and write."

"Why in tarnation don't you attend regular school? I'm starting Central School next month . . . aren't you old enough?"

Her cheeks went bright pink. "I'm almost nine," she said. "And I did start at Central School . . . but now my father thinks it best that I don't go back."

"Why?"

"Because she's a dirty Indian, silly," a voice said behind them.

Jamie turned to see a pale, thin girl about his age grinning at them. A short distance down the wharf a man and woman stood talking, waiting as a deckhand brought their hand satchels from the steamer.

"None of us wants to associate with Negroes or Indians," the girl went on, her faded blue eyes glinting maliciously.

"Who're you?" Jamie demanded, sensing Martha's humiliation.

In a flash the grin vanished and a pointed chin lifted with disdain. "Mara Appleton. My father owns railroads and . . . and is very important."

"So what?" Jamie said. "You're mean. . . . You apologize to Martha!"

"How dare you—" she began, her narrow features tensing with anger. "I'm going to tell my parents."

"Who cares. . . . Just leave us alone," Jamie snapped.

Mara whirled away and ran down the wharf, pausing only

to spit out a last insult. "I'm glad I'm attending Holy Names Academy and not Central School with a harlot's son."

"Come on," Jamie said, taking Martha's hand. "Don't feel bad; see, she insulted me too."

"Jamie's right," Damon said, striding toward them. "Pay no attention to Mara. . . . She's spoiled and needs a spanking."

Martha blinked quickly, but not before Jamie saw the tears sparkling on her thick lashes.

Shortly before noon Joseph came for Jennifer. With her trunk and paintings, she accompanied him to his modest frame house near Front and Seneca Streets. As she stepped from the buckboard to the ground, she felt a cold finger of apprehension touch her spine.

Where was Annie?—and Rachael, her niece? Hadn't they heard their arrival? The front door was closed despite the heat of the August day. Nervously she watched as Joseph lifted her trunk and dropped it onto the street, where it landed with a burst of dust. As he grabbed the small bundle of crated paintings Jennifer cautioned him.

"Please be careful. Those are the only belongings I was able to take from High Bluffs."

His hands stilled as his dark eyes shifted to hers. "What's in them?"

"My mother's paintings," she replied.

"I see," he said, a odd tone edging his words. "I find it surprising that you didn't take the valuable paintings instead."

"I explained that." She tried not to sound impatient with him. "Father had borrowed against everything including the contents of the house."

"Humph . . . very foolish." Joseph placed the crate next to her trunk.

"I'm sure he had his reasons; he didn't expect to die before paying back the bank," she replied, glancing at the unpainted house, anxious to avoid further talk about the past. The future was what concerned her now.

"We'll leave your things here for a spell," he said. "I'll fetch them after you've met Annie and Rachael."

As she was following him up the steps to the porch she

felt a moment of panic and wished she'd stayed with Nellie and Jamie.

Joseph reached for the knob, then hesitated. "Don't expect anything like High Bluffs," he said, his manner friendly for the first time that day.

She smiled back at once, hoping his better humor would last. "There aren't many places like High Bluffs. It was special."

His eyes darkened with remembering, reminding her how quickly his mood could change. "You're right, Jennifer. And somehow, I never thought we'd lose it. I always believed it would be there to go back to one day."

"I wish you'd done that. The place needed a man after Father died." Yet, even as she spoke she knew her words weren't exactly true. She could have managed the plantation if the community had been willing to recognize that a woman was capable of doing a man's work.

The hall, smelling of furniture polish and lye soap, was unexpectedly cool, but she knew the temperature had nothing to do with the chill rippling over her hot skin. She waited while Joseph strode to the back of the house, reminding herself that good manners precluded her fleeing the place as she suddenly felt like doing.

"Annie," Joseph called out, then paused and glanced back. "I can't understand where she could have gone, she expected me right back." His words were threaded with irritation, a tone she was coming to recognize.

She altered her position, so that she saw into a sparsely furnished sitting room, which she hoped didn't match Annie's personality. The faded brown settee and matching parlor chairs blended into the deeper browns of the braided rug and oak side tables, a brass and red-glass oil lamp being the only color in the room. Joseph had disappeared through a doorway, and now she could hear him talking to someone. Jennifer ran a hand over her hair, pushing a loose strand back into her chignon, a style she'd chosen to set off the fashionable straw hat Nellie had given her.

"This is my wife, Annie," Joseph said, startling her.

Jennifer turned to see him standing between his wife and daughter, both of whom stared at her with . . . curiosity? or hostility?

"My daughter, Rachael," Joseph went on, his eyes reflecting parental pride in the slender girl whose pretty features were marred by a petulant expression.

"And this is my sister . . . Jennifer," he told Annie and Rachael.

Annie mumbled something, not returning Jennifer's smile. Painfully thin and small in stature, Annie was entirely different from what Jennifer had expected. Her lips were compressed into a bloodless line and her narrow face was framed by brown hair that had been pulled into a severe bun. Mother and daughter looked nothing alike; Rachael was a beauty, while Annie was as drab as a gray pussy willow. Rachael was a Carlyle . . . from her dark hair and large brown eyes to the aristocratic tilt of her chin.

"I'm so glad to meet you both." Impulsively Jennifer moved forward.

Annie recoiled, ignoring Jennifer's gesture of friendship. "I should think so," she said coldly. "After living as you have in a saloon, and with a—a madam . . . humph."

Jennifer opened her mouth, then closed it again, biting back the retort that trembled behind her lips. It was obvious from the expression on her niece's face that Rachael's opinion was the same as her mother's.

"Enough of that," Joseph said sharply. "Jennifer is family." He moved forward and took Jennifer's arm. "Annie has a meal ready, and it'll get cold if we don't eat it. Then I'll have to get back to work."

Good manners prevailed again, and she allowed him to lead her into the dining room. "We all need time to get used to each other," he said, his tone low and meant for her ears only.

A terrible beginning, Jennifer thought, unable to do more than pretend to eat.

"Why did you move to Seattle?" Jennifer asked Joseph the next afternoon as she walked with him along the wharf.

"Because hop lice destroyed the hop crops in the Puyallup Valley and I subsequently lost my contracts to ship hops. As my other contracts were in northern Puget Sound, I bought the house and wharf here and relocated.

Annie was happy about it. She says there's more society here."

Jennifer watched as Joseph joined Noah on the *Annie C*, his shallow draft stern-wheeler. As its scow-shaped bow headed out against the tide she returned to the clapboard shack she'd been cleaning all day. By tomorrow she would be ready to set up Joseph's office. She locked the door and started toward Front Street.

"So, Jamie was right, you are here," Damon said, falling into step with her.

She stopped, and so did he, the tall, sometimes enigmatic man she'd come to associate with dark jersey and steamships and sudden sensations to her nervous system.

"Hello, Damon," she said, immediately conscious that he'd noticed the soil on her cotton dress and the dirt smudges on her face from her hours of cleaning. Why did he always catch her at these times? Disapproval flickered in his eyes.

"Your brother has you doing work?—other than setting up ledgers?"

"Not really," she replied, her tone cool. "I didn't want to work in a dirty room . . . so I cleaned it." When he started to speak, she went on quickly. "I'm used to hard work, and scrubbing floors is easier than hoeing cotton."

"My God, Jennifer. You worked in the fields?"

She blushed furiously. She hadn't meant to say that.

He grabbed her hands, gently turning them over to look at the palms. As he rubbed his thumb over the calluses that had never completely gone away, his expression softened.

Before she could reply, he took her arm, and they began walking. As though sensing her embarrassment, he changed the subject, telling her about steamship races on Puget Sound and how he'd almost invited her to watch one with him. When they reached Joseph's front door, he broke off suddenly.

"I want to see you, Jennifer." He hesitated, and she knew that what he was about to say was important to him. "Can I call on you?"

Her gaze was caught by his, holding her in a pool of warmth that had nothing to do with the sun that was lowering over the bay. Her body swayed toward him, obeying some primitive urge within her to be held by his strong arms, feel his lips against hers. Mutely she nodded.

Seconds stretched between them. Then he seemed to give himself a mental shake, abruptly stepping back. "I'll see you soon," he said, then turned and strode down the board sidewalk toward the bay.

Slowly Jennifer mounted the steps to the porch, aware that Damon's words had been spoken without a smile, almost sternly. Yet, for a moment, she'd never felt closer to any other human being in her entire life. Damon understood her.

During the next few weeks, Jennifer was busier than she'd been since leaving High Bluffs. But she took time each day to be with Jamie, and Nellie had once joined them for lunch. She wondered about Damon, why he hadn't come calling as he'd promised, but Jamie had mentioned that Damon had been dealing with labor problems and had gone to Port Angeles up on the Juan de Fuca Strait.

Two days later, the shadow of a man fell over Jennifer and Jamie as they ate their lunch on the wharf. Jennifer looked up to see Damon, sunlight gleaming on his black hair, his expression reflecting his pleasure at seeing her.

"Hello, Jennifer," Damon said, and before she could answer, he sat down beside her on a stack of boards. He was dressed in work trousers and a plaid cotton shirt that was open several buttons down his chest, exposing sunbrowned skin the exact shade of his face and arms. When his lips curved into an amused smile, Jennifer's bones suddenly felt like they'd turned to liquid.

"I told Damon we'd be here," Jamie offered, his words like pebbles, dropping into a pool of silence. "I told him we'd both enjoy having him join us."

"Of course," she agreed, her glance darting from Jamie to Damon. Somewhere on the hillside the bark of a dog vibrated against her eardrums, while above them a lone gull cried out to its mate somewhere on the tideflats south of town.

"How're you doing with your work?" he asked casually.

"I've got it all set up . . . and running smoothly." She looked down at her clasped hands, aware of the undercurrent beneath their words. "And I love being involved in the business . . . it's fascinating."

"Jennifer said she'd hate being stuck with that prude Annie," Jamie said, grinning, "and her spoiled daughter."

"Jamie!" Jennifer cried. "That wasn't to be repeated!"

"I'm sorry, Jennifer. I didn't think that meant Damon."

"Don't worry about it," Damon told him, but his eyes, again twinkling with amusement, were on Jennifer. "I can keep a secret."

Nervously, she pushed back a strand of hair, suddenly unable to look away from him. God, he was handsome, she thought: the firm lines of his mouth that smiled at her, the lean hardness of his limbs, and the long fingers that idly tapped against his knees. She wondered if there was a woman in his life, why he had not yet married. Many times she'd wanted to ask him that but hadn't; she'd realized he had a strong sense of privacy.

Confused by the turmoil of her feelings, Jennifer jumped up, her dandelion cotton dress flaring around her. "It's all right, Jamie," she began. "I know Damon understands that I don't dislike Annie—and that I enjoy being able to work—getting to know Noah."

Her words trailed off as his dark, slanting brows shot up. "Of course," Damon said, and got to his feet, facing her. "Will you accompany me to a dinner party next Friday night?"

She stared, taken aback by the unexpectedness of his invitation. "I . . . I don't know if I can," she said, and hesitated, wanting to go, yet apprehensive of the event itself.

"Say yes, Jen. I bet you'll have a great time."

Jamie's words startled her. For a moment she'd forgotten him.

"I won't take no for an answer," Damon said. "The dinner and dance is at the Appletons—" he broke off, his expression suddenly unreadable. "This'll be a good chance to introduce you to the leading Seattle families."

"I suppose I can."

"I'll come for you at six o'clock on Friday," he said, and before she could utter another word, he saluted her and, taking Jamie with him, strode off toward Yesler Wharf.

Jennifer stared after him, watching the confident set of his long-limbed body. He was the most attractive man she'd ever known, she decided. So vital and alive and caring . . . and he seemed trustworthy. Nothing at all like Judson Carr, she reassured herself.

During the next few days she wanted to mention the Appleton party to her brother and sister-in-law, but the opportunity didn't present itself. Somehow she knew that her friendship with Damon wouldn't meet with approval from Joseph and Annie. When she heard that Joseph was taking the steamship to Bainbridge Island, she asked to go along, thinking the trip away from the busy wharf would be a good time to tell him.

But Joseph did not want her along, telling her that she couldn't establish a good reputation flitting over the bay with stevedores: Annie had said it wasn't proper. Jennifer held her temper but reminded him that he'd already taken her on several short trips. He finally agreed when she pointed out that it was her only way of seeing Puget Sound, and that no one would think it was improper when she'd be accompanied by her own brother.

The next morning Jennifer stood on deck, the salt spray cool on her face, missing Noah, who always pointed out places of interest. He'd had to stay in Seattle and a deckhand had been hired for the day to take his place.

She sighed deeply as the wind blew through her hair and molded her clothing to her body. The little steamships that skimmed over the bay like waterbugs fascinated her, just as the wooded islands and mountains awed her. One of these days I'll paint it all, she decided, despite knowing that the pure light of the Northwest and the changing hues of the eternally snowcapped Mount Rainier wouldn't be easy to capture with watercolors.

The *Annie C* steamed into Port Blakely harbor on the incoming tide. While the crew unloaded supplies for the lumber mill, Jennifer walked through the town. When she returned the tide had gone slack, poised for its outward thrust, and the crew had already loaded the deck with lumber. The new deckhand looked familiar to her, but as the ship got under way and he limped into the cabin, she forgot about him. Instead she watched Seattle grow on the horizon and realized she still hadn't told Joseph about the Appleton party, which she was so looking forward to. She needed an evening away from Annie's never-ending complaining. How her brother could stand it, she reflected, was beyond her. All of her attempts at friendship with Annie and Rachael had proven futile. If it weren't for her work and her hopes for the future, she would move back with Nellie and Jamie in a second.

"Well lookee here," a man's voice snarled behind Jennifer, startling her. "If'n it ain't the whore who shot me."

Jennifer whirled around. The man's name came back to her instantly. "Al Cox!" she gasped, realizing now why the deckhand had seemed familiar.

He nodded and limped toward her. "Finally caught ya alone, huh?" He jerked his head toward the front of the ship, indicating that Joseph and the engineer were both out of sight.

"Leave me alone, or I'll call my brother," she told him coldly, but fear rippled through her.

"He ain't gonna hear ya, sister," he retorted.

"This is a small ship . . . lay a hand on me, and everyone'll know it," she said, trying to bluff him.

An ugly grin twisted his lips. "Not if you're out in the bay where no one can hear ya."

Her heart lunged in her chest. He meant to throw her overboard . . . kill her.

Jennifer tried to dart around him, but the small deck, rocking from the choppy water, made escape impossible. He grabbed her arm, twisting it as he forced her toward the rail.

"Think you're gonna get away with crippling Al Cox, you're crazy." His breath was hot and foul on her face.

"Let go!" she screamed. But her words were snatched by the wind to be cast over the wake behind them, away from the ears of others on board.

Suddenly Al Cox was yanked backward. "Let go of her, you goddamned waterfront rat!" Joseph yelled, and, with a swing of his fist, knocked the man to the deck.

Jennifer clung to the railing, her limbs trembling uncontrollably. "He wanted to push me overboard."

Joseph's eyes glittered dangerously. "Not anymore he doesn't."

She stared wide-eyed as her brother hauled the man upright and slammed him against the wall of the cabin. "You're fired, Cox—if I'd realized who you were, you'd never have been hired. But I know now, and if you set foot on my property again"—Joseph took a ragged breath—"you're a dead man."

Then Joseph's gaze shifted to Jennifer. "This is your last trip with me," he said coldly. "Annie was right. You had no business being on board."

She stared at her brother's angry face, knowing she couldn't contradict him now . . . or mention Damon and the Appleton party.

As Cox was led away she knew by the rigid set of his body and the flush of his pox-scarred face that she hadn't seen the last of him. She turned away, shivering, hoping she was wrong.

But she wasn't wrong about being denied the freedom of being on the bay. She knew Joseph would never relent now. God, God . . . nothing seems to last anymore, she told herself and concentrated on not crying.

Chapter Ten

"The Appleton party?" Joseph stared, stunned.

She nodded nervously. Since the incident with Al Cox, Annie had been more curt than usual and Rachael had ignored her altogether. "Damon said I'd meet the leading families of Seattle," she said, realizing she had their complete attention.

"You're invited to the Appletons? . . . and we weren't." Annie stared, her embroidery needle poised in midair.

"You can't go, Jennifer. It wouldn't look right, when my parents aren't there," Rachael announced.

Abruptly, Annie jumped up. "I . . . I'm going to bed," she whispered, and, to Jennifer's amazement, burst into tears and fled the room.

Rachael followed her mother to the door, where she whirled around to face Jennifer. "You—you've ruined our lives."

"Rachael!" Joseph cried, but she ignored his reprimand and disappeared into the hall.

Jennifer's gaze was fixed on the green and blue pattern of her skirt. She'd expected opposition, but not this. "I think it's time for me to reconsider being here. Having me in your house isn't working out."

Joseph leapt up. "That's out of the question . . . everyone would wonder why you left." He dropped a hand on his sister's shoulder in an unexpected gesture of concern. "Pay Annie and Rachael no mind. . . . They're just feeling slighted, but they'll get over it."

Joseph didn't fool her, she told herself; he was in perfect agreement with his wife and daughter. She also knew why he didn't want her to move: he'd be humiliated if she went back to Nellie now that everyone knew she was his sister, and besides, he'd lose his cheap office help.

"I can understand Annie wanting to go," Jennifer began, "but not insulting me because I was invited."

His arm dropped, and she saw that he was no less upset than his family. "I'd like you to consider staying home that night," he said, ignoring her words about leaving. "Aside from saving hurt feelings, it's too soon to appear at that kind of function—people still remember you arrived in Seattle with . . . with Nellie Thornton."

She was beginning to think her father had been right: Joseph was entirely self-serving. The last thing he wanted was new gossip that might jeopardize the social position he was striving to attain.

"I'll think about it," she said finally, and went upstairs to her tiny bedroom under the eaves.

But she knew she was going with Damon. Staying home wouldn't change the fact that her days in Joseph's house were numbered. She had everything to gain by venturing into society: if people got to know her, they'd realize the gossip was not true.

I won't disappoint Damon, she told herself, a man she was coming to . . . what? Respect?—or something much deeper than she dared to admit?

She awoke to a morning of misty rain that covered the countryside like a veil of silvered gauze. "Typical of August rain in the Northwest," Joseph said.

Jennifer nodded, too annoyed to comment that it was already the first of September. Both Joseph and Annie had been upset at breakfast when she'd reaffirmed she was going to attend the Appleton party.

"We have to talk," he told her as he held the door for her to enter the office. "I disapprove of you being escorted anywhere by Damon Polemis."

"You mean to the Appletons?"

He shook his head. "Just what I said . . . anywhere. Believe as you will, but I do have your best interests at heart, and Polemis, my competitor, is not the man for my sister."

"I can't believe you, Joseph," she retorted. "First it's the party you disapprove of, then Damon himself. Unless you can give me a valid reason, I'm going with Damon on Friday night. It's my chance to prove the gossips wrong about me."

"I've already been working on that," he replied, his tone tight with anger.

"On what?"

"On clarifying your position—that you were an orphan who came to the Northwest looking for your only relative . . . me."

She ran a hand over her hair, smoothing away tiny droplets of rain. "When did you start spreading that around?"

"Since you came to live with us." He shifted his weight from one foot to the other, as though he were uncomfortable with the turn of conversation.

"What else have you said?"

"Only the truth—that you were an innocent girl who lost the family plantation and was taken in by a woman who misrepresented herself . . . Nellie Thornton."

"That's a lie. Nellie was the only person who helped me, and you know it." She almost hated him at that moment.

"Don't be dramatic, Jennifer," he said coldly. "You don't owe her, or her bastard, anything."

"Jamie's not a bastard . . . he's our brother."

"The hell he is! And—and," he continued, his anger confusing his words, "I forbid you to see that boy again—or—or his mother!"

She spun away from his hateful face, grabbed her cape from its peg, and ran back to the door. "Then I'm done with you and your precious little family."

Before she could make good her escape, he blocked her way. "You can't go back to Nellie. . . . I won't have it."

"You forbid too much, Joseph," she said between clenched teeth. "I'm not a child to be twisted to your will. If living with you means never seeing Jamie and Nellie, then I'm leaving. It's as simple as that."

"You'd live in a brothel?"

She snapped her finger in his face. "Just like that."

He studied her face, looking for any sign of weakness.

When he saw none, he said, "You win, Jennifer. I can't let you go back now."

"I'll continue to see Jamie and Nellie."

He nodded, but she could see he didn't like it. "But you'll have to agree to stay away from that boarding house. And I want your promise that you'll never mention Jamie's claim of being a Carlyle."

She could return to Nellie's and seal her fate forever or stay with her original plan to make a decent place for herself—one that would eventually include Jamie.

"I'll stay," she said finally. "And I agree to your terms about the boarding house . . . for now."

He nodded, abruptly switched the conversation to shipping orders, and then left. He did not return to the office for the rest of the day.

During the next few days Jennifer's efforts to be congenial met with cold indifference from Annie and Rachael. But she managed to keep her temper, never rising to their remarks and not giving in about the Appleton party.

Now, as Jennifer stood before the mirror in her room, powdered, coiffured, and gowned for the party, she knew she looked her best. She'd taken her time with her preparations, wanting to look her most attractive when Damon introduced her to First Hill society.

"This is a beginning," she told the blond girl whose long-lashed blue eyes sparkled back at her in the mirror. "I'll show Seattle that I'm a woman of background after all." For a moment she allowed herself to think back to the elegant balls and parties she'd attended in Georgia before her father died. It all seemed so very long ago.

Then she looked back into the mirror, pleased with the alterations she'd made on an old party gown. The shimmering peacock blue silk of the skirt dropped away from the high bustle in the back to form a wide sweep just above her matching satin slippers. For the past two nights she'd been busy attaching pink and blue silk roses, strung together by brilliant green velvet leaves, to the low-cut gown. She had painstakingly outlined the neckline with the flowers, bringing them over the sleeveless shoulders and down to the bustle to fall with blue velvet ribbons over the folds of the skirt, creating a gown stunning enough to have come from Paris.

Joy bubbled up inside her as she pulled on the long, white, tight-fitting gloves, which were a gift from Nellie. She whirled away from the mirror, practicing a few dance steps before curtsying to the pink-cheeked girl whose delicate features were framed by elaborate curls and a stylish fringe over the forehead.

Grabbing her lace shawl and a silk fan, she went out the door to wait for Damon in the sitting room. Joseph leapt from his chair as she reached the doorway, his eyes widening at this vision of beauty.

"God, you're the picture of your mother, and I never thought anyone could be as beautiful as she was." He crossed to her, placing his hands on her bare upper arms. "I hadn't realized you owned such an elegant gown. You'll be the belle of the party."

"Then you're not still annoyed?"

He shook his head, although he'd sobered at her words. "No, but I still have my doubts about the whole thing."

She looked away, not wanting another conversation that could lead to angry words. "Where is Annie?" she asked, suddenly realizing Joseph was alone.

"She's in the kitchen—uh—making pies and—" He broke off as a knock sounded at the front door. "That'll be Polemis," he said, his tone abruptly stilted.

As he walked into the hall Jennifer forced her mind from Annie's snub to Damon. Her heart was beating like a drum. Oh, God, she pleaded silently, please, let me stay calm. I can't be reduced to a blushing schoolgirl, not for such an important night.

Then Damon was standing before her, almost unrecognizable in his black evening jacket, maroon silk waistcoat, and gray, striped trousers. His stiff-collared white shirt was a striking contrast to his gleaming black hair and eyes— eyes that had found Jennifer's the moment he'd stepped into the room.

Their gazes were locked, and neither spoke as the silence expanded, then narrowed again to hold them prisoners in the grip of some strange emotion that rocked Jennifer's being.

"Ahem." Joseph's clearing his throat broke the spell.

"You're looking beautiful—very beautiful tonight," Damon said, a smile curving his mouth while he drank in her loveliness.

She smiled, lashes fluttering as she tilted her chin at him. "Thank you, Damon. You're looking quite splendid yourself."

He grinned and took her shawl, draping it over her shoulders. "It's time we were on our way."

The September evening was unusually beautiful, its fading brilliance deepening toward the half-light between day and night. The whistles of steamers on the bay mingled with the cries of gulls, the sounds drifting over the city on slow air currents. She walked with him to the buggy, where Damon took her arm and helped her onto the well-sprung leather seat. Then he leapt up beside her and grabbed the reins, setting the horse in motion. At the corner they turned south for several blocks, then up the steep grade to First Hill.

Jennifer sat quietly with folded hands, occasionally darting a glance at the man beside her. When they reached the top of the hill, there was no mistaking the Appleton mansion. All the outdoor lanterns were lit, and the street in front was crowded with buggies and carriages. The sound of voices flowed out through the open door of the huge house, a magnificent structure of gables and bay windows and porches.

"You'll be the most beautiful woman here tonight," he said softly, helping her from the buggy, and she knew he sensed her nervousness.

Her gaze lifted to his. "I—Thank you, but—" She broke off, her thoughts fragmented by a sudden fear. Damn— some of those women had scrubbed floors, or come with the Mercer party, or in covered wagons from the East—why should I be worried about their accepting me? she reminded herself.

Unexpectedly, Damon pulled her closer, brushing her forehead with his lips. "You're with me . . . and I take care of my own."

She stared. His own? What did he mean? The strange

spell that had claimed them earlier lowered around them again. Her body swayed closer as his hands tightened on her bare flesh.

"Jennifer," he whispered hoarsely.

At that moment a servant appeared to take the buggy, and Jennifer pulled back. Damon's black eyebrows arched over his eyes, which were brimming with amusement at her reasserted sense of propriety.

"Let's get on with it," he said, and, taking her elbow, led her up the wide walkway, which was edged by rosebushes blooming with clusters of scarlet blossoms, up to the front porch, where another servant waited by the door.

Jennifer was introduced first to the Appletons and their painfully thin daughter Mara, a high-strung girl of Rachael's age. Then she and Damon were ushered into an elegant drawing room, where Jennifer met Arthur Denny, Mayor Yesler, and Edwin Woodrow and his wife, who was Annie Carlyle's only sister. The Woodrows, who owned a lumber empire, made no attempt to acknowledge Jennifer's relationship to Annie. As Jennifer moved among the guests the conversations she heard ranged from railroad regulation and land grant forfeiture, to Edwin Woodrow's desire to buy railroad land for its timber, to political talk about Senator Voorhees, who felt the government subsidization of the railroad had checked immigration into the territory. Jennifer smiled. Her eavesdropping was giving her an expanded view of the Northwest.

Jennifer glanced around the room, aware that Mara was watching her. The house was not elegant in the way High Bluffs had been, but opulent in the way of people who'd not always been rich. She caught the eye of Seth Andrews, who stood by a bay window, and he grinned a welcome. That the doctor was there didn't surprise her; the old bachelor seemed at home in any group and was liked by everyone.

When a servant announced dinner, everyone rose and walked in couples into the dining room. Jennifer could hardly eat the many-coursed dinner; there was too much to see and hear and take in. Her gaze jumped from the bejeweled women to their escorts, important men in Seattle. No wonder Joseph and Annie had wanted to be included. To her surprise, no one was shunning her, although she was aware that it was the men who were being friendly, not the women. After desert and coffee everyone moved to the mirrored ballroom on the top floor of the house. There, under the flickering candles in the crystal chandeliers, a small string band tuned their instruments for the first dance.

Damon swept her out onto the floor as the music began, whirling and dipping to a Brahms waltz. Being in his arms only made the evening more perfect. She almost regretted having to dance with the other men who claimed her for a partner. Then, as the band struck up the notes for the last dance, she was again in Damon's arms, her silk roses crushed against his chest. As the black-coated men and brightly gowned women swirled around them in a kaleidoscope of color, Jennifer closed her eyes and rested her head on his chest, her happiness complete.

When the music ended Jennifer excused herself to find her cape. She was directed by a servant to a small room off the huge entry hall. As she was putting it on a voice spoke behind her.

"You're the woman who came to town with a madam, aren't you?"

Jennifer turned to face Mara Appleton. The girl stared back, her small eyes narrowed with malice. "You have nerve coming here. I can't imagine my parents allowing it."

Momentarily speechless, Jennifer knew that an angry retort would place both her and Damon in an awkward position. "I beg your pardon, but my escort is waiting."

"Damon Polemis is the only reason you were allowed to come."

Anger scorched Jennifer's face, as a shivering sensation took hold of her. My God, the girl was trying to cause a scene . . . was she crazy? Jennifer wondered.

"Just because you're beautiful doesn't open the doors to the homes of decent people." Mara stepped closer, and Jennifer could see that the girl trembled from the force of her—what? Anger? . . . Jealously? "You're a whore!"

"Mara!" her mother cried from the doorway. "Go upstairs at once."

Mara hesitated, her eyes darting wildly between the two women. Then, picking up the skirt of her gown, she fled into the hall.

"I'm sorry—" Jennifer's apology froze on her tongue as the woman glared at her from behind wire spectacles.

"My daughter was out of place, Miss Carlyle." The woman was an older version of Mara both in her looks and in her obvious dislike for Jennifer. "But she was right—you aren't welcome back to this house, even if you're escorted by Damon Polemis, a man whose integrity we've always respected until now."

Jennifer's chin came up disdainfully. "I won't be back." Then, shoulders stiff and head high, she flounced past the woman whose drab yellow gown obviously reflected her personality and did nothing for her sallow complexion. At the door Jennifer turned to face Mrs. Appleton and said in her haughtiest southern drawl, "I thank you for the evening all the same . . . even if it was a backwoods imitation of a high society ball." Adjusting her cape over her shoulders, she went to join Damon, aware that she'd just made a few new enemies in Seattle.

The trip down the hill was made in silence after Damon's few attempts at conversation were not pursued. At the door Jennifer thanked him politely. She could not tell him what was wrong. It was too humiliating, and she was too close to tears.

He stood waiting, his expression hidden by the darkness of the night. She sensed his movement before he pulled her into his arms. Then his mouth was on hers, kissing her with a passion that claimed her breath, her body, and her mind. Her lips moved under his, accepting his desire with her own, a silent plea for him to never let her go, to keep her safe forever.

"I . . . I care for you, my Aphrodite, my Diana," he whispered against her lips. Then, as suddenly as he'd kissed her, he stepped back. "And I'll see you soon. . . . We'll go out again."

She felt his questioning gaze for long seconds before he left her to climb back into the buggy. A minute later he was driving away to the sound of hoofbeats and wheels against the hard dirt of the street. Would he really escort her again?

she asked herself. A woman who might be shunned in polite society?

She was glad the house was dark. She could not have faced Annie, or even Joseph. Her wonderful night had ended in humiliation, she thought miserably. Oh, God, she hoped Damon would never find out.

She knew he'd wondered about her sudden silence on the ride down the hill. Did he think her ungrateful? she wondered. She tiptoed to her room and took off her lovely gown. Then the tears came, and she sobbed into her pillow.

Chapter Eleven

Monday morning Jennifer was relieved to have the office to go to. She hadn't mentioned the scene at the Appleton party, but she sensed that Joseph and his family had heard about it. She'd felt like running back to Nellie's and hiding, but that would only have made matters worse. Nellie had brought in girls from San Francisco, and the self-righteous women of the town were trying to close her down. In fact, Nellie and her boarding house had become the focus of the current political campaign; the women of the territory, who had been voting since '83, were backing the reform ticket.

Low-flying clouds were threatening rain, and a brisk wind that smelled of salt and seaweed was scalloping the bay into froth when she left at noon to meet Jamie. When she reached the wharf, she sat down on a pile of boards and pulled her fringed shawl tighter over her serge dress. When Jamie arrived, she was startled to see Damon with him. She wondered if they'd heard the gossip, but when Jamie told about his first day at school, and then Damon talked about a new contract in Port Townsend and then went on to explain to Jamie about the annual autumn canoe trip that the Indians made down Puget Sound to pick hops in the Puyallup Valley, she decided that maybe they hadn't. She stared at Damon; she knew he was good for Jamie, who needed a strong male figure in his life. Having become lost in her own thoughts, she was startled when she suddenly realized that Damon had been speaking to her.

"I invited you to Bainbridge Island with us on Sunday," he repeated with a grin. "I'm taking my new steamer on a test run."

She met his eyes, slowly shaking her head. "I'd love to, but I don't think I should . . . not right now anyway."

"Surely Joseph wouldn't care," Jamie said, a hint of anger in his tone. "There'd be others on board. . . . It's not like you and Damon would be alone."

"Jamie!" Jennifer stood up abruptly, frantically trying to think of an adequate excuse. "I—I have something else I must do on Sunday." The whistle of a steamer echoed across Elliott Bay, and she saw Joseph and Noah returning to the office. It was time for her to go.

Then Damon grabbed her hands. "Don't let narrow-minded people affect you, Jennifer." His words were stiff with anger.

"The Appletons aren't worth your looking so sad, Jen," Jamie agreed. "Who are they anyhow?"

Jennifer stared. They did know. "Is—is it all over town?"

Damon nodded. "I wish you'd told me when it happened; I'd have demanded an apology on the spot, which would have placed them in the wrong . . . instead of you."

Jennifer's lashes lowered. "I know I seemed ungrateful for the evening. . . . I didn't mean to. But I felt humiliated—I just couldn't repeat what they'd said."

All at once the wind blasted in off the bay, heralding a rain that began to fall with a suddenness that reminded Jennifer of the torrential storms in Georgia.

They grabbed up their things and ran for shelter. At the office Jennifer paused for good-byes before dashing to the door.

"When it stops raining, I want to take you for a buggy ride if not a boat ride," Damon called after her.

By the time she and Joseph went home, she was filled with new resolve; she'd try harder to please her family. Respectability was of utmost importance, she had decided. Especially when a young woman wanted to be courted by a respected man. Besides, she knew that her parents would have wanted her to persevere.

Over the next few days Jennifer sensed a slight improvement in her relationship with Annie, if not Rachael, once she'd acknowledged to them that she shouldn't have gone to the Appletons. Damon was true to his word, escorting her to a September performance at the Frye

Opera House, then to a Sunday picnic at Lake Washington, with Andy and Martha and Jamie, followed by a tour of the school with Jamie. Jennifer adhered to all the social proprieties, yet Joseph still made his disapproval clear.

As the days shortened into fall Jennifer's friendship with Damon deepened. One Sunday in late October he came to take her for a buggy ride around the city, offering her a brief history of the waterworks, the electric light company, and the gas plant as they drove. By late afternoon, when he stopped the buggy at the Occidental Hotel, Jennifer was ready for supper. After dinner she finally got up her courage to say what had been on her mind.

"What about you, Damon? . . . You know about my family and background—I'd like to hear about yours."

He lifted his cup and drained the last of his coffee. "You know everything there is to know. . . . I live in Seattle. . . . I've got a successful business . . . am a respected businessman."

"I meant before that. Didn't you say you lived in New York?"

He paused and considered his reply before speaking again. "Yes, I did. My father is dead, but my mother and her family still live there."

"You have a mother?—relatives?"

His expression was suddenly guarded. "My father was a Greek immigrant and my mother's people are of English descent."

She wanted to hear more, but he abruptly pushed back his chair and stood up, and his stern expression put an end to the conversation.

As he drove her home a red sun glowed on the horizon, beginning to disappear behind the Olympics, taking the daylight with it.

"Thank you for the afternoon . . . and supper . . . and the history lesson," she said softly as she hesitated by the door, her hand on the knob.

He nodded, the warm smile banishing a gloom that had been with him since she'd asked about his family.

"I'm . . . sorry if I seemed too inquisitive about your life," she said suddenly, somehow wanting everything to stay right between them.

"Forget it. It's now that counts for me . . . and my future family when I get married."

"After you meet the right girl?"

He stepped closer and dropped a kiss on her nose. "I've already met her, Jennifer . . . the woman I'm in love with."

Then he left her, bounding down the steps to the buggy. With a crack of the whip he was off, leaving Jennifer staring after him, wishing he'd return and reassure her—that it was her he loved.

"That goddamned Polemis stole my contract—the one I need for the new ship," Joseph cried, as he burst into the office the next afternoon.

Jennifer jumped up, sending her oak chair into the wall behind her. "What happened?"

Joseph paced the room. "Polemis gave the Whidbey Island Company a cheaper price to ship the supplies and equipment to the logging camps. Christ! How did he know what my bid was? That I hadn't signed the contract yet?" Abruptly, he stopped, whirling to face Jennifer. "God! . . . You didn't tell him, did you?"

"Joseph," she cried. "How can you even think that? I never discuss your business . . . with anyone." She hesitated, horrified by his question. "And Damon never asks about your affairs either." Jennifer struggled against anger. Last night she'd returned home to find both him and Annie upset that she'd been out with Damon. Annie had insisted that she was flouting conventions, that she must stop seeing Damon, a man they'd never liked . . . and stop working. Joseph had quickly dismissed the latter demand.

For a moment Joseph seemed uncertain. Then he shook his head. "No, he stole the contract; it's the only answer. And we'll not associate with him again . . . none of us."

"It's a business coincidence, Joseph. I know Damon wouldn't do this to us." She hesitated, then repeated the same words she'd told Annie the night before. "I care about Damon, and I can't agree to not seeing him—even though I'm sorry you lost the contract."

Joseph's anger slipped the leash of his control. "You can't

be loyal to both of us, Jennifer. If you see Damon Polemis again, I'll disown you."

As the days passed Joseph proved adamant. She must either obey him or lose her family.

By the end of the week Jennifer knew that, whatever the cost, she couldn't stop seeing Damon; the very thought sent waves of fear through her. She could no longer conceive of a future without him. She remembered her father once saying that every person needed to feel warmth from another, from someone you love and who loves you. She wanted Damon to love her.

After discussing the situation with Jamie, Jennifer went to see Damon, knowing she must be honest with him. The risk of being seen with him and fueling gossip, or having Joseph find out, was not as frightening as losing Damon. He heard her out, then explained that he'd gotten the contract fair and square, that he hadn't known Joseph's bid, that his underbidding Joseph was a coincidence.

"I'd never hurt you, Jennifer." His words fell into a sudden silence, an invisible force that melted her bones to water even while it inflamed her flesh.

She tensed, knowing she was in danger of . . . what? Being unable to tell him no—to anything he'd ask of her, including her love . . . or her body?

Now was not the time for them. She turned away. "I have to get back." She grabbed her cape and threw it over her shoulders. "But I'm glad I came; I know Joseph will get over his anger when he wins another contract."

Then he stood beside her, his expression mirroring her thoughts, his eyes on her face, lingering on her lips, and she saw what she'd hoped for . . . love. Oh, God, she thought, let his love for me be as deep as mine is for him.

"We mustn't let this keep us from seeing each other," he said. "Nothing must do that."

She nodded, her long hair fanning her face. "But it'll have to be without Joseph's knowing, until he's calmed down."

"We'll talk about that when there's more time." He hesitated, his lids lowering to hood his eyes. "Can you spend Sunday afternoon with me?"

She stared, outwardly calm, inwardly shivering, knowing that Joseph and his family had been invited for dinner with friends—knowing her answer instantly.

"I'll pick you up a block from your house, and we'll have a few hours out in the bay on one of my steamers . . . where we can discuss all this and make some decisions for *our* lives."

"I'll be at the corner at noon." She smiled, suddenly shy, wanting to stay, but knowing they both had work to do. He strode to the door, but before he opened it, he bent and brushed her lips with his. For a moment she wondered if her legs would hold her, let alone carry her back to the office. But seconds later she was on the street, knowing God himself couldn't alter the course she'd set for herself.

"This is my newest stern-wheeler," Damon told her proudly as he helped her on board the *Nereus.* "Ninety-eight feet of steam power. Named for an old Greek sea god." His thick black hair was ruffled from the wind, giving him a rakish look. Like a pirate, Jennifer thought.

He looked younger, his expression alive with excitement. "It's beautiful . . . handsome," she corrected, meaning the ship, though the huskiness of her voice seemed to indicate other things.

He smiled down at her, his gaze lingering on her face. "You're beautiful, Jennifer," he said, as his eyes blazed, sending her senses reeling. Abruptly he took her elbow, a familiar gesture, and proudly showed her over the whole ship, from stern to bow. One of Damon's captains stood in the wheelhouse, waiting the signal to get under way. As Damon gestured to the man the ship's engines sprang to life, and the steamer moved into the current of the tide.

Jennifer stood beside Damon at the rail and watched the bay widen between the ship and Seattle, the two connected only by a sun-tipped wake. Behind the hills of the town majestic Mount Rainier towered above the Cascade Mountain Range, stark white against the November sky. Suddenly a whistle blew, startling Jennifer. She jumped backward, tripping over a pike pole that lay at the edge of the deck. Damon caught her, pulling her up against his chest.

"Can't have you falling and breaking a leg," he told her huskily, his face only inches above hers.

She opened her mouth, but words wouldn't come. Her mind seemed to have shut down even though her heart raced, pumping blood through her veins with a speed that weakened her limbs.

"Come, Jennifer," Damon whispered, a rich thread of passion in his voice. "We'll go to the stateroom and have some lunch."

She nodded and walked with him along the deck to the cabin under the wheelhouse, suddenly feeling too warm in her navy wool suit. She was vaguely aware of the smoke from the stack trailing on air currents behind them, of a long-necked, long-legged heron swooping toward the southern marshland, but she was acutely aware of Damon's hand holding hers.

Inside the cabin the sounds of sea and ship were shut out. Only the engines below their feet could be heard powering the vessel across the surface of Elliott Bay. The room was warm and cozy with a narrow bed along one wall and a desk built into the opposite one. A small table had been set for two, and bread, cheese, and cold meats were arranged on plates. He helped her out of her jacket and placed it over a chair.

"Hungry?" He turned back to her, his dark brows arching over his eyes in a question.

She shook her head and swallowed. She shouldn't have come. As much as she loved him, she was too vulnerable . . . and now she was suddenly afraid. Afraid of being alone with him and where that might lead. But if we're only going to talk it'll be all right, she argued mentally. Talk . . . that's all.

"Some wine then?" He moved to the table, his long powerful limbs molded by the corduroy of his stevedore pants, and uncorked a bottle. Then his glance shifted back to her. "Will you join me, Jennifer? It's very good French wine." She nodded.

"To . . . us," he said before they sipped from their glasses. "And to our future."

She watched him over the rim of the goblet. He'd never looked more attractive to her, the dents and creases of his lean face gave him an expression that took the strength from her bones. He licked the wine from his mouth, and she wanted to do the same, remembering the feel of his lips on hers.

She moved away from him, looking for a place to sit, choosing the bed. "This is good wine," she said, aware how inane that sounded. "My father and I used to have a glass when he'd bring a bottle from Savannah."

He watched her from across the small cabin, his eyes intense, as though he were formulating his thoughts. "We must talk, Jennifer," he said finally, and came across the room and sat down next to her. "Or the time'll be gone, and you'll be back on the wharf."

Her hand tightened on the stem of her goblet. She had flouted convention to be with the man she loved, but she knew she was playing with lightning. She was alone with a man, out in Puget Sound, and she suddenly realized that she'd placed her whole trust in him . . . and in her love for him.

Gently, he took the goblet from her hand and set it with his on the floor. Then his hands came down on her shoulders, turning her to face him. For long seconds he looked deeply into her eyes, his expression tender, exposing his own vulnerabiliity.

"I love you, Jennifer," he whispered, but his words soared into the silence of the room, expanding the sound into trumpets of joy that played a love song in Jennifer's heart.

"Damon—oh, Damon," she whispered. "Damon . . . I love you in a way I've never loved anyone."

With a low moan, he pulled her into his arms, burying his lips in the thickness of her long hair. Then his mouth was on her throat, her eyes that had fluttered shut, her lips, stopping any more words of love before she could utter them.

His arms tightened, while his hands moved over her body, possessing her with his touch. Her blood surged through her veins, heating her skin until her flesh became one long sensation of longing and need . . . need for the man beside her, the man who'd just professed his love for her . . . need that couldn't be denied.

"Damon," she whispered under his mouth, but was unable to go on, unable to utter her need to belong to him, to give herself completely.

His eyes, black with passion, searched her face, reading the surrender reflected there. Then his mouth closed over hers again, sending her newly awakened sensations to even greater heights. Slowly his free hand unbuttoned her shirtwaist and unhooked her skirt. The lacy undergarments took less time and Jennifer was only vaguely aware that she was lying naked on the bed while Damon quickly removed his own jersey and pants. In seconds, he lay beside her, his flesh dark against the ivory perfection of her skin.

"I've wanted this for months," he said, feathering her body with kisses, tracing the outline of her breasts with his tongue. "You want it too, don't you?" he asked hoarsely.

In that moment Jennifer knew the power one human being could hold over another—that she wielded that power over Damon now. But she was humbled by it too, knowing they were both equally exposed, open to hurt, at the mercy of the other.

"If I didn't would you stop?" she asked quietly. Although it was the last thing on earth she wanted, she felt compelled to ask . . . to test him.

Something flickered in his eyes, something that reminded Jennifer of a helpless child. He started to speak, but she placed a finger over his lips. "Damon, I'm sorry," she whispered. "Forgive me."

He made a small animal sound, then pulled her back into his arms, possessively, almost violently. Then Jennifer was moaning too, calling out his name again and again, soaring beyond her flesh into a dimension she'd never known before—the heights where the pain of her lost maidenhood was drowned in a wildly boiling sea of ecstasy.

Later, when they were past the first passion, Jennifer was the first to speak. "I love you Damon," she said again. "More now than before."

He propped himself on an elbow, looking down at her with eyes still bright from passion. "I want to marry you. That's why I brought you out on the bay . . . to ask you to be my wife." He hesitated, his expression suddenly troubled. "I hadn't planned to seduce you."

She smiled at him, savoring the fact that he would explain, that he genuinely loved her. "I know," she said finally. "But I can't marry you . . . not yet."

"Because of Joseph?"

She nodded. "I know things will be different when he gets over his anger about that contract."

"And I don't want you working on the waterfront much longer," Damon said, his tone hardening, proving what she'd always suspected—he'd never liked her working for Joseph. "It's no place for a decent woman."

"Now you sound like Annie," she teased.

"On that she's right. I want you married to me, having my children."

Jennifer's face went hot at his words, embarrassed even though he'd explored every curve and swell of her body. "Oh, Damon, I want that too, and soon. But for right now, we'll have to wait."

"But under protest," he muttered into the long strands of her hair.

Jennifer forgot everything as Damon's fingers once again began a search of her body. It was much later, after the ship was back at the wharf and she was hurrying toward Joseph's house, that her doubts began. No, she told herself as she turned to wave at Damon. Everything will be all right. I'll soon be married to Damon, the man I love. Nothing could alter that.

Chapter Twelve

"Don't let Joseph come between you and Damon," Nellie said, angrily. "He's not worth sacrificing your future happiness."

Jennifer nodded. "I know, but I thought—"

"He'd get over it?" Nellie asked, interrupting her. "Let me tell you, Jennifer, Joseph never gets over grudges. Did he ever forgive his own father?"

"What exactly was it that Joseph couldn't forgive? It had to do with you, didn't it, Nellie?"

Nellie dropped her gaze, staring at the rag she'd been wiping over the bar. "He found out that your father and I loved each other . . . and he didn't approve." She turned away, dropping the cloth into a bucket of soapy water. "Joseph is unforgiving—as bad as my own brother."

Jennifer watched as Nellie straightened chairs under tables. She had suspected Joseph had known about Nellie and their father, and she knew there was more to the story than Nellie was telling.

Abruptly Nellie faced her, returning the conversation to Damon. "You've asked my opinion, and my advice is to put your own life first. Marry Damon . . . forget Joseph's ultimatum."

Nellie's words echoed her own feelings. Her hope of Joseph forgetting his anger had faded as first Thanksgiving and then Christmas and the New Year came and went without change. She'd spent part of the holidays with Jamie and Nellie, bringing more disapproval from Joseph and Annie, and now her stolen hours with Damon had taken on a sense of desperation. But she knew she couldn't lose the man she loved.

"Don't depend on Joseph for anything, Jennifer. If you

lose Damon because of him, you might find yourself out on the street anyway . . . the next time he makes an unreasonable demand." She hesitated, her tone hardening. "Some brothers are capable of that."

Jennifer had put on her cape to go, and now she stopped short. Was Nellie referring to Seattle?—or when she was a girl? Jennifer knew her question was on her face, if not her lips.

Slowly Nellie nodded. "Both. We were orphaned when I was seventeen; my brother was older and working in New Orleans, trying to make enough money to go to California."

"You're from Louisiana?"

"Born in Natchez, under the hill." She paused, her expression tightening. "The rich always live on the hills, the poor under them."

"And then?"

"When my mother died, I took her place as housekeeper in one of the mansions above town and lived in a little room behind the kitchen. But it proved to be a short job. . . . The man raped me, the wife caught him at it, and I was thrown out into the street. I had done ironing for an old madam who'd lived near us, and she took me in until my brother replied to my letter telling him of Mother's death and my situation.

"He never answered the letter, and in time I assumed he hadn't gotten it, that he had already gone to California. By then I knew I was pregnant; I miscarried several weeks later and almost died. If it hadn't been for the madam, I would have."

"Wouldn't he have sent word he was going?"

Nellie shook her head. "My brother was ashamed of our background, but I always believed he'd have helped me had he known. But I realized I was wrong after seeing him in Seattle. He'd gotten my letter and had to make a choice: take the ship he had passage on to California, or lose that money and come help me."

"My God!"

Nellie glanced out the window. "I suppose I could say he left me to my fate. I had to live, so I stayed with the madam, and she grew to depend on me; I saw to the kitchen and housekeeping, but I had nothing to do with the

men. The thought of sex had become abhorrent to me
. . . until I met your father. When she moved back to
Savannah, I went with her, and shortly after that she died,
leaving me everything she owned. I took her place, as the
madam, but . . . I was never a prostitute, even though
I've been involved with running brothels all my adult life."

"The woman helped you as you helped me," Jennifer said
softly, moved by Nellie's story and surprised that she'd told
it. "But after all that time why did you think your brother
would help you establish a new life?"

"When your father died, I knew I had to make a decent
life for Jamie. I'd run into someone who knew my brother
and learned that he'd married, was successful, and a
leading citizen in San Francisco. I expected him to want to
help me, and of course I was going to tell him I was a widow
and nothing about my occupation. And . . . you know the
rest."

"That . . . bastard!"

Nellie stepped closer, grabbing Jennifer's hand. "I
wanted you to know my story so that you could make the
right decision in your life. Don't let Joseph steal your
chance for happiness."

Before Jennifer could reply, loud shouts sounded from
the street.

"Jesus!" Nellie ran to the door and flung it open to reveal
Seth Andrews arguing with a group of well-dressed women;
Mara Appleton and her mother were in the forefront. "It's
those damnable 'proper ladies' again," Nellie cried. "Ever
since the People's ticket won the election last November,
they've been trying to run Seattle . . . and close me
down."

As Jennifer followed to the door Nellie blocked her way.
"If they see you, it'll mean more gossip," she whispered.

Jennifer stepped back to watch from behind the curtains.
Nellie was right. She didn't want Joseph finding out she'd
visited the brothel.

"We intend to run Nellie Thornton out of town!" Mrs.
Appleton shouted.

"And Jennifer Carlyle!" Mara added, her gaze on the
front window.

Jennifer jumped back. Had Mara seen her? she wondered, aghast. God, she hoped not. She suddenly thought of Mrs. Pickett in Savannah.

"I don't think so, not in the light of my news," Seth said. "You'd better leave before Nellie calls the law."

The door slammed behind him, and Jennifer could no longer hear. The women started off down the street, their signs reading "What price shame" and "Run harlots out of Seattle" now hoisted less defiantly above their heads.

Jennifer peeked around the curtain, startled to see Mara's backward gaze still on the window. She shuddered.

"How did you get rid of them?" Nellie asked, surprised that they had been discouraged so easily.

Seth Andrews grinned. "I just told them something they didn't know."

"What was that?" Jennifer asked.

He raised his brows. "I believe Nellie will find that her troubles with that group are about over. The suffrage issue has been terminated. A ruling was made yesterday that the legislature was wrong in assuming women were eligible for the vote."

"But they had it for over three years." Nellie shook her head.

"Three years too long," Seth said, his grin suddenly wiped from his face. "And those damnable women are proof of that."

Jennifer's talk with Nellie had helped; she knew marrying the man she loved was more important to her than abiding by Joseph's demands. Once her mind was made up, she went to Damon's office, anxious to tell him her decision. But she was greeted by an angry Damon who didn't give her a chance to speak. She stood in shocked silence as he paced the room.

"We've been sneaking around, worried about Joseph being mad over a contract I supposedly took from him, and he has now taken one of mine. Only I *know* Joseph was underhanded."

"What happened?" It was the first time she'd seen Damon really angry.

"Luke Olson up on LaConner Flats canceled our contract when my steamer, loaded with bales of hay and sacks of oats, started taking on water while still tied to his dock." He stopped in midstride, facing her. "Christ. She'd have sunk but for the tide being out."

"Luke Olson lost his cargo?"

Damon shook his head and continued to pace. "Coincidentally the *Annic C* had just unloaded down the slough and was able to take Olson's cargo before it got wet. But Joseph would only take it if Olson was under contract with him." Abruptly Damon faced her. "Shrewd . . . eh?"

Jennifer stared. "And that's when your contact was broken? Can Luke Olson do that?"

"The contract has a clause about cargo being in jeopardy. Legally he could do it, and I don't blame him for wanting to save his crops. But Joseph—" He broke off as though he suddenly realized his words weren't for Jennifer's ears.

"Damon, can't you see that this is just the same as last time, when Joseph accused you of taking his contract." When his eyes narrowed, she went on quickly. "I admit Joseph is hotheaded and took unfair advantage of the situation, but it was all in the open, he wasn't underhanded."

"Jesus Christ, Jennifer, that isn't the point."

"Then what is?"

"The hole in the hull of my steamer . . . how did it get there when we hadn't run aground or hit a snag?"

She tried not to feel offended, or angry. "Are you saying that Joseph was responsible for that?"

For a moment he seemed frozen . . . uncertain of his reply. But as she looked at him she knew: he believed Joseph had damaged his ship.

She took an involuntary step backward. "You're as bad as Joseph, Damon. Both of you are like two little boys competing in a game. Don't you remember your own words about there being enough work for all Puget Sound steamers?"

"You don't understand what's involved here—that if my ship was tampered with, I'd—"

"Joseph wouldn't do that," Jennifer cried, interrupting him. "Can you prove he did?"

His expression tightened; he looked . . . dangerous. "If a man could stoop to such treachery, then . . . I could almost kill him."

"Damon!" she cried, shocked.

"I don't want to discuss this with you. I shouldn't have brought it up."

"Because you can't prove it?" She whirled away toward the door. "I don't want to discuss it either, Damon. Not until you can talk about it calmly." Before he could stop her, she was out on the street. Tears stung her eyes when she realized she hadn't told him her decision . . . that she wanted to be his wife more than anything else in the world.

Jennifer was miserable. Friday morning she decided to apologize, but as she left the office she saw Joseph coming toward her, his face red and angry.

"I want to talk with you, Jennifer," he said, and taking her arm, led her back inside. "I know where you're going—to see Damon Polemis." His hand tightened painfully. "I'll not have this going on under my nose."

Jennifer jerked her arm away. "How—"

"How?—Luke Olson just told me he'd seen you with Polemis when he was there to pay his final bill the other day."

"I don't know Mr. Olson."

"But he knows who you are . . . saw you on the wharf and was asking after you. Luke's the kind of man you should be seeing . . . not Damon Polemis."

"I admit I've seen Damon without your knowing it, but only because you were so angry about that contract. I thought you'd get over that, and now you've taken his contract. I think—"

"Enough about that. Business is business and doesn't change the fact that I insist you stop seeing that goddamned Greek."

Her legs trembling with anger, she backed away. "I love him, and *no one* is telling me I can't see him. I intend to be his wife."

"Christ!" Joseph's features twisted with mounting rage. "Then you're not welcome in my house."

"Joseph," she began.

"I don't want to hear it!" he cried. "You have no morals since meeting Nellie and her bastard."

"Don't call Jamie a bastard. He's your brother."

"The hell he is. . . . For me he doesn't exist." Joseph stepped closer, a strange expression on his face. "Nellie isn't to be trusted, no more now than back in Savannah when she threw my love back—" He stopped abruptly, turning away to stare out the window. "She's no good."

"What are you saying, Joseph?—that you were in love with Nellie?"

His shoulders stiffened. "Don't ask questions that don't concern you, Jennifer."

"You were," she whispered. "But Father—"

"Was having an affair with her," he said. "And I'll never forgive her for that . . . or him."

"And you . . . did you as well?"

He faced her, his eyes filled with old hurt and old grudges . . . and hate. "No. . . . She looked upon me as a boy—my father's boy—throwing my feelings back in my face." His hands knotted into fists. "They—Father and Nellie—are the reasons I left Georgia, and I want no reminders of them . . . including Father's bastard."

"But it's not Jamie's fault."

"Enough! The subject is closed . . . forever." He hesitated, his dark eyes malevolent. "And I want your promise to start behaving like a lady—not like one of Nellie's harlots."

Her chin went up. "If that means giving up Damon, then I refuse."

Their gazes locked. Seconds passed. Then he turned and strode to the door, where he hesitated, trying to rein in his anger. "I have to go, the crew's waiting. But I'll be back in a few days, and we can talk. Would you promise me not to see Polemis until then . . . until we can discuss this like a brother and sister?"

It was his words, brother and sister, that decided her. If she could talk, it would be a beginning. "I'll wait until then," she said finally. "But no longer."

With a curt nod, he went out to the wharf where his newly acquired steamship, his third, *The Carlyle*, was being loaded for its maiden voyage to Port Angeles on the Juan de Fuca Strait.

* * *

"Whore's bastard . . . whore's bastard!" The leader gave Jamie a shove.

"You stop saying that!" Jamie cried, close to tears, knowing he was no match for the bigger boys. "My mother isn't a whore."

"Ain't a whore?" The boy clucked his tongue. "You ain't that dumb."

Blind anger propelled Jamie into their midst, his fists flailing. But within seconds he was on the ground, his nose bleeding, his body being kicked by booted feet.

"Goddamned bullies. Get the hell out of here!" a man shouted as he pushed his way into the crowd.

The boys stepped back and, muttering that Jamie deserved it, fled down the block toward school. Damon helped Jamie to his feet.

"Are you all right?"

Jamie nodded, trying hard not to cry while he brushed dirt from his coat. It was bad enough that the kids always picked on him, but to have Damon see it humiliated him even more. Before he could explain, the school bell rung. "I'd better go . . . or I'll be late." He forced a smile. "Thanks, Damon . . . for—uh—scaring them off."

Damon placed an arm around him. "I have to catch a steamer for Victoria, but we'll talk about this when I get back . . . all right?"

Jamie nodded again, anxious to be alone.

Damon thumped him on the back. "Forget them, Jamie. You're a better person than all of them put together."

When Damon had disappeared, Jamie altered his course and went toward the waterfront; he wasn't showing his bloody face at school to be laughed at again.

By afternoon, when he ran into Jennifer on the wharf, he'd managed to wash his face. She looked tired and unhappy after he mentioned that Damon had gone to Victoria. When she asked about school, he evaded, letting her think classes had been dismissed for the afternoon. After she was gone, he wandered over to the empty wharf where Joseph's steamer had been docked. He knew he couldn't go home yet without his mother knowing he'd skipped school. And he could never tell her why.

Absentmindedly he plunged a hand into his pocket and

pulled forth a watch. He'd found it on the wharf weeks ago
and forgotten about it. Seeing Noah down the wharf, he ran
after him.

"Mr. Noah," Jamie began, opening his hand to reveal the
pocket watch. "I found this on your wharf, and I thought I
should give it to someone."

"Thanks, Master Jamie," Noah said, a wide smile on his
face. "I'll see to it."

Jamie stared. "You know who I am?"

Noah grinned even wider. "No mistaking that, Master
Jamie. You's the picture of your papa."

"You knew my father?—You'd recognize me as his son?"

Noah's face sobered, and he put his huge hand on Jamie's
shoulder. "I recognize what's right, Jamie. But what's right
ain't always recognized by everyone."

Jamie swallowed hard, then blurted out the very thing he
hadn't wanted anyone to know. "Like the kids at school;
they call me names."

Noah's eyes clouded. "I know, Jamie, I sho know how
that is." He hesitated, as though considering his words.
"But you come and visit me sometime, and I'll tell you
'bout your papa, and my grandpappy Zeb in Georgia . . .
and we can talk 'bout why you ain't gonna git no place in
this world if'n you ain't got your schoolin'."

Jamie's face went hot, but he smiled. "Joseph wouldn't
mind?"

"I've knowed Joseph all my life. But I'm no slave no
more. You come and we'll talk. Miss Jennifer knows where
I live."

Jamie nodded and started back to the boarding house.
Things didn't seem so bad now.

Four days later the door to Jennifer's office burst open.
Noah hesitated in the doorway, his expression stricken,
unmindful of the rain lashing past him into the room.
Behind him stood a stevedore.

"Miss Jennifer, we've got trouble . . . bad trouble," he
said hoarsely, his speech reverting to his southern upbringing. "It's Mist' Joseph. He—he—"

Jennifer stared, momentarily paralyzed by what he was

about to say. Something was terribly wrong; she'd never seen Noah so upset. "He what, Noah?"

"He dead, Miss Jennifer, he dead." Noah shook his head as if in a daze. Tears rolled unchecked down his cheeks. "I knowed him since we been boys . . . now he dead."

"Dear God! . . . No!" Jennifer ran to him and yanked him into the room. The stevedore followed, closing the door behind them.

Noah's huge chest heaved with silent sobs. "It's true, Miss Jennifer. *The Carlyle* went down in the strait . . . and took Mist' Joseph with it."

The air seemed to go out of her lungs, but her heart fluttered with alarming speed. Jennifer sat down; she was near fainting. "How . . ."

"Reports say the ship was destroyed by a boiler explosion," the stevedore said softly. "It was stormy, and that hundred miles of strait that connects Puget Sound with the Pacific Ocean can be treacherous, especially in February."

Striving to control her own emotions, Jennifer asked the necessary questions and learned that the ship and bodies had washed up on the beach near Port Angeles.

Blind with tears, Jennifer grabbed up her shawl and, together with Noah, went to break the news to Annie. The next few days were a nightmare, but for the first time Jennifer and Rachael and Annie were united . . . in their shared grief for Joseph.

Two days after the funeral Jennifer went down to the office. Noah had more bad news. The ship was a total loss. An investigation indicated the engines might have been tampered with, and one of Damon's captains, a man who hated Joseph, was rumored to be a suspect.

Shocked, Jennifer pressed him for more details.

"It only waterfront rumors, Miss Jennifer, but—"

"But what?"

"Some of the stevedores believe Damon was behind it— that he wanted to git even for his ship's accident on LaConner Flats when he lose Luke Olson's contract." Noah glanced away, his face suddenly old and sad.

Within minutes Jennifer was out of the office, hurrying

past Yesler Wharf toward the Polemis Steamship Company. She had to clear up the accusations at once.

"Damon . . . I've heard some terrible gossip and—"

He closed the door behind her, then moved to his desk and coolly lit up a cigar. Did he already know about the gossip? she wondered.

"The stevedores are saying that one of your captains tampered with *The Carlyle.*"

Behind the cigar smoke his eyes were suddenly remote and cold. "And?"

"That you're involved because of the accident to your ship and losing the Olson contract to Joseph." She looked away.

He ground out the cigar and crossed the room. Grabbing her chin, he tilted her face upward, forcing her to meet his eyes. "Yes, I heard the gossip . . . and it's not true. My captain would never have done such a thing. I trust my men. Did you also hear that there's not enough evidence to arrest anyone or to ever determine why the boiler exploded—that the gossips are saying I bought my way out of the mess?"

She shook her head, her mind in turmoil. She stepped back, away from his hand. "Why didn't *you* tell me this?—before I heard the rumors?"

"I was going to, later."

She stared, unable to ask the question trembling on her lips.

"I'm not responsible for Joseph's death," he said, anticipating her question. "Surely you can't believe I was."

Could she believe him, knowing how angry he'd been over the Olson contract?

"If you trusted me, you'd know I'm innocent," Damon said coldly, disbelief edging his tone. "I disliked Joseph's underhanded ways of doing business, but I'm not a murderer."

Abruptly Jennifer went to the window, where she watched a squall dance across Elliott Bay. She wanted to believe him; she loved him. But her feelings were clouded by doubts; Damon was an ambitious and aggressive man in his business dealings. Hadn't he said he could almost kill a man who endangered his ship? A gust of wind heralded the first drops of rain on the glass, little beads of moisture sliding down the pane like the tears down her cheeks.

She struggled for control. I can't lose Damon as well as Joseph, she told herself. Yet, she realized how little she knew about this man and his past. Conflicting thoughts washed in and out of her mind. Until she'd put them into perspective, and the gossip had died down, she couldn't marry the man accused of being responsible for her brother's death. Slowly she faced Damon, and then she told him.

The silence swelled, building an invisible wall between them. When he spoke his voice was low and sounded far away. "I'll give you time but—" His words trailed off as he looked beyond her. "Don't take too long, Jennifer."

She nodded, grabbed up her cape, and fled into the endless winter rain. As more tears came and heaving sobs shook her body she knew she couldn't tell him it was all right . . . because it wasn't. She had to trust the man she married.

Two weeks after the funeral Annie tearfully announced she was expecting a baby. Jennifer was surprised, then pleased. Annie had wanted another baby for years, and now with Joseph gone, the event might be a blessing in disguise. Another child might help Annie accept Joseph's death, something she'd been unable to do so far.

That night as Jennifer got ready for bed she had another shock. "It can't be!" she cried as she stared at her image in the mirror. But as she counted back over the months since November and realized how many times she'd passed up breakfast because of an upset stomach, she knew: she was as pregnant as Annie. She climbed into bed and stared wide-eyed at the ceiling, knowing she still hadn't resolved her feelings about Damon, the father of the life within her body.

When she awoke in the morning, her first thought was her condition. She couldn't eat, and as she walked through the morning fog to the wharf, she wondered how on earth she'd handle her latest problem. It's my own fault, she told herself. That afternoon with Damon on his ship had been perfect, their future assured; she'd been sure of marriage.

Now if she told Damon about the baby, he'd insist on marrying her even though the gossip was growing stronger every day. That he'd been exonerated for lack of evidence hadn't stopped the talk or eased her doubts. As Jennifer reached the Carlyle wharf and entered the office Noah glanced up from a pile of monthly statements, work he'd assumed when Jennifer had gone into mourning.

"Miss Jennifer, we's got problems."

She listened to him tell her that there were nightly thefts on the wharf, vandalism that was causing shipping delays, and that he had no authority with employees and business associates, who wouldn't deal with a "nigger."

All thoughts of her own condition vanished, as she realized she must take command of the company or they'd lose it. Annie's help was out of the question; her first pregnancy had been fraught with complications, and she was now spending most days in bed. Besides, she'd never shown any interest in the business.

"Do you think our troubles are caused by one group?—or person?" Jennifer tried not to jump to conclusions.

"'Fraid so," he said, the strain of the past weeks obvious on his face. "But I doan know who."

"What do you suggest?"

"Hire a night guard," he replied. "But we's still need someone to submit the bids and talk with customers . . . someone not black."

Jennifer felt his humiliation. "It's not fair," she said softly. "The company couldn't run without you . . . not now or when Joseph was still alive. But if you'll help me, I'll take over."

"It won't be much easier for you than for me . . . but I'll stay," he said with the same innate dignity she'd always respected in his grandfather.

She nodded, knowing he was right. Then they got busy, planning the strategy to keep the company going. The days that followed were so busy that Jennifer had no time to dwell on her own problems. When she explained the financial situation to Annie, her sister-in-law begrudgingly agreed to let her try to keep their two steamships moving across the sound.

* * *

Several days later the labor problems came to a head; the men threatened to walk off the job. At work at the office, Jennifer heard a commotion on the wharf and ran out into the blustery March afternoon.

"Wait!" she called to the men who were picking up their tools. "I want to hear your reasons for quitting . . . aren't we paying you higher wages than the other companies?"

There was a murmur of voices, all agreeing the pay was good.

"Well?" she prompted, striving to maintain her authority.

"We ain't working for a girl . . . or a nigger—even for higher wages," one of the stevedores yelled.

Jennifer boldly stepped forward. "I know you all have families . . . and so did my brother." She saw that she had their attention and continued. "My brother's wife and daughter need the income from this business to live."

"Then why ain't Mrs. Carlyle down here 'stead of you?" She read the accusation in their eyes; she was a fallen woman to them.

Jennifer hesitated, knowing her next sentence was critical. "My sister-in-law is in bed, grieving for her dead husband, and trying to keep the baby she's expecting next summer, a baby who won't have a father."

A hush fell over the men. Jennifer waited, not allowing her gaze to falter even though her legs shook and her stomach churned.

"Hell, I'll stay," said one tall stevedore, who shuffled his feet while the others agreed with him. "Ain't right to leave Mrs. Carlyle without an income."

As suddenly as they'd quit, the men went back to work. Jennifer's body trembled as she hurried into the office, but she hesitated at the door when a man stepped forward to meet her.

"I'm impressed, Miss Carlyle. I guess I'll leave my business with the Carlyle Shipping Company after all."

She stared at green eyes that crinkled as a smile curved the man's lips. "Our service will stay dependable, Mr. Olson. And I'm relieved that you aren't canceling our contract as you did with the Polemis Shipping Company."

His smile faded. "I had no choice there, not if I wanted to save my cargo."

"I understand," she said, finding it difficult to be cool to Luke Olson, a man whose sincerity was so evident.

"And, as I've changed my mind about moving my business elsewhere, I'd best get on with my other errands . . . have to catch the evening tide into LaConner." He tipped his cap, his eyes crinkling again, and strode outside, passing Noah at the door.

"Miss Jennifer, you just won over the men; they's gonna stay. And with Luke Olson on your side, telling how you handled things, you've guaranteed keeping most of the contracts . . . so long as we keep our bids low and don't have no more vandalism."

She nodded, suddenly exhausted. As Noah went back out she returned to the ledger, wanting to finish the page of figures before going home.

Then the door opened again, and Damon stepped into the room.

"You've been avoiding me," he said coolly. "It's been weeks since the accident. . . . Have you come to a decision about my guilt?"

She stared at the face she remembered so well, the strong features she'd feathered with kisses, his hard body that had lain next to her naked flesh. Then she looked away, knowing she'd resolved nothing. She loved him but her doubts were stronger than ever . . . and she couldn't lie to him.

"Surely you can't still believe I was responsible for Joseph's death."

"I don't think you're a murderer, but—"

"You think I told my captain to tamper with *The Carlyle*." The lights in his eyes seemed to go out.

He looked . . . ruthless? she asked herself. Jennifer's doubts flooded back. That she carried his child seemed unreal—a situation to be faced later. Right now she couldn't make a commitment of marriage.

They stared at each other, neither giving ground.

"Since you don't know what to believe, I can't help you," he said coldly.

"I need more time . . . to sort out my feelings, and get Joseph's company back in the black."

"I'll buy it from Annie—take over the two steamships and get you out of all this."

"No!" His words had sent a chill down her spine. "We need this business to make a living."

He rounded the desk and grabbed her. "Why do you want to compete in a *man's world*?—set yourself up so that you'll never be socially acceptable?"

"This is respectable work, even if it means my being in a *man's world*, as you call it." She shook her head furiously, her blond hair feathering across her hot face. "It's either steamships or working for Nellie."

"You'll marry me then," he said, his tone frustrated and angry. "And I'll take care of both companies."

She jerked free. Was he offering to marry her only because he wanted to eliminate a competitor? she thought suddenly. Or because he loved her? God, her doubts about him only got worse. If Joseph were still alive, Damon would have had no opportunity to control his rival company—by buying it, or marrying her.

"No," she said simply.

His eyes burned into hers for long seconds. Then he stepped back around the desk and strode to the door. "I'll give you more time, Jennifer. But don't wait too long, or we might both be losers . . . forever." Then he was gone into the sunlight that flickered in and out of the wind-chased clouds.

Jennifer stared at the closed door, not wanting to believe she might have been fooled by two men: first Judson Carr and now Damon.

Chapter Thirteen

Once again Jennifer tried to bury herself in work, foolishly hoping that everything would be resolved if she gave her mind a rest. But by April she realized she was no closer to a solution, and the life within her had begun to move. Now she *had* to face the fact that she was pregnant. The next morning she started to the office, then altered her course and headed for the boarding house, hurrying through the fog like a specter out of her own nightmare—a nightmare that hadn't gone away. She confided in Nellie, who advised her to tell Damon at once.

"My God, Jennifer! I can't believe you haven't already told Damon. The man loves you."

"But the gossip—"

"The hell with the gossip," Nellie interrupted. "You should know how distorted gossip can be. Damon never believed you were a prostitute because you lived with a madam."

Nellie was right. She must tell Damon immediately, but her stomach fluttered with fear. Surely he still loved her . . . still wanted to marry her. As she left the boarding house and walked along Front Street, she was surprised to find it already late afternoon. The sun had burned the fog away, giving the day a warm feeling of spring, and after leaving a letter to Zeb at the post office next to the Post-Intelligencer Building, she didn't feel like going down to the wharf.

She stopped to watch a ship, loaded with coal from the mines near the east shore of Lake Washington, steam out of the harbor on its way to the Pacific Ocean. A block away, a train whistle sounded above the noise of buckboards and horses, and she glimpsed huge fir and cedar logs from the

122

Cascade foothills being pulled by the engine along the tracks of the Seattle, Lake Shore and Eastern Railroad.

Impulsively she decided to let Noah handle the day's work and turned toward home, stopping along the way to buy clams and a small fresh salmon from Suquamish Indian. As she opened the front door she heard Annie call from her bedroom.

"Is that you, Rachael? Please come in here."

Jennifer dropped her things onto a hall chair, wondered where the housekeeper was, and walked quickly to the back room. "It's me," she said, hesitating in the doorway, her gaze on Annie, who sat propped up in her bed by two large pillows. "I'm home early."

"Oh," Annie said, her tone dropping. "Mrs. Scott left early, and I wanted Rachael to see to supper . . . I don't feel well."

"I'll cook something," Jennifer said, even though she knew she wasn't good in the kitchen. Annie was thinner than the week before, her eyes sunken into pale cheeks. God, don't let anything happen to the baby, Jennifer pleaded silently. Annie was distraught enough without having to cope with a miscarriage.

"I didn't know you cooked." Annie's tone was edged with sarcasm.

Jennifer tried not to show her annoyance, a task that took more discipline each day. The widowed Annie had become almost unbearable to her.

"I'll manage, and Rachael can help when she gets home."

"You're getting fat," Annie said suddenly, her gaze narrowed on Jennifer's waistline. "You used to have a flat stomach. . . . You're the one who looks pregnant."

Jennifer's face was suddenly burning with fire. Annie's words had taken her aback.

"My God!" Annie cried, twisting her body higher on the pillows. "You aren't . . . are you?"

"I—" She broke off, unable to answer. Although she had dreaded this moment, she had nothing prepared to say.

"You are!—I can tell by your expression."

Jennifer nodded slowly. The truth was bound to come out sooner or later. She could no longer pretend she wasn't expecting a child.

"Oh, no!" Annie cried, her eyes darting about wildly with fear. "Who else knows?"

"No one . . . yet." Jennifer's voice broke as she struggled to maintain her control. She straightened her shoulders and said she was sorry she'd gotten pregnant but not ashamed of what she'd done. Her love for Damon wasn't shameful, even if it had been overshadowed by problems.

"It's not like you think, Annie. I—"

"No, I won't listen to any more," Annie interrupted, covering her ears. She began to rock back and forth while little sobs came from her chest.

Jennifer rushed forward, knowing Annie was becoming hysterical. "It's going to be all right—let me explain."

"Slut! I always told Joseph you were a harlot like that Thornton woman." She buried her face in the pillow, sobbing harder. "What'll happen to Rachael and me when this gets out? We'll be snubbed . . . by everyone."

"I'll see that nothing happens to your position in Seattle," Jennifer said, trying to calm her. "I'm—I'm going to marry Damon, and no one will know."

Abruptly, Annie jerked her head up, her expression venomous. "You'd marry the man responsible for Joseph's death? Isn't it horrible enough that you're the mistress to a murderer?"

Trying to disregard Annie's vicious attack, Jennifer went on. "I love Damon, and I've come to realize he couldn't have been involved in Joseph's accident."

"But he was . . . I know he was."

"Then why didn't you file charges against him?" Jennifer demanded, her patience suddenly gone.

"Because I couldn't prove it." Then in a rush of words, she went on to say that Damon had threatened Joseph in her presence. "Damon Polemis said that the practice of bribing customers to reveal bids and then undercutting that price was dangerous . . . could get Joseph killed." More sobs shook Annie's body. "Your lover killed my husband."

Seeing that there was no way to calm her, Jennifer left saying, "I'll go see to supper."

"If you dare see that man, I'll tell everyone that you're with his child." Annie flung the ultimatum at her back.

Jennifer faced her. "You just said you were afraid of what would happen if that fact got out."

Annie's blue eyes burned feverishly as they met Jennifer's. "I want you to leave Seattle . . . within the week!"

Jennifer wondered if the woman's mind had become unhinged by Joseph's death. She felt a wave of panic. But she knew Annie was bluffing. Why would she bring a scandal down on her own head, especially when she set so much store in gaining acceptance with the "important" people on First Hill.

"I'm not leaving," Jennifer said coldly. "Whether you like it or not, I'm the only one who can run Joseph's business. If you make trouble for me, then I'll be the one who tells everyone I'm pregnant." She narrowed her eyes at her. "Don't interfere in my life, unless you want to face the consequences."

Hatred glazed Annie's eyes, but she nodded, knowing she was temporarily defeated.

Jennifer went to the kitchen, her hands shaking as she placed pans on the stove. She wondered why Rachael was late, but her thoughts returned to Annie's words about Damon, his threat to Joseph's life. Was Annie lying? She meant to find out.

The next day Jennifer made discreet inquiries about Joseph's business dealings. Luke Olson and several other men indicated that her brother had undercut bids but assured her that the practice was not new to the waterfront. That Damon had been right about Joseph only brought back her old doubts. Had the man she loved decided to get even with Joseph, who'd been double-dealing at Damon's expense?

As she sat behind her desk that afternoon, trying to decide whether to bid on work with Jackson, Myers and Company, a fish cannery opening at Mukilteo, Damon walked into the office. Her heart lurched. How could I have doubted him, she wondered. Even in black jersey and corduroy trousers, no man in Seattle compared to him.

"Nellie said you wanted to see me." His dark eyes were remote, his expression set in lines deeper than she remembered. "Is there something we haven't already discussed . . . before it was too late?"

She nodded as a foreboding stole over her. "Something important."

"I'm still interested in buying Joseph's company. Aside from that we have nothing to discuss."

Frozen by his words, her hands tightened into a knot. He wasn't making it easy to tell him about the baby, and she was glad the desk hid her so that he couldn't see her thickening waistline. Her cheeks flamed at the thought, remembering when his hands had moved lovingly over her flesh—when he'd whispered about the perfection of her body—her small waist. God, what had happened? What was to become of her . . . and the baby?

She glanced up, searching for a glimpse of the love he'd once had for her. She saw nothing but cold indifference, the one emotion she could not conquer. All she had left was her pride.

"We aren't selling," she said, her tone low with defeat.

"Jesus Christ!" he cried. "Why do you want to run a business rather than be a wife and mother? What in hell's wrong with you anyway?"

"Get out!" she yelled, rescued from defeat by a sudden surge of anger. "I foolishly wanted to talk to you about just that . . . wife and mother." She leaned toward him. "But I see that's hopeless—and I intend to continue running this company."

He strode to the door, where he shot her a final glance. "I told you not to wait too long, Jennifer. But you did—you believed I murdered Joseph. And now I can't forgive you." He took a ragged breath. "I'm going to force you out of business."

"Like you did to Joseph?"

Damon stiffened and fear washed over her. Had she gone too far? He looked as if he wanted to strike her.

"Think anything you like, Jennifer; you never trusted me anyway." He hesitated, as though struggling with some powerful emotion. "You were the first person in the world I trusted completely, and you turned out to be like the others—only your deceit was worse. . . . You let me believe in our love. Now—now I don't give a damn." He almost collided with Noah on the way out.

"Is everything all right, Miss Jennifer?"

Jennifer shook her head, desperately blinking back tears.

"Did Mr. Polemis—" He broke off as Jennifer waved her hand.

She stood up and walked to the window to stare at the bay she'd come to love. The clouds, colored in infinite shadings from silver to charcoal, hung low over silky water, poised to disturb the smooth surface with ripples of wind and dimples of rain. Slowly, she turned away from the mountain-ringed, amphitheater of the harbor to meet Noah's gaze, knowing she'd need his help over the next few months. She told him everything: her suspicions of Damon, Annie's accusations, and her own pregnancy.

For long seconds after she'd finished Noah seemed frozen with disbelief. "Then you won't be marrying Mr. Polemis?"

She shook her head.

Noah was silent, formulating his thoughts. Finally he spoke, telling her that a pocket watch had been found on their dock shortly after Joseph's departure on *The Carlyle*, a watch later claimed by Damon.

"Do you believe he was somehow involved?—maybe went on board and tampered with the engines?"

Noah shrugged. "It's possible, I s'pose. But Mr. Polemis was—"

"Exonerated?"

Noah nodded. "I gave the watch to him when he got back from Victoria. It was after that we hear about the accident."

Jennifer glanced back over Elliott Bay, knowing there was nothing she could do about any of it now; there was no way to prove Damon's guilt . . . or innocence. And a black man's word wouldn't stand up against a respected citizen's in any case.

"Noah, can I have your promise that you'll never tell anyone about the baby?"

"Your secret's safe with me," he replied. "But I doan know how you'll keep others from knowin'."

"I'll manage, with your help." She met his worried eyes, knowing her next problem would be explaining the baby

after she had it. But she'd settled one thing forever: she'd
never marry Damon now, never tell him about their child.

Jennifer struggled to maintain a margin of profit, but her
advancing pregnancy hindered her. She gradually let Noah
take over the negotiations with the customers and workers.
The bedridden Annie remained silent about Jennifer.
Surprisingly, she didn't even confide in Rachael, who hadn't
noticed her aunt's thickening body.

May brought the first hint of summer, an occasional
sunny day that burned away the early morning wisps of
vapor that snaked along the shoreline and veiled the distant
islands. But late spring also brought more labor problems.
She decided Damon was behind them. The loss of some of
their labor had caused delays to their schedules, and they'd
lost business because of it. All the contracts had gone to
Damon.

When the door opened suddenly one morning, she knew
it was Noah, as few people came into her office anymore. "I
hired new men," he said, his expression tight with worry.
"But we's paying high wages to get 'em."

She nodded, frustrated by not being able to confront the
stevedores as she'd done in the past—hating being confined
behind the desk. "We'll make it if we can keep both ships
on a tight schedule."

He nodded and went back out to oversee the loading of
the *Rachael C* for its trip to Port Madison on Bainbridge
Island. As Jennifer resumed her work the door opened
again and uneven footsteps on the board floor brought her
gaze to the man who'd entered the room.

A finger of fear touched her spine, pushing her erect on
the chair. Al Cox limped forward to her desk.

"I come to offer my services," he said slyly. "Ya can
protect the Carlyle interests by hiring me."

"What do you mean?" she demanded, surprised that he'd
show his face. She glanced to the window, hoping to see
Noah nearby. Al Cox was a man who'd never forget a
grudge.

"Jest what I said, missy," he replied, his small eyes
glinting maliciously in a way Jennifer remembered all too
well. "Protect you from problems like vandalism or theft—

anything that might happen to a woman who's mixing in where she ain't wanted."

"Are you threatening me?" Jennifer glared at the stocky man, whose greasy clothes smelled of sweat and whiskey and stale tobacco.

He shrugged, grinning his jagged-toothed grin.

"I don't hire thugs. Get out . . . and don't come back." Her words were strong, belying how vulnerable she felt, trapped behind the desk so he wouldn't see her condition.

His eyes narrowed to slits. "You'll be—" He broke off as Noah strode into the room.

"What is you doing here?" Noah loomed over Al Cox, speaking harshly. "Git the hell outta here . . . now."

Al Cox glared up at him for a moment, then moved off as quickly as his limp would allow. But Jennifer knew he was still a very dangerous enemy.

As June approached, Jennifer's worries about the business lessened. In her advanced condition she saw no one. On-the-scene problems were left in Noah's capable hands. Business questions they decided together. For her brief appearances on the street Jennifer wore her long full cape. She'd managed to conceal her pregnancy from everyone, although Rachael was now commenting about Jennifer's weight gain.

As the life within her grew Jennifer avoided any thoughts about Damon and what they had once shared. He'd tried to see her several times, but she'd refused. Jennifer knew she still loved him and sometimes dreamed about him, but she just as often had nightmares about Annie exposing her. Annie had become totally unreasonable, complaining that she'd hoped to attend Tacoma's Fourth of July activities to celebrate the Nothern Pacific's completion of the transcontinental railroad and jealous that her sister and her wealthy husband, the Woodrows, had membership in the new Puget Sound Yacht Club. She blamed all of her troubles on Jennifer.

The first of June brought an opportunity to buy another steamship. With financial help from Nellie, Jennifer bought the ship, registered it as the *Katharine C* after her mother,

and became an equal partner in the company. The trans-
action infuriated Annie.

"You're trying to squeeze me out," she cried. "You want
Joseph's business for yourself and that . . . nigger."

Jennifer's frustration equaled her anger. "We bought the
ship for the same reason Joseph bought the others . . .
we need it."

Her face twisted with malice, Annie spit out her retort.
"I'm going to see to it that everyone knows about you,
Jennifer. After my baby is born and I'm on my feet, I'll ruin
you."

The next morning Jamie came with Nellie's shiny new
carriage and moved Jennifer back to the boarding house. As
he carried her trunk up to her room on the second floor she
realized that his resemblance to their father had become
more pronounced. He was only fifteen, but he sometimes
seemed much older. She hoped that he would join the
Carlyle business when he finished his schooling. Jamie was
smart and creative, and both she and Nellie agreed that
Jamie should have every opportunity.

"That's it," Jamie said, placing the trunk on the floor. "Are
you going to the office today, Jen?"

She shook her head.

"Coming down for lunch?"

She shook her head again. "No, I'll just stay and unpack.
You know how I feel about eating with the men. I'm just
glad your mother no longer has boarders up here."

"Don't explain, Jen," he said. "I understand . . . and
it's all right." Unexpectedly he hugged her and kissed her
cheek. "I love you, Jen." Then he was gone.

Jennifer stared after him. A knot of sudden panic
tightened in her stomach. Would he tell Damon? She knew
that Jamie saw him often. . . . They'd become close
friends.

No, she decided. She trusted Jamie to remain silent.

But fear gripped her. Where does it all end? she asked
herself. Will it ever end?

Chapter Fourteen

In the final weeks of Jennifer's pregnancy she set up an office in her room, where Noah came each day to keep her informed about the progress of the company. Seth Andrews had become her doctor after Nellie had taken him into her confidence.

Although Jennifer's pregnancy had progressed normally, she was troubled by one thought that now consumed her waking hours: what would happen to the baby? How could she conceal the existence of a baby who shared her last name? She and Nellie spent hours talking and never found a good solution.

The evening the labor pains began Nellie hovered over her, running between the saloon and Jennifer's upstairs bedroom. "I'm going to telephone Seth," Nellie said, when by ten o'clock, the doctor hadn't made his nightly appearance downstairs.

"No, not yet," Jennifer said, glad that both Nellie and Seth were among the few people in the city with telephones, but worried that Nellie's telephone was in the saloon. "Someone will hear you and wonder why you need a doctor. They'll ask questions and—" she broke off as another pain gripped her, bathing her body with sweat.

Nellie rushed forward, placing her hand on Jennifer's stomach. "The pains are closer. We can't wait much longer, then I'm calling him."

Jennifer nodded, and Nellie promised to be right back. Jennifer stared at the window, where the night beyond the lacy curtains was alive with crickets and boat horns and voices from the street. Jamie was with Damon somewhere in northern Puget Sound en route to Vancouver. She sighed, the sound suddenly catching in her throat as

131

another pain tightened her stomach. She was glad Jamie wasn't here. By the time he returned she'd have had her baby and would be somewhere else. But where? Tears flooded her eyes . . . from pain, and from fear of what the future held.

Suddenly the door burst open, and Nellie hurried into the room, followed by Seth who went to the bed and quickly examined Jennifer.

"Christ!" he murmured. "I'm here none too soon." he spoke to Nellie as he flipped open his bag. "Bring a bowl of hot water . . . immediately."

The next hour was a succession of pains for Jennifer, and each one seemed worse than the last. When it was over, Nellie stepped forward with the tiny, blanket-wrapped figure she'd just bathed. "She's a perfect little girl," she whispered, placing the infant in Jennifer's arms.

Suddenly humbled by the miracle of the birth, Jennifer lovingly examined the delicate-featured baby, who waved little fists and puckered her mouth. She was only minutes old and already hungry.

"Go on." Seth grinned. "Give her something to eat."

Nellie helped Jennifer free a breast, then stepped back, a gentle smile curving her painted lips. "I must be getting old—I feel like a grandmother."

"But a very attractive one, nevertheless," Seth said, winking at Jennifer. Then he closed his bag, unrolled his sleeves, and put on his jacket. "Now I'll have a drink." He strode to the door, where he glanced back. "Your delivery was an easy one. . . . I just hope Annie does half as well."

"Seth?" Jennifer began, bringing the doctor's gaze back to her. "You won't mention my baby to anyone . . . will you?"

His usual grin was replaced by a serious expression. "I promised Nellie that I'd preserve your privacy, and as I don't know the circumstances, I can't give you advice." He hesitated, and Jennifer knew he'd guessed the baby's father. "Just don't let pride stand between you and your future happiness."

"I'll leave you alone for a few minutes with your new daughter," Nellie said, and followed Seth into the hall.

Jennifer stared at the closed door, knowing Seth would

keep her secret. Nellie had told her about him—that he'd grown up in an orphanage in New England, worked his way through medical school, and then migrated to Seattle, where he enjoyed the unusual distinction of being accepted by all levels of society. Not only was the old bachelor trustworthy, but he was also in love with Nellie.

Jennifer lowered her gaze to the infant who suckled at her breast. A great sensation of love overwhelmed her suddenly, a desire to protect her child whatever the cost. Then as she watched the tiny face she was hit by the resemblance to Damon.

"My sweet baby," she whispered, "can't help how she looks." Gently, Jennifer moved her so that she could kiss the blond fuzz capping the round head. But, as the child fussed, she again gave her a breast.

"Diana, born August 11, 1887," Jennifer told the sleeping baby a short time later. "Your name will be Diana Katherine Carlyle, after my mother." She held the baby closer. "And after the name your father used to call me."

Jennifer swallowed hard. "And I'll protect you, little Diana . . . from gossip and loneliness and fear." Her eyes blurred, as the picture of the moss-draped live oak and two graves surfaced in her mind. "And, Mama and Papa, I know you would have understood—would have loved Diana too.

"And Damon . . . Damon. You'll never know Diana."

A week later Jennifer received a call in the middle of the night that Annie had gone into a difficult labor. Despite Nellie's protest that she shouldn't be out of bed herself at that hour, Jennifer dressed hurriedly and rushed to Annie's house. There she found Seth frantically trying to save the lives of both Annie and her baby, while Mrs. Scott, the housekeeper, in nightgown and robe, hovered in the hallway, wringing her hands. Annie had sent Rachael to the Woodrows hours ago.

"Will she be all right?" Jennifer whispered.

The doctor shook his head, sending beads of sweat down his face. "Jesus, I hope so. She should be in the hospital, but it's too dangerous to move her now."

"She was fine when she went to bed," Mrs. Scott said. "It happened so fast."

"Jesus Christ," Seth said hoarsely, as a baby girl was born, bringing with it a flood of brilliant red blood from the birth canal. He handed Jennifer the crying infant without looking up, trying desperately to stop the flow. But within minutes it was over; Annie was dead.

Mrs. Scott burst into loud sobbing, and Seth ordered her from the room. "Go to bed. You'll need to fetch Rachael when it's light, no need to tell her until then."

In a daze Jennifer bathed the infant, so frail compared to her Diana. The baby was lethargic after its first burst of wails, and not inclined to the natural instinct of sucking even though Jennifer tried to force her to suckle from her own breast.

Seth shook his head, his hazel eyes clouded from fatigue and failure. "There're times I detest being a doctor. I don't think the baby'll make it either."

Stricken with a horrible sense of loss, Jennifer tried harder to entice the infant to eat. She knew how she'd feel if the baby were Diana.

As the doctor and she worked over the baby Nellie arrived with Diana, informing Jennifer that her own baby needed to eat.

The morning was a flush of light on the eastern horizon when the baby joined its mother in death. Shortly afterward Nellie left with Seth, who promised to see about the bodies after he'd had some sleep. Jennifer put Diana to bed in her old upstairs room, then awakened Mrs. Scott to go for Rachael. She didn't mention the baby's death and cautioned Mrs. Scott not to tell Rachael anything. As the housekeeper left, Jennifer told her she wouldn't be needed until after things had calmed down.

When the woman had gone, Jennifer wrapped the dead infant and placed it under the blanket next to Annie's body. She then braced herself for the ordeal that was yet to come.

Rachael burst into the house just after sunrise and ran directly to her mother's bedroom. She was hysterical, and when Jennifer tried to calm her, Rachael lashed out.

"You slut!" she cried. "Since you came into my family everything has gone wrong." Rachael crumbled to her knees, throwing herself onto the pillow next to her mother's head. "Mama, Mama," she cried. "You can't be dead . . . you and Daddy can't both die."

"Come, Rachael," Jennifer said softly, remembering how she'd suffered knowing both her parents were dead. Gently, she led the sobbing girl to the sitting room. "We'll face this together. . . . I'll help you." But even as she said the words, apprehension was clawing at her stomach. How would she tell Rachael about the baby who'd also died?

Rachael twisted away from Jennifer. "I don't want your help—you—you—harlot! My other aunt will help me." She whirled away, her body convulsed with sobs, and rushed from the room. A moment later Jennifer heard the front door slam. Startled by the noise, Diana began to cry.

Jennifer ran to pick up her frightened infant, and as she sat on the bed with the child at her breast, she had a thought, one that grew into a possible solution to her own dilemma. Why not let everyone believe that Diana was the child of Annie and Joseph?

As Diana again drifted off to sleep Jennifer's idea expanded in her mind. No one except Seth and Nellie knew that Annie's baby had died. Her own child was a secret, and as Diana's name was also Carlyle, no one would be hurt by giving Diana legitimacy in the eyes of the world.

Jennifer placed Diana back on the bed, then looked down at the perfectly formed little girl. Her plan would guarantee that neither Diana's nor Rachael's life would be ruined by gossip.

Moving to the window, Jennifer looked out at the flawless morning sky that was mirrored on the surface of the bay. It was a dazzling morning, fresh and clear as only a morning could be in the Northwest.

Glancing back at the bed and her daughter, Jennifer made her decision.

Annie's coffin was closed for the funeral; she and her baby were buried together in a grave next to Joseph. No one questioned Diana's legitimacy, although Rachael mentioned that the name Diana hadn't been the one she'd thought her mother intended naming the baby. Preoccupied with grief, Rachael didn't bring the subject up again.

By September, Jennifer had resumed her work at the

steamship company, a business that was completely in her hands even though half of it, together with the house, was in trust for Rachael.

"What about Diana?" Rachael asked one evening after Jennifer had explained about the trust. "Doesn't she get half of everything too?"

"You were the only one mentioned in your mother's will as Diana hadn't been born yet," Jennifer said.

Rachael's dark eyes were thoughtful. Then her glance shifted to Diana, who lay on the settee next to her. "I think she'll have dark eyes like me and Dad even though she has blond hair from my mother's side." Her tone softened. "She's all I have, and I'll see that she has half of everything when she's older."

Jennifer turned away. She hadn't realized how one lie could feed on itself, breeding more lies.

To Jennifer's surprise, Rachael picked up the baby. "She's eaten so can I put her to bed?"

Jennifer nodded. How she missed nursing her baby, but she couldn't take the chance.

She shivered, feeling the dampness. Crossing to the fireplace, she put another log on the fire, watching as the flames leapt hungrily at the wood and wondering if Rachael would return to spend the evening with her. The girl was her biggest problem; she cared for no one but Diana and the wealthy aunt who'd taken an interest in her since Annie's death. When Rachael had stated that she preferred to live with her Woodrow relatives, Jennifer had been frightened, knowing the Woodrows could claim both Rachael and Diana. But Annie's sister had immediately stated that her age and health precluded assuming responsibility for an infant, relieving Jennifer's mind and leaving Rachael no alternative but to stay with the aunt she considered a harlot.

As Jennifer looked in on Diana later she realized that Rachael had gone to her room without even saying good night. Jennifer shivered again. Rachael was disrespectful, but Jennifer could cope with that. She just hoped to God she'd never have to deal with Rachael's finding out the truth.

Chapter Fifteen

The fall brought Nellie's trouble with social reformers to a head: she was on the verge of being closed down. "I can't lose my business, or I won't be able to afford to send Jamie east to school next year," she told Jennifer one evening after surprising her with a visit. "How can I convince the city fathers that Seattle needs my establishment? It's elegant and clean, and men don't have to worry about disease or being robbed."

"Can't you tell them that?—that Seattle still lacks women and needs such a place?" Jennifer paused, considering the problem. "Would you be willing to pay to stay open?"

"As much as I can afford." Nellie's eyes widened, as she waited for Jennifer to continue.

"Why not make them an offer—that in return for providing a place like yours, you want their assurance that you'll be free of harassment. And if they'll agree to that, you'll be willing to contribute money each month toward the betterment of Seattle, starting immediately with a large contribution to the struggling school system."

"Jennifer . . . that's bribery!"

"Not really . . . if you word it right. They might go for it, especially since you'd be a heavy donor to city projects."

"And I might get thrown in jail."

Jennifer hesitated, her thoughts on her own past business dealings. "It's been my experience that the enemy camp collapses if there is something to gain by moving to the other side of the question. Besides, don't some of the leading citizens of the city frequent your place?—and know you are true to your word?"

Nellie nodded. "But they'd sure as hell be upset if I burst in on the meeting tomorrow. I don't think I'd get past the front door." She stared at the flames in the fireplace that leaped and fell with a life all their own. "If I were a 'proper' lady they'd at least have let me in and heard what I had to say."

"They'd let me in," Jennifer said at once. "I'm still acceptable in some circles." She took Nellie's hand, remembering the times Nellie had helped her. "What time do we go tomorrow?"

"You'd do that, Jennifer? Risk being with me when I make such an offer?"

Jennifer smiled. "I've been seen with you before."

The next afternoon they had surprisingly little opposition in gaining entrance to the meeting room. The men were shocked at first but after Nellie explained her proposition, all but Edwin Woodrow seemed interested; the lumber baron was abrupt and rude. Nellie ignored him, and Jennifer wondered how she dared when she needed his approval. As Nellie finished, they were asked to wait in the hall for the decision. Minutes later, Edwin Woodrow, the husband of Annie's sister, told them the deal had been accepted. While Nellie worked out the amount of money she'd contribute each month, Jennifer realized she'd judged right; men always seemed to go for the deal that benefited them most . . . professionally or personally.

"Miss Carlyle?" Edwin Woodrow stepped next to her. "I don't approve of Rachael's aunt being here with Nellie; it's not proper and I intend—"

"You intend nothing," Nellie said tartly from behind him, "or things will change in Seattle . . . quite suddenly."

Jennifer's gaze darted between them. Old enemies? she wondered. Then as she stared something else occurred to her . . . a thought she dismissed as far-fetched.

"My business here is complete." Nellie took her arm and they went out to the street. As they hesitated, saying their goodbyes, Nellie suddenly hugged her.

"I thank God for the day you became part of my family," she said seriously. "And yes, even I believe in God . . . sometimes."

Then Nellie was gone, hurrying past the Occidental Hotel on her way back to work, leaving Jennifer wondering about Nellie's threat to Edwin Woodrow, knowing he was fully capable of causing her more problems with Rachael.

Rachael had lost interest in Diana and all winter and spring was rebellious about attending school. It was a relief when school was dismissed for summer and Rachael began to spend all her free time with the Woodrows. "If Diana weren't my sister, I wouldn't watch her," she told Jennifer one day when Mrs. Scott was unable to stay. "I'm sixteen, too old to be under your thumb."

The next time Jennifer needed help, Rachael flatly refused. She blurted out angrily that she knew Diana was Jennifer's child, not her mother's—that her own sister had died at birth. "I've put it all together: your weight gain, going to live with that Thornton woman, and then your sudden weight loss. Doctor Andrews said that Mother's pains were putting a strain on the baby—that he hoped it would be all right." Jennifer denied her accusations, but her heart sank when Rachael slammed out of the house saying, "If you've lied, Jennifer, you'll be sorry."

That summer Jamie left Seattle, taking Damon's freighter *The Polemis* to San Francisco, where he was to catch the train to New York and school. It was a tearful goodbye, Jennifer couldn't believe her brother was already sixteen, and that it was 1888, two and a half years since they'd arrived in Seattle. Jamie would not return until he had finished his education and was a man. Jennifer's sadness was mixed with fear when she heard that Damon was sailing with him. She just hoped Jamie wouldn't voice what he'd been hinting at for months: that he knew Damon was Diana's father, that Damon had a right to know, and that Jennifer should tell him.

For weeks after Jamie left, Jennifer was tormented with worry: would Jamie tell Damon, would Rachael reveal her suspicions? But when some time had passed and Rachael hadn't mentioned the subject again, Jennifer relaxed, dividing her attention between Diana and the business. By September, Rachael was back at school, spending her spare time with her other aunt, and Jennifer was leaving Diana with Mrs. Scott during the day. Then one Monday morning in early October brought disaster. Jennifer arrived to find no one but Noah on the dock. He explained that the men had walked off, demanding more money to work for a woman and nigger.

"My God! They're blackmailing us again." But angry as she was, she knew that they had to get the ships moving to satisfy their contracts . . . or they'd be out of business.

Jennifer turned and ran to the street, where she'd left the buggy, scrambled onto the seat, and jerked the reins so hard the horse reared before lunging forward. She knew where her employees had gone: Lou Graham's place. She was oblivious of her flying hair or of startled glances as her vehicle shot up the hill.

At Third and Washington, Jennifer reined in, tied up to the hitching post, and ran through the front doors. Her gaze darted over the elegant saloon, coming to rest on her men, who sat at a table drinking whiskey. Standing beside them was the establishment's short, plump madam, who was gowned in crimson silk, jeweled in diamonds, and looked as startled as the men were to see her. All eyes in the house were on Jennifer.

"How dare you walk off my job," she told them. "You've broken our agreement, and I'm already paying the highest wages on the waterfront." While the men stared, mouths agape, and Lou's blue eyes twinkled in sudden amusement, Jennifer went on. "What more do you want?—Speak up."

"More money," one of the stevedores said. "Working for you ain't worth being made fun of."

Jennifer went over her profit margin in her mind; she'd have to pay more somehow. "I can't give you higher wages, but I'll give you a percentage of my profit . . . a bonus for each contract I fulfill."

The men talked among themselves while she waited, aware that everyone in the room was watching her. Tilting her chin, she pretended they weren't there. They could think what they wanted; she had to make a living for herself and Diana. Finally her men agreed to her terms.

"Good," she replied curtly. "But this time you'll all sign contracts: to protect you in getting your bonus and me so that I won't have to hunt my crew down in a brothel." She hesitated. "I'll expect you back to work within the hour; the contracts will be ready to sign in the morning."

Without looking to right or left, she strode out. Noah had arrived in time to hear the final negotiations, and he helped her into the buggy. Halfway down the hill she heard a muffled sound and turned to find him laughing. "You sho looked funny tellin' them men off," he said. "They was unnerved."

Jennifer began to giggle, and by the time they reached Front Street, she was laughing as hard as Noah. But the whole episode didn't seem funny later that evening when she was confronted by Rachael, who announced that the whole town was gossiping about Jennifer's scene. "I hate living here," Rachael said, "and I'm not staying much longer."

Rachael was a constant irritation over the winter and spring months; she still blamed Jennifer for all the unhappiness in her life. Since the ten-year-old Woodrow son had gone away to school and the older half brother, Edwin's son by a first marriage, had gone into the family business, Rachael spent even more time with her other aunt, whose health was failing.

Jennifer didn't have time to worry about Rachael's absences; once the labor disputes were settled, Noah and Jennifer won more contracts, several on the recommendation of Luke Olson, who'd become a friend. One day, as she told him how much she appreciated his help in landing a big job with the San Juan Island communities, his eyes crinkled, and she knew he was about to smile. "Enough to have supper with me some night?"

She grinned back but shook her head. "You know how I feel about that, Luke. I don't mix business with my private life."

"'Fraid I'd start trying to blackmail you . . . marry me or I'll take my business elsewhere?" His grin broadened, but she knew he was half serious.

Jennifer laughed, but after he was gone she thought about her situation. She couldn't accept Luke's invitation without angering the other men she'd refused. There were always men, married and unmarried, who sought her attention, but she was not interested in any of them. So she told herself and her would-be suitors that she did not want to mix her business and personal life.

She had enough problems without adding new ones, she decided, and glanced at Diana who'd been playing quietly in the corner. She was anxious to finish the monthly accounts; when Diana became impatient, she'd have to take her home. Now that Rachael wasn't helping her at all, she had Diana with her on Mrs. Scott's days off.

Suddenly the door burst open, and a tall man stepped into the room with a cold gust of November wind. His gaze pinned Jennifer to her chair.

"You just signed a contract that should have been mine," he said curtly, not bothering her with a greeting.

"Hello, Damon," she said coolly, but a shaking began deep within her, like one of the small earthquakes that shook Seattle occasionally. "You're talking about the San Juan contract, I presume?"

"You presume correctly." His eyes glinted like sun on black marble. "I won't comment on *how* you got the goddamned thing, but I will discuss your position on the waterfront."

"And?"

"It's dangerous," he said, his tone a note higher than before. "If you'd taken a contract out from under anyone else, you'd be a prime target for trouble."

"Such as?" she asked coolly, but her face had gone hot. God, it was hard to believe that everything had gone wrong between them, she thought. Words of love had been replaced by angry ones.

"Being robbed . . . burned out . . . assaulted by a man like Al Cox who tells everyone that you're—uh . . . never mind." He strode to her desk and placed both of his hands on its surface. "I want to buy you out, Jennifer. Now, before you find yourself with more trouble than you can handle."

She jumped up, sending her chair sliding backward. "Are you threatening me—as you threatened Joseph?"

He straightened abruptly, his expression more forbidding than she ever remembered seeing. "Christ," he exclaimed. "You never give up, do you? I'm sorry I came. In the future I'll treat you like any other business competitor."

"And do you threaten them also?" she asked, her tone as cold as his expression. "Or create labor problems for them? . . . or try to bribe them? . . . or buy them? . . . or destroy their credibility? Like you've been doing to me?"

The words had barely left her lips before he'd rounded the desk, grabbed her, and pulled her against his chest. A moment later his lips closed over hers, kissing her with brutal passion.

She struggled, her emotions spinning, as liquid fire licked through her veins. As his head lifted she twisted free, stumbling backward, eyes wide, heart pounding with . . . fear, or a great throbbing need for him?

He seemed to give himself a mental shake. Then the light died in his eyes. "One day, when you're able to think beyond steamships, you'll realize what you lost," he said finally.

Shaken, Jennifer watched mutely as he strode toward the door, wanting to call him back, but uncertain about his motives or her own feelings. But when his gaze fell on Diana and he suddenly paused, all other emotions were overpowered by one . . . fear.

He spoke softly to Diana, and she lifted her face to answer in unintelligible baby talk. Jennifer was unexpectedly overwhelmed by emotion; he was seeing his daughter for the first time. Dark eyes met identical dark eyes, two pair of brows arched in a similar manner, and Jennifer was struck with a desolation that closed her throat and burned her eyes. Her baby, and the man she . . . Oh, God! . . . still loved.

But then Damon continued out the door, unaware that he'd spoken to his daughter.

Jennifer picked up the curly-headed toddler and hugged her. Despite her strange desolate feelings she knew she'd passed a crucial test. Whether she loved Damon or not didn't change the fact that he must never know Diana was his child.

He just declared war on my company, she reminded herself. She'd do well not to let the issues become clouded by old feelings of love.

Men, she thought, she trusted none of them except

Noah. First Judson Carr had deceived her with his offer of help, then Damon with his offer of love, and even that scum Cox with his offer of protection.

I'll work hard, and I'll make it, and then I won't need any man, she told herself. But her eyes suddenly blurred, and tears sprinkled the child in her lap.

Chapter Sixteen

"The Pontius Building up on Madison Street is on fire," Noah announced as he strode into the office one afternoon in the first week of June.

Jennifer looked up from the monthly bills. "Is it bad?"

Noah shrugged. Fires were not infrequent in a city of wooden buildings and planked streets. "They sent the horse cart out, and that new contraption, the steam fire engine."

"That should take care of any fire," Jennifer said, her thoughts shifting momentarily to Diana who, for the first time in months, was in Rachael's care.

Noah nodded. "I's keepin' my eye on it. Doan want a fire to really git goin'; the wooden buildings and sidewalks would spread it fast."

Noah went back to the wharf, and Jennifer went back to her work, hoping to finish the June's accounts before she went home. But she couldn't concentrate; her thoughts kept jumping to the fire; the Pontius Building was only a few blocks south of their house. Why didn't I get telephones put in here and at the house? she asked herself. Three hundred people in Seattle already had them. But she knew why: she was trying to keep expenses down. She'd even economized recently by selling the buggy and horse.

Throwing down the pen, she pushed back her chair and walked to the front window, which faced the city. She could see smoke belching into the bright cloudless sky, but it was billowing southward away from their house. The fire seemed to be contained.

Relieved, she moved back into the room, pausing to glance out the opposite window at Elliott Bay and the distant islands that lay at the feet of the ragged-edged

Olympic Mountains. She sighed, watching the final loading of the *Rachael C*, which was due to leave port within the hour. They'd kept busy since last summer when Jamie had gone east but had been unable to buy a fourth ship. Labor costs and frequent vandalism had taken a big cut of their profit. Despite the night watchman's presence, they still had problems. Was Damon behind it? she wondered. He had the most to gain if she was forced out of business. Damon's company was expanding with phenomenal speed; he'd added bigger steamers to his fleet, ships for the California and Alaska routes. Being a woman in a man's world was an obstacle to success, she reminded herself. People in a straitlaced community didn't want their women running businesses. There were still certain farmers and businessmen who refused to let her ship their cargo because she was a woman.

The day was warm, and Jennifer felt hot and sweaty in her long-sleeved, high-necked cotton dress. There'd been no rain for a week, and she found herself wishing for it. "I've become a true Seattleite," she decided.

Glancing at the clock, she was surprised to see it was almost three. Jennifer forced her mind back to the ledgers, forgetting everything but her work.

But a noisy commotion on the wharf soon disturbed her concentration. The fire . . . she'd forgotten about the fire, she realized. She leapt up and ran outside. Jennifer stopped short, terror jolting her. "My God!" she cried, her eyes on the mushrooming cloud of dense black smoke that was poised like a giant fist over the city. The whole town seemed to be on fire.

"Whole goddamned block is burning!" a man shouted as he ran past her to the street.

She stood for a moment, uncertain. She'd never seen so much action on the waterfront: men were throwing down their tools to run to the streets; deckhands were hastily moving ships away from the docks to safety; and orders like "Man the fire lines!" and "We gotta save Seattle!" were booming out everywhere.

"I done sent the *Rachael C* out," Noah said as he came up behind her.

"Do you think they'll get it stopped—before it reaches

the waterfront?" She glanced frantically over their wharf. She couldn't lose her business . . . not after all her hard work.

Noah shook his head. "Doan know. But we's all sho gonna try."

Her heart fluttered with fear. How would she make a living for herself and Diana if . . . Diana!

"I've got to get home. Rachael is alone with Diana."

"The fire's movin' this way, so they is safe," Noah said, but deep worry lines etched his face. "You's best git back an see 'bout 'em." In his excitement, his words slurred even more than usual. "I'm goin' wit da men to fight it."

But Jennifer was already running to the office to lock up. She knew she had to find a way around the orange giant that was gobbling up the wooden buildings and sidewalks of Seattle; she had to get to Diana and know her baby was safe.

She grabbed her things and turned to go just as a man entered the office and carefully locked the door behind him. When he turned around, she saw it was Al Cox.

His narrow eyes glinted as his lips twisted into a grin. He limped toward her. "Knew I'd have my day. No one's gonna save ya this time."

Jennifer sucked in her breath, her gaze flying to the windows. There was no one left on the wharf; she was alone. She darted behind the desk for protection. "Get out!" she cried.

He laughed harshly, rounding the desk as she jerked open the drawer. But he slammed it shut before she could grab her gun.

"Trying to shoot me again—eh?" He yanked her against his chest; she gagged from the stench of his sweat. Squirming and struggling, she tried to free herself as his lips lowered to hers. Finally her foot found his ankle. He yelped in pain and retaliated by twisting her arm until she screamed in fear and agony.

"Let me go," she pleaded, her fear for Diana outweighing her fear of him. "I've got to get home to the girls . . . the fire—"

"I don't give a shit about your girls," he sneered, his breath foul on her face. "Let 'em burn."

His words flashed through her like a bolt of lightning, inciting her. She kicked him, scratched his face, and elbowed his soft stomach, but still he hung on to her, trying to bend her backward over the desk top. All at once Jennifer realized she was fighting for her life, not just her virtue.

With a quick motion, she brought her knee up with a sharp blow to his crotch. He cried out, doubled over, and stumbled backward onto the floor, pulling Jennifer down on top of him. Then his eyes rolled back into his head and his body went limp.

Suddenly free, Jennifer rolled away from him and leapt to her feet. Her chest heaving, she stared down at him. He'd struck his head on the corner of the desk and was unconscious.

The sleeve of her dress was torn loose, and her hair hung in disarray, but she had survived. However, as she glanced out the window she gasped, struck by a new terror. The sun was now clouded by an advance guard of smoke that had drifted with the wind and engulfed the buildings along the waterfront. But beyond the roofs she could see a wall of fire and smoke looming over the city.

"My God!" she whispered hoarsely. "The whole city is on fire."

Forgetting Al Cox, she rushed outside. A large section of the business district was blazing, and although the fire was moving south, it had also moved against the thrust of wind to spread flames back toward her house . . . and Diana and Rachael.

Horrified, she stood rooted to the ground for a moment, remembering another fire: the burning cotton fields. Unless this fire was stopped soon, she would lose everything for the second time in her life. Then, recalling how fast her crop had burned, she sprang into action.

Jennifer ran toward the fire, trying to find a street that wasn't closed off by burning debris. There was unbelievable confusion everywhere; Seattle was burning down around its citizens. The closer she got to the flames, the more deafening the roar, like train engines straining against a high, howling wind. Suddenly a man grabbed her arm.

"You can't go that way, lady," he cried. "The street is blocked by fire fighting equipment."

There was no time to explain, and no other way past the fire. She twisted free and continued her flight along the street, surrounded on both sides by blazing buildings. The soot raining down on Jennifer felt like hot needle jabs on her face and hands.

At the next corner she hesitated, for a moment unsure of her route, staring in horror at the destruction everywhere. Frye's Opera House on the corner of Front and Marion was on fire, as was the Colman Building, the Commercial Mill, and saloons and hotels.

"There's no water!" a man with a hose shouted. "The goddamned water mains are too small to give us water pressure!"

"I heard the wooden pipes burned through!" another man shouted back. "And Josiah Collins, the fire chief, is out of town."

"Dynamite! They're gonna dynamite to stop the fire!" someone else cried. "Everyone out of the way!"

"Mary, Mother of God," a woman murmured, her voice barely audible above the confusion. "Seattle is doomed." She stood, dazed, until her husband pushed her up onto their buckboard stacked high with furniture and bedding.

Jennifer's eyes watered from the heavy smoke and her throat burned. But she saw that she'd have to go up on Second to get around the fire. "Oh, God . . . let Diana and Rachael be safe," she chanted under her breath.

She ran up the hill, elbowing and pushing her way through crowds of people who were desperate to save whatever belongings they could carry or load on wagons. A man in a torn frock coat stood in the midst of the pandemonium shouting, "Repent! Or be swallowed into the fire of Hell!" The sounds were deafening, and she wondered if she'd ever hear normally again. Finally at Second Street, she paused to glance back at the monster that was consuming Seattle. Her breath came in ragged gulps as she gathered her strength, her gaze on the red flames blooming against the afternoon sky like giant, eerie poppies. Below the looming specter of destruction, dozens of buildings were already charred ruins while others quivered like

scarlet tissue paper before falling in on themselves with a
thunderous roar and a fountain of flying embers. As she
looked down at the waterfront she knew it was doomed.

She began running again. Each breath ripped painfully
from her chest, and one thought stabbed at her mind: could
she reach her baby in time? The fire had spread several
blocks against the wind. She reached her street. Houses on
it were already burning. The Carlyle home was only
minutes away from being ignited.

She didn't break stride as she ran up the walk, her heels
pounding on the boards, then onto the porch and into the
house, where she stopped abruptly. The sudden quiet
seemed to thunder louder in her ears than the roar of the
fire. Had Rachael taken Diana and fled to safety? She stood
panting, her limbs trembling from exhaustion.

As she heard the walls of a neighbor's house crash to the
ground, Jennifer was propelled into action again. She
searched the house to make sure it was empty. "Rachael?
. . . Is anyone here?" Only silence. Then she heard it.

"Mama?" Diana's voice answered softly from behind a
closed bedroom door. "Me home."

Jennifer rushed to Diana and grabbed her up from the
floor, where she was playing contentedly with her doll.
Horror-stricken, she clasped the chubby body against her
chest. She realized Rachael had left Diana, a two-year-old
child who could not have even opened the door, and run to
safety, leaving the little girl trapped. Jennifer could hardly
believe that Rachael had been so heartless.

The sound of burning buildings crashing to the ground
told Jennifer that they had to get out immediately. Trembling with fear and anger, she started toward the door and
stopped. Her mother's paintings. . . .

Seconds later, the paintings under one arm and Diana in
the other, she fled to the street, glad she was able to
manage the small pictures. As she moved in a half run up
the hill, the flames jumped from building to building
behind her. She couldn't allow herself to think about what
would have happened if she hadn't escaped Al Cox. Diana
clung to her, subdued, her large dark eyes looking over
Jennifer's shoulder, watching the flames destroy their
home.

"Diana," Jennifer whispered to the child. "My own sweet Diana. Nothing on earth will ever come before your safety again . . . not people or steamships." Tears welled in her eyes. Never again would she trust Rachael.

The fire burned throughout most of the night, and by the next morning over sixty-four acres of business area was in ashes, including the Carlyle house and wharf and Nellie's boarding house and saloon. Sometime in the night Noah had found Jennifer and Diana huddled on someone's lawn further up the hill, Diana wrapped in a borrowed blanket, asleep in Jennifer's arms. Gently he'd led them to his two-room shack out on Jackson Street, just beyond the fire area.

Noah left at first light to see if anything could be salvaged on their wharf. When he returned, he told Jennifer that Al Cox was dead, that his remains had been found in the office ruins. It was assumed he'd been looting and was trapped by the fire.

Jennifer nodded, her gaze fixed on the food she was preparing for Diana, afraid to look up. Afraid that Noah might realize from her expression that she already knew about the dead man. "I wonder if he was the one responsible for all the other problems we've had in the past?" she said. "Maybe I was wrong to blame Damon for all of our troubles."

"I always suspected Cox," Noah replied. "Now we'll never know fo' sho.'"

Jennifer knew it was best not to mention what had really happened. Even though she hadn't intentionally left Al Cox to die, she did feel guilty. The man might still be alive if she'd told someone he lay unconscious in her office. The fear and guilt of the day of the fire would remain with her forever, alongside the bitter memory of the burning cotton.

"Was there anything left of our wharf?" Jennifer asked hesitantly.

He shook his head. "The whole business area is done gone, the waterfront and everything south of Union Street and west of Second Avenue, even the Polemis Steamship Company. Nuthin' left but rubble and charred telephone poles. It be a disaster. Mayor Moran is declarin' martial law and askin' that the National Guard be called out to prevent lootin'.'"

Jennifer tried not to feel defeated. God, everything gone, she reflected. "But we still have our lives, and we aren't quitting, Noah," she said finally. She couldn't quit. She had to support Diana. "We still have the three ships."

He nodded, but looked doubtful. "It ain't gonna be easy, Miss Jennifer." He hesitated, as though wanting to spare her from the destruction she'd soon see for herself.

"The banks and stores and warehouses, newspaper offices and the railroad station—" He broke off, waving his arm. "They all gone . . . even the gasworks above Fourth and Jackson."

She swallowed hard, lowering her lashes so that he couldn't see her fear. "I'm hanging on to the steamship company; I'm not giving up." Her mind shifted back to another time, under the moss-draped oak by the graves of her parents. She'd made a similar vow then—to keep High Bluffs—and she'd lost the plantation. But not this time, she told herself. She hadn't let Judson or Damon defeat her, and she wasn't about to let this fire do it either, even though she knew that this day, June 6, 1889, would go down in Seattle's history.

After Diana finished eating, Jennifer took her to Mrs. Scott's house beyond the smoking ruins. Then Jennifer climbed First Hill and paused at the summit to look out over the horrible blackness that had once been the business area of Seattle. Everywhere people were busy, poking through the ashes of their homes and businesses. She could hear a woman crying.

She turned away and headed toward the Woodrow mansion, which had survived. Her knock was answered by Rachael, who stepped out to the porch and closed the door behind her.

"What are you doing here?" Rachael demanded, smoothing the skirt of a pink and white dimity dress Jennifer had never seen before.

"I'm here to talk with you," Jennifer retorted, her anger surfacing. "I want to know why you left Diana yesterday. If

I hadn't gotten to the house when I did, she'd be dead now."

"Diana is your responsibility . . . not mine," Rachael replied coldly, unruffled by Jennifer's words. "And you might as well know that I'm not living with you again. I'm staying here, with my aunt and uncle."

Jennifer wanted to slap her, make her admit that what she'd done was wrong. But Jennifer could see that Rachael didn't care about Diana, or her. But, thought Jennifer, she'd be damned if she'd let Rachael get what she wanted. With deliberate calm she informed Rachael, that at seventeen, she was still too young to decide where she was to live.

"You . . . slut." Rachael's expression tightened with anger. "If you try to stop me, Jennifer, I'll make my suspicions about Diana known to everyone in Seattle. If I can't live here, where I can have money and social status, then I'll destroy whatever is left of your reputation . . . and Diana's hope of a decent future."

"Your suspicions are unfounded," Jennifer said carefully. But Rachael remained silent, waiting for the answer she wanted. Suddenly Jennifer was scared. Rachael was too much like Annie, insecure, desperate for a social position, ruthless toward anyone who stood in the way. Her mind could also become unhinged by hatred. She was dangerous and always would be.

"All right, Rachael, have it your way." Jennifer stepped forward and grabbed her arm. "But not because you're right about Diana . . . you're not. I'm agreeing because I can see we'll never get along, never be friends."

"Whatever the reason, my dear Aunt Jennifer, you're being very wise. And you're right, I'll always hate you." She opened the door. "One more thing, my aunt doesn't want Diana, doesn't want to be bothered with a toddler. So you can rest easy that you aren't about to lose your brat." She turned around and slammed the door in Jennifer's face.

Chapter Seventeen

Six and a half months after the fire, on Christmas Day, Jennifer saw a startling announcement in the *Post-Intelligencer:* Rachael was marrying Edwin Woodrow. Rachael's aunt had passed away only last August, and Rachael was still seventeen compared to Edwin Woodrow's sixty years. Nellie looked grim when Jennifer told her. "The old bastard," she said, and so abruptly changed the subject to the statehood celebration of the month before and the rebuilding projects that Jennifer's curiosity was aroused.

The new year of 1890 brought more contracts; Jennifer's business, like Seattle and its population of forty-five thousand people, was growing. Feeling more financially secure, she bought a summer cottage at Port Blakely on Bainbridge Island. But before she could buy a house in town and move out of the rented one she had been sharing with Nellie since the fire, the Woodrows claimed Rachael's inheritance and seized half of the company. Although Jennifer had always intended that Rachael would have her fair share, she had to make a stand on Diana's behalf or risk substantiating Rachael's suspicions about Diana. After a heated argument Rachael finally threatened, "I want everything that belonged to my parents, or I'll expose Diana." Jennifer was forced to agree. "But only because I won't see your sister destroyed by malicious gossip," she told Rachael, and was relieved to see uncertainty flicker on her face. Half the company was gone, but Diana was safe.

Rachael promptly sold her two steamships to Damon. Left with only the *Katherine C* and the wharf, Jennifer and Noah were unable to fulfill most of their contracts. That business went to the Polemis Steamship Company. As winter ebbed into spring Jennifer faced severe financial problems. Unwilling to devote herself to saving the business at the price of being away from Diana, she placed the company in Noah's hands and moved to her Bainbridge Island cottage at Port Blakely. The mill town inhabitants were emigrants from all over the world and accepted her into the community without question. Jennifer hung lace curtains on the windows and her mother's paintings on the papered walls. For the first time in years she entertained friends, including Luke Olson, who visited whenever he came south on business.

Jennifer soon settled into a routine, painting every day while Diana played on the beach. She did pictures of the mill with its big saws cutting through Douglas firs and cedars, ships in the harbor with Mount Rainier in the background, the Japanese settlement up the hill on Fort Ward Road, and the Indian village across Port Blakely harbor. She painted bright summer scenes, then hazy autumn ones when the island was changing toward the fog and rain of winter. In spring her work reflected the island blooming with wildflowers and new growth.

Their first sixteen months on the island passed quickly. Just before Diana's fourth birthday Jennifer took the morning steamer to Seattle to shop for presents. After a business meeting with Noah she headed toward the Bon Marche, marveling at the growth of the city. Seattle had annexed Fremont, Edgewater, Latona, and Greenlake just this past June, and opened four new public schools and chartered the Seattle Pacific College.

Soon after she had entered the store, she regretted having left her island. The problems she'd fled came rushing back to her. Two well-dressed women standing next to her at the hat counter were discussing the Woodrows in low tones. "It's scandalous. The servants say that Rachael was caught in bed with both Edwin and his oldest son . . . at the same time." The women wandered away but their words stayed with Jennifer. She tried to remind herself how people liked to gossip and how stories became distorted. As nasty as Rachael had always been, and as ambitious for social recognition, Jennifer couldn't see her involved in such an ugly situation.

But Rachael was soon forgotten in the excitement of

Diana's birthday. Nellie and Noah came from Seattle and Luke Olson from LaConner. "Diana needs a father; someone to marry her aunt," Luke told Jennifer later. Jennifer joked his words away, but she noticed both Noah and Nellie looked pleased. She just wished that she cared enough about Luke to marry him. Was she capable of loving another man? she wondered desperately.

By her second fall on Bainbridge, Jennifer was displaying her paintings at a large store in Seattle. The owner was impressed when all of them had been sold by the following spring and invited her to give a show at a new gallery in town. But the event proved to be a disaster, even though the critics raved about her work and she received good reviews in all the newspapers. Not one socially prominent person in Seattle had turned up at the gala opening, although they'd all been invited. She'd been blackballed, humiliated by the citizens of Seattle who hadn't forgotten her past. Her only good memory of the day was meeting Justin Brinker, a tall, thin handsome man who owned several art galleries in California. He'd complimented her most graciously on her navy silk gown and upswept hair and then added, "You have a great talent. I'd like to handle some of your work." She'd agreed hastily before leaving to catch the evening steamer, but was too upset to discuss the possibility in more detail.

Her name as an artist was growing, just as her interest in the shipping company was waning. When Seattle became the western terminus for the Great Northern Railroad in June, Jennifer considered selling the company. The depressed economy had further weakened her struggling business. But after consulting with Noah, she decided to wait: money was scarce and there were no buyers except Damon, who wouldn't pay full value in 1893, a year of national financial panic. All of Seattle was suffering from the depression. "Except Nellie," she told Noah. "The men of Seattle don't forgo their fun."

When the economy began to recover the following year, Jennifer sold her business to the Polemis Steamship Company. Accompanied by her lawyer, she went to Damon's office to sign the final papers. Her stomach churned with both eager anticipation and dread of their first meeting in years.

An older Damon looked up from his desk as they were ushered into the room. She was suddenly glad she'd worn her new blue wool suit with the bell-shaped skirt and wide hem, that her casual hairstyle looked well with her plumed hat.

He stood up and rounded the desk to greet them, as tall and lean as the day she'd first met him. "It's a long time, Jennifer," he said in his low cultured voice, the voice she'd heard on that first day in Seattle, the voice that had once spoken love words to her, the voice— She broke off her thoughts, not wanting to recall what had happened almost eight years ago.

"Hello, Damon," she replied, suddenly remembering he was the most attractive man she'd ever known. The prematurely gray wings at his temples and the deeper lines on his face only made him look more distinguished. Her moment of uneasiness passed when her lawyer began laying out the final requirements for the sale. Within minutes they reached an agreement, one that included a small percentage of ownership for Noah in Damon's company.

As she bent to sign the papers Damon watched, his eyes unreadable. Was he remembering all the times she'd refused to sell? the accusations she'd flung in his face? she wondered, and felt a prick of sadness. It all seemed so far away . . . so unimportant. He now escorted society woman like Mara Appleton. We live in two different worlds, she told herself sternly, and signed away the business that had once been her hope for the future.

After Damon signed, he shook her hand; the feel of his skin lingered, sending a tingling sensation coursing through her veins.

"Ah," Damon said. "Old business is finally completed— on paper—the sure way to maintain trust."

Jennifer's face went hot, understanding the connotation of his words: her lack of trust in Damon, and whatever had happened to him before he came to Seattle to build his empire.

Seconds later Jennifer and her lawyer were thanked by

an abruptly cool Damon and then escorted to the door by his secretary. Once on the street Jennifer headed for the steamer, anxious to return to the peace of Bainbridge Island and Diana.

While the sale gave Jennifer financial freedom, it also allowed Noah to continue working with steamships. By 1897, when word reached Seattle that gold had been discovered in the Klondike, he'd become invaluable to Damon. She was happy for Noah who had no relatives now that Zeb had died, and contented with her own life. But despite her friendships with men like Luke Olson, she was aware of a vague longing she tried to bury in her work and in raising Diana.

But it was a losing battle. Each time she looked into Diana's face she was reminded of Damon and knew that some part of her would never stop loving him.

III

Endless Mountains

Chapter Eighteen

Jamie stood in front of St. Patrick's Cathedral, his gaze on Lottie Harrison, the young women he had hoped to marry. Behind her the Sunday traffic moved along Fifth Avenue, but to Jamie the warm April day in New York had turned cold. Lottie had just announced that she was marrying someone else, that things might have been different had he gone into law, not aeronautics, which her father considered a pursuit for dreamers.

"I'm sorry, Jamie, but I've come to agree with Papa," Lottie said, the stubborn expression on her round face precluding any argument. The lacy high collar of her shirtwaist creased her chin as she glanced down. "Winston is rich and respected and won honors for bravery in the Spanish-American War . . . and I'm marrying him in December, just before the turn of the century."

Jamie stared at her, stunned by the announcement. He'd met Lottie the year he'd started his university studies. She'd been only fifteen then, but he'd liked her at once, not minding her tendency to plumpness or that she was a spoiled only child. The daughter of Damon's cousin, one of the most wealthy men in New York, Lottie had had her choice of suitors, but he'd assumed for the past two years that she favored him.

"What about our plans?" he asked finally.

She waved her hand, and a huge diamond glinted in the sunlight. "I warned you it was a mistake to get involved with those . . . dreamers. Papa might have agreed to our betrothal if you'd gone into a respectable law practice. But when you turned it down for this . . . lark, my parents were suddenly reminded of your background—that you were—"

161

"Illegitimate?" He plopped his derby hat back onto his head. He'd realized that working in a law firm would benefit him financially and socially. When he'd graduated with honors from Harvard, he'd received offers of employment from several top law firms in the city. But he'd also privately pursued studies in aeronautics with a man who'd worked in Germany researching heavier-than-air machines. The concept of air travel had fascinated him since first reading about Otto Lilienthal's gliding reseach a few years earlier. When he'd also been offered a position with a small American company involved in aeroplane research, he couldn't turn it down. He'd discussed his dilemma with Lottie, had mistaken her silence for acceptance, her strained smile for an enthusiasm to match his own, her softly voiced warning as only words.

"Then all these years your family has only tolerated me because of Damon?"

She nodded. "But I cared for you, Jamie . . . truly I did." Her voice shook suddenly. "And not just because Uncle Damon insisted we accept you—that it was one of the stipulations when he kept Papa from bankruptcy back in the depression of 'ninety-three."

A great wave of humiliating heat flooded Jamie's face. People were still as unbending and critical as they'd always been. And Lottie, at twenty-two, was still a daddy's girl; she would never marry him over her father's disapproval. He realized how blinded he'd been by his feelings for her. He'd even attended church each Sunday to be with her, hoping the Harrisons would invite him home for dinner. He'd been a goddamned fool, he thought now.

"Your parents are waiting," he said wearily. There was nothing more for him to say. It was over.

She prattled on, told him not to worry, that they'd still see each other on Sundays, oblivious to Jamie's shattered dreams and that, in fact, she'd never see him again. Then she ran to join her parents in their waiting carriage. Jamie watched it disappear down the street, until the red rosettes in Lottie's bonnet had blurred into the ribbons and straw.

He turned away and went back to his rented room, and for the next few months he buried himself in his work. When the head of the company, pleased by his imaginative approach to aeroplane research, offered him the opportunity to study in Germany with men who knew the Lilienthal brothers, Jamie knew he must make a decision about his future.

Then, days later, two exciting letters arrived from Seattle, one from his mother and one from Jennifer, both telling about how the Klondike gold strike had created a business boom for the Northwest, that there was a great future waiting for him in Seattle.

Jamie immediately decided to go home before making any decisions that would affect the rest of his life. He'd been reading about the gold rush in *Harper's Weekly* and other periodicals and was suddenly anxious to be in Seattle, the city now being called the gateway to the gold. But more than anything he longed to see his family for the first time in over a decade.

Standing on the deck of the Bainbridge Island steamer, Jamie stared across Elliott Bay to Seattle, happy to be home, amazed to realize that it was a new century, and that he'd been gone over eleven years. He'd arrived several days earlier on The Great Northern from New York, and he still couldn't believe the changes to Seattle. Everything was different: the University of Washington had been moved out by Lake Washington, the tidelands south of Yesler had been filled, the Duwamish River had been dredged, and seven hundred old street names had been abolished to establish an orderly system of names.

His mother hadn't changed except for a few more gray hairs and lines on her face. Jennifer, although still beautiful and slim, was another story; she seemed somehow unfulfilled. He knew about Diana, even though no one had ever told him the truth. Once he'd almost confessed the truth to Damon but decided he must respect his sister's privacy. He looked forward to seeing Diana; she'd not been with Jennifer and his mother to meet the train.

As the January sky lowered and it began to rain Jamie went inside the cabin, his thoughts shifting back to his mother; she was more notorious than ever since she'd expanded into the box-house business. John Considine had opened the first box-house in Seattle, and Nellie had soon followed; she'd had a stage built in the basement, where scantily clad women performed each night. The room in front of the stage was broken into small boxed-in areas where the men could watch the stage action in privacy with women supplied by his mother.

He shook his head. His mother was a contradiction: a madam on one hand and a benevolent, civic-minded businesswoman on the other. She'd accumulated a fortune in investments while still donating large sums of money each month for civic improvements. She believed whole-heartedly in the future of the Northwest. When he'd hesitantly explained that his professional ambition was in the field of aeroplane research, she'd supported him: "The Northwest needs men like you to develop new industries."

"If I hadn't sold the business to Damon, you could have run my steamship company," Jennifer told Jamie as they sat in the sitting room that evening. "Then you'd have a reason to stay."

Jamie grinned suddenly. "I've already told my mother . . . I'm staying. But not to work with ships or lumber. Eventually I want to establish an aeroplane company, here in Seattle."

"I'm so glad," Diana cried. "Now we'll be a *real* family . . . like everyone else."

Jamie glanced over Diana's blond head, meeting Jennifer's eyes. He knows, she thought. Her lashes fluttered nervously as she lowered her gaze. Of course, she reminded herself, he can't know for sure; he'd been out to sea with Damon when Diana was born . . . and he'd never asked questions.

Later, when Jennifer was in bed, she went over the events of the day. Although she had sold out her dream of a shipping empire to Damon, the Carlyle family had other aspirations. Maybe Jamie's aeroplane dream and her painting career and Nellie's civic benevolence would establish places for them in the history of the Northwest after all.

She sat up suddenly, plumping up her pillows before she lay back down. Who knows? The family, its roots transplanted from Georgia, might yet build empires.

* * *

"I hear Rachael is a close friend of Mara Appleton," Jamie said as they walked down the hill to meet the morning steamer.

Jennifer nodded, taken aback by his abrupt change of subject. She'd already filled him in on the current gossip about Rachael, how she was manipulating Simon, her bedridden husband's oldest son.

"Mara's about my age . . . late twenties, isn't she?"

Again Jennifer nodded. "I understand she's more high-strung than ever, and desperately anxious to be married."

Jamie paused, his gaze suddenly direct. "Jen . . . I have something to say, and I'm not sure how to do it."

An alarm went off in Jennifer's mind; why was Jamie looking so serious, so troubled? she asked herself. "Maybe you should just say it, Jamie."

He glanced beyond her, as though he were forming thoughts only to dismiss them. When he did speak, his words stabbed her with a strange foreboding.

"I talked to Damon the other day," he began, then went on quickly. "He's a very lonely man, Jen. A man who wants sons."

She waited, her heart fluttering, wanting Jamie to continue and fearful of what he was leading up to. Above them the gulls circled, their cries echoing across the gray sky to touch Jennifer with loneliness, a foreshadowing of sadness yet to face, she suspected.

"He's asked Mara to marry him."

Jennifer swallowed back a cry. Damon who'd made love to her, who'd always respected trust and honesty . . . marrying Mara? she thought in bewilderment. She turned away from Jamie, trying to stop the flow of despair, fighting desperately for composure.

Jamie put his arm around her. "Are you all right, Jen?"

"Yes," she said after a long pause, her tone hardly above a whisper. "I'm just surprised, that's all." Seconds later she was able to face him again. "But why Mara?"

He shrugged, but his expression showed concern. "I don't know, Jen. Maybe he's in love with her. Or maybe she just wore him down. In any case, I understand she's been trying to land him for a long time, always reminding him that he needs heirs, that they share a similar social position."

The whistle of the steamer shattered the sudden silence that had dropped around them. There was no time to continue the awkward conversation; Jamie had to run or he'd miss the ship.

Her limbs trembling, Jennifer waved Jamie out of sight. Then, as she climbed back up the long hill to her cottage, the tears came unbidden, sliding down her cheeks to fall on her breasts, which heaved from the sobs deep in her chest.

I have a future too, she told herself. One that holds the joy of being a part of her twelve-year-old daughter's life, and of helping Jamie find his destiny, and of painting pictures of a beautiful land.

But as she mounted the steps to her porch and turned to look out over the bay at the little ship steaming toward Seattle, she knew she'd never be able to completely erase her feelings for Damon.

She went into the house, glad that Luke was coming for supper. She'd think about him again, the decent man who'd asked her many times to marry him, proposals she hadn't been able to accept because she didn't love him.

But I wish you well, Damon, she thought as she went to her easel. And I hope you are marrying Mara because you love her . . . because I hate her.

Chapter Nineteen

For the first time since moving to Bainbridge Island Jennifer felt frustrated and unsettled over the following weeks. She found it a chore even to paint. The winter rain kept her indoors, and with Diana in school, she was lonely and longed for a diversion, one that would occupy her thoughts. Instead she was dwelling on the past, on what might have been. She kept reassuring herself that Damon would never marry Mara, that they were totally unsuited. Even Jamie's weekly visits didn't lift her spirits. Luke came each weekend, but Luke's insistence on an answer to his proposal only made her uncomfortable; the thought of being his wife gave her a trapped feeling. When she realized Luke's presence did not alleviate her loneliness, that she would never love him, she knew marriage was out of the question.

She also knew that she had to go on with her own life and decided the time had come to move back to Seattle. She bought an elegant two-story house on Queen Anne Hill near the end of the First Avenue streetcar line and moved in the spring. When Diana protested, saying that she did not want to leave her school and friends, Jennifer pointed out that they would still use the cottage on weekends and in the summer.

Jennifer smiled now as she glanced around her large sitting room, which was furnished with Louis XVI tables and satin brocade upholstered chairs. It was very different from the cottage; she'd bought the house with money she'd earned from her paintings. Her mother's canvases now hung against pale gold French wallpaper.

"Oh, Mama," she whispered into the silent room, her thoughts shifting to the news she'd read in the morning paper, news she didn't want to think about. "So much has happened since High Bluffs; so many things didn't turn out as I'd hoped." She walked to the window and looked down at the city, so changed from the mid-eighties. Her gaze followed the northly course of a steamer on the bay, and she wondered whether it belonged to Damon or was bound for Luke's place at LaConner Flats. If only she could have married Luke, she thought. But she no longer even saw Luke; she'd decided it was unfair to let him hope she would marry him one day. And now Damon might marry Mara, Rachael's best friend. Although she hadn't seen Rachael in years, Jennifer hadn't forgotten her threats against Diana.

Hearing a buggy stop in the street, she forced her depressing thoughts aside and hurried into the oak-paneled hall to greet Jamie.

Jamie hesitated on the front porch. He'd received an invitation to Damon's wedding, and he was uncertain how to break the news to Jennifer. He'd always hoped for a marriage between Damon and Jennifer, and their long estrangement had bothered him. Although Damon had arranged his admittance into Harvard, and they'd stayed in touch during the years Jamie was gone, Jennifer was never mentioned in their letters or conversations. Jamie had always respected Damon's silence on the relationship, just as he had Jennifer's.

Jennifer met him at the door. She wore a brown silk dress that molded her high breasts and small waist. As she stepped into the light her blond hair shone like spun silver, and Jamie was reminded of the first time he'd seen her in Savannah. She was ageless, one of those rare women whose beauty didn't fade with the years. He smiled and then hung his mackintosh on the coatrack.

Abruptly the door he'd just closed burst open, and Diana rushed into the house, her long white-blond hair plastered to her head by the rain.

"Heavens above!" she cried. "Sometimes I think it never stops raining in Seattle; spring is almost worse than winter."

"Surely you didn't walk home from school," Jennifer said.

Diana nodded as she struggled out of her wet jacket. "I

stayed after to help the nuns and missed my ride. I always forget that a misty rain is just as wet as drops."

Jamie laughed, watching as Diana unbuttoned her calf-high shoes and then pulled the wet leather from her feet. Diana, who wouldn't be thirteen until August, was already a beauty. Jennifer had made the right decision in moving back to Seattle, he thought. Diana was an excellent student who needed more advanced classes to prepare her for future university studies.

"Your skirt looks soaked. I trust it's not the shrinking kind of wool," Jamie said.

Diana's large dark eyes sparkled with humor as she met his gaze. "I think it is."

"Just get it off, and we'll stretch it while it dries," Jennifer said, and winked at Jamie.

With a flip of wet hair, Diana turned to skip barefooted toward the back of the house.

"And we'll have a sherry while we wait for supper," Jennifer announced.

Jamie poured the liquor, his mind formulating a beginning to the conversation about Damon. For months now he'd known this day was coming. If only Jennifer had married Luke Olson, it would be easier now, he reflected.

He walked to the window and stared out over Seattle so she could not see his face. He didn't understand Damon's attraction to Mara, who was as snobbish and meanspirited as ever. Jamie suspected that she'd been putting on a false front for Damon, playing a desperate game to win herself a rich husband. And Damon, who wanted children to inherit his empire, had been ripe to fall into Mara's trap.

"What's wrong?" Jennifer asked. "Is it about Damon—that he's getting married in May?"

He turned to face her. "How did you know?"

"I saw the announcement in the newspaper," she said softly. Even though she appeared composed, Jamie could tell by her pale face and the way her fingers clasped her glass that she was not as calm as she wanted him to believe.

"I received an invitation," he began, deciding it would be cruel to be other than direct. "Damon's been very good to me over the years, and I feel I should attend his wedding . . . for him, not Mara."

"I agree," she replied, and glanced away. But he'd seen the hurt in her eyes; Damon was marrying another woman.

His thoughts returned to the day in New York when he'd been hurt by Lottie. He'd believed himself to be in love with Lottie, but after he'd returned to Seattle, she'd faded from his mind, and he'd come to wonder if he'd really loved her—if his feelings had been prompted by loneliness. Time is the great healer, he thought. But as he watched Jennifer, Jamie knew that it didn't heal everyone, that sometimes loneliness could become as much a part of a person as their way of walking and talking.

"I don't have to go—" He broke off as she interrupted him.

"Yes, you must; it would be awful if you didn't." Jennifer's lashes fluttered as she stared at the flames that leapt and plunged around a log in the fireplace. "Damon needs his old friends," she said wistfully. "I don't think he trusts many people. Once he said an odd thing, that I was the only person he'd ever completely trusted."

Jamie nodded. "Damon suffered a terrible childhood, shunned by his mother's prominent family because he was the son of a poor Greek immigrant. That's why he left New York and why he's so driven to be a success, to show them they were wrong." He turned away. "I understand; I want to show the world that an illegitimate son of a madam can succeed too."

Jennifer went to him and hugged him. "Come on, Jamie, it's time to eat."

Christ, it was a hell of a world sometimes, he thought. His mother had loved a man, bore him a son, and was still an outcast. His sister—he broke off, not wanting to speculate further.

Several weeks later Jamie attended Damon's wedding, sitting in the back pew for the ceremony, and reluctantly following the other guests to the Appleton mansion on First Hill for the reception. He planned to stay only long enough to be polite, wondering as he glanced over the people if his mother's brother was somewhere in the crowd. He grinned wryly. He had his own suspicions about the identity of the mysterious brother, and if he was right, they were better off without him. As a maid moved among the guests with a huge tray of filled champagne glasses, something about her suddenly caught Jamie's attention.

"Aren't you Martha?" he asked the young woman, who was dressed in a high-buttoned black gown with a stiffly starched white apron. "Andy's daughter?"

The young woman lifted her gaze, recognition curving her lips into a smile. "Jamie Carlyle," she said, her tone as gentle as the expression in her brilliant blue eyes.

Momentarily speechless, Jamie stared, realizing he'd never seen a more beautiful woman. She stood with the regal bearing of both her Swedish and Nootka ancestry, but her raven hair and dusky complexion were reminders of her Indian background, a striking contrast to her eyes. "My God!—my little waterfront playmate all grown up."

Her smile widened, revealing perfect teeth and an expression that reminded him of the child Martha. "And you have grown into a handsome man. My people would say that the lines that mark your face with maturity also say that you are a good man . . . one to be trusted."

Something lurched in his stomach, sending tentacles of some strange emotion into all his limbs. Abruptly he led her to the edge of the room and out of the crowd, then took her tray and placed it on a table. "Now, what are you doing here?"

"Working . . . as you see. Damon got me the job after I returned to Seattle."

"Returned?"

She nodded. "I've lived with my mother's people for several years, up on the northwest coast of Vancouver Island in Canada." She hesitated, her long lashes lowering to sweep the top curve of her cheeks. "I'm not staying long in Seattle . . . but I had to get away from the tribe."

"Was there trouble?"

She glanced up, her distress obvious. "I was being pushed into a marriage with a man I didn't love. So I ran away . . . before I was forced to marry him."

"Are you betrothed?"

She shook her head, the shiny black strands of her hair shimmering under the lights from the massive crystal chandeliers above them. "I couldn't—I didn't know if I really belonged with my mother's people. Now I'm trying to see if I belong here, with my father's people."

As Jamie sensed her inner turmoil he felt a sudden desire to protect her. He'd always felt Martha's hurt. "I hope you decide to stay in Seattle," he said finally, his words hiding the intensity of his feelings. Seeing her again had made him feel like the sun had come out to shine on his life.

Nodding, Martha glanced beyond him, as though her thoughts were far away from the room where they stood. "I do feel I could help my mother's people by staying in Seattle," she began slowly. "Times are changing, and Indians must find a way to live among the white people . . . and still retain their dignity and self-respect."

"And you feel you can help bring that about?" he asked softly.

"I would like to be a bridge between both worlds," she said simply.

Jamie smiled down at her, suddenly knowing he'd never loved Lottie, hadn't felt the emotional jolt that he was feeling right now. He'd cared for Martha when she was a shy child, and now he realized he was falling in love with the twenty-year-old Martha. He hated seeing her as a maid to the Appletons, remembering how cruel Mara had been when they were children. A flash of anger shot through him, and he vowed that Martha would not be a maid for long.

Before he could resume their conversation, a member of the bridal party stepped forward to reprimand Martha. "You're being paid to work, not socialize," the woman said, her pretty face twisted by a scowl. "Get back to your job."

"Wait a minute," Jamie retorted, recognizing Rachael, who was his niece by blood, if not by law. "Martha was only being polite to a guest . . . me."

"It's all right. Mrs. Woodrow is quite right. I am being paid to work." With a final smile, Martha picked up the tray and was gone, again moving with innate dignity among Seattle's most affluent citizens.

For a moment longer Rachael stared at Jamie, her gaze poisonous, but without a flicker of recognition. He realized she knew him and didn't approve of his presence. Then she turned away to rejoin Simon Woodrow, her stepson, putting her arm through his possessively. Jamie left soon after, realizing that his own status among the guests was no more acceptable than Martha's.

In the weeks that followed Jamie didn't see much of Damon, and it saddened him to think his old friend might be influenced by Mara, who disapproved of their relationship. But he saw Martha many times, often taking her bicycling on the fifteen-mile path over First Hill to Lake Union and Lake Washington, stopping each trip at the Good Road Lunchroom that was on the route. They also went on buggy rides, took walks in the city, and spent several weekends at the Bainbridge cottage with Jennifer and Diana. One day Martha took him to see a totem pole that had been erected in a square by the waterfront and explained that it had been stolen from the Tlingit village of Tongass in Alaska by a group of Seattle businessmen. She told him about growing up among the Indians, and he told her about his years on the East Coast and was delighted when she didn't scoff at his views about the future potential of air travel.

"I think it's what you should do," she said one sunny afternoon in July, as they sat on the grass at Woodland Park.

He nodded, then went on to tell her about his ideas for the future, about the glider flight feats of the German engineer, Otto Lilienthal, and the pioneering work of the American aeronauticists, Chanute and Langley.

"It's my hope to establish an aeroplane company," he said. "Just think what flying could mean one day: passenger service all over the country, maybe eventually the world, a faster way to ship cargo and mail, not to mention what an aeroplane industry could mean in terms of jobs and growth to a city." He was anxious to see her reaction to his dream, remembering Lottie's. "Once I thought I'd have to stay in the East to do that."

"Why not in Seattle?" Martha suggested softly, her eyes aglow with his enthusiasm.

He smiled, satisfied. "That's exactly what my mother and sister asked."

As they walked arm in arm Jamie felt happier than he'd

ever been in his life. He was glad he'd decided to stay in the Northwest. Now he knew he'd be there forever. He glanced down at the gentle woman at his side. I'll never let her go, he told himself. Not ever.

Chapter Twenty

"I don't know what to do," Martha said, glancing over her shoulder at Jamie as she led the way up the steps to the front door of her father's small frame house. The fading sunlight sent crimson rays across the purpling sky, but the summer evening was warm and fragrant with roses from the trellis by the porch. "I hate hurting my mother like this. I wish Papa weren't out on the ship. They waited until they knew he was gone, you know."

Jamie caught Martha's arm as he came up behind her, turning her to face him. "You're doing the right thing," he said softly, looking down into the brilliant blue eyes of the young woman who had come to mean more to him than his own life. "Your mother will understand that your ties to Seattle are as great as those to her village on Vancouver Island."

Martha shook her head. "She insists I return with her— that I marry the man from the tribe. She says I don't belong here any more than she did, and she's sorry she left me here with my father when I was a child."

"Yes, I am sorry, my child," a woman's voice came from behind, startling them. "You should not have lived in the white man's world."

They both spun around to face the speaker, Martha's mother, a small woman with a deeply lined face and straight, graying hair. Behind her stood a lean man, garbed in a *Kutsack*, which cloaked him like a blanket from the shoulders, where it was tied, down to scuffed, dusty boots. The man's black eyes glinted dangerously, leaving no doubt in Jamie's mind that he was the one who expected to become Martha's husband. In seconds, the two Nootkas were standing on the porch too, one on each side of Martha.

"You will come with us, Daughter."

The Indian man grabbed Martha's arm, forcing her toward the steps. "We take boat on the night tide."

"No." Martha twisted away from the man.

The Indian man scowled. "You will come." As he strode forward to grab Martha's arm, Jamie blocked his way.

"Martha isn't going with you," he said coldly, trying to control a surge of anger so strong that it quivered within him, like a wild beast poised for attack.

The Indian's eyes narrowed, his body tensing as though he'd read Jamie's thoughts and was preparing for a fight. "She belongs to me." He waved an arm in the air to punctuate his broken English. "I pay grandfather many blankets. Now she mine."

"I'll replace your blankets," Jamie told him, his gaze level, unwavering before the black hatred reflected in the Indian's eyes. "But Martha stays here . . . with me."

In a flash the Nootka's hand had dived under his *Kutsack* and reappeared with a long-bladed knife. "Move aside, white man."

Martha stepped between them. "You'll have to kill me first."

He hesitated, his eyes measuring her, not wanting to hurt the woman he'd already paid for with his blankets.

Jamie took hold of Martha's upper arms, trying to move her out of the way, afraid that she'd get hurt. "Stay out of this, Martha. This is between him and me."

"No." She resisted him, trying to shake off his hands. "I won't have blood shed over me."

Suddenly her mother stepped forward, motioning for the brave to put his knife away, speaking rapidly in her own tongue. The man seemed to consider the situation, his gaze darting between the other three people on the porch. With an abrupt retort in his own language, he replaced the weapon.

Martha's mother nodded and turned away from the man to Martha. "You still will not come with us?" she asked, and Jamie could hear the sadness in her voice.

Martha shook her head. "I must stay. I can't marry someone I don't love."

The quiet of the evening seemed suspended between them. Finally the old woman sighed and turned to the Nootka brave. "We go now . . . alone." As the man stiffened into a posture of defiance, she continued, "Martha is only half Nootka. The half of her that is white would always want to flee back to her father's people." She hesitated, her gaze returning to her daughter. "I am sad for you, my daughter. You will never truly belong in either world."

"Mama," Martha cried, hugging her. "I love you, Mama—I've always loved you. But I can't live in the village."

The woman patted Martha's back. "Yes, I know that now." She paused, her gaze shifting to Jamie. "I only hope the Great Spirit will forgive me for going against my father long ago—and look kindly on the seed of that union so that my daughter will know happiness one day." The expression in her eyes intensified. "The man who marries my daughter will be scorned by his own people. But still I will hold him responsible for Martha's happiness."

Jamie inclined his head, acknowledging her words, knowing she'd read his intentions. He felt a great respect for her. Martha's own strong and sensitive traits had obviously been inherited from her mother.

"Come," she told her young companion, and as the man hesitated, his face tight with rage, her tone sharpened. "As daughter of a chief, I tell you that we go . . . without Martha. My father will repay the blankets."

Jamie wanted to tell them that he'd pay for the blankets, everything he owned, for the privilege of being Martha's husband. But he remained silent, leaving the situation in the hands of the Indian woman, knowing that ancient tribal rules were now dictating the actions of the two Nootkas.

Martha stepped back, aware of the significance of her mother's words. "When will I see you again, Mama?"

Again the older woman's gaze shifted to her child. "When you marry, come back to the village." She flicked a glance at Jamie. "If your man cares for you, he will not mind the Indian ceremony among your people."

Then, her posture erect with all the dignity of her

people, she stepped from the porch, the angry young Nootka brave beside her. As they moved into the gathering dusk, he shot a glance over his shoulder to Jamie, telegraphing a warning that their next meeting would be very different.

Jamie expelled his breath in a long sigh. "My God . . . I can't believe they wanted you to marry that man. White, black, or red . . . he's a barbarian."

She nodded, not meeting his eyes. "But he is Nootka . . . and so am I."

His arms slipped around the slim form, pulling her against his chest. "Forgive me, Martha. I—I—" He broke off, wanting her to know that he didn't care who her ancestors were—that he loved her for everything she was—her dark beauty, her sweetness, her sensitivity.

He felt her head nod against his body. "I understand, Jamie."

"Do you?" he asked. "Do you understand that I love you?—that I want to marry you?"

She stepped back so that she could look into his face. "But it is as my mother said: you would be scorned and shunned by your people if you married me."

Her brilliant eyes shone like gems in the strange half-light of the dying day, the black silk of her hair very dark against the deepening gray of the sky. He smiled down at her. "My beloved Martha, my little playmate, my confidant, my love. To be shunned or scorned doesn't scare me in the least." He paused, his expression sobering. "Do you love me?" He asked the words, and it seemed as though the crickets went silent, the breeze stilled, and the steamer whistles faded away as he waited for her reply.

She stared at him, and to Jamie the seconds seemed like hours. Then that shy smile, the same one she'd had as a child, curved her lips. "I've always loved you, Jamie, since that first day when you rushed into the crowd of men to defend your mother."

"But how could you have—?"

She stepped closer, her tilted face only inches away. "My people would have an answer—that it was the will of the Great Spirit."

He lowered his face, lightly brushing hers with feathery

kisses. Then, as his feelings burst into uncontrollable passion, he claimed her lips, parting them with his tongue, sensing her instant response in the way her body molded to his, taut breasts against his chest, stomach against his throbbing manhood.

Abruptly, she pushed him back. "No, Jamie, we mustn't."

For a moment he couldn't speak, gathering his sanity, controlling his desire for her. Slowly, he nodded. "Will you marry me soon?"

"Yes," she whispered. "Whenever you say."

He pulled her back into his arms, this time with tenderness and loving concern, wanting everything to be exactly right for them. "We'll announce our engagement to the family and be married as soon as it's possible."

"Yes, Jamie," she whispered against his mouth. "Oh, yes."

Jamie stood for a moment after she'd gone into her father's house, listening to the night sounds, feeling like the richest man in the world. He and Martha would be married within the month, he decided as he started back to Jennifer's house on Queen Anne Hill.

"I did it, Seth. Sold the whole damn works to that fellow who thinks he's gonna compete with John Considine's boxhouses." Nellie laughed and glanced around the saloon. "Maybe he can import entertainers from New York or Europe like John does, but I can't afford it."

Seth shook his head. "I never thought I'd see the day . . . Nellie retiring. Wish I could get up the courage to do it. . . . Instead, here I am, past my mid-sixties, and I just finished sewing up a cut on a man from the Ninth Cavalry at Camp Lawton who's going to China to help stop the Boxer uprising. Even thinking about the energy of young people makes me tired."

She put her arm around him. He'd been her friend for many years; she would have married him had things been different. "We've got some good years left. Because I sold out doesn't mean I won't be working. I have several projects in mind for helping the poor, and now that my monthly contributions to the city coffers is stopping, I'll have that money to use as I see fit."

"I still can't see you away from here."

She shrugged. "Did you know the dirt from the next hill regrade is to be dumped on my street?—probably burying me up to the second floor. Think what that'd cost if I had to change my building so that the second floor would be on street level."

He nodded. "I've never seen eye to eye with the city fathers about lowering Seattle's seven hills. But maybe they're right. The regrade projects did make the business district more accessible to the outlying areas, and the dirt was used as fill to reclaim tideland and expand the waterfront."

"Well, I think they went nuts," Nellie said. "That Alaskan mining method of sluicing made washing away the hills too easy . . . and they just didn't know when to stop."

"Come on, Nellie," Seth said, his eyes crinkling with affection. "It all made a new sewer system possible. And we need that down here now that the hills are becoming more populated."

"Well, sewerage on the waterfront is no longer my concern," Nellie said, turning away. "With Jamie getting married, I'll have my hands full planning the wedding. Besides, I'll be living with two former prostitutes who are the cook and housekeeper for a woman who owns a First Hill mansion."

Seth stared after her. "I don't understand. . . . You're moving? Who owns this mansion?"

She paused, shooting him a grin. "Who else? . . . Me."

For a moment his expression was incredulous. Then his face collapsed with a loud howl of laughter. "My God . . . I can't wait. Nellie Thornton . . . on First Hill."

"There are bedbugs in our mattresses," Jennifer told the captain of the steamship that was taking her, Martha, and Jamie to the Nootka Indian village on Vancouver Island for the tribal marriage. Nellie had stayed in Seattle to prepare for the legal wedding in September. Damon had offered the use of the steamer for the trip, but it was a relief to Jennifer when she'd realized he wasn't going along to Canada.

"The vermin came from hauling them goddamned Indians up to Vancouver Island a couple weeks ago," the captain said as he turned over his own cabin to Jennifer and Martha. "Get bedbugs from those savages every time."

Beside her Martha stiffened, and Jennifer felt her humiliation and anger.

"I beg your pardon," Jennifer said coldly. "Not all Indians are savages, just like all whites aren't trash."

Taken aback, the captain stared at them, then shrugging, turned and walked out.

Martha stood in silence, her eyes downcast. "Jennifer, maybe this is a mistake—that is, maybe Jamie is making a mistake."

Jennifer put an arm around her, knowing she was alluding to her marriage. "No, Martha, he's not. The only mistake would be in not marrying you. Jamie loves you very much."

"And I love him . . . have always loved him. It's just that—"

". . . Nothing. You love each other, and that's all that's important."

Then Martha was hugging her. "Thank you, Jennifer. I guess I'm just nervous because I'm so happy. Sometimes I feel that it won't last."

Jennifer smiled, but her thoughts returned to when she'd been in love and it hadn't lasted. "It will last, Martha. Because you are both honest and open with each other." She crossed to the narrow window. "Yes, it will last for you."

Jennifer enjoyed the primitive beauty of the San Juan Islands as they steamed north into Canadian waters, following the inland passage through the Strait of Georgia to the northern tip of Vancouver Island, then into Queen Charlotte Sound for the turn south along the Pacific side of the island. The captain brought the steamer into a small bay and dropped anchor. The shoreline was steep and wooded on two sides of the inlet; a deckhand rowed them toward the cluster of untidy planked houses that squatted above the only strip of accessible beach. Waiting to greet them were a middle-aged woman and an old man.

Jamie stepped ashore as the boat nosed up on the beach.

Then he helped Martha and Jennifer ashore and instructed the deckhand where to place the luggage and his gifts to Martha's family. Martha's grandfather came forward then, his whole bearing denoting his position in the tribe, that he was a respected chief. Both Indians wore the traditional *Kutsack*, as did the other members of the village, who stood some distance away, watching the return of Martha, the half-Indian girl who'd run away.

As they walked up the slope toward the houses Jennifer was conscious of the solemn, brown-skinned people who'd closed in around them, staring, in silence. She felt appalled by what she saw: dirty children, crude living conditions, and a sense of isolation that was frightening. The tribe lived in the worst poverty. She caught Jamie's shocked expression.

"Wait!" a man shouted as he shouldered his way through the crowd.

Martha sucked in her breath sharply, and Jennifer saw fear in her eyes. The old chief turned to face a young Indian man who suddenly blocked their way. The brave spoke in Nootka, a spate of angry grunts and gestures. But there was no mistaking the object of his wrath: Jamie and Jennifer.

"What's going on here?" Jamie demanded.

"It is the brother of the man who bought me with blankets," Martha whispered. "He is saying that I've disgraced his family—that the white eyes cannot stay—that it is my duty to marry his brother."

Jennifer glanced over the crowd; she could see they were moved by the brave's words. Fear rippled through her; she was reminded of Big Sam's threatening her at High Bluffs. But there was no one to help her this time; she and Jamie were the only whites, the ship had already gone and wouldn't return for three days.

Jamie stepped forward to confront the brave, but Martha grabbed his arm. "No, Jamie, you mustn't. My grandfather would lose face; he will handle this."

Jennifer had her doubts. The chief seemed too old and wizened to stand up to the lean strength of the brave. The men in the crowd murmured and nodded, obviously impressed by the man who had dared to defy his chief. She watched with dread, wondering what was to happen next.

A small boy near Jennifer blew his nose in his ragged shirt, and when she glanced in his direction, she saw his mother pick lice from his matted hair. My God! she thought. What was she doing here?—at the mercy of such filthy savages!

"Easy, Jen," Jamie whispered. "Don't let them see you're afraid."

The chief suddenly held up his hand, silencing everyone. He pulled himself up to his full height before speaking in a tone that commanded even Jennifer's respect. She watched in awe as the old man chastised the crowd. Although she didn't understand his words, there was no mistaking their meaning. Dark glances moved from the chief to Jamie, Jennifer, and Martha. Then the crowd dispersed, leaving the brave without supporters.

"Christ!" Jamie said quietly to Jennifer. "I can see why the old boy is the chief; he is quite a character."

The brave jerked his head in Jamie's direction and said in stilted English, "But do not fool yourself, white eyes. He will not always help you." His black gaze lingered for a moment on Jennifer before he strode after the others.

"It will be all right now," Martha told them, although Jennifer could see that she was still upset. "My grandfather has assured me." Her words didn't calm Jennifer's fears.

Jennifer and Jamie were assigned a deserted house near the beach, where they were to stay until certain proprieties had been observed. The first was that Jamie must present Martha's grandfather with pairs of blankets. If the old chief kept them, then he would be accepting Jamie's proposal of marriage to Martha. Martha's mother told them that she had seen to it that their house was clean and free of bugs. "I remember that your people like clean houses and bedding," she said proudly.

"This is horrible," Jennifer said when they were finally alone. "I can understand why Martha can't live here. I feel as though we stepped into a different world."

Jamie nodded. "If she'd never lived in civilization, it might have been different. Now it would be a living nightmare for her, not just because of the filth and disease, but because of their primitive beliefs . . . like arranged marriages."

"And shamen who treat sickness with incantations and

hocus-pocus," Jennifer added. "Did you see the man in that frightful costume who was peering out of one of the houses we passed?"

Jamie nodded. "Martha said he's trying to heal a woman who gave birth to a dead baby."

Jennifer shuddered; she wouldn't feel safe until they were back on board ship. While Jamie gathered his gifts in readiness for his meeting with the chief, Jennifer examined the rough interior of the timbered room. The supporting posts were carved in the shapes of beasts and imaginary animals, similar to those on the totem poles scattered throughout the village. There were sleeping mats on the floor and a carved wooden chest in one corner. She couldn't imagine sleeping there; not only was it crude and uncomfortable, but she wondered if they'd be safe. The door had no lock. The windows had no glass.

"How many blankets are you giving him?" she asked, as Jamie prepared to leave for the chief's house later that day. "Martha said one to five pairs was traditional for the *tsi'as*, when you ask to marry her."

Jamie grinned. "I want to make sure, so I'm giving the old boy twenty pairs. I won't risk him saying no. God only knows what would happen to us if he did."

Jamie needed two braves to help him carry the blankets. Jennifer walked partway with him, then altered her course toward the beach, where she was to meet Martha. She found herself looking over her shoulder with each step. She had a horrible feeling of being watched, although she saw no one. She had a strong urge to run . . . but there was nowhere to go.

"Over here," Martha called, slipping off the huge boulder where she'd been sitting. "Is Jamie with my grandfather?"

Jennifer nodded, relieved to see her. "He took twenty pairs of blankets."

Martha's eyes widened. "But that wasn't necessary."

"It was for Jamie. He's making sure your grandfather doesn't say no."

Martha glanced down at her *Kutsack*, the loose cloak was tied under her chin. Her hair had been pulled back into two braids, a style that took years from her age. "My mother says that Grandfather will accept—that he only goes through the ceremony for the sake of the tribe." She looked up, her eyes sparkling with tears. "But they believe my marriage is doomed, like my mother's was. I can't convince them that the future will be different—that someday Indians and white people will live as equals."

Jennifer looked out over the Pacific Ocean, where the late afternoon sun shimmered on the edge of the breakers. She wasn't as optimistic as Martha. People were cruel to those who were different, and she doubted that prejudice would disappear, and, not for many years if ever. No one in the village was happy about the marriage; Martha's mother acted as though she were preparing for a funeral, not a wedding. Martha, as if trying to lighten the mood, had explained the Indian ceremony in great detail to Jennifer, explaining that most of the marriage rituals, like *topati*, where the groom performs dances, speeches, or feats of bravery, wouldn't take place because she wasn't marrying an Indian. The only thing Jennifer felt good about was that the Indian brave who'd wanted to marry Martha was gone and not expected back for a month. His brother was dangerous enough.

"I'm always sad when I'm among my people," Martha said. "Please forgive my somber ways."

Jennifer smiled, wishing Martha's family could allow her to feel the joy of the occasion.

Martha waved her hand in a gesture of futility. "I love them . . . but I hate the dirt and poverty. You see I'm used to the white man's ways, and now I can't live here."

"You'll never have to," Jamie said softly, coming up behind them.

Martha took his hand. "Are you sure, Jamie . . . absolutely sure you want to marry a woman who belongs nowhere?"

Without a moment's pause, Jamie pulled her into his arms and kissed her tenderly. "My Martha . . . you belong to me. I'll always want you."

Jennifer moved away to lean against the rock Martha had been sitting on, suddenly feeling lonely. God, she lamented, why couldn't I have belonged to someone . . . who'd have loved me regardless of anything else . . .

like Jamie loves Martha. She moved off to walk on the beach, forcing her thoughts into other channels, forgetting her fear of the Indians.

When Martha's grandfather didn't reject the blankets, the wedding plans for the simple ceremony were made without delay. The next day Jennifer watched Martha being given to Jamie and then Jamie speaking to the tribe about his background—that what was his was now Martha's. She felt strangely moved, respectful of Martha's Indian heritage despite the differences. She saw her feelings reflected on Jamie's face.

Their final hours in the village passed without incident; the Indians remained stoic in their acceptance of Martha's marriage. Jennifer was just glad the hostile brave was not present; she imagined the old chief had banished him somewhere.

When they were leaving the village, Martha's mother placed a hand on Jamie's arm before he climbed into the waiting boat. "Do not forget your promise," she told him solemnly. "There will be many times when my daughter will need your strength. Do not fail her."

"I never will . . . not ever," Jamie said.

Then they were off, a deckhand rowing them to the steamer that would carry them back to Seattle and their other wedding.

Chapter Twenty-one

Three days after their arrival in Seattle the *real* wedding, as Nellie called it, was held at her new First Hill mansion. Although the Carlyles were still shunned by society, the event became one of the biggest and most magnificent in the history of the city. The guest list included the governor and two former governors, McGraw and Semple, and continued all the way down the social ladder to stevedores and prostitutes. Nellie was well liked by the men of the city, if not their wives. The only missing Carlyle was Rachael, who hadn't been invited.

It's like she doesn't exist . . . or we don't, Jennifer thought as she watched Martha and Jamie exchange vows. Stunning in a pale blue gown, Martha looked totally different from the Indian maiden who'd been bought with twenty pairs of blankets. Yet, Jennifer couldn't help but feel that the simple ceremony among those primitive people had somehow been more meaningful than the one she was watching now.

She glanced at her daughter, who stood next to her, a beautiful bridesmaid in a buttercup silk gown and white elbow gloves, which were complemented by the yellow and white roses adorning elaborately coiffured upswept hair. Diana was dressed exactly like Jennifer, who was the maid of honor. She swallowed hard as her gaze wandered over the wedding party, small out of consideration for Martha's lack of friends in Seattle.

Beside Jennifer and Diana was Fred Aeschliman, a friend of Jamie's from New York who'd come for the wedding and to look into potential employment in Seattle, and next to him, Damon, darkly handsome in his double-breasted black waistcoat. Suddenly Jennifer knew he was watching

her. Her lashes fluttered momentarily before she glanced
away. She'd been plagued by conflicting emotions ever
since Jamie had told her he wanted Damon as his best man.
One minute she would anticipate seeing him, the next,
dread the thought. Her real fear was Diana. But she told
herself that worry was ridiculous; neither Diana nor Damon
suspected the truth. Nevertheless she meant to see that
Diana was never alone with Damon.

After the ceremony Jennifer helped usher the guests to
the ballroom, where a band was playing music of the Old
South. The top floor of Nellie's elegant mansion had been
turned into a fairyland; garlands of yellow roses and lacy
ferns decorated the room, while hundreds of twinkling
lights from three huge crystal chandeliers were reflected on
the mirrored walls.

As the music paused, signaling the first dance, Jamie and
Martha moved out onto the floor. Soon the ballroom was a
kaleidoscope of shimmering gowns and flashing jewels and
black-suited men, their reflections swirling on the highly
polished floor and in the gilt-framed mirrors.

Jennifer danced with Seth Andrews after he'd first
partnered Nellie, then with Luke Olson, who announced
he was soon to be married. The band played surprisingly
good waltzes, and when the next one began, Damon
appeared at her side and swung her out on the floor before
she could think of an excuse.

"Remember this one?" he said softly, his breath ruffling
her hair. "It's the same Brahms waltz we danced to at the
Appletons."

She nodded, not daring to meet the dark eyes that
watched her. She could hardly believe he had remembered
after all this time.

His arms tightened, and she trembled as they whirled
into the dancers. Then she relaxed, allowing herself the
magic of being in his arms. When the waltz ended abruptly,
she felt a moment of confusion, a strange desolation as
Damon led her back to the edge of the floor. With a nod he
was gone, leaving her with the realization that their dance
had only been a "duty dance" after all.

As she stood beside Noah she watched Diana, who was
undoubtably the most sought after young woman in the

room. Jennifer smiled with pride; it wouldn't harm Diana to enjoy herself, even if her gown and hair made her look more mature than her thirteen years. Turning to Noah, she voiced her thoughts.

"No, Miss Diana is just having fun," he agreed, smiling fondly as he watched her. "She's a real beauty. Jus' like her mama."

Jennifer grinned back. "You're just partial to the Carlyle women." Even though they laughed, they both knew it was true. She and Diana and Jamie and Nellie were his "family." But as hard as she'd tried to make him feel an equal, including him in family celebrations, there were some lines he wouldn't cross. Even now, she knew he felt awkward about being at the reception, and would probably leave early. She sighed, then went to make sure the long table of food was well supplied.

Jennifer went to the far side of the ballroom and sat down on the window seat built into the bay window that overlooked the garden and the city. She leaned her forehead against the cool glass, glad that a decorative trellis of roses and greenery gave her privacy. When would Damon finally leave? she wondered. Mara wasn't with him. Surely he'd want to go home to his wife soon.

Then she heard two voices on the other side of the trellis. She stiffened. Jamie and Damon were only steps away. She shrank back into the shadows, not wanting to make her presence known, hoping they'd wander away before she became an eavesdropper.

"Martha's a fine woman," Damon was saying.

Jamie must have nodded because Damon went on after a brief pause. "I've been wondering about your decision on my offer. I'd sure like to have you join my company, Jamie."

"I'm sorry, Damon," Jamie began; she could picture the solemn expression on his face. "I appreciate your wanting me, but I don't think so. I've never had much interest in ships, aside from loving to watch them as a kid. I know Jennifer used to want me with her company, but my intentions are still what they were when I was in New York. I plan to get into aeroplane development as soon as I can."

"Won't that be difficult? What'll you do for all the years

it'll take before an aeroplane industry takes hold in this country?"

Jamie gave a short laugh, and Jennifer detected his nervousness. "I'm trying to convince Fred to stay and help me, and in the meantime I'll be forming a construction company with my mother to build modest houses for working people and helping her take care of other holdings, like several office buildings and warehouses she rents out. My aeroplane company is still off in the future, but I'll be looking for a big chunk of land to buy, and trying to interest backers."

"Sounds like you've thought it out pretty well," Damon said, his tone vaguely annoyed—or was it disappointed? Jennifer wondered. "I've heard that your mother has acquired a few investments."

"You probably also know she's given sizable amounts of her profits away over the years, to civic projects." Jamie's tone was cooler; Jennifer knew he didn't tolerate even a hint of criticism of his mother.

Damon said something Jennifer couldn't hear as the men moved away without having discovered her presence. Again she leaned her face against the glass, trying to cool the heat in her cheeks, her gaze on the lights of the city. A half-moon hung in the sky, sending narrow beams across the bay. "I still love him after all this time," she whispered against the pane.

She'd been fighting the realization since coming face to face with him before the ceremony. He'd arrived with Noah, and she'd suspected Mara's sense of propriety wouldn't allow her to attend a wedding that united two people of different races, not to mention boasted a guest list that included prostitutes, laborers, and the black man who worked with her husband. Mara was not the only wife to stay at home.

Jennifer stepped back from the window. She'd heard rumors that Damon's marriage, though still only months old, was not highly successful. But she also knew gossip wasn't reliable. It was hard to believe that Mara wasn't completely happy with Damon, who was still lean and handsome, although his black hair was graying. Yet, Jennifer couldn't help but still wonder why Damon had married Mara—because he loved her and wanted a family?—or because she'd fooled him into thinking he'd be happy with her? Jennifer sighed and stepped from the alcove, knowing Damon would probably leave soon, and then she could relax.

Her gaze turned to Diana. Jennifer's heart fluttered a warning when she saw her daughter deep in conversation with Damon. Without hesitation she moved to Diana's side. But as she reached them she realized her fears were groundless; they'd been discussing Diana's classes. But Diana seemed captivated by him, and he had obviously found her enchanting.

Suddenly his eyes were on Jennifer, pinning her with that strange intensity she remembered. "You've done a good job in raising your brother's daughter. I was just telling Diana that very thing."

Diana giggled, her dark eyes dancing with an expression identical to Damon's. "I told Mr. Polemis that he's only seen me at my best. I have days when I try my aunt's patience, don't I, Jennifer?"

Jennifer nodded, smiling in spite of the fact that her face felt like cracked porcelain. She felt like a liar and cheat and was amazed that everyone else in the room did not see the resemblance between Damon and Diana. Then, from long habit, she got hold of herself. It *was* for the best. Even after all this time her doubts remained; there was no way she could have married the man who might have murdered her brother.

"I have this dance with Fred," Diana said as Jamie's friend claimed her for "The Blue Danube" waltz, leaving Jennifer alone with Damon, just the situation she'd been fearing all evening.

He fumbled in his inside pocket to pull out a cheroot, which he lit, the sudden burst of smoke momentarily obscuring his face.

"Had we married, we might have had a child like Diana," he said, his glance shifting to the laughing girl who danced past . . . with her captivated partner. "She's as beautiful as you were . . . still are." Abruptly his tone was cooler. "Why did you do it, Jennifer? Why did you destroy what we could have had together?"

Her thoughts shattered, she retorted in the only way she could—with anger. How dare he, a married man, bring up that subject, she fumed.

"Because . . . of my brother's death."

"But I *wasn't* responsible." His tone was low with resignation, with his belief that he could never change her mind about the question of his guilt.

"Your pocket watch was found on the dock the day Joseph left," she said, trying to sound aloof, but her old anger had lost its power over the years.

At that moment Jamie came up behind her. "What did you say, Jennifer?" he demanded.

Glancing at her brother, she explained and was chilled by the horrified expressions of both men.

"Christ all mighty!" Jamie cried. "You're wrong, Jennifer. I'm the one who found the watch . . . two weeks before the accident. I tried to give it to Joseph, and he told me to leave it with Noah. I put it in my pocket and forgot about it." Jamie hesitated, his shock intensifying in his eyes. "I didn't know it belonged to Damon until he mentioned he'd lost his watch, and that was after I'd finally remembered to give it to Noah, the day Joseph left on his new steamer."

Then, with awful suddeness, Damon's face darkened. "My God. . . . Why didn't you tell me about the watch, Jennifer?—why didn't you trust me? You were more important to me than my own life. Didn't you know that? I could never have hurt you through your brother?"

"Damon . . . I'm so sorry," she began, knowing there were no words to take away what she'd done to him . . . to them both.

He waved a hand. "It's too late now—too late for anything." His gaze locked with hers, and all that might have been, and all the lost years, flashed through her mind.

Then, without another word, he turned to go, leaving her with Jamie. But she knew, with horrifying clarity, that the wound would never heal. It was her fault. . . . She was the one who'd destroyed their love.

No, she'd had help, although that thought was little consolation now. Joseph had planted the first seeds of distrust, and then Annie had added the final words to undermine her love for Damon.

She stared at the dancers, who suddenly blended together like the oils on a palette. Then Jamie placed his arm around her. "It'll be all right one day, Jen. Just hold on to that thought." Then he was gone, leaving her standing in a pool of despair.

But she knew he was wrong. . . . He didn't understand. How could she ever right everything? Damon? And Diana? The dancers came back into focus as the threatened tears were forced away. The depth of her feelings had gone beyond the luxury of tears.

Chapter Twenty-two

"I loved Joseph like a brother," Noah told her one evening as he slipped on his coat to leave. "But I always knew that he was self-centered and stubborn." He hesitated, his expression pensive. "I's sorry that I hadn't realized the facts behind Jamie finding that watch . . . things might have been different."

Jennifer handed him his derby, knowing that was why he'd stopped by: he felt somehow responsible for what had happened over the watch, and wanted to apologize. "Don't worry about it. . . . It wasn't your fault." She knew he felt bad, but over the weeks since the wedding she'd come to accept that the past was past and must stay that way.

He reached for the doorknob, then paused, and she noticed that he was looking older, almost drawn. "But you sho should have married, Jennifer. Wasn't there ever anyone else? Nellie and I both hoped you might marry up with Luke."

A sudden burst of windswept rain rattled the door window. "I never loved Luke, and I never met anyone else I was interested in as more than a friend. And as I've always believed it's wrong to marry without love, I didn't marry," she replied finally.

Slowly he nodded. "I understand, Jennifer. The world is unfair sometimes . . . mighty unfair."

The next few months brought more changes. After the first of the year Jamie and Nellie formed their construction business, then Jamie purchased the land for his aeroplane company, and Martha announced she was pregnant. In June she gave birth to a baby girl they named Elizabeth, after Nellie's mother. By mid-August Martha had hired a housekeeper to help care for the baby, and she went to work in the Indian community.

"I must help my people," she said months later, one afternoon when she'd stopped to pick up some old clothing Jennifer had donated for needy Indians. "Somehow I want to make everyone aware that Indians are people—that they need jobs and an education and a decent place to live."

Jennifer had helped Martha carry the bundles of clothing to the buggy. Now, as they stood in the street, Jennifer hesitated, realizing that Martha had become painfully thin over the fall and winter months. "How can you get that involved? Doesn't it take too much time away from Elizabeth?"

"I do worry about that," Martha said slowly. "And Jamie is worried that I neglect her. But the baby is well taken care of and—" She spread her hands. "The need among my people is great, and there's no one to help them."

"Babies grow up fast," Jennifer said.

Martha smiled suddenly. "Don't worry, Jennifer. Elizabeth won't be neglected. I missed having my mother during my childhood, and I won't let that happen to her."

Jennifer nodded, but she wished Martha could be content as a wife and mother and leave her charity work to others. Suddenly she remembered Damon telling her a similar thing once—words she hadn't listened to either.

"But that's just it," Martha went on. "My mother didn't abandon me, she left because she thought I'd have a better life without her. It's a terrible thing when a mother must leave her child because she's an Indian and, as such, not acceptable. That's what has to change."

Jennifer knew she had no argument. Martha's words were too depressingly true. Someone had to help those who were in no position to help themselves, as Noah was doing, finding jobs for black men on the waterfront.

"I've got to be on my way," she said, giving Jennifer a hug.

Jennifer watched her go, marveling how Martha had changed from a shy child to a determined woman. Since visiting the Indian village she could understand the need, but she just hoped Martha didn't carry her crusade too far.

Suddenly Jennifer felt the chill of the March wind and hurried back to the porch.

That evening Edwin Woodrow died, leaving Rachael a widow. Several days later Seattle was rocked by the accusations of Edwin Woodrow's youngest son, Rand, who claimed that Rachael had poisoned his father. The story made the front pages of the local newspapers.

"Jesus, what a scandal," Nellie said, settling back into the cushioned seat of the carriage that was taking her and Jennifer home from a shopping trip. "And the gossip is even worse: Rand claims that his older half brother, Simon, and Rachael had a sexual relationship during the whole time his father was bedridden." Nellie hesitated, an odd expression on her face. "The dumb old bastard. Serves him right for marrying his wife's niece."

Jennifer was silent. She could believe the sexual part, but not the murder.

"Rand's accusation was investigated, but no charges were brought because there wasn't any evidence to back up his story," Nellie continued.

"I can't see Rachael murdering her husband, even if he was old," Jennifer said finally.

"I disagree. That woman is capable of anything." Nellie paused, catching her breath, and Jennifer realized she was angry—at Rachael?—or because she thought Rachael might have killed Edwin Woodrow?

"She's a real bitch. She and Mara Polemis have launched a campaign to discredit Rand, spreading it around that he wanted to seduce her and when she rebuffed him, he tried to destroy her reputation." Nellie shook her head. "Rand quit the family business, leaving it all to Simon and Rachael."

"Who still lives with her in the house?"

Nellie nodded. "Simon's weak when it comes to Rachael, just like his father was. The servants say he follows her like a puppy."

"It's amazing that Rachael gets away with it," Jennifer said.

"She will," Nellie said. "Simon is a powerful man, and all he has to do is tell people that the gossip is untrue, that he lives in the house with his widowed stepmother so that she's not alone and unprotected, that it's completely proper, and they'll believe him . . . because they want to. The topper is that Damon has given Rand a job."

Jennifer's eyes widened with surprise. Yet she felt pleased with Damon as well. It was like him to see through Rachael's lies, even if he hadn't believed Rand's accusation about his father being poisoned. "My God, what do you suppose Mara thought about that?"

"Probably went into one of her rages. I've heard she has lots of them."

As they crossed Madison on Third Avenue, their carriage passed another one going in the opposite direction. For several seconds Jennifer's gaze was caught by the eyes of the passenger in the other vehicle. Rachael was even more beautiful than Jennifer remembered. But in the instant before she was gone, Jennifer saw her features twist as recognition flashed on her face. A feeling of foreboding stuck Jennifer. Rachael hadn't forgotten her old enemies.

Rachael sat back against the cushion, trembling. She hated her, the woman her father had brought into their home over her mother's objections, the woman who'd almost destroyed her life.

The carriage stopped in front of her house, and she waited for the driver to help her to the ground. Then she swept up the walk to the front door and into the mansion that now belonged to her.

"Maggie!" she called, and immediately a buxom woman hurried into the hall, her huge breasts heaving above the white apron.

"Yes, Mrs. Woodrow?" she said, blinking nervously.

"Get my bath ready at once." She flung her fur muff and coat onto the seat of the mirrored hallstand and her purse onto a table before starting up the steps to her bedroom. As the woman hesitated Rachael turned back, velvet skirts flaring. "What are you waiting for? I want a bath now, not tomorrow."

"I've always hated Jennifer," Rachael said later to her image in the dressing table mirror, searching her face for signs of aging, pleased when she saw none. Jennifer hadn't looked a day older than the last time she'd seen her. The realization infuriated her.

Problems always came in batches, and old enemies didn't go away . . . or die very fast, she thought—take Edwin, for example, who'd become an enemy by insisting she still sleep with him, a whiny, smelly, bedridden old man. She shuddered. As far as she was concerned, he should have died sooner; he'd outlived his usefulness to everyone.

Restless, she moved back to the long mirrors on the closet doors, slipping out of her clothes so that she could study the lines of her body. She knew that men found her perfect; hadn't Edwin first told her that long ago?—become a slave to her body? And Simon . . . Simon couldn't get enough of her; his lust knew no bounds.

For a moment her spirits lifted. She'd convince Simon that Rand was wrong and that the story she and Mara had concocted was true. Picking up a crimson wrap, one of Simon's favorites, she put it on. She had everything to lose if she lost Simon's support. Rand had planted seeds of doubt that she must destroy before they sprouted into a ruined life for herself.

She was not a harlot—like Jennifer and the Thornton woman. She was respectable, with a social position to maintain, a position she must protect at any cost, she told herself. The scandalous gossip would be forgotten if Simon stood by her. If Simon believed in her innocence, then so would everyone in Seattle.

Finally Maggie brought the water, and Rachael took her bath. After completing her toilet, she turned a lamp on low and closed the velvet drapes against the winter afternoon. Then she waited on the bed, knowing her crimson negligee and flowing black hair provided a vivid and appealing contrast to the white satin spread.

When the door opened, Rachael was calm, ready to do what she knew must be done. "Hello, Simon," she said softly, her eyes meeting those of the balding man whose thickening waist denoted his passing into middle age.

He hesitated, uncertain when he saw her on the bed. "Maggie said you wanted to see me."

She twisted slightly, so that one leg was bare all the way

to her thigh. Then she patted the bed next to her, lowering her lashes seductively.

"You know I'm still upset," he began, but a slow flush was creeping up his neck to his face.

"Which is very silly of you," she said in a low tone. "If you think about me—about how loving I've always been, first to your father and then to you, you'd realize I'm what I've always been . . . a person who couldn't hurt anyone."

Something flickered in his blue eyes, as though he needed to believe her, and with a muffled groan, he stepped into the room, locking the door behind him.

It was then that Rachael knew she'd have no further worry about Simon. She smiled, contriving a proper response to his touch, allowing her wrap to slip from her shoulder so that her breast was exposed to taunt him further.

His hands fumbled with his clothing, and for an instant she thought of Rand with his strong, lean body, so different from his older brother's. She'd never managed to seduce Rand, and one day he'd pay for rebuffing her. As would Damon, who by hiring Rand had fanned the flames of the gossip.

She lay back, watching Simon through half-lowered lashes. And she'd make Jennifer sorry for what she'd done. She knew Jennifer had lied about Diana. Somehow she knew Diana wasn't her sister. But for now she welcomed Simon into her arms . . . the others would wait.

Chapter Twenty-three

Jennifer continued to capture scenes of Northwest history on canvas: new parks, new buildings, and the growing waterfront. She painted a crowd of streetcar strikers in front of the Bon Marche, President Theodore Roosevelt when he visited Seattle in 1903, and the Navy battleship *Nebraska* as it moved across Puget Sound after being launched at the Moran Brothers Shipyard in 1904. The following year she did one showing the construction of the Alaska Building, which was Seattle's first skyscraper.

She couldn't keep up with the demand for her paintings; most of them were sold to people outside the Northwest. After Justin Brinker began selling her work in California, she'd been receiving invitations to hang her work in galleries all over the West. But the old families of Seattle didn't recognize her as an established artist; to them being a woman artist was hardly more respectable than being a businesswoman, or madam.

Jennifer filled her days with her work and with Diana, who was rapidly growing into a young woman. Her thoughts of Damon had faded, and she found herself thinking more about Justin Brinker, a man whose gentle nature and quirky humor appealed to her.

As her reputation as an artist grew she found herself making occasional trips to openings of her exhibits. Diana had become involved in helping Martha with charity work now that Jamie's wife had delivered a second child, a boy they named Gregory, but Diana managed to accompany Jennifer frequently.

Early in the spring, Jennifer picked up the telephone and heard a welcome male voice.

"Hello, blue eyes. Care to do a lonely old bachelor a favor?"

"Justin . . . where on earth are you calling from?"

"The Butler Hotel, down on Second and James. How about joining me for supper." She heard the familiar note of humor in his tone. He loved surprising her with his visits.

After agreeing to meet him, Jennifer put away her paints and hurried to get ready. She put on a high-necked lace blouse and a brown mohair skirt, styled her hair, and placed a large oval hat with orange ostrich feathers atop the curls. Then she left a note for Diana and ran to catch the streetcar. Justin was waiting for her at the door of the Butler.

His hazel eyes twinkled with pleasure when he saw her. His Harris Tweed suit complemented his long limbs, and as they walked to the dining room she felt proud to have him as her escort. He ordered oyster cocktails to be followed by prime beef rib roast, then he told her why he was in Seattle.

"I'm opening a gallery in Seattle," he said seriously. "I intend to live here until I've developed it into a paying business, like my others."

"That's wonderful news."

He covered her hand with his. "I'm happy to hear that, Jennifer. Because you're the main reason I decided to do this."

Her lashes fluttered, but she held his gaze. His long narrow face, though not as handsome as Damon's, was expressive. She knew that his feelings for her had grown beyond friendship.

"I want us to have the opportunity to become closer," he went on. "Do you mind?"

She shook her head, smiling into his eyes. "I'll love seeing you more often."

Her words brought a smile that lit his face. Suddenly she realized that her feelings for him had deepened as well.

Jennifer helped Justin settle into a rented house out on the Madison Park Streetcar line and a small gallery several blocks from the waterfront on Yesler. She showed him where to shop for groceries, and for fun took him to Ye Olde Curiosity Shop, which was located on the Colman Dock.

He bought her a dainty tea set from China and said, "My appreciation to the woman I . . . I care about."

With Justin living in Seattle, Jennifer's days were suddenly filled with activities. He took her to concerts and plays and art exhibitions, and they spent many leisure hours discussing literature and politics and world events. She began to wonder how she'd managed before Justin became a part of her life.

One evening, after he'd brought her home from a symphony performance, he came into the house for cake and coffee, a ritual they'd established after each evening out.

"I've been wanting to ask you something, Jennifer," he said after they'd finished their cake and were talking. "Something very important to me."

She nodded, watching the changing expressions on his face, the eagerness reflected in his hazel eyes and his hesitancy. She glanced away; she suddenly knew what he wanted to ask, and she was frightened. She hadn't allowed herself to think past friendship.

When he finally spoke, his words ran together in his haste. "I'm in love with you, Jennifer. . . . You must realize that by now."

"Yes," she said softly. "But—"

He interrupted, as though he didn't want to hear her doubts. "You know my parents died and left me with a sizable fortune, and—and I'm capable of supporting both you and Diana." He hesitated, spreading his hands in a gesture of supplication. "I want to marry you, Jennifer. I'm forty, neither of us are getting any younger, and I don't want to waste any more time. I'm impatient now that I've found the woman I want for my wife, and I'm jealous of the time spent away from you."

"Oh, Justin . . . I don't know." His hand covered hers, and even though he didn't interrupt again, she felt the tenseness of his body as he waited for her next words. "I care about you; I love being with you . . . but I'm confused about how I feel." She broke off, trying to examine her feelings. She cared deeply for him, but did she love him? She was comfortable being with him, and they shared the same interests. She'd told him everything about her background: how she'd lost High Bluffs, her early years in Seattle, and her life on Bainbridge Island. He'd been sympathetic about the deaths of Joseph and Annie and praised her for raising Diana. It would never cross his mind that she'd lied to him.

"We'd have a good life, Jennifer," he said, his tone almost pleading. "There's no one else . . . is there?"

"Oh, no." Unable to sit still, Jennifer moved to the fireplace. "But I've always felt I shouldn't marry without love." She faced him. "I'm not sure I love you, Justin."

He came to her and took her into his arms, reassuring her that love meant many things other than what schoolgirls dreamed it was. "It means liking and sharing and caring . . . and that's really what love is," he said fervently. Then he was kissing her with a passion that surprised Jennifer and kindled a feeling of desire for him. She found herself responding, though it was not with the same all-consuming emotion of the past.

He stepped back to look down into her flushed face, his expression triumphant. "See, Jennifer. If you don't love me now, then you will in the future. . . . I'll see to that."

His slow, crooked grin was somehow endearing to her; maybe she would fall in love with him, maybe she loved him already and didn't know it.

He picked up his derby and coat. "I won't press you for an answer tonight; just think about it . . . how happy we'd be . . . what a good life we'd have." He grinned and dropped a kiss on her nose.

She smiled back; his enthusiasm was contagious. That's one of the nice things about him, she told herself. He always sees the good side of everything. After promising to give his proposal serious thought, she walked him to the front door and saw him out into the June night. Then she locked up the house, turned out her recently installed electric lights, and went to look in on her daughter.

For a moment she stared at Diana, her blond hair splayed over the pillow, her dark eyes closed. In two months Diana would turn eighteen. Jennifer's throat tightened, remembering her deceit. Would Justin have to know about Diana if she married him? But, as she looked at Diana, she felt the familiar calming effect of knowing how

important her daughter's future was to her—as much now
as when she'd perpetrated the lie.

Slowly she went to her room, her thoughts on Justin's
proposal. She suddenly knew that she'd like to be married
to him, share her life with a gentle man who loved her. She
admired and respected him and in a way *did* love him,
although not in the way she'd once loved Damon.

Climbing between cool sheets, her thoughts spun in her
head. If she confessed her real relationship to Diana, then
she'd have to reveal her love affair with Damon. And how
would Justin react to that?—with disgust?—revulsion? He
might not understand; she'd already recognized his one
flaw: he was jealous of any man in her life. She twisted
around, trying to find comfort for her body, if not her mind.
And what would happen to Diana if she found out she was
illegitimate? Would she lose her respect for Jennifer, and
ultimately her own self-respect?

Finally, as Jennifer drifted toward the welcoming arms of
sleep, she came to a decision. She'd marry Justin, but she
wouldn't reveal the truth about Diana. For Diana's sake,
the past must remain in the past forever.

The wedding was set for a Sunday afternoon in late
August of that year, 1905. Because of Justin's social status,
the *Post-Intelligencer* ran the announcement on the front
page. But Jennifer's pleasure was diluted by the article next
to it reporting that Damon had been contracted to ship
Woodrow lumber abroad.

When the day of the ceremony arrived, Nellie, gowned
in navy silk and a matching plumed hat, arrived early to
help Jennifer with the final preparations.

"How do I look?" Jennifer asked when she was finally
ready to go down to the parlor and the ceremony.

Nellie smiled. "You couldn't be lovelier if you were still
twenty."

Impulsively Jennifer hugged her. "Thanks, Nellie. I
needed that even if it isn't quite true. She turned back to
the mirror to fasten pink rosebuds in her carefully coiffured
hair. Then she stepped back to examine herself. She had
chosen a long, simply cut, blue brocade gown and matching

satin high-heeled slippers for the occasion; the pink flowers in her hair and bridal bouquet accented them.

"Everything's perfect," Nellie said behind her.

Jennifer met Nellie's reflected gaze in the mirror, suddenly remembering the day when Nellie had saved her from Judson Carr. Nellie had been beautiful then, not gray and lined as she was now, her buxom figure altered by a gradual weight gain over the years. So much had happened since Jennifer had set fire to the cotton field . . . another lifetime. She glanced back to her own image in the glass, seeing the fine lines near her still brilliantly blue eyes, noting that her hair was still blond, though not as bright as before. At thirty nine her figure was still slim, and Jennifer was satisfied with her appearance. But as she examined herself she wondered if children would ever be a part of her marriage to Justin.

"I wish you much happiness . . . you deserve it," Nellie said.

Jennifer's lashes flickered. She knew that Nellie was referring to Damon. "Thank you, Nellie. I'll be happy with Justin. . . . I know I will."

"Good. With Diana starting school at the University of Washington, I'm glad you have him."

Jennifer smiled and picked up her bouquet of roses. "Come on, Nellie. I can't be late for my own wedding." As she walked toward Jamie, who waited at the top of the stairs, she heard the pianist begin Mendelssohn's "Wedding March."

Seconds later she stood next to Justin and repeated her marriage vows, seeing such love in his eyes that she felt tears in her own. Oh, God, thank you for Justin, she thought. I'll be a good wife . . . maybe even come to love him more than I ever loved Damon.

Then it was over, and Justin's mouth was on hers, kissing her with a passion that surprised Jennifer. "I love you, my darling," he said against her lips. "My own Jennifer, the only love of my life."

She kissed him back. "And I love you, Justin." But she couldn't repeat his words about being the only love.

"It was a wonderful wedding," Diana told her later as they were being served an elegant dinner in the dining room. "I'm so happy for you, Jennifer—I couldn't be happier if you were my own mother." She laughed suddenly, and then continued, "As far as I'm concerned you're the only mother I have."

Diana's words were bittersweet for Jennifer. "And I've always considered myself your mother. . . . I couldn't have loved you more if you'd been mine."

Diana patted her hand. "I know that."

"What's all this?" Jamie interrupted from across the table. "Did I hear something about children?" He gestured fondly toward his own Elizabeth, who sat between her parents, and Gregory, who sat on Martha's lap. Both were chattering and dripping food onto their clothes. "Anyone care for a child?" he asked with mock seriousness.

"You'd soon retract your words if we did," Diana said, grinning.

Noah, sitting next to Martha, nodded. "Jamie loves his children."

"But they grow up fast," Jennifer said soberly, her eyes meeting Jamie's. "We can't bring back the time we spend away from them. Don't miss their childhood."

He nodded, his expression troubled. "I know that, Jen. But then my family is my reason for wanting to make my dream of an aeroplane company a reality."

"And my reason for wanting to make life better for my people," Martha added softly.

Jamie shot his wife a strange look, and Jennifer realized that he felt as she did: Martha was spending too much time away from the family. "As long as the price isn't too high, Martha," he said.

Martha glanced down, but not before Jennifer saw the hurt in her eyes. Martha was torn by love, for her family and for her race, a dilemma that didn't bode well for their future happiness.

"How's the aeroplane business?" Noah asked, changing the subject.

"Progressing slowly," Jamie replied. "My friend Fred Aeschliman is in Germany keeping abreast of the latest research. In the meantime, I have the property I need and I'm still talking things up with potential investors and looking at building plans."

Soon it was time for Jennifer and Justin to leave on their honeymoon to Victoria. Diana and Nellie accompanied her upstairs, where they helped her change into a white, lacy waist and a dark blue traveling suit.

"Time to go," Diana said, a sweet smile curving her lips.

Jennifer stared at the dark-eyed young woman whose blond hair was as bright as hers had once been. Oh, how I love my child, she thought. She realized that the day was bringing all her feelings to the surface. "It *is* time to go," she said, knowing she was beginning another chapter in her life, one that now included Justin . . . one that closed the book on Damon forever. She went down to join her new husband.

Jennifer's new life with Justin was filled with interesting people, trips, and quiet weekends at the Bainbridge Island cottage. Justin had agreed to live in Jennifer's Queen Anne house but had insisted on adding a housekeeper and cook.

As the city grew with the opening of the Seattle Public Library and the Waldorf Hotel in 1906, Jennifer's name as an artist was growing as well. Never had she dreamed that her paintings would bring her such success.

"Your style has had a subtle change," Justin remarked one afternoon as he hung one of Jennifer's paintings. "You're creating a softer and more intimate mood now, a more mature and confident style."

Suddenly he turned to her, his eyes alight with love. "Your work tells me that you're happy, Jennifer, that you're contented."

She nodded. Her work had been her salvation many times, and now her quiet kind of love for Justin was reflected in the growth of her talent. The passionate bold strokes of the past were gone along with the love she'd once had for Damon.

Justin pulled her into his arms and kissed her tenderly. "I love you, Jennifer . . . and I'll be with you for all the months and years of our lives." But as he kissed her again she felt an icy touch to her spine. To predict a happy future isn't to tempt fate, she told herself firmly, but she couldn't stop the memories of the times it had.

* * *

At Christmastime in 1907 Jennifer invited the family for a special holiday reception at the gallery. Justin had asked a select group of patrons. In recognition of the season he was displaying winter landscapes by local artists.

As Jennifer watched a black-coated waiter move among the guests, she realized the party was a success, as was everything Justin did, and a very different experience from her first art exhibitions. A memory of that pain and humiliation swept through her momentarily.

Jennifer turned to watch Diana being a hostess, displaying a combination of beauty and intelligence, dignity and grace . . . hers and Damon's. She was startled. She rarely thought of Damon these days.

Then, strangely, she overheard Jamie mention him to Noah. "Damon sees the potential of air transportation and has pledged his support."

"I hear he's quite successful in his own type of transportation . . . shipping," Justin said, and as he caught Jennifer's eye he smiled fondly.

Her glance returned to Diana, who was now discussing the organization of an Indian school with Nellie and Martha. For a moment longer Jennifer let her thoughts wander into the past. She knew that Damon and Mara didn't have children, that Damon spent most of his life at the office or aboard his ships, that the gossip said he wasn't happy. As she watched Diana punctuate her words with hand gestures, as her father did, she wondered how no one had ever noticed the resemblance.

She saw Jamie turn to Martha. "People are beginning to leave, and I think we should too."

"In a few minutes." Martha smiled up at him. "We're right in the middle of an important discussion."

Jamie's expression tightened. "It's also important that we promised Elizabeth and Gregory they could wait up for us."

She nodded but kept on talking.

"So I'm going now . . . with or without you," he said, a note of anger in his tone. "Our children should come first once in a while."

Startled, Martha said a quick good night to everyone and hurried after Jamie. Jennifer felt a sudden qualm about the children . . . and about her brother's marriage. Surely

Martha wasn't becoming obsessed by her causes, Jennifer tried to reassure herself; she'd realize that she couldn't deprive her own children of her presence, wouldn't she? Jennifer fervently hoped so.

Everyone seemed to leave at once. "You take care of yourself," she told Noah as he stood at the door. "You're looking a little tired."

"I'll do that," he said, smiling. "But I's just fine."

She returned his smile, noticing that he seemed thinner and that his words sounded more southern than usual. He looked much older than the sixty-two she knew him to be. After he'd gone she felt uneasy. Something didn't seem right about Noah.

Chapter Twenty-four

Don't let Noah die, Jennifer prayed over and over as she sat next to Nellie in the carriage. The moment Jennifer had heard that Noah had collapsed, she'd flung on a coat and headed toward Providence Hospital. Impatiently, she peered out at the gray January sky, wishing the horses more speed up Spring Street.

Minutes later she pushed open the door to Noah's room and allowed Nellie to go in first. As Jennifer stepped into the room she stopped short, her glance darting from the still form in the bed to the man who sat in the chair by Noah's side . . . Damon.

Slowly Jennifer moved to the side of the bed opposite Damon, forgetting him as her gaze fell on Noah's face. Was Noah alive? she wondered, her heart racing with fear. Reaching out, she covered his hand, which lay motionless on the blanket, wishing her strength into his body. She felt tears brimming in her eyes and an aching tightness in her throat.

"Noah?" she whispered softly. "Noah, it's me, Jennifer."

"He's asleep now," Damon said quietly. "The doctor said he's had a heart attack and it's important that he sleep."

Her gaze lifted to his, dark, penetrating eyes she remembered so well, holding her prisoner as they'd done so many times in the past. For a moment the shadowy room, and Nellie, and Noah seemed to slip away, leaving her alone with Damon, a man whose black hair was half gray, whose lean face was lined by the years, whose mouth, those same lips that had kissed her with such passion, turned down at the corners. His whole expression seemed carved from stone by a loveless sculptor. Then, as sudden as a flash of Northern Lights across the night sky, she saw the little fires flicker to life in his eyes.

Abruptly the door opened again, shattering the spell. Jennifer's gaze shifted to Diana, who had stopped short just inside the room, her eyes on Noah. Behind her, Martha and Jamie paused, their attention also focused on the bed.

Then Diana crossed the room and stood next to Jennifer. "Is he—is Noah—" She broke off as her words whispered off across the silence like dead leaves scuttling before a winter wind.

Diana was trying hard not to break down. Jennifer placed her free hand around Diana's waist and pulled her close, knowing how much she loved Noah. "It's all right . . . for now. He's asleep."

She felt Diana's slim body tremble under her long wool coat, and vaguely she heard Nellie's whispered explanation to Jamie and Martha, but her gaze had returned to Damon, who watched them with inscrutable eyes. Jennifer's stomach knotted with another fear, one as old as the girl beside her.

Then the door opened once more to admit Dr. Quine, Noah's physician. When he saw them clustered around the bed, he stopped short in astonishment. "This is a sickroom, not a family reunion," he said tartly. "I'll only allow one person in at a time. Noah needs absolute quiet."

Damon stood up immediately and moved toward the door, followed by everyone but Jennifer and Diana. "I'll stay with Noah," Jennifer whispered.

As Diana hesitated Jennifer gave her a gentle nudge. "Go on home, Diana, and tell Justin what's happened. If anything changes I'll telephone at once."

The doctor waited at the door, and Diana had no choice but to go. She turned away, then back again, and rushed to the bed, stooped and brushed a light kiss on Noah's cheek. "I love you, Noah. Please get well soon because—because we miss you already." Then she was gone, following the others into the hall. Dr. Quine nodded before closing the door, leaving Jennifer alone with Noah.

Time seemed suspended with only Noah's ragged breathing to denote the passage of minutes . . . then hours. As Jennifer stared at his face, so like Zeb's, her mind turned

backward to those days in Georgia when she'd believed that
the whole world began and ended at the borders of High
Bluffs. Her thoughts whirled, as images from the past
surfaced in her mind: the gleaming white mansion, the
shell drive lined with live oaks, the sleepy Savannah River,
and the graves of her parents. The Carlyles of the Old
South were no more. Only Jamie, the illegitimate son of a
madam, was left to carry on the family name, but he was on
the other side of the continent from the plantation that had
been in the family since before Washington was president.
She sighed and then became aware that Noah's hand had
moved and was now holding hers.

Startled, she realized that his eyes were open and he was
watching her. His lips moved in a brief smile.

"You's thinking of High Bluffs," he whispered.

She nodded. "How did you know?"

"Always know," he replied, but his words were fainter
and spoken with difficulty. "Certain look you get."

"Noah, don't talk now," she told him, alarmed by the
blue tinge to his lips and the way his words were slurring.
"Just rest so that you're better soon." She paused, fighting
back the foreboding that edged her thoughts. "I'll be right
here if you need anything."

His lashes fluttered down over his eyes, and for several
minutes she thought he'd drifted back to sleep. But his
hand again gave hers a weak squeeze.

"Little Jennifer," he begun, his voice stronger. "I's
remember when you be born. Who'd of thought you'd be
sittin' by my bed all these years later . . . the mistress of
High Bluffs and her slave."

"But you're part of the family, Noah," she said softly, and
despite all her attempts at control, the tears rolled unchecked down her cheeks. "We love you—and want you
back with us."

"I wanted you to know—" He broke off, resting before he
went on. "That you and Diana mean the world to me—that
I 'ppreciate you giving me the chance in business—and I's
sorry 'bout Damon—'bout the watch and all."

His words had run together in his need to tell her, and
before she could reassure him, he'd gone into a deep sleep,
so deep she wondered if he'd slipped into unconsciousness.

She sat on, not knowing how many hours had passed or how many times a nurse had poked her head into the room. Then Dr. Quine came back, and after a brief examination of Noah, motioned Jennifer out to the hall.

"It would be wise for you to go home and get some sleep. You can return tomorrow."

She nodded, suddenly exhausted.

"Do you have a ride home?" he asked.

"I'll take Mrs. Brinker home," Damon said behind her.

Startled, she turned to face him, suddenly aware of her crumpled appearance. Her hair hung limply around her face, and her wool skirt and plaid waist were work clothes she wore under her smock, not what she'd have chosen for a meeting with Damon.

About to protest that she could call Justin, she changed her mind, realizing how tired Damon looked . . . and how worried. He'd been waiting because he cared about Noah, and her refusal would be rude.

"I promised Diana that I'd see you got home safely," he said.

The doctor spoke up. "I'll be on my way then. Mrs. Brinker can explain about Noah's condition." With a final nod, Dr. Quine strode off down the hall, leaving Jennifer in an awkward situation—alone with Damon.

But before she could say a word, he'd helped her into her coat and was leading her out to his buggy. As they walked she told him about Noah, forgetting her apprehension about being alone with Damon.

In the buggy, its canopy top protecting them from a misty rain, Damon tucked a lightweight rug over their legs. Then he took up the reins and signaled the horse, who started off down the street toward Queen Anne Hill, which stood beyond the business district. As the wheels rattled over wet bricks they sat in silence. Jennifer was acutely aware that their shoulders and legs were touching. Suddenly an old longing, one she'd believed had died long ago, was coursing through her veins.

When the vehicle turned onto the street where Jennifer lived, Damon finally broke the silence.

"Diana is terrified that Noah won't make it," he said, and although she didn't glance at him, she felt his eyes on her.

She nodded. "Diana loves Noah very much. He's always been an important person to her."

"Yes, that's what she told me," he replied softly. "But then everyone cares about Noah . . . Indians, poor people, and all the others he's helped."

She felt emotionally drained. Another silence dropped between them, broken only by the whine of the wheels, hoofbeats, and the whisper of fine rain from the midnight sky. But Damon's next words broke the unreal spell.

"Diana is a lovely girl," he began, and again she felt his gaze on her. "She has many of your traits, Jennifer: beauty and intelligence and breeding, not to mention gestures and ways of expressing herself."

Her heart lurched in her chest, but when she spoke her voice was normal. "She's taken after me because I'm the one who raised her."

"Probably so," he replied with a short laugh. "Similarities can be strange. Diana even reminds me of my mother in some indefinable way."

"That is strange," she said, and realized her tone was stilted. What had he meant? Was he suspicious about Diana?

The buggy came to a sudden stop. Damon secured the reins, then jumped down and came round to help her to the ground. "Get a good sleep, Jennifer," he said, changing the subject so completely that she realized he'd attached no significance to his comment about Diana.

As he stood looking down at her, his hands still on her arms, she felt he wanted to say more. Then, with a quick motion, he dropped a light kiss on her lips. "You're still the only goddess I've ever known—ever—" He broke off and leapt back into the buggy, and a moment later it was moving away from her.

She stared until he was out of sight. Then she walked into the house; her whole body was trembling. Had he been going to say *ever loved*? she asked herself over and over.

The days that followed saw no improvement in Noah's condition, and by February, when she'd planned to accompany Justin to California, Jennifer decided to stay in Seattle. Several days later she was glad she had, when

Noah suffered another serious heart attack. A nun met her at the door with the news when she arrived to visit. Once again, Damon was already there, awaiting the verdict. They were both ushered into a small waiting room, while Dr. Quine worked to save Noah's life.

Every nerve in Jennifer's body seemed conscious of the lean man who sat beside her in the closet-sized room. But strangely, as the time passed and they talked of Seattle and its growth, she began to relax, remembering the long ago day when he'd taken her on a tour of the town. Then, after all the intervening years of estrangement, their conversation gradually moved to more personal topics.

"It was lack of trust on my part." Jennifer hesitated, glancing down at the black velvet of her suit skirt, glad her hair was coiffured and she was looking her best. "And of course I had too much pride."

"I'm equally guilty. You had your reasons, Jennifer. . . . I realized that much later, I'm sorry to say." He spread his hands in a gesture of acceptance. "You had Joseph and Annie trying to poison your thoughts about me, and then there was that man in Georgia who'd deceived you, making you overly suspicious of men."

"But I was still wrong . . . maybe too young to see through the lies . . . or trust in my own feelings."

He stood up suddenly and walked to the window, his back to her as he stared out at the late afternoon sky that was already darkening toward evening.

"Did I ever tell you that my father, a poor immigrant, fell in love and married the wrong woman? . . . my mother." He turned, facing her, his eyes glowing like black coals. "But she deceived him, leaving him because that's what her rich and powerful family wanted her to do." He paused, his gaze unwavering, and Jennifer knew the worst was to come.

"He committed suicide shortly after that, when I was a small boy."

"My God . . . I wish I'd known that."

"When I believed you'd deceived me, as my mother had done to my father—you the one person I'd trusted—I was totally disillusioned."

Damon's tone was calm even though they both realized

that all the words they'd left unsaid, the thoughts and feelings they hadn't shared, the trust that hadn't been strong enough between them, had become a force powerful enough to alter their lives.

"And I felt the same way," she began slowly, and went on to tell him the whole story of Judson Carr.

A silence fell between them, broken only by the wall clock that gonged the six o'clock hour, its louder sound racing ahead of the steady ticking into infinity. Then, as their eyes locked, the tiny room was charged with all the feelings and passion of the past. Jennifer's breath seemed trapped in her lungs, stopping all her words in her throat.

Abruptly she stood up, suddenly wanting to comfort him, make his world happy as she sensed it had never been. He'd always been reticent to speak of his past, and now she realized he'd been afraid of making himself vulnerable to being hurt again.

The mood was broken as Dr. Quine stepped into the room. "Noah is holding his own, and I think he'll make it. But he's resting, and I'm not allowing visitors tonight. It wouldn't be wise."

"We understand," Damon replied. "We both want what's best for Noah."

Damon took her arm as they went out into the damp winter night. Jennifer fastened the buttons of her jacket, then slipped her hands into her fur muff.

"Will you have something to eat with me?—supper?" Damon asked hopefully.

He held her gaze as she considered his offer. She felt unsettled; they'd been interrupted before being able to tie up the loose ends of their past.

She smiled, suddenly shy. "I'd love to . . . if you think it's proper for us to do so."

He grinned, reminding her of the old Damon. "You . . . worried about being proper?" He clucked his tongue. "Don't tell me you've changed that much."

They laughed together, setting the companionable atmosphere for the night. This time they drove in his new Ford to a nearby hotel and dined at a restaurant with a wonderful view.

As they sat by the window that looked out over the seven hills of Seattle and Elliott Bay, Damon talked about his life. Although he didn't come right out and say so, Jennifer sensed his desperate unhappiness with Mara, whose whole life consisted of one social event after another . . . and his disappointment that he'd never had children.

"I thought Mara had changed, that I'd grow to love her once we were married, that we'd have a good life . . . and children. But it didn't turn out that way; it was soon apparent that Mara had only been playacting to land a husband." He glanced away but not before Jennifer glimpsed his hurt. Her knowing that he'd suffered brought back all of her own guilt.

Jennifer's throat throbbed with a need to tell him about Diana, but she knew it was too late to confess. There was no longer only Diana to consider, there was Justin . . . and Mara.

"This is where I spend most of my evenings," Damon said softly as he opened the door to an apartment in his office building. "I often work late and instead of going home just stay here for the night."

"I feel a bit awkward," Jennifer began. "Like I'm intruding into Mara's domain." Even though she knew that Mara and Damon had a strange and unhappy marriage, she also knew it wasn't right for her to be with Damon in his apartment in a deserted building.

His features tightened momentarily. "Don't be. Mara doesn't bother me here except to telephone; she thinks the place is drab, uncomfortable, and depressing."

Nervously Jennifer glanced around, wondering if she should have accepted his invitation for a brandy. As on the last occasion, they'd both visited Noah and then gone to supper. Although she'd seen Damon many times in Noah's room during the intervening weeks, this was the first time Justin had again been out of town. In a way she felt deceitful; she had been careful that when Justin accompanied her to the hospital they didn't run into Damon. Somehow she couldn't face being with Justin and Damon in the same room.

"Don't worry," Damon said as he took her cape. "We aren't hurting anyone by becoming friends again."

She nodded but was suddenly unsure when his fingers accidently brushed her neck and the tingling sensations began in her veins. Although he'd never kissed her again after that first night, and she'd come to believe he did look upon her only as a friend, she was pricked by guilt. She still loved him, and she was married to Justin, who loved her— Justin, who was jealous of any man who seemed overly interested in her. It was wrong to be with Damon, yet she couldn't bring herself to refuse to see him.

"Would you care to look around . . . I have a great view."

When she murmured a yes, he took her elbow, another of his old habits, and led her from the parlor to the kitchen and on to the small office and then the bedroom.

"This is the room with the best view," he said, suddenly so close that his breath fluffed her hair.

She stood frozen, terrified by the powerful emotion that swelled within her. Then slowly, almost of its own volition, her body swayed toward him. His arms shot out to clasp her against his chest. For a moment her eyes were caught by the fires blazing to life in his, the naked desire on his face. Then his head lowered and his lips claimed hers in a kiss both tender with longing and savage from the deprivation of years.

"My goddess, my love," he whispered hoarsely. "God, how I've missed you."

She moved closer, molding her body against his, raising her face to meet his lips. With a low moan, he began to fumble with the buttons of her dress, slipping it from her shoulders, so that he could feather her neck with kisses, then lower to her breasts.

"No, Damon, I didn't mean for you to—" What? she asked herself. Go beyond kisses? . . . make love to her? She struggled, trying to free herself from the hands that traced her flesh with fire, the lips that reduced her to a quivering mass of sensation.

"Yes . . . yes, we can," he whispered, pinioning her arms gently but firmly. "Say you can refuse me now," he said, his tongue tickling her top lip before thrusting into her mouth in a long, passionate kiss. "Say you don't want my love after denying me for over twenty years." His hands freed her breasts that heaved with a longing all their own, taut nipples tingling for satisfaction deeper than the touch of his hand.

Liquid fire erupted within her as her arms went around him, pulling him closer. She wanted him—his naked body next to hers—the ecstasy she'd only known when he'd possessed her completely. At that moment she forgot everything else but that Damon wanted her, and she couldn't refuse him her love.

He moved her toward the bed, his low throbbing voice caressing her as ardently as his hands or lips. "Forget everyone . . . only you and I exist tonight . . . for each other. Don't think about Mara . . . or Justin."

She stiffened, then twisted out of his arms to stumble backward away from him, her eyes wide with love and desire . . . and sudden guilt. "I—I can't, Damon. Oh, God, why did you mention Justin?"

"Jennifer—" He took a step toward her, then hesitated, his black eyes clouding as he read her stricken expression. "Christ." He turned away, as though it took all of his strength to pull himself together, to cool the heat that had almost devoured his reasoning power. When he turned back, his eyes were hooded and the lines and planes of his face tight with control.

"Damon . . . please don't look like that, please understand I can't do this to Justin . . . he loves me."

He nodded, then arched his black, slanting brows. "I quite understand, Jennifer. And I think it's time I took you home."

She stared for a moment, knowing she'd hurt him deeply and that he'd retreated behind his veneer of coldness. Moving away she adjusted her clothing and repinned her hair. Then she put on her coat. In silence they went down to his Ford, their brandy forgotten.

Jennifer continued to see Damon during her visits to the hospital. Noah was gradually regaining his strength, and Jennifer made arrangements to take him home. Justin was in complete agreement with her plan, but as he was involved with spring art shows at all of his galleries, he was constantly traveling, a situation that didn't please him because he felt he should be with Jennifer.

By the time the daffodils and tulips were blossoming in April, all signs of awkwardness had vanished between Damon and Jennifer concerning the night at his apartment. Closing her mind to any feeling of wrong, she again had dinner with him. Their conversation included everything but personal subjects, and by the time he took her home she didn't hesitate to invite him in for a nightcap, knowing both Justin and Diana were away.

After stirring up the fire in the sitting room and pouring whiskey for Damon and brandy for herself, Jennifer sat down on the velvet divan, facing Damon.

"Are you in love with Justin?" Damon asked, surprising her with his directness even though she realized that he'd probably drawn that conclusion when she'd rebuffed him.

Jennifer hesitated, lowering her long lashes to screen her eyes. She'd told him about Justin, what a wonderful man he was, and that she deeply respected him. But now, how could she answer Damon's question and still be honest?

As she formed her answer, Damon was suddenly beside her, pulling her toward him. "You don't love him, do you, Jennifer?"

"I—I—that is—I care for him, Damon," she said, her eyes seeking his understanding. "And I have a good marriage."

"But do you love him?" His hand moved upward, over her shoulder to her chin, where his thumb gently traced the lines of her mouth.

She stared, terrified by what she knew was going to happen, what she might not be able to stop this time. God, she thought, she should have known better than to be alone with him again. Her body was tingling, her bones melting under the heat of her flesh that burned with fire. Her lids drooped as his other hand caressed her back, then moved upward to gently nudge her head closer to his.

"Do you love him?" Damon repeated softly, insistently, his breath warm against her mouth.

"No . . . oh, God . . . no." Then her lips parted as

his came down on hers and reclaimed that which had always belonged to him.

With a moan that seemed torn from his soul, Damon's passion mounted to meet hers. He carried her into the bedroom, unable to control the love that had lain dormant for too long, she unable to resist the need she shared.

He laid her on the bed and then stood over her, his face pale as he studied her face. "Are you sure, Jennifer?" he asked softly.

She stared into the bottomless black of his eyes. Slowly she nodded and took the pins from her hair, so that it cascaded around her face. She wasn't sure that it was right, but she was sure about wanting him. She couldn't hurt him again, not for any reason.

Then he bent over her, his eyes brimming with love, and carefully removed her clothing. With each touch, Jennifer's need grew until she could have screamed for him to hurry. But, like a great artist who knew creating a masterpiece was not done quickly, Damon took his time.

When she lay naked, he undressed, unabashed that she watched, that she saw his desire in the throbbing hardness of his manhood. Then he was beside her, his mouth on her face, before moving lower to her nipples that waited taut and quivering on the soft mounds of her breasts. His tongue flicked over them before moving lower yet.

"Damon . . . oh, Damon, please." She clasped his body, pulling it down onto hers, and for a moment his gaze was triumphant. But as he saw the little smile trembling on her lips, his eyes went soft with love . . . humbled.

As he entered her they soared together beyond the confines of the house, Seattle, and the world, knowing the joining of their flesh was the culmination of their love.

Later, their passion spent for the moment, they lay talking for a long time, coming to no conclusions except that they loved each other, even more than before.

The first light of dawn was sending an advance guard of light from the horizon when Damon finally left her house. As she closed the door behind him she felt as though the past had been suddenly erased by a benevolent God, that she'd been given a second chance for the love denied her all those years.

But as she went back to her bedroom, she wondered. Was she really a whore after all?—as she'd been called so often in the past? She shook her head, still incredulous that Damon had made love to her in the bed she shared with her husband, a good man who loved her. As she slipped back under the warm covers Jennifer snuggled against the pillow; the smell of Damon was still on the sheets. My God, she thought. I must be the harlot Rachael always accused me of being. Because I feel no guilt whatsoever . . . only the warm sense of finally belonging to the man I love.

Yet, after Justin returned from California and Noah came from the hospital to their house, Jennifer knew she must stop seeing Damon.

"I love you, Damon," she told him at his apartment. "But this is madness."

He grabbed her, pulling her naked limbs against the lean hardness of his body. "You can't mean that, Jennifer. We'll each get a divorce so we can marry."

She shook her head, tears spilling from her eyes. "It's no use, Damon," she said, her voice breaking while the words dropped between them like stones in dead water. "It's too late for us—too many people would be hurt."

"No . . . it's not too late." For the first time since she had known him, Jennifer heard a pleading note in his voice and saw fear in his eyes.

She glanced away from his stricken expression, hating herself, but knowing she must have the courage of her decision—they must end their affair. "I'm forty-two and you're forty-seven—too late to begin again." Her words trailed off as she fought her emotions: love and desire and a need to protect him from more hurt. But what about Diana? she asked herself, and Justin? . . . even Mara?

"We have responsibilities to the people who depend on us, Damon. We can't afford a scandal."

He started to speak, then stopped, seeing her resolve. The fire in his eyes went out, like a candle flame suddenly extinguished. "You're right, Jennifer," he said finally. "But if I'm to keep my hands off you, then I can't be alone with you . . . not ever."

She swallowed hard, then nodded while everything

within her screamed a protest. "I know," she whispered, and then after dressing, she walked out of his life for the second time.

The spring blossomed into summer, and Noah slowly began to recover. Diana and Jennifer spent many hours with him, reassuring him that he'd be back to work by fall.

Then, without warning, Noah suddenly died in his sleep. The funeral was attended by blacks, Indians, business people, as well as family and friends. A week later, in early September, his will was read. Noah had left everything to Diana, including his part ownership in Damon's shipping company.

Jennifer was startled, and then apprehensive of the latest turn of events. But she knew that Noah, in his own way, had been trying to right the wrong of Diana's birthright. When Jennifer returned home after the session with they lawyer, she went to her room and gave in to a rush of tears. I'm going to miss Noah for the rest of my life, she told herself. He was everything to me . . . and to Diana.

"I love you, Noah, just as I loved Zeb," she whispered into the silent room, thinking that everyone she ever loved seemed to die too soon.

Shortly before Diana was to begin her last year at the University of Washington, she brought up the subject that had been bothering Jennifer: Diana's interest in Damon's company.

"You know I loved Noah," Diana began, then paused to take a ragged breath. "And I take my inheritance seriously."

Jennifer nodded, waiting.

"I'm not going back to school," she said, abruptly direct. "Damon has offered me the opportunity of taking an active part in the company, and I've accepted." Her dark eyes were serious, but Jennifer saw uncertainty in their depths as well.

She wants my approval, Jennifer suddenly realized. She's made up her mind, but she doesn't want to hurt me. Oh, God, how I love her . . . more than my own life.

"Do you know what it means to be involved in a 'man's world' of business?" Jennifer asked softly.

"Yes, I believe I do."

"It's not easy, you know." Jennifer watched the changing expressions on Diana's face, knowing she'd inherited her strength of purpose from both Damon and her. The realization gave Jennifer an immense feeling of pride.

"I realize that," Diana replied, her gaze steady on Jennifer's face.

"Then you have my blessings," Jennifer said, and dropped a kiss on her daughter's cheek. History repeats itself, she thought as she watched Diana, anxious to get started with her future. Diana was bringing her mother full circle. Diana was now entering a business Jennifer had left long ago . . . because of Diana.

Chapter Twenty-five

By Christmas, Jennifer relaxed: there was no reason for her to worry about Diana's working with Damon. Diana was enjoying her involvement in the company, and neither of them suspected their true relationship. Even if it had been possible to reveal the truth without destroying Diana's reputation, Jennifer couldn't bear to have her deceit exposed to Damon now that she'd finally regained his respect. He'd despise me forever, she told herself.

After the year passed from 1908 to 1909, her worries faded as she worked furiously to complete a series of Northwest paintings for a one-woman show in March. The event was designed as a forerunner to the Alaska-Yukon-Pacific Exposition, which was scheduled to open on the first day of June on the University of Washington campus.

On opening day Jennifer and Justin stood in the waiting crowd. At precisely ten o'clock in the morning President Taft pressed the nugget key in Washington, D.C., the gates swung wide, and Jennifer and Justin moved with thousands of surging people onto the landscaped grounds. Jennifer could only glimpse the French and Spanish renaissance buildings that had been constructed for the event.

Justin shouted above the noise, "At this rate we'll be a huge success. Do you know that at this very minute a fleet of automobiles are leaving New York for a transcontinental race to Seattle?"

Jennifer grinned, feeling pride in her adopted city. Seattle was proclaiming to the world that it was aware of its Alaskan, Indian, Eskimo, Chinese, and Japanese neighbors—that it was a city on the move upward.

"First to Martha's booth?" Justin asked as he glanced back at her.

"Yes," she replied. "It's over next to the amusement concessions on Pay Streak."

They wormed their way through the crowd, finally arriving at the booth where Martha and Diana were passing out pamphlets on facilities available to minorities. Most of the people taking sheets were either Chinese or Indian, the former garbed in loose black trousers and high-necked jackets, the latter in the usual blanket wrap over shabby trousers or long skirts.

Martha, who was speaking with an Indian man, looked upset.

"What's wrong, Martha?" Jennifer asked, concerned, as the Indian gestured in a threatening manner, then spoke angrily in words she couldn't understand. He glowered at them all, then turned and strode off into the crowd.

"It's all right, Jennifer—he was—" Martha broke off, as though at a loss for words.

"How long was he here?" Jamie demanded as he reached the booth. "I saw him leave, but I couldn't get through the crowd in time to stop him."

"Who was he?" Diana asked the question that was also on Jennifer's tongue.

"The man the tribe had wanted Martha to marry," Jamie replied before Martha could open her mouth. "Was he threatening you, Martha?"

She nodded slowly. "But I'm sure he didn't mean it." She hesitated, and Jennifer could see Martha was shaken. "He's still angry about the past," she went on. "And—"

"And?" Jamie prompted.

Martha glanced down at the handkerchief she'd been knotting in her hands. "He said my two children should belong to him . . . not a white man."

"Christ!" Jamie cried, and his eyes narrowed on the hundreds of people that were moving like a sluggish river toward the natural amphitheater and the dedication ceremony. "I'd like to get my hands on that bastard."

Although Martha left the booth in charge of two young Indian women and reluctantly went off with the family, Jennifer was uneasy. It wasn't normal for a man to be angry after all these years . . . unless his mind was unhinged.

That thought sent a chill down her spine, and she was glad of Justin's warm arm that suddenly pulled her closer.

The exposition closed in mid-October, and Martha's former suitor hadn't been seen again. By the first of the year, he'd been forgotten.

In March, Jennifer and Justin drove their new Franklin automobile out to the meadows south of town to watch Charles Hamilton's biplane flight. Jamie was interviewed about his new company for the newspaper, and the coverage helped Carlyle Aeroplane Company gain new investors. Seattle was changing fast: construction had begun on a ship canal to link lakes Washington and Union with the Puget Sound; the Chicago, Milwaukee, and St. Paul Railroad had come to the city; the population of 1910 had grown to about two hundred and forty thousand. Jamie had been right: aeroplanes would be a part of Seattle's future.

Jennifer turned from arranging her spring flowers when a knock sounded on the front door. As she opened it she smiled, thinking it was Nellie, as both Diana and Justin were at work.

"Rachael!"

"Obviously," her niece answered crisply.

Startled, Jennifer said the first thing that came into her head. "What do you want?" Then, remembering her manners, she stepped aside, allowing Rachael to sweep into the hall, her French plumed hat bouncing, and her full skirt of lightweight tweed swirling around the tops of her shoes.

Rachael's dark eyes narrowed. "I want Diana out of Damon's company . . . immediately. Or I intend to tell the whole town that Diana is Damon's bastard daughter."

"What? . . . That's ridiculous!" Jennifer cried. "Are you crazy?"

Hatred sparkled in Rachael's eyes. "I can prove my accusation," she retorted, all her old resentment of Jennifer mirrored in her face. "But I'll keep quiet if Diana leaves Damon's company."

Jennifer strived to stay calm. What was the motive

behind Rachael's sudden demand? she asked herself. And could she prove her accusation? "I can't tell Diana what to do. . . . She's an adult. And I can't imagine why her actions would bother you at this late date."

"Because Mara wants her gone," Rachael began, her cheeks flushing dark red. "Mara doesn't approve of Diana being in Damon's office."

"My God . . . Mara's as crazy as you are."

Rachael whirled away toward the door and then glanced back. "You've got a week to get her away from Damon, or I'll destroy all of you." She hesitated. "How do you suppose the town'll react when they hear that Diana is Damon's bastard daughter, a woman he might be considering for a mistress . . . if she isn't already his mistress."

Anger enveloped Jennifer; she tried to expel the obscene implication of Rachael's words. There must be more behind the visit than these threats . . . something vital to Rachael. Rachael would go to any extreme to maintain her social position. Like her mother, Rachael had always believed that wealth and status were all that counted. It's all she has, Jennifer thought, and suddenly felt sorry for her.

"Why didn't you tell Mara your ridiculous suspicions in the first place?" Jennifer asked, glad her voice didn't reflect her shock. "Wouldn't that have been easier than threatening me? And more to the point, why are you involving yourself in Mara's marital problems?"

"None of your damned business. Just get Diana out of Damon's office or else."

"How can you hate Diana that much?"

"Because I've always hated you, Jennifer . . . right from the first day. And one day you'll pay for pawning your bastard off as my sister." Then she was gone, slamming the door behind her, leaving Jennifer terrified for her daughter's future.

Rachael was blackmailing her. But why now?—after all this time? Jennifer wondered. And why was Rachael doing Mara's dirty work? Was it possible that Damon *had* fallen in love with Diana, *was* considering an affair with her? Oh, God . . . she couldn't begin to guess; all she knew was that she had to preserve Diana's happiness and secret . . . somehow.

* * *

After several sleepless nights and tormented days, Jennifer knew what she must do. Hearing Diana's glowing reports about Rand Woodrow, she gratefully realized that her daughter wasn't romantically interested in Damon, but Jennifer knew she had to tell Diana the truth. She couldn't risk giving in to Rachael's blackmail attempt; if Rachael succeeded once, she'd do it again. Giving in would also be admitting the truth.

When supper was over, and after Justin had gone to the sitting room to read, and the cook and housekeeper had retired to their rooms, Jennifer sat down in the kitchen with Diana.

"I don't think I've ever seen you look so grim, Jennifer," Diana said.

"I don't know quite how to begin."

"Why not just say it . . . whatever it is," Diana suggested, her dark eyes puzzled. "You and Justin aren't having difficulties, are you?"

Jennifer shook her head.

"Are you sick?" Sudden alarm altered Diana's expression.

Jennifer ran her tongue over her lips, knowing she'd just have to say it. She felt color stain her cheeks, her heartbeats drummed in her ears, and her shame left her limp as a fallen sparrow.

Diana's hand reached across the table to cover hers. "Jennifer, it can't be that bad, just say it."

Jennifer's lashes fluttered, but she kept her gaze steady on Diana's face. "You're not my niece, Diana . . . you're my daughter."

Diana's expression froze.

Knowing that she must go on or burst into tears, Jennifer spoke quickly, telling Diana about her birth—that she wasn't the child of Annie and Joseph—that Jennifer had perpetrated the lie thinking it was the only way to protect her baby.

"I'm illegitimate," she whispered. "But who was my father?"

Jennifer hesitated. "It's best you don't know," she whispered brokenly.

"But I must know—Can't you see that? Or I won't be able to face this."

"I—can't."

"Yes, you can," Diana insisted. "This lie had gone on for too many years already. Now it's time for the whole truth."

With faltering words, Jennifer related the rest of it. "Your father is . . . Damon."

Diana's eyes widened. "Damon's daughter . . . I can't believe it. Does he know?"

Jennifer lashes fluttered downward. "No," she said simply.

"Why are you telling me now?" Diana asked suddenly. "Couldn't you have kept up the lie forever?"

Once again Jennifer explained, this time about Rachael's suspicions and her visit.

"The bitch," Diana said, angrily. Then, as a silence fell between them, a slow smile suddenly lit Diana's face and tears welled in the dark eyes. She jumped up, scraping the chair legs on the floor, and ran round the table to hug Jennifer.

"I love you . . . Mother," she said, the word sounding strange on her lips. "Now I understand why you gave up so much just to raise me—to give me a secure childhood."

Jennifer hugged her back, tears streaming from her eyes. Diana had forgiven her.

"I know the lie was wrong, but I believe I'd have done the same in those circumstances." Diana sat back down but still held Jennifer's hand. "And odd as it might sound . . . I'm proud to be the daughter of you and Damon."

After Diana had gone up the back stairs to her room, Jennifer struggled to regain her composure, knowing she must join Justin soon or he'd wonder what had happened to her.

"Jennifer?"

She glanced up, surprised to see him in the doorway to the hall. "How long have you—" She broke off when he interrupted.

"Long enough to hear most of your conversation with Diana," he said in a low tone. His expression was distorted by shock, disappointment, and jealousy.

Her stomach lurched. Oh, no, not this, too, she prayed.

Then he stepped into the room, and Jennifer knew that nothing would be the same between them again. His thin face looked ravished by what he'd heard, and she could see his pulse beating frantically in his neck.

"I want to know the whole story, Jennifer." He hesitated, his normally kind eyes expressionless for the first time since she'd known him. "I can't believe you kept this from me, your husband."

She swallowed hard, her shattered emotions unequipped for another scene. "I couldn't tell you," she began, and broke off, biting her lower lip.

He shook his head. "Damon Polemis is Diana's father? . . . I can't believe it." Then he moved closer, his eyes narrowing. "You saw a lot of Damon while Noah was sick; has there been anything between you since our marriage?"

"I—I—" she began, hesitating to say another lie.

"There has been!" Sudden color suffused his pale cheeks. "My God! Did he make love to you?" Justin's voice cracked as though he were close to tears himself.

Unable to lie to Justin, who valued truth, Jennifer slowly nodded, but went on to explain that the affair began and ended during Noah's illness.

Stunned, Justin began pacing the kitchen. Only his footsteps and the ticking clock penetrated the ominous silence of the room, a silence Jennifer dared not break, knowing their marriage was in his hands. Abruptly he stopped short, facing her. "I can forgive you the affair as long as you're not in love with him."

Jennifer knew she couldn't meet his gaze without his reading the truth in her eyes. "I love you," she told him instead. "I've never lied to you about that."

"But you love Damon," he said, with a finality that sent her hopes crashing to join all the others that had been destroyed over the years. "And you've loved him for most of your adult life." He moved to the back window and looked out at the empty blackness of the night. "I can't fight that, Jennifer." He turned back to her, his eyes sad with resignation. "And, regardless of the cost, I can no longer live with you. My pride won't allow me to be second to another man."

Jennifer jumped to her feet, trying to make him understand her feelings, knowing he was about to walk out of her life, and the thought shattered her.

"I can't listen to any more," he said brokenly. Then he rushed from the room, explaining as he went that he'd be taking a room in a hotel, that he needed time to think.

She stared at the empty doorway. Her life had just drastically changed again. But this time she didn't know if she had the strength to go on, or if it was worth the try.

Chapter Twenty-six

"Jennifer, what's going on? Why has Justin moved into a hotel? Jesus! I couldn't believe it."

She sat opposite him, her gaze lowered to the bright red plaid of her skirt. "Oh, Jamie . . . I've destroyed the lives of everyone around me."

"Christ, Jennifer. Just tell me what in God's name has happened."

Then her words dropped from her lips, faster than the sudden spring shower that was hitting the house with soft drumbeats of rain. She told him everything, from Diana's birth to Rachael's visit to Justin's decision to leave. Her last word fell into a sudden silence as the rains abated.

A moment later he was beside her on the settee, embracing her gently. "Oh, Jen, you haven't destroyed anyone. You only did what you had to do and . . . I always knew that Diana belonged to you and Damon."

Through a haze of tears, Jennifer stared at him. "Who else—"

"No one," he said gently.

"What'll I do?" Jennifer's hands knotted in her lap. "I've hurt Justin terribly. . . . He loved me."

"Give him time, Jen, and he'll understand."

She swallowed. There was one thing she hadn't told Diana or Jamie, that she'd had an affair with Damon and Justin knew about it. Jennifer squeezed her eyes shut, trying to halt her mental pictures. Jamie's words couldn't help her; she knew that she'd never be absolved of her guilt. She hadn't trusted Justin enough to tell him the truth years ago, just like she'd once not trusted Damon.

Jennifer became aware that Jamie was patting her clenched hands. "I'll talk to Justin," he said. "Make him understand." He stood up. "Don't worry, Jen. It'll be all right."

But by the end of the week she still hadn't heard from Justin, and her pride and shame wouldn't allow her to seek him out. Diana also felt terrible, reproaching herself for demanding to know the identity of her father.

"But it wasn't your fault, Diana," Jennifer insisted.

"But it might have been different for Justin if Damon hadn't been mentioned," Diana replied, her dark eyes troubled. "Knowing who my father is changed nothing for me. I can't tell Damon the truth and chance destroying his marriage."

Jennifer nodded, moving her fork around her plate, pretending to eat. She knew Damon's marriage was already sour, but she didn't want Diana to know.

"I've come to a decision," Diana said slowly. "I'm leaving the company, because we can't risk Rachael's making the situation any worse." She pushed her plate of untouched food away. "I can't jeopardize my father's future. So I gave notice—told them I've decided to continue my education."

"And he accepted?"

Diana shook her head. "Not at first. In fact he was quite upset when I placed my company stock in his hands." She smiled sadly. "He's genuinely fond of me . . . ironic, isn't it?"

Jennifer looked away, her eyes burning.

"But I told him I'd finish out the month."

Silence engulfed them, holding them in its grip until they retired to their separate rooms for the night. The next morning Diana went off to work, while Jennifer moved from room to room, feeling like a ghost of her former self, unable to concentrate on anything.

When the telephone rang, she picked it up, hoping it was Justin. But her hopes sank when she heard Rachael's voice. Abruptly Jennifer informed her that Diana, for her own reasons, was leaving the company at the end of the month.

"Don't ever threaten us again. Diana knows all about your absurd claims and doesn't give a damn . . . and neither would Damon. You seem to forget that Damon would also know he wasn't Diana's father, since he's never made love to me." Jennifer slammed the phone down before Rachael could utter another word.

For Jennifer it was an anticlimax, and the feeling continued throughout that day and the days that followed. For the first time in her life she was truly depressed. The guilt of knowing she'd never loved Justin as she'd loved Damon hung over her. Even though Damon had discussed divorce, she knew it was now out of the question.

When the mail brought a letter from Justin, she held it in her hands for a long time before opening it. When she read that he would seek a divorce, she wasn't surprised . . . only resigned. The following week he left Seattle to return to California, leaving another letter to inform her he was making no claim on her house and that he'd turned the Seattle gallery over to her. Within several more days Seattle was gossiping about Jennifer's new, socially unacceptable status—divorcée.

By the first of June, Diana had left Damon's office to spend the summer helping Martha, who was involved in more charitable causes than she could handle. Both Diana and Martha tried to interest Jennifer in their work, but she couldn't be persuaded. She had no desire to face the gossip. Damon called her, but she couldn't face him either; it would only fan Rachael's and Mara's hatred. Even Nellie's chatty gossip couldn't shake Jennifer out of her depression.

Finally Jennifer made a decision: she'd go to the cottage on Bainbridge. Maybe she could paint there . . . to be able to paint again would help.

Several weeks later she was informed that several of the gallery artists had canceled their fall exhibitions. The news suddenly snapped her out of her depression. She needed the income from the gallery and realized she'd better take command of the situation.

That day she went down to the gallery and was appalled to discover it wasn't even open. Going around to a side entrance, she used her key and let herself into the back office, where she startled the two employees, who sat gossiping and drinking coffee.

"What's going on here? Why isn't the gallery open?"

The men jumped to their feet, staring openmouthed at her. "There isn't any business," one of them informed her, abruptly cool now that he'd recovered from his surprise.

Jennifer glanced around. The office was a mess, littered with stacks of bills and unopened letters. At the showroom door she stopped short: the walls were bare and the glass cases empty. "What in God's name has happened? You didn't inform me that we'd sold everything."

"We didn't sell it. Mr. Brinker took some of the things with him, and some of it was removed by the owners because"—the young man shrugged indifferently—"of the gossip about you and your husband."

"You mean the two of you just sat here and let this happen without informing me?—still collected your salary?—for doing nothing?"

"See here, Mrs. Brinker, we don't have to take your upbraiding—"

"That's right," she interrupted coldly. "Because you're both fired."

The man's thin face tightened with anger. "What about the wages you owe?" His assistant nodded agreement.

"How dare you mention that." Jennifer gestured with her hand. "You've already been paid for weeks when you did nothing."

"This was your fault, not ours," he said curtly. "And you'd better send our wages, or I'll let everyone know that you don't pay your help."

"You'd better not, or I'll see to it that everyone knows how you cheated me."

His eyes glinted, but he and his assistant left without another word, leaving Jennifer to straighten out the accounts, regain her artists, and attract new customers.

Jennifer worked hard, and by November her gallery was once again filled with paintings, prints, and sculptures, and she'd rescheduled all the exhibitions that had been canceled. But most important was her own healing process.

By the time Mayor Gill was defeated by Dilling in the recall election in February, Jennifer had landed a contract to display ancient Chinese art objects, a coup for her as well as for Seattle.

"I'm really excited about this," she told Diana that night at supper.

Diana grinned at her enthusiasm. "I'm glad to see you happy again—that you've realized your life isn't over because Justin left."

Jennifer glanced away. "But I don't think I'll ever stop feeling guilty about hurting him, even though I hear he's doing well in San Francisco."

Diana put down her fork. "You had good reasons for not telling him about me. Now you have to stand by your original decision, Mother. After all, you didn't know then how things would turn out later." She hesitated, smiling again. "Remember when I'd have a little problem while growing up and you'd always remind me that I was like everyone else—that I had to cope with whatever life placed in my path? You've been a good example of that lately, and it's been helpful to me to watch you."

"Is something wrong?" Jennifer asked, with motherly concern.

She nodded slowly. "I still see Damon now at board meetings . . . and Rand Woodrow." She paused, and Jennifer felt a sinking sensation in her stomach. "You know that I've always liked Rand. But because he's a Woodrow, I know I shouldn't like him too much . . . but I do."

Shock sent ripples of fear into Jennifer's body. Was Diana interested in Rand Woodrow as more than a friend? As she watched Diana's face and heard the soft tone to her voice, Jennifer knew: Diana was in love with him.

What next? Jennifer asked herself. It was as though an angry God were punishing her. Maybe she's not really in love with him, Jennifer argued mentally. Maybe it was just a flirtation.

As the weeks passed Jennifer's hope proved futile; Rand began escorting Diana to concerts and plays and dinners at leading hotels, such as the Perry, which had been designed by a French architect for its First Hill location, and the Frye Hotel, which supposedly was the handsomest building in the Northwest, and the Sorrento with its dine-in-the-sky restaurant.

As she watched their friendship grow Jennifer became more apprehensive. How would Rachael react? When

Diana told her that Rand and his brother Simon had begun to resolve their differences, Jennifer was even more worried. Rachael could cause trouble at any time.

Finally Jennifer decided to broach the subject directly. "Are you in love with him, Diana?"

Diana's response was immediate. "Yes, I love him."

Jennifer was suddenly at a loss for words and deathly afraid for her daughter's happiness. Please, God, don't let Diana be hurt, she prayed silently.

"It'll be all right," Diana said softly, knowing what her mother was thinking. "Rachael won't dare interfere."

"The most important thing in the world to me is your happiness," Jennifer said, softly.

"Thanks, Mother . . . for understanding."

Jennifer understood all too well and was frightened. She didn't want her daughter to be punished for loving the wrong man.

"NEW EVIDENCE FOUND IN DEATH OF EDWIN WOODROW. HIS WIFE RACHAEL SOUGHT FOR QUESTIONING," Jennifer read aloud. "My God," she said, her eyes scanning the front-page story.

"It's all over town," Jamie said. "Mara Polemis told some of her cronies that Rachael had poisoned Edwin Woodrow and that she could prove it. Naturally, she claims she hasn't associated with Rachael since learning about it."

"But it doesn't say how she found out, or if she could prove her accusations," Jennifer said, looking up.

"Christ!" Jamie was pacing the room angrily. "I feel for Damon . . . being married to that bitch. I don't know who's worse . . . Mara or Rachael."

"How's Damon taking it?"

"That's just it. Damon's out of town and not due back for several days. I don't know if he's been told, but I'm sure as hell not doing it."

Jennifer's thoughts were spinning. "So that was it—Rachael's reason for doing Mara's dirty work. Mara must have known Rachael poisoned Edwin."

Jamie whistled. "And when Rachael didn't succeed in getting Diana completely out of Damon's life, Mara got even with her."

"Who knows . . . maybe there's even more to it. Otherwise, why did Mara wait so long to speak up? Diana left Damon's office almost a year ago."

Jamie stopped pacing, his eyes narrowed in thought. "I know Damon and Mara had an argument shortly before he left. He told me that she'd wanted to go with him to Alaska and he'd said no."

As Jennifer walked home that night she had one thought: I hope Rachael didn't tell Mara her suspicions about Diana.

That evening Diana reported on her conversation with Rand. "He told me that Mara has focused her rage about her marriage problems on Rachael, and no one can understand why, because they were good friends. But Mara's raging at everyone, like she's lost her mind."

"What did you tell Rand?"

Diana's dark eyes were troubled. "I . . . I didn't explain about Rachael coming here, if that's what you mean."

"Mara needs to believe that her husband is interested in another woman, because he's not interested in her. But she doesn't dare bring you into it for fear of losing Damon for good," Jennifer added. "She must be eaten up with jealousy, crazy from feeling rejected."

"Poor Father," Diana said, her eyes suddenly bright with tears. "It must be a nightmare being married to that witch."

Jennifer moved to the window, her gaze on the bay, where the evening sun had gilded the water with pathways of reflected gold. Poor all of us, she thought. Because she hadn't trusted, she'd perpetrated a lie that had affected the lives of everyone involved. The price had been too high. If she'd been Damon's wife, then Diana would be his legal daughter, Mara wouldn't be tormenting him and Rachael would never have been a threat. She turned back to the room where memories of past mistakes hovered in the shadows of the dying day; she knew the magnitude of what they'd all lost . . . because of her.

The next morning Jennifer listened to the growing gossip with resignation. There were rumors about Rachael and Simon being lovers. The police had questioned Mara, but Rachael had supposedly disappeared, and Simon claimed he didn't know where she'd gone.

By the time Jennifer locked up the gallery for the day,

she wished she hadn't agreed to have dinner with Nellie. But once outside in the sea air, her spirits lifted. She ran to catch the cable car that went up First Hill, knowing she'd pass within a block of the Woodrow mansion.

Quietly Rachael let herself out through the back door of her house. Simon was already fast asleep; she'd seen to that, even though his flabby body had become repulsive to her. She glanced around before starting down the street. No one must see her, she told herself, not after she'd convinced Simon to tell the police he didn't know where she was.

The night was without a moon, but she'd know the way to Mara's house if she were blindfolded, she mused, and it was vital to her position in Seattle society that Mara say she'd lied. She would get Mara's retraction, she reassured herself as she touched Simon's revolver hidden in her pocket.

At the back entrance to Mara's house she fumbled for the spare key she knew was always kept under the mat. Before unlocking the door, she looked around the dark yard once more; Damon's Ford was gone.

She closed the door softly behind her. Before starting up the back stairs she took off her shoes. Once again she went over her plan: Mara would sign a confession saying that her stories about Rachael were all lies.

Rachael's hand tightened on the railing. She had trusted Mara with too many of her secrets, she reminded herself, confiding in her that she'd intentionally given Edwin too much medicine. But she wasn't a murderess; he was already dying, and she'd only speeded up the process. Rand had not been able to prove his accusation because the doctor had found no evidence of any drug other than the medicine he'd prescribed.

At the second floor she hesitated. Her thoughts switched to Jennifer. At times she hated her father for bringing Jennifer into their lives. She had been delighted when she finally thought to check the birth certificates at the courthouse, a long process that had eventually revealed the truth: Diana was Jennifer's child. But she still didn't know who had fathered Diana. She suspected it was Damon, and that was why she hadn't exposed Jennifer; that information would have destroyed high-strung Mara. Everything had calmed down after Diana had left the company, but when Damon had asked for a divorce recently, Mara had gone to pieces, irrationally blaming Rachael, assuming Damon was in love with Diana.

Rachael stepped into Mara's room. A small bedside lamp cast a swath of light across the pink satin coverlet, and she saw that Mara was asleep. Rachael shook her gently. Mara sat up immediately, the blankets falling from her, her eyes wide with alarm.

"Rachael . . . what are you doing here?"

"Get up," Rachael said coldly. "You're going downstairs."

"I'm not going anywhere." Her momentary fear had turned to anger. "How dare you break into my house in the middle of the night. The police are looking for you, and I'm going to call them . . . right now."

Without hesitation Rachael pulled the revolver from her pocket. She hated to threaten Mara, even after what Mara had done to her, but it was necessary if she was to clear her name.

Mara stared, measuring Rachael and the gun. "What are you going to do?" she asked, her face crumpling from sudden fear. "You wouldn't hurt me, would you? . . . We're friends."

"Friends don't destroy each other," Rachael retorted.

"I didn't mean to destroy you. I just told a couple of women, to get even with you, and then they reported what I'd said." Tears flowed down her face, and she began to tremble uncontrollably. "It wasn't my fault."

"I'm giving you a chance to retract what you said."

Mara mumbled all the way down to the dining room, where Rachael lit a kerosene lamp. She ordered Mara to sit at the table. Then she brought out a sheet of paper and a pen.

"What is it?"

"A confession that you lied, and why."

"But I didn't—you know you really killed Edwin."

"I said sign!" Rachael cried, losing her patience.

Mara burst into sobs as she read what Rachael had written. "If I sign this, Damon will hate me. He'll know that I'm jealous of Diana, that I had you get her out of his office." Her voice had risen to a hysterical whine. "This paper will destroy me. I won't sign . . . I won't."

Mara leapt from the chair and grabbed Rachael's arm, trying to wrestle the gun from her. They struggled, Mara scratched at Rachael's face and beat against her arms and body. Fear shot through Rachael; she knew Mara was out of control. She would shoot Rachael if she got hold of the gun.

Twisting suddenly, Rachael knocked her captor off balance, freeing herself, while Mara fell backward against the table and crashed to the floor with the lamp.

Mara lay stunned. Rachael bent over her, calling her name, trying to bring her friend back to consciousness. At last she became aware of a sound behind her. Jerking her head around, she saw that the fallen lamp had ignited the curtains. Within moments the flames were licking up the papered walls. She sprang to her feet; the room was filling with smoke.

For a minute she didn't know what to do. While she hesitated, the fire spread. Dropping the gun, she ran to the door and yanked it open, only to see the rush of air fan the flames into an inferno. Dry sobs shook her. She knew she'd failed; she hadn't gotten Mara's signature.

Mara . . . she couldn't leave her to burn, she thought desperately. She turned and ran back to the woman who'd been her friend. But before she could bend to take hold of the lifeless form, Mara's hand shot out and grabbed her ankle. For a suspended second, Rachael struggled to regain her balance. Then she was falling, falling toward the fingers of fire that were snaking all around her.

As Rachael hit the floor the brilliant orange and red and yellow of the room snapped off, sending her to a dark place that struck a moment of pure terror in her soul. The last sound she heard was her own scream.

Jennifer and Nellie hurried along the sidewalk toward the fire. They'd seen the glow and knew the fire was in the vicinity of Damon's house. They were following all the other people who'd been called out of their beds by the fire alarm.

"My God, it *is* Damon's house," Jennifer cried.

The whole lower floor was blazing and the flames were eating their way toward the high, pointed roof. The yard was illuminated by the fire blossoming against the night sky.

"Mr. Polemis is away on a trip!" a man shouted near them.

"But his wife is home . . . may be trapped in there!" another voice cried.

The words paralyzed Jennifer. She remembered the great fire of 'eighty-nine, when Al Cox had died in her office, and the day she'd burned her own cotton. Fires always seemed to change her life.

The fire exploded through the roof with a boom of thunder. As they watched in horror the front doors burst open to frame a figure engulfed in flames and screaming in agony. Arms spread in supplication, it tumbled down the steps to collapse on the ground.

A hush fell on the crowd as the firemen rushed forward to smother the flames. A strange aroma of roasting flesh mingled with acrid smell of smoke.

"It's Mara Polemis," someone whispered, as Mara's shrill screams rose above the roar of the fire.

"Rachael—it was Rachael—she tried to kill me." Mara's words were broken by her screams. "I'm dying . . . but she's in there . . . in the fire." Abruptly her convulsed limbs stilled as she lost consciousness.

Simon arrived in time to hear Mara's words and immediately darted toward the house that now quivered like scarlet gauze. He was restrained from running into the fire.

"Rachael!" he cried, struggling against the hands that held him. At that moment the walls fell inward upon themselves, sending a shower of sparks up through the flames to the night sky, where they exploded like Chinese rockets. If Rachael was indeed in the Polemis house, she was dead.

Damon rushed back to Seattle and sat at his wife's bedside while she hovered on the verge of death. When Mara was able to speak, she told him that Rachael had tried to kill her—that Rachael had knocked her unconscious and then set fire to the house. The authorities ruled that

Rachael had been trapped by the fire she'd set, and died by her own hand.

Jennifer had a strong feeling that there was more to the story than what Mara had told. But with Rachael's death, no one would ever know what had really happened; Mara would never jeopardize her own position. The investigation of Rachael's involvement in Edwin Woodrow's death had also been dropped, and Jennifer vowed to lay her old fears to rest as well. Rachael could no longer hurt her or Diana, and despite her relief she felt a lingering sadness for Rachael. Life should have been different for Joseph's beloved daughter.

In July, when the Golden Potlatch was celebrated with a week of carnival and parades and street dances, Jennifer knew her sorrow was lifting. The Potlatch, based on an Indian tradition, was a huge success, and when Jennifer heard Martha addressing the crowd as a spokesperson for her people, she was moved to tears.

"Remember the words of the great Chief Sealth, after whom Seattle was named," Martha said. "'At night, when the streets of your cities are silent and you think them deserted, they will throng with the returning hosts that once filled and still love this beautiful land. The white man will never be alone. Let him be just and deal kindly with my people, for the dead are not powerless.'

"I add my words to those of a noble and wise chief. May we all live together in peace while we reap the bounty of the beautiful land we all love." As Martha sat down applause shook the rafters.

Jennifer often thought of Martha's words as summer passed into fall. There *was* a place for everyone in Seattle.

Shortly before Thanksgiving, Jennifer heard that Mara's burns were healing, but her mind was not. Mara was unable to accept her disfigurement. Jamie reported that Damon was exhausted from trying to cope with Mara, a woman who'd always been high-strung, critical, and selfish. When Jennifer heard that she'd finally had a nervous breakdown, she wasn't surprised. The term of Mara's hospital confinement was extended indefinitely, and when she didn't respond to treatment, she was transferred to a mental institution.

As the fall rains intensified, heralding winter, Jennifer's thoughts were constantly with Damon, a man married forever to a woman whose prognosis for recovery was poor . . . a man who was all alone with his grief.

Chapter Twenty-seven

"Well, Mother?" Diana prompted, waiting for Jennifer's response. "I wouldn't have brought this up, but I'm worried about Damon . . . about . . . my father."

Jennifer pushed her chair away from the table, picked up their Sunday breakfast plates and took them to the sink for the housekeeper to wash later. Her hand trembled as she turned on the faucet. She knew that Damon had been through hell since the fire. She'd wanted to go to him many times over the fall months but hadn't dared. Now Damon appeared to have lost interest in everything.

"I wouldn't have suggested this, but—"

Jennifer turned, waving a hand to silence her daughter. "I know, Diana. But to tell him—to have him know that I lied . . . I'm scared."

"I understand that, Mother. But he needs to know that he has someone in the world, something to live for," she said softly, her dark eyes troubled. "Both Rand and Jamie say that he's not even interested in his company—that he's just going through the motions, as though he's waiting for his own death."

Another kind of fear rippled through Jennifer. "Is he sick?"

Diana shook her head. "Not yet. But it's time to tell him the truth."

She stared at her daughter. Although she knew she couldn't deny Damon hope, Jennifer also realized he would hate her for having deceived him . . . for her unforgivable lie.

Slowly Jennifer nodded, her fear for the man she loved taking precedence over her guilt. Diana was right; she could no longer consider only herself.

"Why don't you call him and arrange a meeting," Jennifer said finally, glancing out at the drizzily January day. "For this afternoon." She knew she couldn't wait now that she'd agreed to tell him. Her stomach knotted. Maybe knowing he had a daughter would give Damon new purpose, she told herself. But she knew that to give him hope would take hers away . . . a frightening thought.

Dressed in a slim gray wool suit trimmed in black velvet, Jennifer paused behind Diana, who was about to lift the door knocker. Diana hesitated, turning to Jennifer. As Jennifer nodded, Diana let the knocker fall.

As the heavy sound echoed into the shadows of the hall like indistinguishable words from the past, the ghosts from Jennifer's memories suddenly materialized to haunt her present. Oh, God, let this be the right thing to do, she prayed silently.

Suddenly, Damon was standing framed in the open doorway, a slow smile softening his face, the angles sharper and creases much deeper than Jennifer remembered. "Please come in." The familiar voice sent heat coursing through her veins. He ushered them into a small parlor, then waited, obviously curious about the visit.

Jennifer glanced at Diana, who was also waiting for her to speak. Then she returned her gaze to Damon, whose dark eyes immediately captured hers. The day was dreary, and he'd turned on the brass banquet lamps that stood on tables at both ends of the overstuffed sofa where she sat. The glow through the silk fringed shade touched Damon's face with a golden tinge, illuminating the silver streaks in his black hair and tiny mysterious lights in his eyes.

Jennifer swallowed, trying to decide how to begin, dismissing each thought that surfaced in her mind. She must tell him. She noticed how painfully thin he'd become.

"Well?" he prompted, a note of humor in his tone. "Surely what you want to say can't be so terrible that you're struck speechless, Jennifer."

"Mother," Diana began softly as Jennifer still hesitated. "I think you must . . . just say it."

"Mother?" Damon repeated, glancing between them.

Diana's eyes widened, realizing the word had slipped out. "That's—"

"The name Diana calls me now," Jennifer finished for her. "It's what we came to tell you, Damon." She took a deep breath, trying to slow her heartbeats. "Diana is my daughter, not Joseph's," she said, and her words grated the silence like the discordant notes of an untuned instrument.

His body stiffened, his face drained of color. "Your . . . daughter?"

She nodded, fear pounding through her as she watched the progression of his thoughts, knowing the exact moment when the truth hit him.

He staggered backward, grabbing the mantel for support. Diana jumped up and went to him. "Are you all right?"

He stared at her, mutely. Then his eyes shifted to Jennifer, as a silent question hovered between them, the grim specter of the lie that spanned over two decades. His expression went from disbelief to anger and finally to sadness. Her vision blurred with tears, but she didn't look away: she had to face it. She was the one who had lied.

She nodded slowly, her voice barely a whisper. "Diana is your daughter."

His lips moved but made no sound. The tension threatened Jennifer's self-control. But the first move had to be Damon's.

Diana stepped back, and Jennifer read doubt on her face. We've made a mistake in coming here, Jennifer cried inwardly. Oh, my God, we shouldn't have come. A moment later she was on her feet, hoping her trembling limbs would hold her up. But before Jennifer could say they were leaving, Diana moved toward her father.

"I know we've shocked you," she began, her face flushed with embarrassment. "I'm sorry we came. I made Mother do this, and I'm afraid it was a mistake." She hesitated, but her gaze, so like her father's, didn't waver. "I was worried about you. You see I knew you were my father . . . and cared about you . . . even though you didn't know about me." She spoke faster, trying to break down the barrier. "You're so alone now . . . so unhappy . . . that I wanted you to know about me . . . that I love you. I wanted you to know that you had someone in the world who is a part of you."

Then, slowly at first, Damon moved toward his daughter. As they embraced, a great wracking sob tore free from his throat, his shoulders shuddered as he cried, a sight that shredded what was left of Jennifer's control. Her Damon, a man who'd always shown an indomitable spirit, an ability to cope with the world and build an empire, a man above men, was weeping over finding a daughter.

She grabbed the table for support as an emotion more powerful than any she'd ever known took hold of her. Damon had been united with his daughter, the one she'd borne for him, raised all those years and was now giving back to him . . . a daughter he was accepting with humility and joy.

"No wonder I always thought you resembled my mother," Damon said as his first wave of emotion passed. "She's your grandmother." He held Diana at arm's length, staring down into her smiling face, the tears already drying on her pink cheeks. "I've always admired you, wished I had a daughter like you and—" He broke off, once more hugging her close. "Now I learn that you are mine. God still lives in heaven after all."

Jennifer turned away, filled with joy that he finally knew about Diana and sadness for all the years of separation. But whatever the cost, she *had* done the right thing. Damon was like a new man: confidence was back in his tone, the rigid set to his body had relaxed, and he'd obviously found a reason to go on with his life.

She walked to the window and stared out over Elliott Bay, remembering the day when she'd first seen it from the deck of a ship, the same day she'd met Damon . . . and fallen in love. Her sobs came then, great heaving, tearing, convulsive sobs that took her breath away. She slipped to the floor, burying her head in her arms, wishing she were somewhere else but not having the strength to go.

Gradually, she became aware of arms going around her, gently pulling her against the lean hardness of a male body. Her lashes fluttered open; Damon's face was only inches above hers. Kneeling next to her, he was dabbing at her face with a handkerchief.

She covered her face with her hands, unable to look into his eyes—eyes no longer like cold black stones, but warm as a summer night. She was humiliated, but she couldn't stop crying, hating herself for what she'd done to the two people she loved . . . Damon and Diana.

"It's all right, Mother," Diana said from behind Damon. "Please stop crying—it's not your fault . . . none of it."

Jennifer shook her head, not able to answer.

Damon pulled her to her feet and led her to the sofa. "Jennifer, I was angry at first, but I'm not now. I can't tell you what this means to me."

She looked at him; he seemed sincere.

"We'll talk this out later," he said softly. "So that I can understand . . . so we can all understand."

Jennifer nodded, and after a few minutes was able to speak, beginning in a quavering voice, gradually explaining. "I don't expect you to understand," she said. "It all seemed so important back then . . . and now so foolish."

Damon was silent. Jennifer looked away, willing her fragile emotions under control.

"I love you, Jennifer," Damon whispered suddenly. "I've never stopped." He paused, taking their hands. "I'm sorry for all the lost years, but I'm also happy for those that are still ahead of us, years none of us will waste." Again he hesitated. "I understand, Jennifer, and I accept half of the blame. We were both wrong."

"And I love you both," Diana said softly. "I wish we'd been a real family while I was growing up, but I have you both now . . . and that's good enough."

Jennifer swallowed hard, smiling for the first time. Whatever happened now, she'd finally exorcised her lie. Even though Damon was a married man and would never be hers in the eyes of the world, they would always love each other . . . and would always share Diana.

They talked for hours, and by the time Damon drove them home, they'd banished the last ghost. But they'd all agreed that it was too late to reveal their secret to the world.

"But that's a small price to pay," Jennifer assured herself. Now that her past was no longer shrouded in lies, she'd placed her guilt into perspective, although she'd always regret what she'd done to Justin. Most of all she was grateful that her relationship to Damon was at long last based on trust as well as love. She was thankful for each day and night spent with Damon, hours of happiness such as she'd never known.

With the coming of spring Jennifer noticed the deepening relationship between Diana and Rand. She liked Rand; he had a quick mind and was considerate, not at all like his father had been. When Rand and Diana announced that they were getting married, it was Nellie who seemed a bit hesitant. When Rand had revealed that his brother Simon had become a virtual recluse, Nellie seemed unusually interested. Simon had even refused to stand up for Rand at his wedding. Simon obviously wanted nothing to do with the Carlyles.

As champagne toasts were being made at the party in honor of the engagement, Nellie suddenly stood up. "What I'm going to say will surprise all of you." She hesitated. Her head was piled high with twists and curls, her face powdered and rouged, and her crimson velvet gown revealed too much bust, making Jennifer suddenly think of the day she'd first seen Nellie.

"I've always had a policy of just speaking my mind . . . so I guess that's what I'll do. I've decided to reveal an old secret, one that might be important to Rand.

"I brought Jennifer and Jamie to Seattle to start a new life, and I believed my only brother would help me." While she paused, little Gregory squirmed in his chair, but he was the only one whose eyes were not glued to Nellie. "My brother was a successful businessman, his second wife came from a respectable pioneer family, however, and he wanted nothing to do with me. In fact, he ordered me to leave town . . . or else." Nellie grinned. "Of course I refused to go. But I did agree that I wouldn't reveal our relationship as long as he left me alone. And I've kept that promise until now, when it might be wise to tell the truth."

Jennifer realized that Nellie was relishing her own performance.

"Edwin Woodrow was my brother."

"My father?" Rand said, his gray eyes wide with surprise. As she nodded he stood up, dwarfing the old woman with his six feet. "You're my aunt?"

"I figured knowing the truth might not embarrass you, that you might like being part of a family again."

Slowly a big grin spread over Rand's face, and he grabbed Nellie and embraced her, endearing himself forever to Jennifer. "Embarrass me? . . . my God. You should be ashamed of *my* family . . . my branch of family."

When Simon heard about Nellie's revelation, he angrily vowed he'd never believe a prostitute's lie. He definitely would not be at the wedding Rand and Diana had set for early September.

"It's too bad about Simon," Nellie told Damon and Jennifer after the ceremony in Jennifer's parlor. "He missed seeing Damon give Diana away and Jamie being the best man."

"And me being a bridesmaid," Elizabeth said, overhearing her grandmother's wry comment.

Nellie stared at the eleven-year-old. "You have a bad habit of listening to the conversations of your elders," she said, but the twinkle in her eyes spoke of pride in Elizabeth who, looking like both parents, was a budding beauty.

Elizabeth sighed impatiently and flounced off.

Another girl with the Carlyle pride and independence, Jennifer thought, hoping it wouldn't be misdirected and cause trouble when she grew up. As she watched Elizabeth she felt a shiver of apprehension, one she quickly dismissed when she saw Diana going upstairs to change into her traveling suit for her honeymoon trip to San Francisco.

"You'd better go up with her," Damon whispered in Jennifer's ear. "These are her last minutes as our single daughter; now she's Rand's wife as well."

Jennifer smiled, wishing she could tell the world that Damon was her lover, that he was Diana's father. She could see the pride and happiness in the glowing lights deep in his eyes. Diana's marriage had brought them even closer. She turned and went to wish her daughter a long life of happiness with the man she'd chosen for a husband.

* * *

Diana and Rand spent a month in California, and when they returned, they moved into a large house only two blocks from Jennifer. Even though Mara's condition hadn't improved, and it was common knowledge that she'd probably never leave the hospital, Seattle society still considered Damon married and frowned on his continued friendship with Jennifer, whose past had not been forgotten. But the family ignored the gossip, and Jennifer felt no guilt about being with the man she loved.

Within a year Diana and Rand had their first child, a boy they named John Randolph Woodrow. Rand doted on Diana and his son, and he spent every free minute with them. He even got up with Diana for the middle-of-the-night feedings. Diana's marriage was happy, giving Jennifer and Damon great satisfaction. Sharing a grandson was a sheer joy, expecially for Damon who'd never raised a child. Even when Simon sent Rand on trips to their distant sawmills and logging operations, the trips never caused a problem in Diana's marriage.

"I want many sons," she told her parents, "so that they can help their father expand the growing lumber industry."

"And one or two of them to take over a shipping company I know about," Damon said, grinning.

Chapter Twenty-eight

"I'm glad we changed the wing design," Jamie said. "This one will *really* fly . . . maybe even seventy-five miles an hour."

Fred Aeschliman nodded as the plane moved across the glassy surface of bay on its floats, its straight wings level, its propeller whirling. As it lifted into the clear June sky the plane tilted dangerously, as though it were about to fall back into the water.

Jamie watched the plane reach altitude and level off before going into a turn. "Think the wings'll hold together when he banks?"

"Christ, I hope so. There's no way of knowing if the weights and stresses and motor power are balanced until it's tested."

Jamie's eyes never left the plane as it circled above them, roaring and sputtering. The engine, which they'd hung between the upper and lower wings, was awkward, and he knew the aeroplane was still a little heavy for its power.

Then the plane made its approach for a landing, hitting the water at a wrong angle, bouncing before nosing into the bay near the dock. The pilot scrambled onto the wing struts and threw his goggles aside, but the plane settled back onto its float and didn't sink.

An immediate shout went up among the people lining the shore. "You did it, Jamie. . . . The goddamned thing really flies."

Jamie and Fred pounded each other on the back, beside themselves with the excitement of success. It was later that the pilot informed them that more work was needed on the trailing edge of the wing to stabilize the plane when it banked.

"If the wind hadn't been right, I think I'd of lost her," he said. "It needs a better balance of propeller pull against machine drag through the air, and wing lift against gravity pull."

"But we're getting there." Fred grinned. "Think how far we've advanced in a short time."

Jamie met his partner's eyes. "And think how far we're going in the next couple years."

On the fourth of July, 1914, William Boeing's pusher-prop hydroplane was given a successful test flight on Lake Washington as Jamie and Fred stood among the crowd who watched. Jamie realized that competition was growing in the aeroplane industry, a fact that inspired him to greater achievement.

By the time the Panama Canal opened the next month, Damon had expanded his shipping company once more, the length of the voyage on the ocean route to the Atlantic having been cut by many weeks. The old ways of Seattle were gradually making way for new ones: saloons had been banished, better building codes implemented, and labor union movements organized by the workers. The completion of the forty-two-story Smith Building was cause for celebration; it was the tallest building west of the Mississippi.

As a war threatened in Europe, Jamie's company had a sudden surge of growth. Jamie and Fred now employed a dozen men and were selling aeroplanes as fast as they could build them. He'd explained to Jennifer that a war needed weapons, and he anticipated a demand for aeroplanes, a point of view he'd used to interest more investors. With the added financial support, he again gambled on the future of aeroplanes, working on a model that could be used as a fighter plane.

"By the time Gregory is old enough to be a part of the company, I intend it to be a huge success," he told Jennifer many times during the following months.

Jennifer had great faith in Jamie, and knew that Martha was behind him even though the two often disagreed on what was best for their children. Jamie opposed Martha's days away from the family. Martha, trying to compensate, began to take her children along with her when she could. But Jennifer was troubled about Elizabeth. Although she was blossoming into a beautiful young girl, she was also too outspoken in her views for one who'd just turned fourteen. Jennifer wondered if Martha had made a mistake by exposing Elizabeth to her charitable work and forceful opinions. Elizabeth announced that she was against the United States becoming involved in a European war, that unions were important for workers, and that the rich should be required to share their wealth with the poor. She stated flatly that the socialist group called the Wobblies had a perfect right to march and wave red flags and speak out against the principles of America. Nellie had laughed Elizabeth's observations away as growing pains, pointing out that she loved to ice-skate on Green Lake and play baseball like all the other kids. But Jennifer hadn't laughed; she'd seen the glint of determination in the girl's eyes.

Jennifer gradually realized that too much of her time was spent running the gallery and not at her easel painting. She sold the gallery and settled down to painting each day and spending as much time with Damon as possible. She loved sharing his life and seldom remembered that they weren't really married, that Mara still lived in the hazy world of a mental hospital.

By April of 1917, when President Wilson declared war on Germany, Jamie and Martha had just moved into their elegant new mansion near Nellie's home on First Hill. On a sunny spring Sunday they held a housewarming party.

"It's a fine home," Damon said, shaking hands with a beaming Jamie. "A symbol of your success."

"And years of hard work," Jennifer added fondly.

"But far too elegant and costly when there are people starving," Elizabeth said coolly, stopping the conversation as all heads turned to her. "America is becoming too influenced by the profiteers who wanted the war," she went on. "If we weren't so concerned with 'things,' we'd have had the sense to stay out of the stupid mess."

"Elizabeth," Jamie said sharply. "That's enough of that foolishness."

Jennifer stared at the abruptly sullen dark-haired girl

who had Martha's brilliant blue eyes. But the resemblance to her mother stopped there; Martha's expression had always been sensitive and gentle; Elizabeth's was stubborn and closed.

Apprehension washed over Jennifer. My God . . . what was happening to Elizabeth? she wondered. How could a young girl be so opinionated, so aligned to groups such as the Wobblies, who maintained that they had been enslaved by powerful employers and were unable to provide for their families despite their long hours of work. Didn't Elizabeth know that the Carlyle family businesses were fair to their workers, even though some of their competitors were not? Elizabeth had occasionally been snubbed because she was part Indian, and Jennifer wondered if perhaps this had created her empathy with downtrodden people.

"Well, I love the house," Gregory said, with his usual optimism. He did a little dance in the wide hall. "There's room for my whole class to attend my birthday party."

Gregory's antics dispelled the awkwardness created by his sister, and soon everyone was once more talking, joking, and toasting the house and family.

As Jennifer watched Elizabeth moving through the group, talking with everyone, she couldn't shake her uneasiness. Elizabeth could be friendly when she chose to be, and she did well in school, but her basic attitude worried Jennifer.

"When she meets the right young man, she'll forget causes," Damon said.

She smiled into the dark eyes she loved. "Perhaps you're right. But you've been unusually quiet today. . . . Is something wrong?"

His lids lowered, guarding his expression. Then, as though forcing himself, he smiled. "Nothing that can't wait until later."

She stared, feeling as though she'd just gone down First Hill in a speeding automobile, and her stomach had been left at the top. A sudden thought hit her. "You already told me about your ship that was sunk by a German submarine on the Atlantic."

"So I did," he said, as though glad to change the subject. "But that wasn't a loss I can't eat."

"Profits soaring?" Jamie asked, overhearing the remark.

Damon nodded, flashing a smile, and Jennifer caught her breath. Nothing must happen to him . . . nothing must come between their love.

"This damnable global conflict has helped my company, though; we've shifted into high gear to meet the demand for more aeroplanes, or airplanes, if you will. At any other time I'd be worried about all my competition, like that new Boeing Airplane Company."

"Has the thought crossed any of your minds that you might have to go fight?" Rand suddenly asked as he and Diana joined the conversation.

"I'm too old," Damon replied, "and the importance of Jamie's company will keep him in Seattle as well."

"Do . . . you think you'll have to go?" Diana asked Rand, and Jennifer saw fear in her eyes.

Rand pulled Diana down next to him. "If it doesn't end soon, it's possible. Simon is head of our company . . . not me."

Jennifer moved away from the group, feeling chilled. She found her shawl and draped it over her shoulders. The day had started out as one of joy and festivities, but now there was something ominous in the air.

That night, as Jennifer sat in her dressing gown having a nightcap with Damon, she saw that he was finally about to tell her what was bothering him. It's a financial problem, she told herself. She knew he'd invested in a huge shipyard on Lake Union now that the locks connected the lake with Puget Sound and the Lake Washington Ship Canal formed a waterway between the two lakes.

Abruptly he placed his glass on the night table. "There's no easy way to say this," he began, his dark eyes trapping little lights from the lamp. "Mara is being released from the hospital."

Stunned, Jennifer stared at him, seeing her own anguish reflected in his expression. The room was suddenly deathly still; only the clock beside the bed and the night sounds beyond the window disturbed the silence. "When?"

"The end of the week. I've known for a couple of weeks, but I couldn't tell you. I'd hoped—God help me—that she wouldn't really be released. And I didn't want to spoil our final days together."

"Final—" The word hit her like a death sentence . . . or worse . . . a life sentence without Damon.

Gently he pulled her into his arms, caressing her body with hands so tender she wanted to cry.

"Oh, Jen, I love you so much. . . . How can I lose you again?"

She couldn't speak—there were no words.

"It'll be hell for us, but—"

"We can't see each other," she whispered, completing his sentence, a thing they often did for each other, so wholly were they bound together: their thoughts, their feelings, and their bodies.

"Not for a while." He stroked her hair, which she'd loosened from its chignon. "My beautiful Jennifer, still as lovely and shining as that first day." His fingers traced the length of her arms, the contours of her face and the curves of her body.

"Not at all?"

He shook his head. "It wouldn't be wise. Mara has focused a lot of hate on you because of something mysterious Rachael had hinted at."

She stiffened. "Has she ever mentioned Diana?"

"Well, yes. You know how she resented Diana in my office. But she's never indicated she knows the real relationship between us . . . and she must never know or she'll cause trouble for Diana and her family."

"Damon, now that Mara is being released, why can't you get a divorce?"

"It won't be possible at first." A haunted expression flickered across his face. "She has no one but me now. She's horribly disfigured, and I think I should help her get back into the world, but when she's well enough to manage on her own, I plan to divorce her, I promise."

By the end of the week Jennifer realized that Damon was right.

But as Mara took her place in Damon's waterfront apartment, Jennifer was bereft, suddenly knowing the true meaning of "being the other woman"—the one who lived in the twilight world of secret meetings, the one who wasn't recognized by the world, the one who came second to a whining, complaining woman.

Jennifer's turmoil was pushed aside unexpectedly when Nellie was stricken with heart problems. Frightened, Jennifer insisted Nellie move into her house until she'd recovered.

Diana decided she'd picked enough roses for the dining room bouquet. She smiled to herself; she wanted everything to be perfect when she told Rand tonight that she was finally pregnant again. As she turned toward the front porch, her glance fell on a woman walking slowly and painfully along the sidewalk. At first her gaze lingered because of the woman's shabby clothing, but it was held when she realized that the woman wasn't as old as Diana had first thought, only stooped and tired from—overwork?—or illness?

To her surprise the woman stopped, her eyes on Diana. "Are you—Diana Woodrow?"

Diana nodded, her curiosity rising.

"I'm—you don't know me," the woman began in a labored voice. "My name is Laura Ryan."

As Diana waited for her to to on she impatiently hoped John wasn't up from his nap and getting into the lemon pies she'd left cooling in the kitchen.

The woman's face was prematurely lined, her complexion like her hair, dull and lifeless. What did she want, Diana wondered, directions? No, Laura Ryan had called her by name.

"I have a ten-year-old son . . . Stephan," she began and broke off with a coughing spasm.

"Can I get you a drink?" Diana asked, suddenly alarmed.

The woman shook her head, the bout passing with little choking sounds as she swallowed back the coughs. "I'm very sick . . . dying." Her gaze lifted, and Diana could see pain in her eyes, both mental and physical. "I've come to you for help."

Diana's eyes widened. "But I don't even know you."

She nodded. "It's for my son. . . . He's a good boy or I wouldn't be here . . . saying things that'll hurt you."

A chill prickled over Diana's sun-warmed skin. "What things?"

"Stephan is Rand's son," she said, and began coughing again.

Diana stared, rooted to the grass, her mind rejecting the woman's words. It was impossible. Rand couldn't have fathered a son with this beggar woman.

When the woman slumped to the ground, unable to stop coughing, Diana ran into the house and returned in seconds with a glass of water. As Laura Ryan regained her composure she told Diana a strange story.

"Years ago I loved Rand. His family was very hard on him, and he needed me, but things didn't work out for us. I knew I wasn't good enough for a Woodrow, and I stepped aside even though I'd given birth to Stephan. But now I'm dying, with no family to take my boy."

Words escaped Diana. But she could see that Laura was telling the truth, that she honestly didn't want to hurt Diana, but she had no choice; she had to find a place for her son after she was gone.

Laura grabbed Diana's hand. "Would you help my boy?—see he's taken care of?—there ain't no one else."

"I'll . . . look into it," Diana replied, still at a loss. Maybe Laura Ryan was lying, she reflected. But the practical part of her mind rejected the thought. Hadn't Laura, sick to the point of collapse, walked up the steep hill from town? If her story was true, then why hadn't Rand— no—she wouldn't allow herself to think ill of the man she loved and respected. She'd wait until he could explain, tell her the whole thing was a mistake.

Quickly Diana wrote down Laura's name and address, then paid the neighbor's gardener to drive her home. In her own house at last she stood alone and trembling in the cool hall.

Somehow she got through the hours until Rand came home. Her stilted efforts at conversation during supper only puzzled Rand. After they'd finished the meal, the one she'd carefully planned to announce her news, and after John was in bed, she forced herself to the parlor, where Rand was reading the newspaper.

"Something terrible happened today."

His eyebrows shot up as he patted the cushion next to him. "What could be so terrible?"

"Stephan." The word hung in the sudden silence between them before it dropped into the void that had swallowed Diana's happiness. She'd seen the truth on his face. She averted her gaze to the window, where the color of the sky was deepening from reds and purples toward the fall of night.

Suddenly Rand was beside her, explaining about Laura, explaining that he'd been involved with her during a bad period of his life, before he was old enough to know any better, that he'd never loved her, even though Stephan had resulted from the affair.

"But you still see Laura?"

He nodded slowly. "But not often. And then only because she's the mother of my son."

"Do you take care of Stephan? . . . financially, I mean."

He moved away, and she felt his distress, but somehow she couldn't reach out to him. She felt she'd been betrayed. . . . He hadn't trusted her.

"I—uh—probably haven't done what I should in these last few years."

Diana faced him, disturbed by the whine she'd detected in his voice. Did she know Rand?—her husband, who knew every inch of her body—had shared her hopes and dreams for the future.

"Do you know Laura is dying?"

Something flickered in his eyes, and she realized that he had known. "Jesus, Diana, don't do this to our marriage. There's been nothing between us for years . . . not since I met you. But I've been trapped because of Stephan."

As she looked at him she suddenly saw a stranger. She didn't care about the past, she could have lived with that. But that he hadn't told her, had ignored his responsibilities to the dying woman and the boy he'd admitted was his son, in her eyes that was something of greater importance, a flaw in his character.

Diana felt a coldness settling over her. Poor Laura Ryan . . . another victim of love, she thought, knowing intuitively that the woman was gentle and honest, but desperate.

"Why didn't you marry her, Rand?—back when she had your child, and you had no other ties."

"She was never acceptable to my family," he began, then stopped abruptly when he saw the disgust on Diana's face.

"I see. You couldn't face the result of your actions, so you ruined everyone's life, mine included." Her words quavered as she thought of the new life her body was nurturing even as she spoke, the baby she couldn't tell him about now.

"What are you saying, Diana?"

"Only that I understand *you* couldn't marry a girl who loved you because she wasn't acceptable to the likes of Simon and Rachael." Anger seared her with waves of heat. "But I expect you to take care of Stephan." She took a quivering breath. "I'll stay married to you, Rand, but I'll never share your bed again."

She ran to the bedroom and threw herself down on the bed. She still loved him. Why doesn't he follow me and make it all right, she asked herself. But when he spent the night in the parlor she knew why: he was a weak man.

As the war raged in Europe the whole United States prospered. In Seattle the Carlyle family became one of the richest and most powerful in the Northwest. Jamie was watching his dream become a reality, yet for Jennifer and Damon, success was secondary.

The war made Gregory wish he were old enough to fight for his country. His sister Elizabeth was involved with a local movement that was revolting against it. Elizabeth had become enchanted with Communism, a doctrine that was sweeping the country, and she had incurred the disapproval of her parents and grandmother.

For Diana, all the success in the world wouldn't compensate for Rand's deceit; she was relieved when he joined the armed forces, almost immediately after Laura Ryan's visit, and soon left for Europe. Closing her mind against her love for him, and the fact that she hadn't told him she was pregnant, she lavished all her affection on their son John.

Yet, despite the unhappiness or joy, success or failure, the family still had one thing in common: the knowledge that the future was still there for the taking—for better or worse—if they had the courage to go on . . . and they did.

IV

The Heights

Chapter Twenty-nine

As the war in Europe accelerated, Damon was spending more time in his office, concerned about the curtailment of shipping to countries involved in the conflict. The company was dealing with labor problems due to a shortage of men. Many of those who were left were members of the Anti-Conscription League and opposed to the war, yet vocal in demanding higher wages. The situation was causing unrest all over Seattle.

When Damon bought a house at the end of Madison Street overlooking Lake Washington, Jennifer realized he was trying to help Mara cultivate outside interests and forget her bitterness while making the mansion a home. But Jennifer also knew from Jamie that Damon was having difficulties being a husband to her. She had gone from a high-strung social climber to a middle-aged shrew, more disfigured by her personality than by the scars of the fire.

"Mara blames the Carlyles for destroying her life," Jamie reported.

"I realize that," Jennifer replied, looking away from her brother's discerning eyes.

"But she hates you more than anyone, Jen," he went on. "You'd better be careful with that woman. . . . She could be dangerous."

Jennifer knew he was warning her about seeing Damon. "It's all right. There's no way she can hurt me." But even as she spoke, she felt a vague fear about what Rachael might have told Mara. That Mara and Simon were friends again worried her even more. But if Rachael had said anything, Simon or Mara would have revealed it by now, unless they'd kept quiet because Diana had become a Woodrow.

She reined in her imagination, telling herself to stop jumping to conclusions.

Exploding shells and staccato rifle fire deafened Rand as he hunched over in the muddy trench. He'd been in France for weeks now—he'd lost count of how many— taking part in the invasion to retake the northern part of that country and Belgium as well. It's hopeless, he thought, as hopeless as his own personal affairs: a wife who no longer cared, who couldn't forgive, who didn't understand that his upbringing among dishonest people hadn't prepared him to be honest always.

"Look out!" a man down the line shouted, and by reflex, Rand dropped into the mud. An instant later, a shell exploded nearby, showering him with dirty rainwater and bits of shrapnel.

"Christ!" the man next to him cried. "We'll never make it."

"We gotta," Rand replied as he resumed firing his weapon, his thoughts returning to the Diana who'd been a devoted wife and mother . . . and a loving woman.

The rain that had been a steady drizzle for days intensified. The trench was no longer just muddy; a puddle covered the tops of his booted feet. He heard a man down the line get hit and gulp a last breath before splashing into the bottom of the ditch.

God, help us, Rand prayed. His ragged uniform was soaked with other men's blood and mud from the incessant winter rain. I must stay alive, he chanted silently. I must concentrate on the peace and beauty of Puget Sound . . . on Diana. I *must* make her believe in me again.

The days passed and nothing changed; they couldn't seem to gain ground from the Germans. The rain continued, filling the trench until the water was up to Rand's knees, and he couldn't regain the feeling in his lower legs no matter how much he exercised them in the confined space. The stench of death filled his days and nights, and he knew his faith in survival was slipping.

When the shell hit the trench, he wasn't surprised, only sad, knowing he was an instant away from death. His numbed body hardly felt the pain as he concentrated on his last thought . . . Diana: I'll never change things—never prove how much I love her. . . . The countryside went dark and quiet, and Rand had no way of knowing that Laura Ryan was also dying on the other side of the earth . . . or that his daughter was being born.

Diana was unprepared for the grief that overwhelmed her at Rand's death. She should have been more forgiving of Rand, she told herself. After the birth of their daughter, Alexandra, she'd written him a long letter, explaining that she wanted to begin again, that she'd been wrong to shut him out of her life, that she needed him and so did their two children.

When the letter was returned unopened, Diana was devastated. The days became a blur of agony, and even her parents couldn't break the grip of depression that held her a prisoner. When her mother hired a nurse for Nellie so she could take care of five-year-old John and the baby, Diana was still unable to shake her despair.

"It's my fault Rand's dead," she told Martha one afternoon while her mother was upstairs putting John and Alexandra to bed for naps. "He joined up because I'd driven him to it."

Martha crossed the oriental rug and sat on the sofa next to Diana. "Don't torture yourself. Rand knew he would be conscripted anyway."

Diana suddenly stood up and walked to the fireplace, where she could see her image in the mirror above the mantel. Her dress hung from boney shoulders, her face was pale, and her eyes sunken from her drastic weight loss. But she felt a slight lifting of her spirits being with Martha. Martha was the only person other than her mother to whom she'd confided about Rand's affair and "other" son.

"I have something to tell you," Martha said, and then hesitated. "But I'm not sure if I should."

Diana faced Martha, her pulse quickening. "Is something wrong with my parents?"

Martha shook her head. "It's about Stephan. . . . He's alone now. . . . His mother died."

Diana's thoughts began to churn, remembering Laura Ryan's request. Stephan was an orphan—but he was Rand's son. And now he belonged nowhere. For the first time in weeks she felt sadness for someone else.

"Where is Stephan?"

"He's living temporarily with nuns in a Catholic parish near the waterfront. I heard they're trying to place him in a foster home."

Diana's gaze followed the floral pattern on the carpet. Rand hadn't arranged for the boy's future before leaving Seattle. He'd been wrong, but she wished very much that he had lived. She sighed and then lifted her eyes to Martha's. "I'll take care of him," she said.

Martha stepped forward and clasped Diana in her arms. "I was worried about telling you, but I'd also hoped knowing would do what it's done . . . given you a place from which to start your life again."

The next morning Diana was up early. When her mother arrived, Diana announced that she had a business appointment downtown. She told Jennifer that she'd explain after she returned. Then she took the cable car down to First Avenue and walked the remaining blocks to the convent. A nun answered her knock and ushered her into a waiting room. A short time later she returned with a tall, thin boy who looked about eleven or twelve even though the expression in his steady gray eyes belied his youth.

"My name is Diana Woodrow," she began, her gaze on the boy, who stood waiting, his bearing calm and polite. She felt her throat tighten as she detected the resemblance to Rand. Stephan had the same strong, well-defined features that hinted of honesty and sincerity. Rand, too, had been honest and sincere, except in his relationship with Lucy Ryan and his son.

He nodded, smiling politely. "I know who you are, Mrs. Woodrow. My father's wife." He spoke simply and without a trace of jealousy or anger, or expectation of being recognized as the oldest son of a very rich man.

He stood quietly as Diana explained that she wanted to help him find a home and see to it that he was well taken care of in the future.

"Thank you, Mrs. Woodrow," Stephan said, his tone cooler, and she could see that the boy was proud. "But don't concern yourself with me. I know Mother went to see you . . . and she shouldn't have done that." He straightened back his narrow shoulders. "I can take care of myself. Please don't think I'll ever trouble you . . . because I won't."

Diana liked him instantly. And she made an impetuous decision: she was taking Stephan into her family to be brought up with Rand's other children. He deserved a chance.

His eyes widened with fear when she told him what she meant to do. Suddenly he was only a small boy. "You can't do that, Mrs. Woodrow; it wouldn't be right. What would your family—your friends say?"

Her feeling for him grew. Finally she put her arms around him. "It'll be just fine. And besides, it's what your father would have wanted." As he heard her final words his expression suddenly brightened, and tears of gratitude appeared in the round, gray eyes. He nodded vigorously, and Diana knew that the little lie was justified; it was the boy's future after all.

The family took the news well, and Diana suspected that they'd all known about Stephan. An ostrich only hides from himself when he buries his head, she told herself with a sad grin. How well she was learning about life as she got older. But after Stephan settled in with Diana's little family, Seattle society reacted with another surge of gossip, which didn't concern her one bit.

Over the summer Nellie had grown stronger, Diana had taken back the responsibility of her children, and Jennifer was once again free to paint. She painted scenes of political confrontations, Wobblies shouting socialism from soapboxes, and strikers fighting on the streets.

By the time the war ended, in November of 1918, Stephan was settling into his surroundings, pleased that Diana treated him like a son. He'd assumed a protective attitude toward John and Alexandra and had indicated to Jennifer his fondness for Diana.

"I'll never forget my mother," he told Nellie and Jennifer one afternoon. "But I mean to take advantage of my opportunities so Diana can be proud of me . . . proud she took me into the family."

Jennifer exchanged glances with Nellie: Stephan would make his mark in the world.

Jamie, however, began having problems. After coping with labor unions during the big General Strike that February, his company was besieged by protests from militant workers. He'd been suffering financial setbacks since the war ended, and the economy had gone into a slump.

"If the economy isn't turned around soon, and these damnable labor problems settled, some of us will face bankruptcy," Jamie announced at dinner.

"Father, I've told you, the answer is compromise—with the workers," Elizabeth said tartly.

Jamie's jaw tightened. "They're demanding jobs when there aren't any . . . and higher wages when they aren't working. My God, Elizabeth. How can you align yourself with protesters who don't know what they're talking about?"

Elizabeth's eyes glinted with anger. "That's why there's a need for labor unions," she snapped. "To counteract attitudes like yours . . . employers who don't want to share profits."

Jennifer sat stunned. Elizabeth, a first-year student at the University of Washington, was actually defying her father.

"During the war there were more jobs than men," Nellie began, trying to calm things down. "And during that time the labor unions gained control of the work force." She paused. "There was a need for unions . . . still is. But now both sides, labor and management, must work together for a balanced solution. It's wrong if employers take advantage of workers, and equally wrong for workers to make demands that can't be met if a business is to keep operating. Everyone has to recognize that the economy has slowed to a standstill."

"That's just the propaganda of big business," Elizabeth cried. "Dad, how can you subscribe to such lies?"

"Elizabeth," Martha said sharply. "This is the last time I'll hear this argument. You've been associating with radicals who advocate overthrowing our government . . . and, even worse, set you against your own family." Martha's voice shook. "I think your father was right: I may have been too permissive. But no more. Your father and I have talked of transferring you to Oberlin College in the East, and now I've come to a decision . . . you're going."

Elizabeth leapt to her feet. "But I'm only doing what you and Grandmother—the whole family—have always done . . . try to help others."

"Our way has never been the way of the mob, Elizabeth," Martha replied tartly.

"Typical!" Elizabeth exclaimed, her gaze darting over her family gathered around the table. "A typical attitude of the rich."

"Christ Almighty!" Jamie cried. "Maybe a school in the East *will* help you regain your objectivity."

Elizabeth stood trembling with a fanaticism that scared Jennifer, who feared that it was too late for an eastern school to alter Elizabeth's radical beliefs.

Jennifer never knew quite how Jamie arranged Elizabeth's transfer to the eastern college, but within the week she'd left Seattle by train for Ohio. She knew that both Jamie and Martha hoped the change would have a stabilizing effect on Elizabeth, a hope Jennifer believed was a slim one. Several days later Martha came to visit, and Jennifer saw immediately that she was upset.

"Do you think I gave Elizabeth the impression I was a radical while she was growing up?" she asked Nellie and Jennifer. "Or that I spent too much time away from her when she was little? . . . I know Jamie always thought so. . . . It was the only thing we ever argued about."

"She'll probably mature past all this once she's away and can think things over," Jennifer said.

"Stop worrying and get on with your life: Jamie and Gregory and your work. Everything'll work out," Nellie added.

Their support was all Martha needed to go on with her projects, efforts that had a huge impact on Seattle during the following months. No longer able to take funds from Jamie's business profits, Martha had been forced to look elsewhere. With Nellie's help, she began the long job of setting up a philanthropic organization that would consolidate all of her projects. Martha believed that such an organization would gain more fund-raising support, and also, a board would decided on which causes and individuals were most in need of help. An organization could undertake bigger projects than Martha had ever attempted on her own.

Damon's shipping company pledged money, as did Jamie's and many other large Seattle businesses. Although none of the pledges, aside from Damon's, was substantial, a great many citizens contributed as well, people representing both the radical and conservative elements of society. It was a response that astonished Martha and the family.

Only Simon Woodrow, among the social elite, refused to contribute to the new organization. His refusal surprised no one.

Chapter Thirty

Jennifer, feeling the chill of the October night, pulled her rocking chair close to the fire in the parlor. Nellie was back in her own mansion on First Hill, and the evenings were quiet unless she entertained. But tonight she felt tired, having worked all day on a new painting. She'd then soaked for an hour in a perfume-scented tub before donning her new blue nightgown.

She tightened the cord of the matching robe around her waist, stretching her feet toward the hearth. The crackling flame was the only sound intruding on the peace of the empty house. As Jennifer stared at the fire, which had cast the room into vague humps and shadowy outlines, her thoughts moved back over her life, from being a girl in Georgia to being a middle-aged woman in Seattle. She'd never expected to be alone, one of those women who had to be strong because there was no one to share the burdens with.

A slight wind touched the shrubs beyond her windows as her thoughts shifted to Nellie. Her old friend had liquidated all of her assets to underwrite Jamie's company. Nellie believed Jamie's business couldn't be allowed to go bankrupt; it was too important to the future economy of the Northwest.

The cabinet wall clock in the hall struck ten o'clock, startling Jennifer. She stood up, knowing she must go to bed. As she walked to the hall stairs her thoughts shifted to Damon and their shared nights in the past. She hadn't been alone with him for over two years. She knew he was busy coping with union problems, working hard to find a middle ground that would benefit both labor and management. She worried about him; his work and Mara were constant stresses on him.

Abruptly a loud knock sounded at the front door below her. Then there was a second one, louder, and sudden fear shot through her. She tiptoed back to the hall; a family member would have telephoned before arriving so late.

"Jennifer?" a man's voice called. "Jennifer . . . are you there?"

Jennifer flung open the door, revealing Damon, his hair blowing from the wind, his dark eyes burning in a face leaner than the last time she'd seen him.

He stepped into the hall, locked the door behind him, and pulled her into his arms. "I had to come," he murmured into the long strands of her hair. "I couldn't stay away any longer."

Overwhelming joy swept over Jennifer; it was almost as though she'd conjured him up out of her thoughts. She couldn't believe he was here, holding her in his arms. As his lips claimed hers, she was swept away on a tide of sudden passion, an emotion stronger than ever.

He picked her up and carried her up the steps to the dimly lit bedroom they'd shared so many nights in the past. She giggled against his coat. He'd be carrying her to the bedroom when he was eighty.

After depositing her on the satin spread, he quickly removed his coat, throwing it over a chair. It was followed seconds later by the rest of his clothing. Soon he was beside her, gently slipping the sheer silk robe and gown from her body.

"Jesus, but you're beautiful, Jennifer." His eyes were lit by a longing too long denied. "You're always the same to me . . . as beautiful as when you were nineteen."

She smiled into his face, only inches above hers. "I love you, Damon. And you still look like the tough Greek shipowner I met that day Seattle was trying to ship the Chinese out on the *Queen of the Pacific*." She hesitated, drinking in his beloved features. "I'll love you when I'm old and cranky and too weak to move out of my rocking chair; I'll love you for the rest of my life . . . and throughout eternity."

He kissed her again and again, from her mouth to her

breasts and lower still. Unable to control her passion, she cried out, "Love me, Damon . . . love me now."

With a low moan he entered her, and she forgot everything else but the touch of his flesh. For tonight he belonged only to her.

As the first rays of dawn touched the fringed window shades, they talked. Damon confessed that his life with Mara was a nightmare.

"She wants sex, and I can't stand the thought of touching her."

"Do you?" Jennifer asked softly, compelled to find out, yet hating the thought of him with Mara.

He shook his head. "I can't . . . and that makes matters even worse." Abruptly he pulled her closer until her breasts were flattened against his chest. "I don't want to discuss Mara with you; it depresses us both. But I want to ask you a favor . . . a life-and-death favor."

She nodded, waiting.

"Can I come to you sometimes?—even if it has to be in the night when no one sees me?"

She smiled slowly, softly. "I'll settle for that because I love you. And because I know you love me." She hesitated, her tone serious. "But if I believed you were using me—looked upon me as a whore—my feelings could die and be buried so deep that even I couldn't bring them back to life."

Something flickered deep in his eyes. "I'll never deceive you, Jennifer. And I already know that about you."

"You know what?" she prompted, needing to hear him say it.

"I know that you don't give your love to a man lightly—that you've only given it once . . . to me." His lips feathered her face with kisses. "And I'd never risk losing it again."

It was Diana who told her the full extent of Mara's insanity. "Did you know that Mara telephones him at the office ten or twenty times a day—that she sneaks around following him to business meetings, as though she expects to catch him cheating on her?"

"My God," Jennifer whispered hoarsely as fear prickled her spine. Had Mara followed Damon to her house?

"But that's not even the worst," Diana continued, not realizing the impact of her words on Jennifer. "She won't go out into society because she's too ashamed of her scars, but she swept into Dad's office one day and fired all the women who work there. It was a terrible scene; she accused them all of trying to steal her husband."

"She's crazy."

Diana nodded. "Of course, Dad hired back all the women, instructing them to pay no attention to Mara, that she was still suffering from her illness." She hesitated, her forehead creased with worry. "It has to be awful for Dad. . . . Do you think he'll ever be free of that woman?"

Jennifer was too upset to do more than shake her head and was relieved when the conversation drifted to the children. But she resolved to see Damon whenever he wanted.

As the fall passed into December, Jennifer was gradually taken up with Christmas preparations. One afternoon, shortly before Christmas, she and Diana came out of the Bon Marche and found Mara standing in the middle of the sidewalk, looking as though she'd been waiting for them.

Jennifer stopped in midstride, shocked. The woman's face was a mass of lumpy, pink scars. Her clothes were long out of date and ill-fitting.

"Rachael knew all about you," Mara said, her tone like the hiss of a snake, her eyes narrowed at Jennifer.

"What are you talking about?" Jennifer asked, trying to be calm, aware of the gathering crowd of people.

"Come on, Mother," Diana said, tugging at Jennifer's arm. "I think we'd better get out of here."

"Mother?" Mara repeated. "So that's what Rachael hinted at . . . what Simon suspected." She stepped closer, her scars turning bright red, her hand shooting out to grab Jennifer's arm in a painful grip. "I know where Damon goes on those nights he thinks I'm asleep. To you spend the night with you . . . his mistress!"

"That's nonsense," Jennifer replied, trying to shake free of her.

"I know because I've followed him—and waited all night until he left."

"My God," Diana said under her breath. "She's crazy."

"Crazy?" Mara repeated, hearing Diana's last words. "Crazy, crazy, crazy," she chanted, and then laughed shrilly. Abruptly, she turned to the silent crowd. "This woman destroyed my marriage, and she calls me crazy?" She gestured wildly with her hand, knocking her old-fashioned plumed hat to the ground. "And this woman"—she pointed a trembling hand at Diana—"is my husband's bastard daughter."

Jennifer jerked away, so enraged she contemplated doing bodily harm to Mara. But Diana stepped forward, pulling her back.

"Don't say anything," Diana whispered urgently. "The best thing to do is get away from her. . . . She's insane."

Shaking with anger, Jennifer knew Diana was right. They moved on down Second Avenue, away from the crowd.

Mara continued screaming after them as they ran around the next corner. They were both ready to cry; Mara's words would be all over town in hours.

Jennifer did not sleep at all that night. By noon, when Damon telephoned, her nerves were shattered.

"I heard what happened," he said, his tone concerned. "And I believe I've smoothed things over as far as gossip is concerned."

"How did you do that?"

"Never mind for now. I can't talk long, but I want you to know what's happened. I've told Mara I'm getting a divorce—that by trying to destroy you and Diana, she'd only hurt herself." He drew in a deep breath, and she could hear how upset he was. But his words had given her hope. "That even if what she'd said were true, she'd canceled out my last reason for staying with her by announcing it in public."

"Does she know it's true?"

"Not for sure."

"Did she go into a rage—when you told her?"

"No," he replied wearily. "She had one of her sudden changes of mood. She was contrite, pleading with me to stay—that she was sorry—that she'd been jealous—that she loves me . . . and on and on."

"Do you think you'll be able to get a divorce in this state?"

He hesitated again, and as Jennifer waited a foreboding stole over her. "I've talked to a lawyer. . . . It's going to be tough.

"But, Jennifer"—his tone lifted—"I love you, and whatever happens, that won't change. I'm back in my apartment—moved in this morning."

"I love you, and I'll be here when you need me."

After they hung up, Jennifer felt her spirits soar. Damon would get a divorce, then they would marry after all.

The year 1920 brought prohibition and even more labor unrest in Seattle. The Wobblies were still causing riots, and Mayor Hanson had resigned; the city was growing, its population now exceeding three hundred thousand. The citizens boasted that their new radio station, KJR, was the second one in the nation; the University of Washington had a huge new stadium, and the Sand Point Naval Air Station had been established.

As the months moved into 1921, and then 1922, Damon struggled to find a settlement that would pacify Mara, who continued to contest the divorce. Jennifer knew Damon brooded over ever being free—that he worried about Mara's causing a scandal. Mara couldn't even keep servants in the house; it was reported that she left every light in the house burning day and night, that she'd become a walking skeleton; her hair and body were unkempt. Both Damon and Jennifer knew that even if a settlement was reached, it was now doubtful a judge would grant a divorce when Mara was clearly insane.

Jennifer saw less and less of Damon, who feared dragging her into the mess. He also curtailed his visits to his grandchildren, grieving him and angering Diana.

But Damon was adamant, and Jennifer feared he was losing his perspective altogether. Then, without warning, Damon was a free man, his wife dead. The morning paper carried the story on the front page, and Jennifer knew Mara had found her revenge. Mara had poisoned herself and left a note incriminating Jennifer and Diana. The note was published intact.

By the next day it seemed that everyone in Seattle had heard the scandal and were avoiding Jennifer and Diana. Jennifer didn't dare see Damon. They talked on the telephone, but they both knew that being seen together would only make matters worse.

As the rains of winter warmed to the blustery showers of spring in 1923, and then to the gauzy mists that watered the blooming gardens of summer, Diana realized that the situation was taking its toll on her parents. When she discovered that Simon was keeping the gossip alive, she vowed to take matters into her own hands and went to confront him. By the terms of Rand's will, half ownership of the Woodrow Company belonged to her . . . and to Rand's children.

Taking a deep breath, she entered the Woodrow Building, one of the tallest in Seattle. When she reached Simon's floor, she stepped briskly past the startled secretary and into the private office of her brother-in-law.

He glanced up, saw her, and leapt to his feet. "Diana, what in hell do you want?"

She nudged the door closed behind her, satisfied that he was his typical nasty self, which would make her job easier. "I came to inform you that I'm taking control of the half of the company I inherited at Rand's death." As his expression turned from disdain to disbelief, she felt a thrill of satisfaction. "From now on I'll be here every day to oversee the interests of Rand's two sons and daughter."

"Like hell you will. . . . I won't have it."

She tilted her chin, narrowing her eyes at him. "You should have known better than to feed the gossip about the Carlyles. Now you have no choice. And when Rand's sons are older, they'll be here as well."

"Rand had but one son, Diana," he retorted.

"Stephan is his son, and you know it. And I intend seeing that he inherits what's rightfully his."

"At the expense of your own son?"

"My son is already heir to another empire. . . . He's not going to be hurt in any way." She stepped closer, feeling disgust not only for his fleshy body that was bathed in sweat but for the ugliness of his personality. "My son isn't like you, Simon. He can share his fortune with his brother."

"I'll fight you on this, Diana. I don't recognize women in my business, nor do I recognize illegitimacy."

She laughed coldly. "You're a pompous ass, Simon. So go ahead, fight me. But from now on keep your mouth shut about Damon and Jennifer."

During the second half of that year Jennifer once again devoted daylight hours to painting, grateful for the work that would help pass the time until the gossips lost interest and she and Damon could marry. Shortly before Christmas she lent Jamie money so that he could complete work on a new airplane model, one he hoped would test out with greater speed and distance capabilities. He needed a successful new plane in order to obtain a government contract. His business was already in a precarious financial position when faltering sales had slowed production. Even Damon had lacked ready cash to help out.

Wanting to display her mother's paintings at her next show in the spring, Jennifer sent them off to San Francisco to be cleaned. A short time later she received a letter from an art dealer who wanted to purchase them for a substantial sum of money.

"Good Lord, can you believe it?" she asked Diana. "It's enough money to help Jamie *really* get his company going again."

"You can't sell your mother's paintings," Diana said. "You'd feel terrible."

"I don't know," Jennifer replied, pushing a wisp of hair back into her chignon. "The man said in his letter that paintings that depict the years shortly before the Civil War destroyed Georgia are rare, and as such are in demand."

"Forget it. You don't need to sell them—that's what I wanted to tell you."

Jennifer waited for her to continue, noticing that Diana had fine lines at the corners of her eyes, that she was still far too thin. My God, Diana was in her mid-thirties, Jennifer reminded herself. It seemed as though the years were passing faster now. Although Diana didn't look her age—

her hair was still bright and her eyes still expressive and beautiful—Jennifer felt a twinge of sadness. Had her daughter done the right thing in taking an active part in the Woodrow Lumber Company?

"I'm lending Uncle Jamie the money he needs."

"Where on earth did—"

Diana grinned and suddenly looked years younger. "From the company. The new bookkeeper I hired found that Simon had been withholding dividends from me, money that he'd put into a separate account to use as reserve against borrowing."

"He was trying to cheat you?"

"No, not really," Diana said, picking a piece of lint from her corduroy dress. "It wasn't illegal, but it wasn't fair to Rand's family either. He was using part of Rand's share of the profit to build up the reserve account and placing his own share in a private account."

"He's really a devious person," Jennifer said. "But maybe he'll mellow as he gets older. People do change."

During the following days Jennifer gave much thought to the dealer's offer; now that she knew the value of the paintings she questioned the sense of keeping them. Then, one day she knew she'd solved the problem: she would give the paintings to the state of Georgia. She knew her mother would have been pleased. She had been born and bred in Georgia and had loved it.

By September her offer had been accepted, and she'd had the paintings crated and sent. Three weeks later, Jennifer received a letter from a member of the historical society, thanking her for her generous donation and inviting her to visit in the future, and signed by . . . Judson Carr.

Jennifer sat on the nearest chair, her heart suddenly thumping in her chest as she pulled two photographs from the envelope. She stared, her eyes misting as she looked upon High Bluffs again—a beautiful High Bluffs completely restored to its former elegance. The second photograph was of the old live oak on the bluff above the Savannah River, the grave markers still sheltered by the Spanish moss draping its branches. She swallowed hard, but the tears streamed from her eyes, and for a long time she didn't notice the old man's shaky writing on the back of the mansion photograph.

"I knew you'd like to know High Bluffs has been restored. . . . I love this plantation, and I'm sorry for the past," Jennifer read aloud. "Please forgive an old man."

Jennifer sat staring at the pictures that brought back so many memories of the past: her father mounting his horse for his morning rounds, her bedroom that looked out over the cotton fields, and old Zeb, the man she'd loved like a grandfather. Then came the later memories: Nellie, infamous Savannah madam; San Francisco and Seattle; steamboats and the progression of many years.

Finally, she stood up and walked to the window, where the evening lights of Seattle twinkled beneath her hill. My city, she told herself. My roots are here now. High Bluffs really belongs to the past . . . to Judson, a very old man. And in that moment, she forgave him, knowing that Seattle had been her destiny.

In the days and weeks and months that followed, she had a new sense of belonging to Seattle. By spring, she and Damon had decided that their wedding would be a summer one. They became formally engaged in April, a traditional gesture that pleased Jennifer. Their engagement spawned another wave of gossip, but they were able to ignore it.

As long as Diana and the family knew better, Jennifer and Damon didn't care. They were too happy to care.

Chapter Thirty-one

"I'm so glad you came along, Jennifer," Martha said, as she dropped her purse and gloves onto a chair. "Having lunch was a wonderful idea." She hesitated, glancing around the stark meeting room of the waterfront church. "My talk will only take a few minutes."

Jennifer nodded; she was anticipating the meal with the female members of the family. It would be the first time they'd all been together in years. Her gaze moved from Martha and Nellie to Elizabeth, who'd just rushed into the room.

"Am I late?" she asked. Then, as she noticed that only a few Indians stood at the back of the room, Elizabeth clasped a hand to her chest and gave an exaggerated sigh. "What a rush. My meeting took longer than I'd anticipated."

Watching her, Jennifer marveled at the dark beauty of the young woman who'd returned to Seattle only in May. Two months later Elizabeth was already making her presence known in Seattle. A graduate of Oberlin College with a Ph.D. from another leading university in the East, she'd stepped into a position with a child-welfare organization.

"Where's Diana?" Elizabeth asked, her bobbed dark hair feathering as she pulled off her tight-fitting cloche hat.

"We're meeting her at the Olympic Hotel," Jennifer replied, placing her pink raincoat and umbrella beside Martha's things on the chair. "Her lunch time away from the office is limited."

Elizabeth grinned, then adjusted the collar of her lightweight pullover blouse and tightened the roll of her silk stockings under her calf-length skirt. "Are you excited about your wedding next month, Aunt Jennifer?"

"Course she is," Nellie piped up, the gay tone of her voice belying the fact that she was in her late seventies. "And about time they tied the knot . . . after all these years." With her gray hair permanent waved, her cheeks rouged, and her belted, navy dress accentuated by her favorite fox fur wrap, Nellie was still the woman Jennifer remembered from their Georgia days.

"Yes, I am," Jennifer said. "I've been looking forward to the day . . . as your grandmother says, it's time."

Martha moved away to talk to the president of the Christian organization that had sponsored this meeting to interest Indians in free medical facilities and schooling for their children. As she watched her Jennifer felt sudden pride; Martha was an outstanding woman, one who'd be remembered for generations to come. She'd never lost her sensitivity and gentleness, attributes that gave her an ageless grace.

"She'll still be doing this at ninety," Elizabeth said, her eyes also on her mother.

Jennifer nodded. "Her organization is doing good things for a great many people."

"But it's all so slow," Elizabeth replied. "They can never make a quick decision without board approval."

"Sometimes that's necessary," Jennifer said softly.

Elizabeth shrugged. "I think the answer lies in giving the downtrodden the opportunity of making their own way . . . giving them jobs . . . sharing the wealth."

Jennifer's eyes widened. My God, she reflected, Elizabeth hasn't changed, all her education and the publicity since arriving home notwithstanding. Elizabeth's recent activities had attracted the attention of the newspapers, one of which had described her as "a young and beautiful woman with brains."

Before she could reply, Nellie motioned them to sit down, as the room was filling up, mostly with Indians.

Suddenly there was a commotion at the back of the room. An older woman, dressed in the traditional blanket cape, was arguing with a wild-looking man who sounded drunk, while a pregnant girl tried to stop the conflict.

"Our daughter needs medical help," the Indian woman aid, resolutely standing up to the man although her voice quavered and her eyes reminded Jennifer of a trapped animal. "I want her to have it."

"White man's help?" the man cried, grabbing the woman and trying to force both woman and girl out the door. "We don't need their medicine—so they can try to make us like them."

Jennifer stared at the man, whose gaunt, lined face was obscured by ragged black and gray hair; vague recognition stirred her memory. Then she saw both Martha and the Christian sponsor move toward the couple.

"Please," Martha told the man. "We want to help your daughter. You must know that I wouldn't harm her."

The man turned on Martha, his eyes narrowing dangerously. "You . . . dare tell me?—a *white indian*?—a disgrace to your tribe?" He loomed over Martha. "Get out of our way. The white man has hurt us enough, soiling my girl by planting his seed in her body!"

Her heart pounding, Jennifer rushed forward, pushing through the people. She *had* seen the Indian before—at the exposition back in 1909. The man was the one Martha's family had wanted her to marry—the one who'd threatened Martha years ago.

As the Indian tried to push his wife and daughter toward the door, Martha stepped forward to place a hand on his arm. "Let her stay so we can help her," she said gently, ignoring the hatred that flared in his black eyes and the sudden movement of his hand under his blanket. "I want—"

Martha's words ended in a high, piercing scream. A second later she slumped to the floor, her hands fluttering around the knife that was buried in her chest, blood staining her dress crimson and puddling the floor beside her. Shock and disbelief shone from her eyes, while her lips moved, trying to speak. Then her long lashes drooped, not quite closing over eyes that were already glazing from death.

"Dear God!" Ripping off one of her petticoats to try to stop the bleeding, Jennifer flung herself down beside her. "Martha . . . Martha!"

But Martha was still, her eyes lifeless. To Jennifer the
sounds of overturned chairs and voices of alarm seemed to
come from a distance. Gently she cradled Martha's head in
her arms as tears streamed from her eyes and great sobs
shuddered through her. The woman she loved like a sister
was gone.

Suddenly Nellie was beside her on the floor, crying
openly. "No, God, no. Take me instead . . . I'm the
sinner, not Martha." Powder and rouge blended with tears,
making grotesque streaks on the wrinkled cheeks. "Send
her back, God. Please, send her back to us."

"She's gone, Grandmother," Elizabeth cried, her eyes
filled with horror. "That bastard killed her." Then she
dropped beside her mother, oblivious to the blood soaking
her own clothes, and sobbed uncontrollably, her head
resting next to the knife still buried in Martha's flesh. "My
God . . . he murdered her before our eyes."

Abruptly, Elizabeth leapt to her feet. "Where is that
murdering red bastard?" Only seconds had passed, but
people were already rushing to get out of the room.

Jennifer scrambled up and grabbed Elizabeth's arm,
fearful that she'd also get hurt. "He's gone."

"But—but we've called the police," the Christian sponsor whispered, trembling and wringing her hands, her
expression frozen with disbelief.

Jennifer's gaze swept over the people still in the room.
"Wait!" she cried, knowing that the police would want
witnesses. But her command only added impetus to their
exodus. Within seconds everyone was gone except for the
small group standing by Martha's body. Jennifer knew the
killer had escaped—that he'd never be made to pay for
what he'd done.

The murder was front-page news, and editorials demanded the apprehension of the murderer. Martha's death
became an example of Seattle's need to crack down on vice
and corruption.

The tragedy had shocked everyone, but Jamie was totally
devastated: the power of his grief frightened Jennifer and
Nellie. By the time Martha's mother arrived from Vancouver Island, Jamie was in seclusion, refusing to see even his

children and refusing to leave Martha's coffin, which he'd insisted be placed in the parlor. He left his vigil only when Martha's mother asked to be alone with her only child. She wailed and chanted all night until, in the morning, Jennifer gently led her away.

The funeral was a nightmare: Jamie stood frozen, his gaze never leaving Martha's face; Gregory's loud crying echoed above the murmuring and weeping of the hundreds who'd come to pay last respects; and Elizabeth stared, unseeing, her eyes filled with tears and anger. And for the first time in decades, Martha's father held his Indian wife in his arms, trying to comfort her.

Later that night Jennifer unintentionally interrupted a conversation between Elizabeth and her grandmother.

"No, don't go," Elizabeth said as Jennifer turned to leave. "I was saying that Mother's way of helping people wasn't always the method she should have used. Oh, God . . . she should have listened to me."

"What do you mean?"

"Mother always went to unsafe places—trying to influence people to her ideas for a better life." Elizabeth spread her hands in a gesture of futility. "You can't change the ways of people by telling them, they must have the means of doing for themselves, having more pay for their work, gaining self-esteem."

"Your mother wanted that as well," Jennifer replied softly. "But she also knew that change doesn't come overnight—that prejudice had to be overcome first. And in the meantime, those people needed to be educated and helped with their needs."

"But if all the wealth in the land weren't in the hands of just a few, then more people could live better, and there would be no prejudice."

Frustration rushed over Jennifer. Elizabeth was right in some of her views and completely wrong in others. She hadn't changed. Jamie needed a daughter now, not someone who viewed his lifetime work through the eyes of Communism and believed he should give away his profits, "share the wealth."

"Elizabeth, one day soon we'll talk about all this," she said slowly. "I'd like to help you understand that because a business is successful doesn't mean the profits should all be given away, or there'd never be a way out of poverty for anyone. A few people have the vision to create jobs by building empires, not just for personal wealth, but to help improve the community and the quality of life for their workers. Successful businesses help everyone—and in America anyone can try to be an empire builder."

Elizabeth stared at the floral carpet. "I loved my mother but I still believe her way was . . . too slow."

"Not so," Martha's mother said, startling Jennifer, who'd forgotten her presence. The woman looked like an Indian carving, Jennifer thought, as though her wizened face had been carved by a primitive artist. "Once I believed Martha was wrong . . . but I was wrong. Martha was chosen, by our Great Spirit, the white man's God, to help her people so the Indian and white man could live together in peace. Martha was a bridge between those two worlds."

Jennifer nodded, moved by the woman's words, realizing now that Martha's sensitivity had been inherited from her mother.

"Perhaps, Grandmother," Elizabeth replied impatiently. "But then why did an Indian kill her? And why didn't the authorities arrest him before he escaped to Canada?" She hesitated, her features tightening. "Because he was only an Indian who'd killed another Indian? . . . and not worth the effort of running him down?"

The old woman chanted something under her breath, words Jennifer suspected were a prayer for her granddaughter, who'd somehow fallen off the bridge, never having established a place in either world.

Jennifer again delayed her marriage. She felt a wedding when the family was in mourning would not be appropriate. Jamie had lost interest in everything, including his work. She knew Fred Aeschliman and the board of directors were keeping things going despite the slow economy and the fact the company was still struggling out of the last major crisis.

Three weeks later when Nellie told her Jamie's company had plunged into the red, she wasn't surprised. But she was alarmed by Jamie's reaction: he didn't care. The next day

Nellie told Jennifer that Elizabeth had taken charge, representing her father at board meetings. Jennifer felt an icy finger of apprehension touch her spine. Within a week Elizabeth had become a strong force in the company's decision-making process; the male board members had been seduced by her "beauty with brains" image.

But over the following weeks, the image began to tarnish as Elizabeth started altering company policy to benefit the employees. She insisted that by giving more of the projected profit to the workers, they would work harder and make more money for the company. Even when the board members pointed out that they couldn't spend what they didn't have, Elizabeth wouldn't listen. Heedless to the fact that her lack of business acumen could destroy the Carlyle Airplane Company, she demanded her instructions be implemented. Two board members immediately resigned, while Fred Aeschliman and the others openly disputed Elizabeth's socialistic approach.

Jennifer, disturbed by the impending bankruptcy, decided to confront Jamie, tell him it was time to let Martha go. One evening in late fall she went to his house. As she knocked on Jamie's door it opened and Fred Aeschliman stepped out.

"It's gonna be all right now, Jen," was all he said as he walked past her to his car.

For a moment she stared after him, but then she heard voices coming from Jamie's study, angry voices.

Suddenly Elizabeth stormed into the hall, her face flushed, her eyes brimming with tears. She rushed past Jennifer without speaking and ran up the stairs, and a moment later a door slammed on the second floor.

"Come in, Jen," Jamie said. His face was even more gaunt than she remembered, and his hair had turned gray, but his eyes glinted with new life, and Jennifer was suddenly heartened.

"What happened?"

"We . . . that is, Elizabeth and I, had an argument." He went to the tray on his desk and poured brandy into two glasses. "I had to tell her to leave the company."

He handed Jennifer a glass, and she saw that he was

upset. A definite improvement. At least he was feeling emotions again.

"Fred was here to tell me exactly what was happening at the plant. He and Elizabeth got into a fight, and I had to stand by Fred because she was wrong." He took a gulp of brandy. "Then Elizabeth got mad at me, started spouting all her radical views."

"You know what's been going on then."

He nodded. "Everything . . . all Elizabeth's communistic ideas and crazy changes." His gaze was level, but there was a tremor in his words as he went on. "She says she's leaving, Jen, going back East to work."

Jennifer put down her glass and went to him, hugging him tightly as she used to do when he was a boy. "She'll be back, Jamie," she said gently. "But if she must go, then she must . . . because you're right about your company."

The following week Elizabeth caught the train for New York. The whole family saw her off, and Jennifer hoped that time would mellow her before she ruined her whole life. Elizabeth telephoned when she'd reached the East Coast, making Jamie feel a little better.

Jamie was gradually regaining his enthusiasm and reestablishing his closeness with Gregory, who showed promise of becoming a fine man.

"Everything seems to be moving smoothly for a change," she told Damon one evening after supper. "Do you suppose we—"

"Could get married now?" he said finishing her sentence, his expression tender.

She nodded.

A moment later she was in his arms, her face against his chest listening to the steady thump of his heart. "As soon as possible, my darling," he whispered. "Before anything else happens."

How she loved him . . . his body, his mind, his soul. There'd been so many delays, so many years of separation, but their lives had been full and rewarding. And most important, their family would continue, Diana's children would eventually inherit Damon's empire.

"I'm a lucky man," he whispered against her hair. "My

business is successful, my grandson John is forceful enough to take over my empire one day, and now I can marry the woman I've always loved." He hesitated, his words catching in his throat. "I must be the happiest man in the world."

As Jennifer slipped into her blue silk wedding gown, she felt a comfortable, mellow happiness enfold her spirit. She stood before her mirror, her gaze on the still slim figure. Her hair, not as blond as it once was and silvered with streaks of gray, had been styled into a simple upsweep.

"Not bad, Mother," Diana said, coming into the room. "If I didn't know better, I'd take you for a young girl going off to wed her fairy-tale prince."

"You're as beautiful as when I first knew you," Nellie said, stepping from behind Diana.

Jennifer turned, smiling at both of them. "Thank you, my good friend," she told Nellie. "And my loving daughter," she added, her gaze on Diana who was lovely in navy chiffon, her blond hair casual, her dark eyes aglow.

"It isn't everyone who can see their parents get married," Diana said, laughing. "Even Simon asked me about the wedding. . . . Can you believe it? I think he's finally taking a step toward being human."

"And you, Diana . . . are you happy?" Jennifer asked.

"Yes, I've made a place for myself in the Woodrow Lumber Company, and there will be one for Stephan one day as well." She hesitated. "Rand would have been proud of him; Stephan has the earmarks of becoming a great man, one who'll reach the heights. Even Simon has been hinting that Stephan will be one of his heirs."

"Humph," Nellie said. "Simon is changing, even if he still doesn't recognize me as his aunt."

"Surely that doesn't bother you," Jennifer said.

"Course not," Nellie replied. "I've got my hands full being proud of Jamie. Say, did you know that he just landed a huge government contract? It might make the Carlyle Airplane Company one of the most important industries in the Northwest."

Jennifer smiled and noticed that Diana was also grinning. Nellie didn't mince words when it came to bragging about

Jamie. "And he has Gregory to carry on his work into the future," she added.

Nellie adjusted the black net of her sheath dress over her silk slip, and Jennifer thought: she'd be overdressed until the day she died—forever their beloved madam. Impulsively she kissed a rouged cheek. "And you, Nellie? . . . you're happy?"

Nellie's lashes fluttered, holding back sudden tears. "Contented . . . I'm keeping an eye on Martha's organization. She was some woman; it was a privilege having her in the family. Her work will endure far into the future."

"As will the Polemis Steamship Company, the Carlyle Airplane Company, and the Woodrow Lumber Company," Diana added.

As Jennifer walked down the stairs to the parlor her thoughts returned to her youth, and she realized how far she'd come since those days in Georgia.

As she and Damon were pronounced man and wife a searing joy flashed through Jennifer. His lips sealed their bond in a kiss that sent electricity jolting along her veins. Thank you, God, she thought, knowing that she'd finally realized her lifelong wish . . . to be married to Damon.

He lifted his face, his dark eyes burning into hers, and she knew that for all the heartache and tragedy, she wouldn't trade her life with anyone else. She had always accepted challenges and gone on, finding the strength to endure. Above all else—wealth and success, power and position—the ability to endure and face whatever life placed in one's path, was the legacy she and Damon were giving to future generations.

"I love you, my Jennifer . . . my life," he whispered against her lips.

She nodded, eyes filled with tears, lips smiling with sudden humility. "Forever and into eternity."

They kissed again, knowing they'd never be parted for as long as they lived. They had set down deep roots in a new land, and nothing could defeat them now . . . not ever again.

Nor would prohibition, strikes, general unrest, or even a great depression dim the shining light of ambition. Just as the Carlyles had conquered their own mountains, in the pursuit of dreams and goals and a place on the heights, Seattle had come of age, the symbol of a continent conquered. Jennifer was correct in believing that her loved ones would keep a wakeful eye on the horizon, looking ahead with unobstructed vision . . . poised for the next challenge . . . ready to meet it.

ABOUT THE AUTHOR

DONNA CAROLYN ANDERS was born in Tacoma, Washington, and later moved with her family to a small town in the northeastern part of the state. After she married, Ms. Anders lived in New Jersey for several years before returning to the Puget Sound area.

While her three daughters were growing up, Ms. Anders began to write. She soon discovered that her love of painting was being replaced by an affinity for other kinds of pictures—word pictures. She sold her first effort, a children's poem, for one dollar, and the thrill of that sale was the beginning of a life-long commitment to writing.

After the dollar poem came other successes. Ms. Anders sold three to four hundred stories, articles and poems before publishing her first historical saga, *From This Land*, in 1980. Aside from two children's picture/coloring books, she now limits her work to adult novels. She loves researching events of the past, bits and pieces of history, to fit into the backgrounds of her fictional characters.

Ms. Anders is currently working on a new saga and lives in a small village on Puget Sound near Seattle.

Sacred Is the Wind

by Kerry Newcomb
Author of *Morning Star*

Dreams of wealth and adventure brought the white man to the snowcapped mountains and fertile valleys of the proud Cheyenne. With their coming, the ways of the Morning Star People were doomed to perish—but not to be forgotten. Not as long as the name and deeds of Panther Burn were whispered by the wind and remembered in noble hearts.

Driven from the home of his youth to the land of the South Cheyenne, Panther Burn met the lovely Rebecca Blue Thrush whose limitless love gave him the courage to strike back against the white men who betrayed his people with treachery and terror.

This is the story of the birth of a legend and an undying love.

Look for it wherever Bantam Books are sold, or use this handy coupon.

BANTAM
SHOP·AT·HOME
C·A·T·A·L·O·G

Special Offer
Buy a Bantam Book
for only 50¢.

Now you can have an up-to-date listing of Bantam's hundreds of titles plus take advantage of our unique and exciting bonus book offer. A special offer which gives you the opportunity to purchase a Bantam book for only 50¢. Here's how!

By ordering any five books at the regular price per order, you can also choose any other single book listed (up to a $4.95 value) for just 50¢. Some restrictions do apply, but for further details why not send for Bantam's listing of titles today!

Just send us your name and address and we will send you a catalog!